Do I Know You?

Pamela Cory

**CALUMET
EDITIONS**
Minneapolis

SECOND EDITION DECEMBER 2022

This is a work of fiction. All of the characters, names, incidents, organizations, and dialogue are either the products of the author's imagination or are used fictiously.

10 9 8 7 6 5 4 3 2

ISBN: 978-1-960250-06-3

Cover design by Sue Stein
Book design by Gary Lindberg
Images licensed from Adobe

Dedicated
to the memory of
Haydn Martin

"And scars will lighten, they'll pale unless
you keep rubbing at them…
wait long enough, they'll fade."

C.F. Joyce, *Persephone in Hell*

acknowledgements

In the eight years that it has taken to write this second book of the Hassie Calhoun Trilogy, I have called on many willing friends, family members and colleagues to read and critique the work in progress. I am grateful to each of these people and would like to extend special thanks to Alun Hood, Bryan Kennedy, Nancy Stancill, David Harris and Minda Dowling for their input and expertise.

I am also very grateful to Lt. Bradley G. Robinson, US Navy, and Paul Northcott for their contributions as military experts. Their input has been invaluable.

To John McManus, I am eternally grateful to Janice for sharing her secrets with Zelda. Her class and elegance make an impeccable role model.

Steve Ostrow's *Saturday Night at the Baths*, Richard Freeman's *A Close Run Thing: The Navy and the Falklands War* and Edmund White's *City Boy* were invaluable resources that helped to credibly underpin the story. Many thanks to those authors.

And to Ian Graham Leask, I continue to appreciate your support and encouragement and (I mean this with all my heart) your nagging. On to the next one.

Also by Pamela Cory

Hassie Calhoun

Do I Know You?

Pamela Cory

CALUMET EDITIONS
Minneapolis

part one

chapter one

New York City, November 1969

They lived in Hell's Kitchen. The neighborhood was a quiet one, officially known as Clinton, which sounded like a nicer place for a single woman with a five-year-old son. When Hassie Calhoun and Kenny arrived from Reno that summer, the view from their fourth floor apartment had been the exact opposite of the one they'd left behind: an expansive, verdant landscape at the foot of the Sierra Nevada mountains versus an urban grid of narrow streets lined with boxy apartment buildings and the obligatory playground where local kids see-sawed or pushed their swings toward the sky. Their minders gathered on worn wooden benches while the older kids noisily played basketball. There were birds and cats and dogs—lots of dogs, some on leashes but most running free. Hassie had taken Kenny to the playground—reluctantly at first, unsure of their safety. But as she began to see familiar faces and nod in polite recognition of the regular denizens, it became routine and comfortable and proved the best way to meet neighbors and playmates for Kenny. Little by little, the modest apartment became their home. And now, the equipment and courts often stood empty but for shadows of near-naked trees; the wooden benches occasionally occupied by sad souls down on their luck, a desolate reminder that their first winter in New York City was on its way.

Hassie awaited a phone call and watched Kenny scribble his index finger in the condensation inside the window, a lonely leaf fluttering past in a rainy drizzle. She walked over to him and said, "If you're going out with Tommy today, you better get dressed."

"I want to go play on the jungle gym."

"Not in this weather, sweetie. Let's get dressed and then you need to have breakfast."

Kenny faced her, stuck his right foot out and said, "I can't find my other boot."

"I'm not surprised. That room of yours is a disaster." She brushed a lock of hair off his forehead, gently touching his plummy cheek. "Go look again, and hurry up." The little boy took off for his room as Hassie called after him, "And put on the clothes I laid out for you."

She went to the kitchen and lit the stove to boil water. She rested her hips against the Formica countertop, crossed her arms over her chest and fixed her eyes on the wall phone as if doing so would cause it to ring. It had been three days since her last audition, and based on recent experience, she had no real reason to expect that it would amount to anything. But her gut told her that this time was different. She believed she'd impressed the man she'd sung for—this Ruben Layne—a dark, brusque man with an unorthodox brand of charm. He'd had the gall to tell her that she was too thin. And he'd promised he'd be in touch.

Hassie shivered and pulled the cable-knit sweater tighter around her body. It was her day off from Rosenblum's Music Store, the job she'd taken to pay the bills while struggling for that first singing job. And she *had* lost weight since they got to New York. Her boss, Myron Rosenblum, made a point of mentioning the fact at least once a week and, lately, he'd come to work laden with homemade prune Danish or cinnamon *rugelach* or chocolate *babka*. He'd guilt her into eating by raising his hands to the heavens and saying, "The wife slaved for hours. You gotta put meat on those bones." She'd smile and send thanks to Gilda, and when he was busy with a customer she'd carefully wrap her share to bring home to Kenny.

Waiting for the kettle to boil, she wiped down the countertop, recalling her audition at a place called the Chelsea Baths. She'd learned that Ruben Layne had taken the basement levels of an old building on the lower west side of Manhattan and turned them into a private club with a cabaret lounge for entertainment. She was to audition for Mr. Layne, and he'd tell her more about the job. When she arrived, she was sent to a cavernous, rectangular room that had the feel of an old-fashioned nightclub; an oversized mirror ball hovered above the dance floor. The room was empty until an elderly black man shuffled onto the stage and said he was there to play for her. He took his time getting situated behind the keyboard, during which time a paunchy, middle-aged man with thinning dark hair and a day's growth of beard walked into the room and eyed her up and down. He introduced himself and then asked her if she knew "People" from *Funny Girl*, which, of course, she did and relaxed with the choice until he sternly told her *not* to emulate Barbra Streisand. The mere suggestion made her nerves kick in, which she struggled to keep out of her voice. But Mr. Layne applauded and then motioned for her to join him.

She thought back on the conversation that ensued, dissecting the meaning of everything he'd said. He'd seemed genuinely impressed with her—maybe a little too impressed with her legs—but she liked him, and now she had to wait. She went into the living room to fold up the sleeper sofa that was her bed. While tucking the mattress back into the frame she called out to Kenny, but his response was lost beneath the shrill ring of the telephone. She rushed back to the kitchen, pushed her hair from her face and answered the call.

"Is that Hassie Calhoun?"

"Yes, it's… yes."

"It's Ruben Layne."

"Hello, Mr. Layne. I've been expecting your call."

"First off, call me Ruben. I told you you'd hear from me, didn't I?"

"Yes, you did, Ruben." She stretched the coiled phone cord across to the stove and poured the boiling water over a teabag.

"You know you knocked me and Joe dead the other day."

"Joe?"

"The piano player?"

"Oh, yes, of course. That's very kind."

"You're a real pro. That Vegas experience shows."

"Is that your way of saying that I might be too expensive?"

Ruben laughed. "I had a feeling you'd be a tough negotiator."

"Are you offering me the job?"

"That's exactly what I'm doing. Are you interested?"

She looked up at the ceiling and mouthed *thank you*, and then smiled into the mouthpiece as she said, "Yes, sir."

"Well, I'm very interested in you. What say we explore this mutual interest?"

She recalled his leering attention during the audition and lightly said, "Now, Ruben. I'm not going to have any trouble with you, am I?"

"Trouble? Oh, I don't think so. But I never make promises I can't keep."

"Neither do I." She paused. "When do you want me to start?"

"We're booked out now until say first of Feb. But we need a contract, and I want to discuss your program."

She poured some orange juice for Kenny while saying, "I already have a pretty strong repertoire. I'm sure it'll work just fine—that is, if you think your piano player is up to it."

"Well, well, Miss Copa Room. You wanna bring your own musicians?"

"Not at all. But who do you have besides… Joe?"

"Bass and drums—darn good players that everybody else gets along with just fine." There was an awkward silence before he asked, "Do you understand what kind of place our club is… who the clientele are?"

"I understand that it's mostly men."

"So you know about these bathhouses here in Manhattan."

"Not really, but from what I saw when I auditioned, it seemed like a YMCA with music."

"Something like that, but the cabaret club is gonna knock the entertainment up a notch or two. You think you're up for that?"

Hassie peered out of the kitchen toward Kenny's quiet room and then casually asked, "Ruben, can you excuse me a minute?"

"Sure."

She muffled the receiver against her hip and called out, "Kenny? Come in here and eat your cereal." She went back to the call. "Sorry about that. You were saying?"

"When can you come in to work out the details? I'll show you around and explain how it all works."

She hesitated, not wanting to appear desperate, and then said, "I could make myself available this afternoon or... tomorrow." There was still no sign of Kenny.

"How about today, say three o'clock?"

"That'll work. Shall I meet you in the club?"

"Ask the doorman to guide you to my office."

"Thank you, Ruben. I'm grateful for the opportunity."

"I think we'll be good together, Hassie. Just remember that we're not the Copa Room."

"Not yet. Just give *me* a chance, and we'll get there."

"That's my girl. See you at three."

She hung up the phone and muttered, "No, Mr. Ruben Layne, I'm not your girl, and you better keep your pants on." She called out to Kenny again and started back through the living room, stepping around the sofa cushions still piled on the floor. His tiny room was a mess, but he wasn't there. The window leading out to the fire escape was open wide enough for a child to squeeze through. She ran over and opened it wider, stuck her head out into the chilly rain and called him again, scouring the rickety, black iron staircase. There was no sign of him anywhere, but she guessed where he'd gone. She stepped back into the room, shut the window and then ran out of the apartment, through the dingy stairwell and high-ceilinged corridors to the Jordan's apartment on the second floor. Someone was cooking with garlic. She knocked on the door, but no one answered. She knocked again, more forcefully with her fist. Carol Jordan opened the door wearing a bathrobe, her hair in curlers.

"Hassie, is everything all right?" Carol asked.

"Is Kenny here?"

"I don't think so."

Hassie sighed, and Carol asked, "Did he come down the fire

escape again?"

"His window was open."

Carol walked toward her son's bedroom, calling out, "Tommy, is Kenny in there with you? Come out here, please." She faced Hassie and said, "Tommy's not allowed on the fire escape."

Hassie looked away. "Kenny's not allowed out there either."

The two boys appeared. Kenny stood a distance from the women. Hassie reached out to him. "Come on. Let's leave Mrs. Jordan to finish dressing." She focused on Carol. "Will you call or come by for him when you're ready?"

"Of course."

Hassie tightly gripped Kenny's arm and led him to the door saying, "Oh, and, Carol, I have a business meeting this afternoon. Can Kenny stay here until I get back?"

The woman faked a smile. "Sure."

When they were back in the apartment, Hassie held Kenny's shoulders. "What have I told you over and over again that you must *never* do?"

"Go out by myself."

"And what else?"

"Go on the fire escape."

"Then why did you do it?"

"You talked on the phone a long time."

"I don't care if I talked for a whole day. You do not leave this apartment without my permission, and you never, *never* go out on that staircase unless I tell you to. It's dangerous, and you know better." She took his hand and led him to his room. They stood in the doorway while she said, "Look at that mess. Your clothes and shoes are piled on the floor. Your toys are scattered everywhere. Why can't you put them away like I've shown you?"

He walked over to the pile of dirty clothes and sat down in that way only a child can do—his legs bent at forty-five-degree angles underneath him. He was wearing a pair of old rain galoshes that must be too small for him now. She squatted beside him. "Is that what you want to wear today?"

He nodded. "They're my crappy weather boots."

"Kenny, we don't say crappy."

"You say it." His lower lip and chin trembled.

She drew her mouth into a straight line and brushed his hair away from his eyes as she said, "I know there's not a lot of room, but we can do better than this, don'tcha think?"

He dropped his head to his chest and cried. "Why can't we go back to Uncle Clay's house?"

She lifted his chin; her heart leapt at his credulous dark eyes. "Do you remember our talk with Uncle Clay when we decided to move to New York?" He wiped one side of his face with the back of his hand and nodded. She picked up a shirt and wiped the other side of his face as she said, "We're going to have an adventure here, right?"

He nodded again. "Why couldn't Uncle Clay come with us?"

"Because his job is in Reno. And Mommy works in New York. And Reno and New York are very different places, right?"

He shrugged. "But couldn't we live in a bigger department?"

She hugged him close as she said, "*A*partment, sweetie. And, yes, we will get a bigger apartment. I promise."

* * *

After sending Kenny off, Hassie finished making up the sleeper sofa, picturing her own bedroom with a nice big bed and a closet full of stylish clothes with matching shoes and handbags. She'd had that room in Clay Cooper's sprawling hacienda. She'd had a nice big bed and more comforts of home than she could ever have wished for. Back then—despite how comfortable and cared for Clay had made her feel—it had represented a life she was trying to forget. And now she didn't need that big bed… because she always slept alone… because she'd had a baby and then a toddler and now a five-year-old. Because the love of her life had died.

She went back to Kenny's room and started to clear up his mess, all the time thinking of the job at the baths and how much having a decent income would do for them. But as she smoothed the knotty chenille bedcover into place, she started to cry. The incident with

9

Kenny had frazzled her nerves. She sat down on the bed; her thoughts and emotions were all over the place. She'd spent so many years of her life letting people down and was determined not to screw things up with her son. But every day there was some kind of reminder that she'd taken him from a normal, safe environment and inserted him into an unstable one. And now having a nightclub singer for a mother? Wouldn't Clay Cooper have a heyday with that one! He'd never supported her decision to move with Kenny to New York and had tried to talk her out of it. She stood up, wiped away tears and, with a rush of determination, said, "Shit. He's my kid. I'll take care of him. I'll take care of us."

She went back to the kitchen, the extent of her loneliness weighing her down. She'd tried making friends with a few women in her building. But they seemed intent on avoiding her and made her feel awkward or foolish, and she didn't feel that she could trust anyone. But she was bursting to tell someone about her new job, which evoked thoughts of her childhood teacher and mentor, Barbara Crumpler. Years after she left Barbara and her family behind in Texas to work in Las Vegas, she went home when her mother died and learned that Barbara had moved back to England. The letter she'd sent from Reno judiciously filled in the years since they'd last seen each other and included a photo of Kenny. Barbara's return response had slapped Hassie's hands for losing touch and let her know that her naïve mistakes and bad judgment under evil influences were not acceptable excuses. It had taken time to get back into Barbara's good graces, and now Hassie treasured their conversations. But the phone calls were expensive, and it had been a while since she felt secure enough with her earnings to spend that money. In a few weeks she'd get that first paycheck from the baths, and the call to Barbara would be full of good news.

She picked up the cup of tea, which was now cold, and poured it down the drain. Clay's monthly phone call was due in a few days. But it was becoming harder and harder to open up to him; the distance between them had grown greater than the near three thousand miles. She simply couldn't shake her guilt about how she'd left things with him. She sometimes thought that if it weren't for Kenny, she wouldn't stay in touch with Clay at all. And then she'd hate herself for such thoughts, remembering that she would possibly have had a nervous breakdown if he hadn't convinced her to leave Vegas and then taken her home to Reno, where she soon found out she was pregnant. And to make matters worse, and for the long torturous period of the pregnancy, she wasn't sure whose baby she carried. The night that she'd left Jake Contrata's bed to seek comfort with Frank Sinatra had been emblazoned on her heart and mind. But when the nurse handed her son to her, his little head of wispy, jet-black hair poking out of the soft, blue blanket, she knew that the love she and Jake genuinely—if not oftentimes furiously—shared had created this amazing little creature, and he would forever represent the union that was never meant to be.

She placed her hand on her stomach, recalling so vividly—remembering how unstable and unhappy she'd been—that the thought of having a child to look after had made her ill. She'd wished it would go away. She'd considered getting rid of it—anything to avoid the reality of what the pregnancy would do to her. She'd never said any of this to Clay, but she felt that he knew what a monster she was. But he never mentioned it or judged or chastised her in any way. Instead, he made sure she was comfortable, demonstrating time and again how he felt about her and carefully suggesting that he would marry her and give her baby a father and a home. But as close as they'd become, Clay was still Jake's half brother, and that connection was bothersome like they were bound to share the evil gene that had caused Jake to hurt her. She simply didn't love Clay enough to take that chance.

The fact remained that Clay had nursed her through a terrible time, making sure that as she got stronger and her newborn son was happy and healthy, she spent at least an hour a day on his grand piano. Immersing herself in her music had been the main factor in her recovery. She'd promised him that she would stay connected to her songwriting. She'd promised that she would find access to a piano, which was a major reason for taking the job at Rosemblum's—a store full of pianos, of which she had her pick. Clay had also introduced her to the volumes of great literature and poetry that lined the shelves in his study, encouraging her to read and comprehend the writings of others while focusing on her own voice—to make her music great.

She read and studied, earmarking pages and passages that touched her emotions, which, at the time, were desperately trying to drag her down. Clay helped her focus on the good things, which eventually gave her the strength to leave the comforts of his love and care and venture off—albeit unsteadily—on her own. She'd believed she was doing the right thing. She still had to prove it.

She went over to the sofa and located her notebook on the coffee table. In the precious few hours she had on her own, she focused on the songs she'd been working on. Her intention had been to pull from the emotions she'd experienced during her childhood in Texas through those tumultuous years in Nevada. Didn't her own love, loss, success and failure have meaning to most people? But, since their arrival in New York City, her songs had taken a turn toward lachrymose—sad and hopeless, with minor melodies that would depress Little Miss Sunshine. Where were the words to describe the depth of emotion that still existed when she allowed herself to think about the intensely volatile, life-changing love that damn near destroyed her?

It had been six years since Jake Contrata died, and in that time she'd given birth to a son he had never known and had become a mother at the age of twenty-two. But when she thought about Jake—when she remembered the good things about their time together—she was right back there with him in Vegas, living in his suite at the Sands, reveling in the high life and spending hours in his arms, where being loved by him was the sweetest, most exciting thing she'd ever experienced until he had become obsessive and irrational and literally almost loved her to death.

She rubbed her finger across the scar just above her eyebrow—the distinct reminder of the power behind the blows that had knocked her out and sent her to the hospital. She needed to forget Jake Contrata. But these days that didn't seem possible. For when she looked at Kenny, she was reminded of his father's mop of black hair, his dark, compelling eyes and thin but firm lips that broke into a determined smile and clouded her better judgment. She'd selfishly dragged Kenny across the country to pursue her dream job in New York. But now, as the opportunity at the baths was becoming real, she realized that her main focus was to give her son a new and better life. She'd be away from him many more hours of the day than either of them was used to, and she'd need someone to help look after him. Babysitters were expensive, and she could impose on the neighbors only so much. It was clear that taking this job wouldn't be easy. But then not much of the last ten years of her life had been easy. She needed this job. She wanted it. She'd make it work.

chapter **two**

February 1970

Warren Zachary entered the Chelsea Baths, escaping the arctic air, the smell of chlorine drawing him toward the Friday night action. The labyrinthine corridors peeled off into function areas throughout the lavish conversion of the old gymnasium. He passed a dozen or so men headed for the sauna or pool, naked but for the standard-issue white towel tightly wrapped around their asses and thighs, secured at their waists. His eyes glided past them, one by one, tempting him. But his cousin, Ruben, was waiting for him in the cabaret club.

Already seated at his table, Ruben waved a cigar in a motion for Warren to join him. "Looks like you've had a busy day of crazy," he said.

"You have no idea. Secretary announced she's pregnant. Two partners took a long weekend, and good ol' Warren will just handle it all. I need a drink."

A young man dressed in a white tank top and black satin hot pants that left little to Warren's imagination stopped by to take his coat and hat. Warren thanked him and watched him walk away and then looked at his cousin who'd screwed his mouth into a disapproving moue and said, "Shameless, you are."

"What?" Warren loosened his tie, slumping into the comfortable chair. "And for what am I being summoned here tonight?"

14

"What do you want to drink?"

"Dry martini, olives. Double up the vodka."

Ruben waved another scantily clad young man over, ordered a couple of drinks and then slapped the guy on his ass and said, "Thanks, Milo."

Warren laughed. "I really doubt his name's Milo. What's going on, Ruben?"

Ruben lit the cigar and made a jerky, sweeping gesture. "Look at this place."

Warren quickly peered over each shoulder, shrugged and said, "It's Friday night."

"But it's early."

"So?"

"Remember that new singer I told you I hired? The one who used to work in Vegas?"

"Honestly, I don't, but tell me now."

A different waiter served the drinks, and Warren told him to bring another round in fifteen minutes. The lights dimmed, and Ruben said, "You're gonna see for yourself."

There were only a few empty seats in the room that Ruben had originally wanted to convert from a seedy dance hall to a venue that could accommodate everything from private parties to themed gala events. His aim was to build a downtown version of the Upper West Side's Continental Baths—a safe haven where homosexual men could gather to enjoy a relaxing spa atmosphere or an evening of music and dancing. Warren had convinced him that a cabaret club was the classier, more lucrative way to go. He'd also convinced him to use an interior decorator friend of his who had a flair for taking the ordinary to the brink of the outrageous without going over the top. The result was this campy throwback to 1940s Hollywood with mirrors and blue and gold velvet curtains and decorative elements of shimmering glass. In the four months the room had been open, Warren had only been in a couple of times and hadn't yet decided if he liked the place or not.

The musicians filled the small stage. Joe Monroe sat behind the white baby grand piano and projected the belief that it was his show.

The bass player and drummer followed his lead; their music was solid. They set the mood with Dave Brubeck-style free jazz, which eventually settled into an easy bossa nova beat and the intro to "The Look of Love." A tall, dark-haired woman came on stage wearing a black Grecian-styled gown with straps across one shoulder, her hair in a messy pile on her head, her lips a delicious red. A pale, rosy lilac spotlight intensified her aura, immediately pulling Warren in, and he wondered if her hair was really that rich, black coffee color and imagined her long, perfect legs underneath the flowing dress. He felt his cousin watching him from time to time, but kept his thoughts to himself, rapt in the woman's performance, which was both sensual and honest.

Toward the end of the first set, Ruben leaned in to Warren and said, "She's gonna take a break in a minute, and you'll meet her."

Warren hinted a smile, nodding approval, but stayed focused on the stage.

She'd been sitting on a stool for a medley of Bacharach-David songs. As the applause died down, she moved forward, placed the microphone in its stand and stood in front of the audience of mostly well-dressed, if somewhat *over-dressed*, men and the odd table of muscle-bound *dudes*.

"Thank you so much," she said. "I'd also like to thank Burt Bacharach and Carole King for their wonderful songs and Dusty Springfield and Mama Cass Elliot for their contributions to the charts, which I've had great pleasure performing for you." She recognized the band members and then waited for the applause to wane before saying, "We're gonna take a break and give you a chance to stretch your legs, so get up and dance. But first, I'd like to leave you with one of my favorites, written by Jule Stein and made popular by the incomparable Barbra Streisand."

Warren swallowed the last of his drink and stuck his open hand in Ruben's face when he attempted to speak. He'd been a fan of Joe Monroe's since the first time he'd heard him play in a basement jazz club in the West Village. In fact, Warren had been instrumental in bringing Joe to work in the Chelsea Baths. During Joe's sensitively rendered intro, Hassie looked as if she might be saying a prayer. She had a way of making Warren feel that she was actually singing to him. He believed that every person in the room felt the same way—not unlike the eyes in a portrait that seemed to follow whomever looked into them. When she sang the first line of the song— "People, people who need people are the luckiest people in the world..."—his skin tingled, and he realized that he'd been totally captivated by this woman. But he also knew that there were better singers with better interpretations of this song, and he was forced to question why she had such a unique grip on him—something he'd not been remotely prepared for and something that, for several reasons, unnerved him.

The band took her out of the song in a flourish. She threw kisses and waved and, for a moment, he questioned her sincerity—was she acting the part, desperate to leave the stage and have a drink or rip off her dress or, generally, get the hell out of that room? About half the guys in the audience stood up, applauding and whistling but Warren remained seated, concentrating on the stage, his fingers interlocked as his hands rested on the table. He relished the moment until Ruben slapped him on the back, and asked, "So? What'd you think? Ain't she the shit?"

"That's an odd choice of words but, yes, she's terrific." He motioned to the waiter. "You say she's coming out to see us?"

"Yeah, which means I gotta get rid of this cigar. She goes all lecturey when she sees me smoke."

"Good. Where's my second drink?" The band stopped, and the piped-in music kicked in with Sergio Mendes and Brazil 66; a mirror ball reflected glimmering light onto the ceiling and walls.

Ruben raised his voice above the music. "You want some food? I can get a plate of something for us."

Warren nodded. "I'm starving." He focused on nothing for a moment and then asked, "Is she married?"

"Who? Hassie? No, not involved with anybody, best I can tell. Anyway, she don't know it yet, but she's got the hots for me."

Warren laughed. "My guess, it's the other way around."

"Can you blame me? Look at her. You can't tell it in that dress she's wearing, but she's got great tits too." Ruben leaned into Warren while he crushed the tip of his cigar in the ashtray and said, "Not that you'd notice that sorta thing."

"You don't know what I notice."

Ruben nodded his head slowly. "Come to think of it, you *were* ogling her a bit."

"*Ogling?*" Warren said, laughing.

"Yeah, I caught a couple of looks like you were ready to tear her clothes off."

"Maybe I was."

"Aw, come on. Who do you think you're talking to here?"

"You don't always know everything, Ruben."

"Hmph. But I know *you* better than anybody, and you know it."

Warren shrugged.

Ruben said, "Anyway, here she comes."

Hassie approached the table, and Warren stood just as Ruben leapt up to kiss her cheek and said, "Honey, you were sensational."

"Thank you, Ruben. I told you the Bacharach medley was ready to go."

"Yeah, yeah. You were right on the money."

Warren stepped closer and proffered his hand. "Hello, Hassie. I'm Warren Zachary, Ruben's cousin."

She shook his hand. "Ruben told me you'd be here tonight. It's nice to meet you." He pulled the chair next to him out for her, and she sat as she asked, "Did you enjoy the set?"

"Very much. You're quite a singer."

"And that's high praise coming from Warren," Ruben said. "He's into that highbrow opera sort of thing."

Warren glanced sideways at Ruben. "I enjoy the opera and the symphony and the occasional Broadway show. I've also been known to go for a jazz fix in the Village."

She smiled at him. "A man after my heart—not that I've had an opportunity to enjoy much of the city's culture."

"That's a shame. Maybe we should work on changing that."

"Oh-kay," Ruben said and grabbed hold of Milo as he walked

past. "What'll you have to drink, Hassie?"

"My usual, please."

"Warren, you feel like joining Miss Calhoun for a glass of champagne?"

"I'll stick with the vodka, thanks."

Ruben chatted with the waiter. Warren asked Hassie how she liked working in the club and listened while she talked about getting to know the band and how skeptical she'd been in the beginning. She was the perfect cross between dynamic and feminine—the way she elegantly talked with her hands when she was trying to get her point across or curiously tilted her head while she listened as he talked. Ruben joined in, saying, "Yeah, you gave me a real hard time about *old* Joe, didn't ya?"

She nodded. "I did. I hate to admit it, but I thought nothing could ever top working the Copa Room in Vegas."

"Well, this might not be *the* Copa Room," Warren said, "but old Joe's a great case of *don't judge a book by its cover.*"

The waiter served Warren a martini and then presented a bottle of Laurent Perrier Rosé champagne to Ruben. He touched the bottle. "That'll do." When they each had a drink, Ruben raised his glass and said, "*Genatset!*"

"That's Armenian for 'cheers,'" Warren said in Hassie's direction.

"Yes, I know." She took a sip.

Ruben twirled the unlit cigar in the ashtray. "So, Warren, tell Hassie what you thought about her set."

"I liked your program. I liked that it was mostly current and popular with this sort of crowd."

"I hear a 'but,'" she said.

Warren smiled. "But I believe your repertoire in Vegas was something quite different. Why don't you sing some of those great standards?"

"Told you he was a know-it-all about this stuff," Ruben said. "But he's not that clever. Tell him, honey."

She sipped the champagne and then said, "First of all, Warren, you're right about my repertoire in Vegas. Except for a few original songs, it was mostly the great standards and honestly, those songs are the basis of who I am as a singer. But Ruben knows his business, too, and we agreed that this place needs diversity."

"So your second set is the old stuff?"

She nodded. "Some of it. You gonna stick around?"

"You bet." He still couldn't put his finger on that *thing* about her that unnerved him.

Ruben motioned for the waiter to pour more champagne for Hassie, after which he stood up and said, "Folks, if you'll excuse me, I'll see what the chef can whip up for us."

"Ruben, you know that I can't eat a thing until after the show," Hassie said.

"I don't think you eat much at any time. But I'm looking after my guest here now. We'll worry about you later."

Warren perused the nearby tables, observing that the few women in the room seemed to be considerably older than the men accompanying them. When he felt Hassie's eyes on him, he looked over to see her smiling. He smiled back and asked, "What's the matter?"

"I'm deciding whether or not you look like a *Warren*."

He gently laughed. "What does a Warren look like?"

"I know that sounds silly, but I'm intrigued by people's names. Ruben looks exactly like a *Ruben* to me. You know what I mean?"

He nodded. "So what name do you think I look like?"

"Your last name is Zachary?"

"Actually it's Zacharian. My grandfather changed it to Zachary when he brought his family over from the old country."

"I'm going to call you Zach. That's a good name, don'tcha think?"

"I suppose so. Although I hope Zach Zachary doesn't catch on."

She put her hand on his forearm and leaned into him. "I think I should be the only one who calls you Zach."

She smelled like fresh flowers. He put his hand on top of hers and said, "You know my cousin's in love with you."

She gently slapped his hand. "He's my boss, Zach. He's been told to behave himself."

"Yeah, well, keep telling him, because I think he has other ideas."

"He's harmless really. And I'm very good at taking care of myself."

"I've no doubt about that." He took the champagne glass from her and set it on the table while saying, "Ruben tells me you're single—or at least that you're not married."

"And that's important because…"

"Have dinner with me."

"Tonight?"

"I was thinking of one of your nights off… somewhere away from here and—"

"Ruben?"

He nodded. "What do you say? We can go anywhere you like."

"You have no idea how long it's been since I've been out like an adult."

"Then does that mean there is no man in your life?"

She squinted, wrinkling her nose and then tentatively said, "I have a five-year-old son."

"Get a sitter." He reached over and brushed a bit of hair away from her eye. "Because as charming as I'm sure your little boy is, I'd like to have you all to myself on our first date." She took a deep breath and Warren said, "Speaking of names, where'd you get a name like *Hassie*?"

"My mother was part Choctaw. She named me Nia Hushi after her grandmother. I think she called me Hushi as a baby, but it eventually evolved to Hassie—or some such story. I only ever remember being called Hassie."

"So, Hassie Calhoun, will you please have dinner with me?"

She smiled and nodded. "Yeah, okay."

He took a card and a pen from his shirt pocket and handed it to her. "Give me your number, and I'll call you tomorrow."

She studied the card for a moment and then said, "You're a lawyer?"

He nodded. "Guilty."

She jotted her number on the back of the card and handed it to him. "Put this away. Here comes the boss."

Warren tucked the card and pen in his pocket. Ruben joined them with a glass of scotch and asked, "What'd I miss?"

"Hassie was just telling me about what it was like to work in the Copa Room."

"You know, it amazes me how much attention I get when I talk about Frank Sinatra," she said.

Warren raised his eyebrows at her as Ruben asked, "Hey, Warren, do you believe that Ol' Blue Eyes didn't chase this woman around the piano a few times?"

Warren winked at Hassie as he said, "I don't believe that for a minute."

"It really doesn't matter what you two believe," she said. "He was a perfect gentleman and treated me like a real pro, which was more important than I actually knew at the time."

"How so?" asked Warren.

"I was just a kid when I went to the Sands. Frank came in, first as a headliner and then with the Rat Pack—I mean, seriously, I was hanging out with those guys… Frank, Dean and Sammy. Frank encouraged me. He's one of the reasons I had the confidence to do my own show at the Tropicana. He used to come in to see me. I didn't appreciate then what his support was saying to the whole of Vegas. And I'm not sure I ever really thanked him."

"How long was he there?" Warren asked.

"On and off for a couple of years. But the day came when he had to move on—to make a film. He came into the Copa Room one day and said goodbye." She sipped the champagne. "I can't believe I'm admitting this now, but I actually thought he might ask me to go with him."

"And you still insist that he didn't fancy you," Warren said.

"Maybe it was me who fancied him." She stood up. "And on that note, it's time to get ready for the late set."

Warren stood to join her and asked, "Shall we save something for you to eat?"

"Thanks, but I can't hang around tonight." She looked directly into his eyes and said, "Maybe another time."

Ruben stood and walked around to hug her. "Have a great show and, honey, flirt with the guys a little more."

"I'm not sure these guys are interested in my flirting with them."

"You know what I mean." He swirled his hands in front of his round belly. "Show 'em some love."

She laughed. "Okay, Ruben." She reached out to shake Warren's hand and said, "It was nice to meet you, Zach. I look forward to seeing you again."

She fluttered her fingers at Ruben and walked away.

Ruben turned to Warren and said, "Zach?"

He shrugged one shoulder. "She says I don't look like a *Warren* and wants to call me Zach."

"I see." Ruben sat down, took a pull on his drink and said, "Sit down for a minute. What did you two really talk about?"

"Her life in Vegas."

"And that's all?"

"That's all. Why?"

"Because you looked awful cozy together."

"We just talked, Ruben, and you're right. She's gorgeous and talented and... I'm wondering why she would want to work here."

"Excuse me?"

"I'm thinking that she can do better—say at the Carlyle or a Broadway show."

"Well, thanks for the vote of confidence, but from what I know, since moving to Manhattan she's been eking out a living selling musical instruments over on 48th Street. In my mind, I've given her her first break in the big time."

Warren slapped Ruben on his back. "That's my demure, completely objective cousin."

"No. No, really," Ruben said, too seriously. "You know I've got a lot riding on this little venture, and we've got a long way to go to compete with what Steve Ostrow's doing at the Continental. We're trying to do something different here, and I'm countin' on Hassie to build a strong clientele."

"Okay. I get it. I thought you were crazy to give her a six-month contract. But your instincts are good for building a business. It's one of the more annoying things about you."

Ruben half-smiled, focused on the stage and then said, "Don't fuck with her, Warren. Or should I say, don't fuck with her, *Zach*?"

"We're all adults, Ruben. I won't be doing anything she doesn't want to do."

"I wish I believed you."

Warren carefully nodded as his prurient gaze landed on a trio of athletic types with bulging physiques with shirts too snug.

Ruben watched him for a moment and then asked, "Now what?"

"I've been thinking about taking up weight-lifting. What do you think?"

Ruben pushed back from the table, stood and said, "I think you're a horny lunatic."

chapter three

On Kenny's sixth birthday—a Saturday afternoon in late May—
Hassie and a couple of the mothers in her building went across
the street to the May Matthews Playground and staked out two of the
square cement tables that appeared to have grown out of the ground.
It was Kenny's first party with other kids, so Hassie let him have his
desired baseball theme. She bought matching plates, cups and napkins
as well as flimsy paper cloths that would do little more than cover
the tabletops. She got balloons from a street vendor and a cake from
a neighborhood bakery—a rectangular cake decorated to look like a
baseball diamond with plastic miniature players in various game poses.
The cost of everything had set her back at least a full day's wages, but as
she watched Kenny running and laughing and having the time of his life,
it felt like the best and most important thing she'd ever done for him.

Hassie waved her arm in a windshield wiper motion to get Zach's
attention and then signaled that they needed to cut the cake. Zach
trotted over to the table carrying Kenny on his shoulders, the batch of
noisy kids running after him like he was the Pied Piper of Hamelin.
When they'd all arrived, Zach turned to face them and asked, "What
do we do now?"

They shouted in unison, "Sing 'Happy Birthday'!"

Zach started singing, the kids joined in, and Hassie stood by,
smiling. Zach's transition into their lives had been easy. Kenny took to

him straight off the mark—started calling him Uncle Zach and wanted to spend most of his idle time in Zach's company. When they finished singing, Zach set Kenny down on the cement bench in front of the table. He blew out the candles with one big breath. The kids cheered. Kenny stuck the knife down the middle of the cake and then handed it to Hassie and said, "Here, you do it."

"You want to keep the baseball players?" Hassie asked.

He nodded enthusiastically and pulled the plastic pieces off the cake one by one, licking the icing off each base. Hassie cut the cake into squares and slid them onto the paper plates that were then doled out by the chaperones, Carol and Jessica. When they'd all been served, Hassie looked around for Zach, who was standing to the side nursing a cup of Hawaiian Punch. She took a piece of cake over to him and said, "You look like you could use a little spike in that punch."

He took the cake from her and focused on Kenny. "Where do they get all that energy? I think herding cattle would be easier."

"Zach, nobody told you that you had to single-handedly entertain all ten kids."

"You're right," he said, but didn't look at her. "That's the thanks I get for trying to take some of the pressure off you."

She took the empty cup from him. "That's not what I'm saying. You're a star, and Kenny's thrilled. In fact, he'd probably rather have you here carrying him around on your shoulders than all the cake and balloons I could buy."

"So that's it. He likes me better than you."

Hassie laughed and knocked her hip into his. "Come on. Eat your cake and then figure out how you're going to entertain them next."

He took a big bite of the cake, leaving a dollop of icing on his upper lip. Hassie wiped her finger across her lip and said, "You missed your mouth."

Zach hooked his arm around her waist and pulled her close, saying, "Maybe you should lick it off." He drew his mouth close to hers while she giggled and squirmed before he kissed her hard.

She pushed back from him, still laughing while pretending to be perturbed and then brushed her mouth with her fingertips and kissed him again. "You're a troublemaker, you know."

He swallowed the last bite of the cake and then wiped his mouth on the back of his hand. "You bring out the devil in me." He handed her the empty plate and fork and jogged toward the playground equipment, motioning the kids to join him, shouting, "Come on you bunch of chuckleheads. Let's work off this sugar high." In a flurry of shouts and squeals, they took their places on the seesaw and swings while Zach helped the littlest guy up the slide's ladder.

Carol and Jessica sat at one of the tables, deep in conversation. Hassie focused on Zach. His dark, brooding sex appeal had her attention from the get-go, and these last months of getting to know him had been anything but conventional *dating*. He was unpredictable and could lurch from treating her like royalty—wining and dining her in Manhattan's finest restaurants and bars—to going for a couple of weeks without so much as a phone call. If she questioned his motives or intentions, he'd say something totally irrelevant but with such charming conviction that she'd practically chastise herself for having negative thoughts. And to make it all more confusing, she usually ended up being much less annoyed than she expected she should be. The fact of the matter was that she didn't really understand what she wanted from the relationship, and there were times when she felt that she might be trying to force something between them for Kenny's sake.

They had jumped into bed pretty quickly, and for a while she was simply lost in the knowledge that she'd been without a man for a long time. But she soon realized that she missed the passion she'd shared with Jake Contrata. Admittedly, she'd gone a little wild when she got to Vegas, something that in hindsight had initially been a reaction to her puritanical upbringing—the proverbial sowing of wild oats. But in doing so, Jake showed her how to love and about making love, and she learned how to be a woman. Remembering some of those reckless times made her blush—how Jake made her feel and what that overwhelming desire could do to her. But that hunger for unfettered passion steadily waned, and for a while she wondered if maybe she'd sown too many wild oats—that maybe she was finished with that part of her life. And then she met Zach, and things changed and it was different and she just didn't know what she thought about sex any more.

Hassie was drawn from her thoughts as Carol walked up and said, "We cleared up the dirty plates and cups. I need to get the Polaski boys home, so if you don't mind, I'll take Tommy and walk them across the street. Jessica will help with the other kids when you're ready for them to leave."

"Thanks so much, Carol. Was it too obvious that I'm a rookie at this kids party business?"

"They all had fun. That's what matters."

Carol took her son and walked away with three other boys—twins and their older brother. Before they crossed the street, Zach ran over to talk to her. Hassie's attention was drawn to Kenny who'd gotten right in one of the other boy's face. She walked over to them and said, "Hey, what's going on here?"

"He called me butt face," Kenny said, pointing at the stocky boy.

Hassie frowned and asked, "Luke, what's wrong? That's not a very nice way to talk."

Luke sneered at Kenny and then said, without looking at Hassie, "He gave Tommy one of his baseball players, but he won't give me one."

"Kenny, don't you think you can share with Luke too?"

Kenny wrinkled his nose and then fiercely shook his head, tightly gripping the plastic figures.

Hassie held his arm and said, "Kenny, this is not how we behave. Luke came to your party and brought you a nice present. I think you should apologize to him and—"

He pulled away from her and ran back to the seesaw.

Hassie signaled Jessica and said, "Come with me, Luke. Mrs. Martinez will take you and the others home."

Zach took a big bag of trash over to the metal cans and then joined Hassie who stood watching Kenny. He had jumped back on the seesaw with the last remaining child.

"I think this was a roaring success," Zach said.

She shook her head. "I don't know what to do with him sometimes."

"Who? Kenny?"

She nodded. "I think he really hates me for taking him away from his happy home in Reno."

Zach put his arm around her shoulders and said, "He could never hate you, Hassie. You're his mama, and you take good care of him."

"Yeah, well. It's time to go home." She focused on the seesaw and then shouted, "Kenny! Come on, we're leaving now."

Zach waited a moment and then asked, "Why don't you come over to my apartment tonight? We can relax and order in—have some good wine, and then maybe I'll let you seduce me."

"That's tempting, but I should probably stay in with Kenny."

Zach made a "that's ridiculous" face and said, "Hass, he's exhausted. He'll be asleep by seven o'clock and, anyway, I've sorted it all out with Carol. She'll keep him for the night as long as you pick him up by the time they leave for church in the morning."

Hassie's mouth tensed. "You shouldn't have made those plans without asking me. Maybe I don't want Kenny staying the night with the Jordans." She walked away, shouting at Kenny. The two boys ran over to her, and they all walked back to where Zach stood. "Kenny, have you thanked Uncle Zach for coming to your party and playing with your friends?"

Zach reached over to him and said, "Was that a super-duper party?"

Kenny nodded, still gripping the plastic ball players.

"Did you thank your mom for all her hard work?"

Kenny looked up at Hassie.

She pushed his hair from his eyes and asked, "It was our first real party, wasn't it?"

"Can we go home now?"

Zach grabbed the two bags containing Kenny's birthday presents, and the four of them walked to the curb. While waiting for the oncoming traffic to pass, Zach leaned into Hassie and said, "You deserve to relax and be pampered. Will you please meet me at my place at eight o'clock?"

They walked the boys across the street. At the entrance to their building, she took the gifts from Zach and said, "Okay, I'll come over. Just don't ever do that again."

Zach waved to Kenny. "Happy birthday, buddy. See you again soon."

Kenny ran in the door. Zach touched Hassie's arm and said, "Don't be late. There's something I want to show you."

* * *

Inside the apartment, Hassie took the gifts into Kenny's room and dumped them on his bed. "You got a lot of cool presents, didn't you?"

He reached for the model of a police car and dropped down to the floor, rolling it around while making siren sounds. Hassie gave him a moment and then said, "Kenny, you weren't very nice to Luke, were you?"

"He's not my friend."

He was so serious she knew there was more to the story, but she was too tired to hear it. She moved closer to him and said, "You need a bath and then you can play with your toys."

He stopped and looked up at her. "Why? I didn't sweat or nothin'."

"You didn't sweat or *anything* and, yes, you did get dirty. Let's have a bath and then I'll help you put away your toys."

He resumed the police car's noisy race around the floor. She sighed. "I'll be back in five minutes, and we're going to the tub."

She fell onto the living room sofa, wishing she hadn't agreed to go out. Zach's assumptive behavior really irked her, but he'd meant well, and he did know how to pamper her. She'd gone through a range of emotions that day, first thinking of Clay, who'd been there for all of Kenny's birthdays, including the day he was born. She was surprised they hadn't heard from him. Surely he hadn't forgotten. Kenny had become too important to him, and there was no way that he could know that Zach was now in the picture, which worried her at times. If things didn't work out with Zach, Kenny would lose another important male connection and, again, it would be her fault.

Her legs felt weighted to the sofa, but Kenny was too quiet. She peered into his room. He lay on his bed, prone and fully dressed like he'd collapsed. His mouth slightly gaped, drooling onto his bedspread. She sat on the edge of the bed beside him—her ebony-haired, onyx-eyed little boy who had come into her world six years ago and changed her life. Now when she watched him and listened to him chatter about nothing that meant a thing to her, she often saw the sheer, unadulterated evidence that Kenny was Jake Contrata's son, and she'd yet to decide if that was a good thing.

She shut the door and went to the kitchen. She meant to make a cup of coffee but took an open bottle of wine from the fridge and poured it into a juice glass—a habit she'd picked up back in Vegas from her friend and ex-showgirl, Dotty, who said it didn't count as *drinking* if it wasn't in a wine glass. It upset her to think about Jake, so why did she do it? Why did she let herself wonder what her life with Kenny would have been like if Jake hadn't died? Because in reality, it wouldn't have been the romanticized version she'd clung to. They would probably have gotten married, and Kenny would've had a mother and a father. But why would she dare to think that Jake would have been anything less than the son-of-a-bitch who had abused her—emotionally *and* physically? What good would that have been for Kenny?

She turned on the radio at the opposite end of the counter. The dial was set on a station that played two hours of her favorite music on Saturday afternoon—the great standards of years past sung by the equally great recording artists. She turned up the volume to hear Sarah Vaughn's recording of "Stardust" with the Count Basie Orchestra. She recognized it from her father's collection, one of his favorites. What would her father think of her life now? Would he have urged her to stay in Reno with Clay and raise her son in a wholesome, loving environment? Would he ever have supported her taking her five-year-old son to New York City to start over again? She'd never know the answer to those questions, and Kenny would never know Jackson Calhoun. In fact, at the rate things were going, Zach was the dominant male influence in his life—at least for now.

She poured more wine and took the glass to the sofa. Kenny could sleep for an hour before she'd need to wake him and start the battle for a bath all over again. She relaxed, propping her feet on the coffee table. The phone rang—Zach? Making sure she was coming over? She went back to the kitchen and answered the call with a flat, "Hello."

"Hello, gorgeous."

"Clay. I was just thinking that we haven't heard from you."

"I called earlier but guessed you were out with the birthday boy."

"Yeah. We had a little party in the playground across the street. Can you believe he's six?"

"No, I can't. I miss the little guy."

"And he misses you. He's growing up fast and getting a little too big for his britches."

Clay laughed. "How are *you*, Hassie?"

"I'm good, thanks. The job at the cabaret club is going well, and the financial pressure has eased a bit."

"Glad to hear it. Any chance you two can come out for a visit this summer? I'll send you airplane tickets."

"That's tempting and very generous of you, but it's such a task to work two jobs and still have time to be Kenny's mother. I've got a rhythm going now, and well, let's just say that I need to stick with it."

"I understand. Where is he? Can I speak with him?"

"He just crashed and is dead asleep. I'd wake him but—"

"No, don't do that. Just tell him I called and give him a big hug."

"I will and thanks so much for calling."

"Take care, Hass."

She hesitated and then said, "Clay? We miss you."

"I miss you, too, Hassie."

She stood at the sink and softly cried, feeling the pain that she heard in Clay's voice and recognizing that the strong woman façade of hers merely camouflaged the gaping hole in her life—a cruel reminder of the vibrant, sensual woman she used to be, the woman that seemed to have died with Jake. Clay knew her better than anyone, and despite the growing distance between them, she knew she could count on him to be there if she needed him. But she still couldn't bring herself to tell him about Zach. And she wasn't exactly sure why.

* * *

She rang the bell at the front door of Zach's building, and he buzzed her in without comment. Halfway down the corridor, the door to his apartment stood ajar; she could hear symphonic music. She knocked and then guardedly pushed the door open to an empty living room. She called out to Zach but felt that she shouldn't leave the room. It seemed odd, and she sensed that someone was in the apartment with him. She laid her handbag on a chair, calling out his name again, and then heard what sounded like the clicking of a woman's heels on the bare wooden floor of the corridor from the bedroom. She felt off-kilter and wanted to sit down but couldn't move. The footsteps got closer; she stayed focused on the doorway from the hall until the figure appeared. She recognized Zach's—albeit distorted—face, but the body was that of a woman. She gasped, steadied herself on the table beside her and then asked, "Zach? Is that *you*?"

He gracefully moved forward while saying, "Call me Zelda." His voice was breathy with the slightest hint of a southern accent. As he got closer to her, she could see that he wore heavy makeup and false eyelashes. The dark wig was a wavy, swept up style like Elizabeth Taylor wore. Pearl and rhinestone earrings were clamped to his earlobes. "Do you like the suit?" he asked. "It's Chanel."

Hassie clasped her hands together to stop them shaking and then took in the classic, black bouclé wool skirt and jacket and low-heeled black pumps. Her face warmed, and it was difficult to manage eye contact, but she finally said, "It's very nice."

He fingered the tie of the white blouse. "Could you tie this into a bow, please? I'm not very good with this sort of thing."

Hassie walked closer, took hold of the streaming ties, but her hands shook too much, and she finally stepped back and said, "I can't do this."

He turned toward her, propped one hand on his hip and said, "Let's have a drink." The overall image was confusing. His demeanor was more like that of Warren Zachary, which made for a frightening sight, as he was dressed as this scary woman. She wanted to grab her handbag and leave. "Wine or vodka?" he asked.

"Vodka. Lots of vodka."

He laughed and then made the drinks without speaking. He moved like a woman and poured the vodka like a female bartender might. He seemed to have become this woman. She sat down as he turned to face her and said, "I know this is shocking, but I felt it was time you knew."

Knew what? That you're a demented lunatic who likes wearing women's clothes? "I wouldn't say I'm exactly shocked, Za-elda."

"Oh, no?" he said, walking toward her.

She took the drink from him, again avoiding eye contact and said, "I've seen... people like you before."

He tittered and then said, "People like me? What do you mean, dear?"

She swallowed a big sip of the drink, fidgeted in her chair and then said, "I worked in Vegas long enough to see a bit of everything—men with men, women with women, men wearing women's clothes. It's nothing to be shocked about."

He controlled an urge to laugh. "Then what would you call it?"

She hesitated and then said, "Okay, I'm shocked. But did you think I wouldn't be?"

"I had a bet with myself as to how you'd react. And—I won. You're freaked out, aren't you?" He sat in his wingback chair and crossed his legs, and she realized that they were completely devoid of hair. When he noticed that she was staring at his legs, he said, "I'll never understand why women gave up the garter belt and stockings for those dreadful panty hose." He rubbed his manly hands—which seemed twice as big as normal—along his thighs. "These feel so sexy. I'd wear them every day if I could."

Hassie took a slug of the drink, set the glass on the table and asked, "So is this a— *hobby*?"

He gazed around the room like he was looking for the answer and then said, "It's something I like to do in my spare time so, yes, I suppose it is a hobby. Does that make it better?"

"I don't know, Zach. Maybe you should have given me a little warning?"

He uncrossed his legs and leaned forward. "Do you really think you would have come here tonight if you knew I'd be dressed as Zelda?"

"Probably not. I don't know." She studied him again before asking, "Why do you do it?"

He sat back and sipped his drink. It was difficult to look at his face—how the makeup exaggerated his features and made him look like a freak. At least his *breasts* were small. He finally looked at her and said, "I've loved wearing women's clothes since I was a little boy. I started by wearing my mother's high heels and hats and then gradually took more things from her closet when she wasn't around. She was a petite woman, and by the time I was about twelve, I could wear her housedresses, as she called them. It was fun and felt perfectly normal."

"Did she know you wore her clothes?"

"She—" He stopped to clear the emotion from his throat, focusing on something on the top bookshelf. "My mother was an amazing woman. I think she just *got* me, if you can understand. To this day, I loathe the *God* that could take such an incredible human being from her place on earth at such a young age. Goddamn cancer." He released a long, sad sigh and then said, "She eventually caught me in full drag. I even had my own makeup by then. But she never chastised or berated me for doing it. Her only real words of concern were that I not let my father see me that way." He set his glass on the table, wiped his cheeks with his fingertips and said, "Come... I want to show you something."

He took her into the second bedroom—his *boudoir*. He walked over to the built-in wardrobe and pulled open the two doors.

Hassie moved closer in to a mélange of color and texture in the shape of long gowns, cocktail dresses and suits along with evening coats and a woolen wrap trimmed in red fox fur. "Good Lord," she murmured *sotto voce* and wondered what she would do if she caught Kenny wearing her makeup or clothes.

He pulled out a fiery magenta, orange and red cocktail dress, a sweetish, floral scent wafting after it, and said, "Valentino and one of my favorites." He held it up to Hassie. "It would look gorgeous on you. Too bad it's not your size."

He hung the dress back in the closet while Hassie backed away saying, "Share clothes with my *boyfriend*? Uh, uh. That's a little too weird." She sat on the chaise lounge in the center of the room, which suddenly felt like a grand dressing room at some fancy boutique. "So what do you do after you get dressed? Do you go out, or do you have friends who—do this?"

Zach removed the wig and placed it on the Styrofoam head. He sat at the dressing table and removed the earrings, catching her eye in the mirror. "Believe it or not, there are places to go where it's perfectly fine for men to be dressed in women's clothes. I've become friends with some of the guys I've met, and we have parties—dinner parties and cocktail parties. But I'm very careful, Hassie. I don't risk my reputation where my job is concerned. It's actually quite a private thing and personally, one that I think is perfectly harmless." He turned to face her and asked, "Do you understand?"

She hesitated and then nodded. "I think so. I think I expected that there was something a bit *kinkier* involved. But dressed like that you look more like a secretary or a librarian."

He laughed. "I doubt a secretary or a librarian could afford Chanel."

She took a deep breath and said, "Okay, I think I get it. But I came here to have a nice evening with Zach."

"Give me a few minutes to change." He stood up, slipped out of the jacket and hung it in the wardrobe. He unbuttoned the blouse, and she could see an old-fashioned bra with pointed, padded cups. She averted her eyes, her stomach queasy, and said, "I'll wait for you in the living room."

She took her drink to the bar and poured more vodka. It felt creepy to think that she'd actually had sex with this—guy. Granted it wasn't the greatest sex she'd ever had, but she thought it was because between her work schedule and looking after Kenny they didn't have much time together and maybe she held an unrealistic expectation. But now, in hindsight and with this new revelation to consider, she thought about that first encounter. For a first time, it was disappointing, which wasn't so strange in itself. But she remembered thinking that he wasn't quite into her—that he seemed to work too hard to stay aroused, and that since then there'd been times when he would never really get hard, and he'd curse and make excuses and ask her to bring him off with her hand. And then there was the fact that she'd never had an orgasm with him, which was disappointing because she was attracted to him. He was handsome and sensuous by nature, and his kisses easily got her going. In the moment, it was all so confusing.

She knocked back the rest of the vodka and poured more as Warren walked into the room. He wore a white terrycloth bathrobe, his hair slicked straight back. This was the *man* that she'd grown quite fond of—the man that she'd hoped to spend an intimate night with.

He walked over to get his glass and asked, "Are you getting drunk?"

"I could probably use some food."

He joined her by the bar and poured a drink as he said, "Good. I ordered a Greek meal for delivery..." He looked at his watch. "...about now."

"Sounds perfect." She was relieved that he looked like he was supposed to look and asked, "Can I ask you a question?"

He leaned over and kissed her. "Of course you can."

"Does Zelda have sex? I mean, have you ever had sex while dressed...?"

He smiled—a small smile that represented a range of emotions. "Are you just curious about this or do you really want to know?"

She wasn't sure what to say. Yes, she was curious, but she also wondered how it was all likely to affect her. She nervously looked in his direction. "I really want to know."

The doorbell rang. Zach went to let the delivery man in as he said, "I opened a bottle of wine before you got here. Grab it, and meet me in the dining room."

They sat in silence while Zach dished out the food. Hassie sipped the wine and said, "You know, you don't have to tell me anything else about Zelda and... the other business... if you don't want to."

He put the fork on his plate and then leaned his elbows on the table as he asked, "Have you told me everything about yourself? Your entire life and past?"

She swallowed a bite of meat and then carefully said, "I don't think I could put my hand on my heart and say that I've told you *everything*, but—"

He took hold of her hand. "Look. I know we haven't known each other all that long and that this might sound a bit premature. But lately I've been having a hard time imagining my life without you in it, and I want you to know the real me—Warren the man, the lawyer, the cross-dresser, even the fool."

"I don't think you're a fool."

"I would be if I let you get away." He kissed her hand. "I think we can be really good together. Like forever, maybe."

"Does that include Kenny?"

"Of course it includes Kenny. Do you think it could include Zelda?"

She sat there, barely breathing, thinking of the moment she'd first seen Zelda and then the realization that Zelda and Zach were one and the same and that Zach had only a few hours earlier made her son one happy little boy. If someone had told her that she would make a life and a home for her son with a cross-dressing, eccentric lawyer, she'd have poo-pooed the idea in two seconds flat. It just wasn't an ideal scenario for her life going forward. But as she considered the dearth of alternatives and allowed her burgeoning feelings for Zach to take hold, she studied him for a brief moment and then nodded as she said, "I think it could."

chapter four

They were to meet at 69th Street and Central Park West after Hassie finished work at the music store. Going that far uptown in the late afternoon was obviously meant to accommodate Ruben, who had an apartment in The Dakota—an up-market residential building on the corner of 72nd and Central Park West. But he'd said it was important and insisted that it was the only time he had free. He'd also promised a drink at the Plaza when they finished their chat, which sounded a little suspicious—like he was offering a prize for showing up or salve for a wound.

Ruben stood on the walkway just inside the park; he spotted her and waved. She walked up to meet him, his face flushed and damp. "I've never known you to arrive early for anything," she said. "This must be important."

His manner was cool as he took hold of her arm and hooked it through his. "Thanks for meeting me. I want to talk to you away from the office, and it's a nice day, so I thought what the hell. A walk in the park would do us both some good."

They strolled a few paces along the stony path in silence before she said, "Ruben, are you getting ready to fire me?"

"Course not. Your contract's rock solid."

"Then what's going on? This is making me nervous."

"Relax. Today I'm talking to you as Warren's family."

She stopped, dropped her arm by her side and said, "What about it?"

"He came to see me this morning." They started to walk again, but Hassie kept a little distance between them, holding onto her shoulder bag with both hands. "He told me that you two are gonna get married." He grabbed her forearm and said, "Watch it. Some dog left his business behind." They carried on a little farther before he said, "I didn't realize that you were so serious. How long have you been seeing each other—three, four months?"

"Four."

"And you're all madly in love now?"

They approached a sprawling building partially hidden in a garden of shrubbery and trees drenched in hundreds of white twinkling lights. Hassie stopped and said, "That's the Tavern on the Green?"

"You never been there?" Ruben asked. "That cheapskate cousin of mine has never taken you for dinner in the Crystal Room?"

She shook her head. "This is as close as I've ever been."

"Maybe you could have your wedding reception there."

Perturbed at his sarcastic tone, she said, "Ruben, please say what's on your mind."

They started walking again. "Is it true? Are you and Warren getting married?"

"Yes. We really care about each other and think we could have a good life together." She hesitated before continuing, "And make a good home for Kenny."

"So is that what this is all about? Kenny?"

"No. But I get that you think it's happened too fast. That is what's worrying you, isn't it?"

"I'm mostly wondering if you really know what you're doing."

"Honestly, Ruben, why does this concern you so much? I'm a big girl and fully capable of making my own—and my son's decisions."

"Hassie, Warren is my family, and I've known him a long time. I dare say I know him better than you do, and I know *a lot* about him."

"I know that, Ruben. I know that the two of you grew up together in the Armenian community and that now you're close friends—more like brothers."

The path was almost deserted but then it was the middle of the afternoon on a Wednesday. The old, leafy trees shaded the winding path, cooling off the summer day. Yet Hassie was perspiring. "I'm a little surprised that Zach came to you with this news so soon," she said. "I thought he wanted us to tell you together—after we've sorted out the plans."

"I probably shouldn't say this, but he almost sounded boastful about it all—like he wanted me to know that he'd bested me—got the prize."

"Oh, Ruben. I can't believe you're right about that."

He slowed his pace and looked over at her, his mouth a painful expression as he asked, "Do you love each other?"

"Of course we love each other."

"You said you *care* about each other. Do you love Warren, Hassie?"

"I love him, and I know he loves me and he adores my son. Why are you going on about this?"

He stopped her, lowered his chin, which caused the excess flesh on his neck to lie in soft folds, and then gently held her shoulders. "I honestly, seriously think you'd be making a huge mistake to marry Warren, and you know I'd do anything in the world for him."

She felt a tantrum brewing over his determination to point out the negatives but was careful not to sound defensive. "Then why can't you just be happy for us? Why can't you just accept that we want a life together?"

"Because I think you're talking yourself into this, honey. I think you're tired of struggling to make ends meet and that you want something better for your son."

"And what's wrong with that?"

"Nothing's wrong with it. But is it enough reason to marry someone?" He took a cigarette from his pocket and lit it and then pointed at the path ahead and started to walk again. "Don't get me wrong. I know how much Warren cares about Kenny. He's told me that he thinks of Kenny as his own son. But something about that worries me too."

Ruben exhaled smoke while they walked along in silence. He'd said some things that were out of line, like he was goading or testing her, which screamed "hidden agenda" and made her uncomfortable. She said, "You sound bitter, Ruben. You wouldn't be trying to sabotage our plans, would you?"

"Why the hell would I wanna do that? You think I'm really capable of screwing over my own flesh and blood?" He kept walking, shaking his head and muttered, "That's cruel, Hassie."

"I'm trying to understand why you're so against this marriage. Warren Zachary is a wonderful man. He's been so good to me and Kenny, and we're very happy together. I know this is right, Ruben. I know we can have a good life."

"He says you're going to move into his apartment and that you've already sorted out a school for Kenny."

She nodded. "PS 41 is within walking distance. It's perfect, and I'll probably cut back my hours at Rosenblum's. I can spend more time with Kenny and still work nights in the club. Zach supports whatever I want to do."

He puffed on the cigarette and then said, "You know, this is good for *his* career as well."

"How so?"

"That hotsy-totsy law firm he works in likes for everything to be tied up in a big bow. They'll love it that he finally has a wife. You guys thinking of having kids?"

"Oh, God, I don't know. It's never even been mentioned. We still need to sort out a wedding."

"You're not thinking about a church wedding, are you?"

"No, we're not thinking about a church wedding. It's more likely to be a simple ceremony downtown and then maybe lunch with a few friends—which, of course, would include you and Isabelle."

"Hmph. Guess you haven't heard. She left me."

"I'm sorry. I thought you'd worked through your problems."

He shrugged. "After three failed marriages, I should maybe consider that *I'm* the problem or at least that I'm not the kinda guy that should be married."

She took hold of his arm again and said, "Maybe you just haven't met the woman who's everything you really need so that you want to settle down."

He didn't look at her. "Oh, I've met her. She's just not interested." He dropped the cigarette butt on the ground and stepped on it.

Hassie asked, "So where do you think we should have this wedding lunch?"

"How about 21 Club? The manager's a good friend of mine."

"Zach's mentioned that as well. I'll tell him to talk to you about it."

"What does Kenny say about all this?"

"He's as thrilled as a six-year-old can be. He wants to wear a suit like Zach's, and he's excited about us all living together in Zach's apartment."

"Did Warren get rid of Zelda's paraphernalia?"

"You know about Zelda?"

"Hassie, I told you. I know *a lot* about Warren, and yes, I know Zelda."

"Well, don't worry. I've dealt with Zelda's *wardrobe*, and Kenny will be none the wiser."

After a long, awkward moment, he stopped, faced her, crossing his thick arms over his chest and said, "If you want to marry Warren and despite everything you know about him you believe that you can have a happy marriage, then you have my blessing. Just promise me that you're sure about this, and I'll never mention my concerns again. Unless it's to say I told you so."

She became tearful and looked away from him as she said, "All I know is that I want us to have a life together."

"Then let's get to planning a wedding. You gonna go away for a honeymoon?"

"Maybe. We promised to take Kenny, whatever we do."

"That's your business. Just give me plenty of notice so we can cover your absence at the club." He put his arm around her shoulder and said, "You still wanna get that drink?"

"Sure."

They reached the exit from the park onto Fifth Avenue and walked toward 59th Street. Outside the domed veil of bushes and trees, the traffic was loud and obtrusive. Ruben put his arm across Hassie's back, guiding her along as he said, "I know you'll tell me that it's none of my business, but how's your sex life?"

She looked at him quizzically. "You're right, it is none of your business. You do have a lot of nerve."

"I'm just asking the obvious. I've felt since the moment I laid eyes on you that you love sex. So it's only natural to wonder if Warren gives you everything you need."

She stared straight ahead, clenching her jaw. When they reached the next corner, she turned to him and said, "I'm going to pretend that you didn't say any of that to me, and I'm going to get in a taxi and go home."

"Did I hit a nerve?"

"No, Ruben. You're just a big, disgusting boor and… what can I say? I'm really disappointed in your attitude." She turned to face the traffic and stuck her hand in the air. A taxi pulled to the curb within a few seconds, and Ruben opened the door for her. Before getting inside, she looked at him and said, "If you're actually *not* happy with our plan to marry, can you at least pretend to be happy for Zach? You're basically all the family he has, and whether or not he's mentioned it yet, he wants you to stand up for him at whatever wedding we have."

"Don't worry. I won't let him down. Go. Make your plans, and have a nice life. See you at the club tomorrow night."

* * *

Kenny had gone to sleep-away camp up in Westchester County—an extension of the summer day camp that he attended at the Presbyterian Church up the street from Zach's apartment. She'd been against it at first, fearful that he was too young to go off without her. But Zach

44

had argued that the other kids his age would be going and that the church knew what they were doing. She eventually gave in, packed a small duffle bag for him and took him over to meet the bus. He'd been nervous and had stayed close to her side until he recognized a few of the other boys and then took off to join them as if she didn't exist. She watched the bus drive away, waving at the back of Kenny's head. She was booked to work both Friday and Saturday nights at the baths and was spending the weekend in Zach's apartment. She grabbed a taxi and went over to Macy's.

Hassie and Zach had tentatively pinpointed the end of July for the wedding, which meant it would most likely be hot and humid, and she had no idea what to wear. Zach told her to get whatever she wanted and that money was no object. But the mere gesture of sorting through the racks of dresses and suits made her think of her mother when she'd come home from one of her shopping sprees with tote bags of more of what she'd bought only a few weeks before. And then her father would fall in from a hard day at work, and she'd explain why she needed another dress and another pair of shoes and another scarf, and her father would just look at Hassie and then pour himself a glass of bourbon. But he never questioned what his wife said, and he never got angry. Despite Zach's lack of concern over the expense, no legacy of her mother's would ever sit right with Hassie. She considered a few options that the saleslady suggested—both dressy and casual with simple lines and pastel colors. But after an hour or so of browsing from floor to floor, she went home with a bag of lingerie.

* * *

Zach came in for her second show on Friday night and whisked her out the door as soon as she finished. They decided to walk home, and she didn't talk. He held her hand and asked, "Are you worried about Kenny?"

She looked at him. "You think I'm silly, don't you?"

"A little. He's in great hands and was excited to go off on his own. It had to happen eventually, Hass."

"I know. But what if he falls or hurts himself?"

"They'll take care of him." He kissed her hand. "Stop worrying and think about spending two whole nights alone with me. It'll be like a dress rehearsal for after we're married."

She held his arm and said, "I did a little shopping today."

"Did you find your wedding outfit?"

"No, but I found some good stuff to wear *under* the outfit."

"Mmmm… is it bad luck to see them before the wedding?"

* * *

He stood at the end of the bed. She came out of the bathroom looking like an ad for Frederick's of Hollywood. The teddy she wore was extremely short, exposing her equine legs. Her breasts were barely covered by the skimpy, transparent top. She lifted her hair off her neck and softly said, "Do you like?"

He nodded, unbuttoning his shirt. He pulled her closer to the bed and said, "Undress me." She slowly removed his belt and guided him to step out of his trousers. When she dropped his shorts to the floor, she looked up at him and said, "I thought you would be excited."

"I am."

She took his flaccid penis in her hand and said, "Then you need to get the message down here."

He pulled her hand away. "Take that thing off."

"Zach, I just put it on."

He kissed her gently. "Please."

She removed the teddy. He took it from her and rubbed it between his fingers and then threw it on the floor said, "Now, take off the panties."

She slid them off her legs and held them up to him. He looked at her but said nothing. She knelt down and held them for him to step into. She pulled them up as far as they would go. He held her close, and she could feel his erection. She whispered, "Is this what you want?"

He cupped her bare buttocks and kissed her neck. "You know what to do."

She stroked him and said, "Get in bed."

He pulled her on top of him. She was rough and aggressive and watched as his eyes rolled back with an urgency that she recognized, having been in this place with him many times before. He finished quickly and quietly. They lay in each other's arms, and when she looked at him he smiled, but there were also tears, and there was nothing left to say.

chapter **five**

On the day of the wedding—their appointment at the town hall was for eleven a.m.—Zach took Kenny out for breakfast to give Hassie some alone time. A beautiful Cypriot named Molara arrived early to style Hassie's hair. She sat at her dressing table while the zaftig brunette looked at her in the mirror and said, "You'll be most stunning bride. We're putting up hair?"

Hassie shook her head. "Zach wants me to wear it down." She reached for a magazine opened to a page of a model with hair about her length. It rested on her shoulders in a light flip; the front swept across her forehead. "What do you think of this?"

Lara, as she liked to be called, studied the photo for a moment. "It so *dramatic*. I love it!" She fussed with the length of Hassie's hair a little bit, asking, "Did Zach tell you dress to wear as well?"

Hassie frowned at Lara in the mirror and said, "No. I picked it out myself. He hasn't seen it yet."

"How's it look?"

"It's a short, sleeveless dress with a matching coat in a pale, beigey-yellow color that the saleslady called maize."

"Hmmm. Sounds lovely. And a little—*safe*. I think hairstyle jazz it up. What you say?"

Hassie nodded. "Let's do it."

Do I Know You?

Within an hour, Lara had left Hassie to do her makeup. She sat at the dressing table and spotted the recent photo of Barbara Crumpler sitting in the garden of her home on the south coast of England. It reminded Hassie of the beautiful garden that Barbara had kept in Angus, Texas, which Hassie hadn't seen since she left Texas for Las Vegas—over ten years ago now. Most women want their mother present on their wedding day. Today, Hassie missed Barbara, who'd been much more the mother to her in all the ways that mattered. But she hadn't told Barbara about her marriage to Zach, and although she'd yet to openly address the reason why, deep down, she knew. She knew that she'd never been able to hide her innermost workings from Barbara, and she feared that Barbara would see right through what she was doing.

In the mirror, Hassie saw a face she didn't recognize. Her skin looked lifeless and dry. The crow's feet at her eyes were too deep for her age, and if she imagined her hair in a shorter, fifties-style coif, she could see her mother. Bonita Calhoun had been a beautiful woman, styled and dressed to the nines. But she'd often looked tired—worn out from the dissolute, duplicitous life she'd led. She'd never had a hard day in her life. She'd never wondered if she could keep a roof over her child's head or if there would be money for food at the end of the month. She had nothing in the world to worry about other than how to spend her husband's hard-earned money and how to cheat on him without getting caught. Had her mother ever loved Jackson Calhoun? Or had she married him because he offered her security and a respectable home for their family, affording her a fancy social life and a charge account at Neiman Marcus in Dallas. Had Bonita Calhoun had a moment of remorse after her husband died? And had her mother ever loved her or her brother the way she loved Kenny?

She dabbed a thick cream along the sockets under her eyes. In less than five months, she would turn twenty-nine. Despite the odds having been against her when she left Reno those months ago, she'd not done too badly. She'd worked hard and kept Kenny safe. She'd landed a job that enabled her to do what she loved most and get paid well to do it, and she'd secured a promising future for her and her son. She was thankful that Zach loved them both and wanted them to share in his life. It wasn't a perfect life, and she knew it. But if that perfect life even existed, she doubted she deserved it.

* * *

They arrived at the city clerk's office about ten thirty. The July air was hot, heavy with humidity. Kenny pulled at his shirt collar but didn't complain. Hassie brushed his hair away from his forehead and said, "You look so handsome."

He tugged on the necktie. "Do I have to wear this?"

"You said you wanted to dress like Uncle Zach. See how nice he looks?"

Kenny dropped his hands by his side and then scuffed his new shoes across the floor to sit in the waiting area. Hassie kept an eye on him as she joined Zach, who appeared to be on the lookout for someone. "Is Ruben on his way?" she asked.

"Ruben's not coming."

"I thought he'd agreed to stand up for you."

"Yeah, well, he changed his mind. Said he was too busy to get away this morning but will meet us at 21 Club later."

She held his arm. "I'm sorry, Zach. I don't really know what to say."

He put his hand on hers and said, "Never mind. I've asked a friend to stand in. Everything will be fine."

He wore a Brooks Brothers dark-grey suit—one usually reserved for serious client meetings or funerals—and one of his many blue and white striped shirts, but she didn't recognize the tie. It was beautiful silk with an elegant red and cream geometric design. She touched it and asked, "Is this new?"

He nodded. "It's Hermés. Do you like it?"

"It's nice but not your usual style, is it?"

"It was a gift. Hey, there's your neighbor."

Carol Jordan walked toward them. Maybe they weren't the conventional definition of close friends but she'd actually been lovely and gracious when Hassie asked her to stand up for her. When she joined them, Hassie said, "Zach, you remember Carol."

"Of course," he said and reached over to kiss the woman's cheek. A few minutes later, a suntanned man of average height with a head of curly salt and pepper hair arrived at the top of the stairs. He wore a cream-colored suit with a pale-blue shirt and a light-yellow printed tie. Warren walked over to meet him. They spoke briefly without emotion and then joined the women. Warren introduced the man as Andrew Callegari and then rushed them toward the clerk's office.

Before they left the apartment, Zach had taken a velvet-covered box from his pocket and opened it to reveal a row of six small diamonds anchored to a narrow, platinum band. It had belonged to his mother, and she'd wanted him to give it to his wife. The gesture touched Hassie deeply, for she knew that Zach wouldn't have taken the decision to give it to her lightly.

The ceremony was short and to the point. As they walked down the steps of the government building, holding Kenny's hands between them, Hassie made a sweeping gesture with her right arm and said, "Say hello to Mrs. Warren Zachary."

When they reached the bottom of the stairs, Kenny looked up at her and pulled on the necktie as he asked, "Can I take this off now?"

Zach stepped in. "Not yet, big guy. Andrew's going to take some photos, and we want you looking great."

Hassie straightened Kenny's tie and asked, "Have I met Andrew somewhere before?"

"I don't know. I don't think so." Zach stood Kenny in front of the two of them and motioned Andrew over.

"He seems awfully familiar, but I can't think where we would have met. Has he ever been to one of your firm's functions?"

"I don't remember. Possibly." Andrew stood before them with a complicated looking camera. Zach put his right arm around Hassie's waist and rested his left hand on Kenny's shoulder. "We just want a couple of family shots. How's this?"

"Stunning," Andrew said. "Now, big smile on the count of three."

* * *

They had booked a private dining room upstairs in 21 Club. Hassie arranged for Kenny's afternoon sitter to pick him up from the town hall and take him home. Two of the partners from Warren's law firm came in with their wives. Hassie greeted them and made sure they had champagne before she saw Joe Monroe, the pianist from the baths, standing at the door. She approached him and said, "Hiya, Joe. I'm so glad you're here. Please, come in and join the party."

She looked around for Zach and then spotted him in the opposite corner talking with Andrew. She motioned to the waiter and asked, "Joe, would you like champagne?"

"I know that's good stuff," he said and leaned into her. "But it gives me gas. Got any bourbon?"

She smiled. "Of course. Tell the waiter what you'd like, and I'll be right back. By the way, have you seen Ruben today?"

He shook his head. "Came straight from home."

Hassie walked over to Zach, focused on Andrew and said, "Zach, I thought you said that Ruben would be here for lunch."

"That's what he said." He checked his watch. "He's only a little late."

"So, Andrew, we haven't really had a chance to speak about anything other than the ceremony. How do you know my husband?"

Zach immediately said, "Andrew's an art dealer. One of the best in the city. Has clients all over the world."

Andrew smiled. "Warren's obviously a fan."

Hassie slipped her arm through Zach's. "That's nice but it doesn't tell me how you two know each other."

Zach looked at her quizzically and Andrew said, "I don't recall exactly, but I'm sure we met at some pretentious fundraiser somewhere."

Hassie half-smiled before saying, "Do you have a gallery here in Manhattan?"

"Galleries are merely resources. Collectors come to me to find certain artists or pieces. I look for good work and match it to collectors."

"Andrew's quite the collector himself," Warren said. He perused the room and then said, "There's your boss, what's-his-name."

Hassie looked over to see Myron and Gilda Rosenblum walking through the door. "They look a little lost. I'd better go greet them."

Hassie introduced the Rosenblums to Joe Monroe and left them to chat. On her way to get more champagne, she saw Ruben talking to the waiter. She stopped briefly to speak to Carol's husband, Dan, before joining Ruben. The waiter topped up her glass as she said, "You made it."

"Of course I made it." He kissed her cheek.

"I'm glad you're here, and I'm not going to dwell on it, but your last-minute desertion of our wedding was a little rude, don'tcha think?"

"Is that what Warren told you? That I deserted you? And at the last minute?"

"Well, I just assumed so. He told me weeks ago that you'd stand up for him and never told me differently."

"I found out *two* weeks ago that a meeting I've been trying to arrange for months was coming together today."

"Really? A meeting?"

"It's a work day, Hassie. Warren said it was fine as long as I made it for lunch."

"Sounds like a lame excuse for missing the ceremony—you know, the one that you don't think should've happened."

He put his arm around her shoulders and said, "Honey, I'm not going to fight with you today. You're being ridiculous. By the way, you look beautiful. I like your hair." A waiter brought Ruben a scotch on ice. He nodded thanks and asked, "Where's Kenny?"

"His sitter took him back to play with his friends," Hassie said. "He'd have been bored silly here after ten minutes."

He smiled, touched her glass with his and said, "So, Mrs. Zachary. This is what you want?"

"Yes, Ruben. This is what I want."

"Then let's go say hello to the groom."

They joined Warren and Andrew. Ruben reached out to hug Warren and said, "Congratulations, cuz. You got yourself a beautiful little family now."

"Thanks, Ruben. We missed you at the ceremony. You remember Andrew Callegari?"

Ruben turned to look at him. Hassie noticed his hesitation while proffering his hand. Andrew shook his hand and said, "Nice to see you again."

"And you," Ruben said.

Andrew smiled, and Hassie studied his face. He looked significantly older than Warren. If she had to guess she'd say late forties, early fifties. He was quite handsome in a rugged, bohemian sort of way. He wore a gold ring on his left pinkie finger embossed with some sort of crest—his family, maybe? His clothes looked expensive, his sense of fashion a little too eccentric for her tastes, a design of tiny elephants dotted his tie. She still couldn't place where she'd seen him before.

"This is a nice turnout," Ruben said.

Warren nodded. "We wanted to keep it intimate."

Hassie brushed a speck of something off Warren's shoulder and said, "You've been holed up in this corner for long enough. Don't you think you should mingle with your guests a little bit?"

"So you're nagging me already," he said, grinning. "Do you think you'll be safe here with these two gentlemen?"

She laughed and said, "Go."

Andrew put his empty glass on a table. "Hassie, Ruben, if you'll excuse me, I need to visit the men's room."

Hassie watched him walk away and then asked, "How do you know him?"

"I've met him with Warren a couple of times. You've never met him until today?"

"No, but I know I've seen him somewhere before."

"Probably at the baths. He's been in to see your show."

She considered the situation for a long moment. "He's the only person in this room that I really don't know, and *he* was one of five people at my wedding. It just seems strange to me, Ruben."

"You're officially part of Warren's life now. You'll get to know his friends."

Zach tapped a knife against a glass to get everyone's attention and then said, "Thank you all for coming. Lunch will be served in ten minutes, so please take a seat. Your places are marked. Could I ask my beautiful bride to join me?"

Hassie walked around to the table where Zach stood. He put his arm around her and said, "I took the liberty of placing Carol and Dan and Andrew at our table as our wedding party."

"Actually, Ruben should sit at our table," Hassie said. "After all, he's family." In what appeared to be an intricately choreographed sequence, she picked up the place card from Andrew's seat, took it to the table where Zach had placed Ruben and exchanged the cards. She walked over to Andrew and pointed as she said, "You'll be sitting at that table for lunch." She then took Ruben's arm, pulling him in the direction of the head table, saying, "Come with me."

chapter six

Changes in Hassie's life seemed to sneak up on her after only one month of marriage. As Zach had suggested, she'd cut back her hours at Rosenblum's, which had given her more time with Kenny and more time to enjoy the comforts of home. So when Zach lobbied for Ruben to give her one weekend night off from the baths, it made perfect sense, and those nights became family nights where the three of them went out to dinner and maybe took in a movie or went roller-skating or anything else Kenny wanted to do. The family unit had come together exactly the way Hassie had envisioned, and it felt good. But then Zach convinced her to drop the agent that she'd recently signed with, arguing that Hassie had done well enough on her own. Why should an agency get a piece of it? And anyway, Zach was a world-class negotiator when needed. She didn't argue with him at the time. But she had no intention of involving him in the renewal of her contract at the baths. That was between her and Ruben, and she had a few new ideas.

Ruben asked her to come in that afternoon. She suggested that they meet for lunch, but he'd said he had a busy day and just wanted to chat in his office. When she arrived, his door was open; she stuck her head in, and he motioned her inside. "Close the door," he said and pointed her to the chair in front of his desk.

"Did you just get some bad news? You look worried about something."

"Just the usual bullshit. Too goddamn many people with their big ideas." He gestured broadly as he said "big" and then sat behind his desk. "Never mind. I haven't really seen you since your wedding day—I mean other than when you're here at work. How's everything? What's it like being a married lady?"

"It's fine. We all have to do a little adjusting, but—no, it's good. We're all good."

"And Kenny? He liking his new home?"

"Oh, yeah. Can you believe he just started first grade? My baby's growing up."

"Hmmm." He pushed some papers around his desk but didn't seem to be focused on anything in particular. She sat quietly until he looked up and said, "We have some business, don't we."

"You sound awfully formal, Ruben."

He levied a weak smile. "Your contract is up in a couple of weeks."

"I know. Aren't you just going to renew it?"

He shifted his weight uneasily in his chair. "Hassie, your contract was never gonna be for more than six months. I thought you understood that. It's the way things work in these kinda places."

"You own the damn place, Ruben. You can do whatever you want."

"Yes, I can. And I want to make a change." If he'd seemed preoccupied earlier, now he was focused, his demeanor cool like he just remembered that he was in control, and he liked it. "It's nothing personal, I swear. Sometimes change is necessary."

"Were you getting complaints about me? Was business down? Because it sure didn't feel like it."

"Not at all. Like I said, it's just time for a change."

"So you already have someone in mind?"

He nodded and lit a cigarette. "You know her. She's been filling in for different acts for a while now, and she's been coming in on the nights you wanted off."

She leaned forward in the chair and said, "You mean that bloated bleached blonde that sounds like Ethel Merman on a bad day?"

Ruben stifled a laugh. "There's no need to be rude. I realize she doesn't have your looks or graceful presence, but she's got a good style for a place like this, and I'm sorry, honey. The audiences like her, and there's a new sort of buzz when she's here."

She focused on her hands, which felt numb and possibly out of her control. "When does *Ethel* start? And, by the way, I didn't want those nights off, Ruben. Zach did."

"Look. Like I said, your contract was for six months, and you've done a helluva job. Of course, I want you to finish out the next two weeks."

She fought the sensation that the slightest move could make her ill. "So I'm really out. Just like that."

"You can always come back later, but in the meantime, get your agent on the case for a new gig. It'll be good for you."

She bit her lower lip. "Ruben, does this have anything to do with my marrying Zach?"

He flicked the cigarette in the ashtray and said, "Course not."

"Does he know? Does Zach know?"

"We haven't discussed it. But he drew up the contract. I'm sure he's aware it's finishing."

Hassie sat dumbfounded and miserable and hadn't the first idea what to do. Ruben ground out the cigarette and pushed back from his desk. "When I've got more time, I'd like to talk to you about something else."

She wanted to say something nasty but kept her mouth shut.

"I know you write music, and from the little bit I've heard, you're pretty good at it. I want to write a musical, and I need a collaborator. I thought that might interest you. What do you think?"

She grabbed the arms of the chair and said, "I think you're out of your ever-loving mind. You're finished with me as a singer and want me to help *you* write a musical." She stood. "No thanks. I'll finish out my contract and then I'll be out of your hair."

She turned to leave. Ruben stood up. "Hassie, having a shit fit won't help you here. Think about what I've said. You need to spread your talent around as well. Talk to your agent today."

She looked at him. "Yeah, okay, Ruben. I'll do that." She started out the door and then faced him again saying, "And I'll have a *shit fit* whenever I like."

She rushed out of the building and started walking. A hot, gritty breeze whirled around her. Everything she'd been thinking and planning had now gone out the window. She followed 23rd Street on to Fifth Avenue. The traffic whizzed by, extremely loud and annoying. Sometimes she hated the city—the noise and the relentless scurry of people, pushing and barreling along the sidewalk like they owned the whole goddamned world. She stopped at the corner, waiting for the light to change, and noticed a little old woman on the other side. She was sitting on some sort of industrial bucket, holding a paper cup. It wasn't clear if she was drinking from it or holding it, waiting for passersby to drop in coins. She sat stooped and alone, wrapped in a ragged shawl, an odd turban on her head, bedroom slippers on her feet.

Hassie crossed the street and slowed as she walked past the woman, who looked up, her crusty eyes unfocused and sad. Hassie smiled at her and then thought *this could've been me.* She took a few coins from her bag and dropped them in the cup and then kept walking. It was her afternoon to meet Kenny after school and take him for ice cream and shopping. He'd had a growth spurt and needed new sneakers. She wished she could buy some sort of magic potion that would stop him growing up.

Right now, she needed the walk to clear her mind before she met Kenny. It bothered her that Ruben had been so matter of fact about letting her go—like it didn't really matter to him that she'd help build the clientele and reputation that made it necessary to instigate a reservation system and that maybe he owed her the loyalty she'd shown him. But then Zach hadn't helped matters. He'd all but dictated that she stop working, and he'd gone out of his way to end her career. Or at least that's the way it felt, and she really didn't know what to do. Maybe her agent would take her back. Or she could do like dozens of other people in the city and go to the open auditions—try her luck at landing a decent part that would at least get her on a Broadway stage. She'd find another job on her own. To hell with Ruben Layne.

* * *

Hassie met Kenny at his school, and they walked to the neighborhood diner. He asked for a black and white sundae, which was so big she knew he'd barely make a dent in it. His thick, black hair was a shaggy mess over his ears and eyes. She'd lost the recent battle to get him in a barber's chair. She ignored the urge to tame it with her fingers and asked, "How was school today?"

He licked the whipped cream off a spoonful of the sundae. "Good."

"Just good? What are you studying?"

"Lotsa stuff. But I like science."

"Oh, yeah? You must be very smart."

He nodded and smiled, revealing the gap where his two front teeth had been. He turned serious and asked, "Do you think Uncle Zach would help me with my project?"

"Of course he'll help you. We'll both help you." She watched him tackling the ice cream and then said, "We're a family now, Kenny."

"So are we still a family with Uncle Clay?"

She nodded. "Uncle Clay will always be your uncle. He'll always be part of your family."

"But Uncle Zach's my uncle too."

She hesitated and then pushed his hair away from his eyes. "Uncle Zach's a different kind of uncle, but they both love you just the same."

Kenny shrugged and said, "I thought so."

When they exited the diner, it had started to rain. "I think we'd better get home before it pours," Hassie said. "We'll go to the shoe store tomorrow." They rushed along Sixth Avenue to 12th Street. Kenny took Hassie's keys and ran up the steps to their building to open the front door. Hassie stopped just inside and told Kenny to wait. The Broadway score from *Cabaret* blared from inside the apartment. Zach had been obsessed with it lately, playing it in the evenings before dinner. But it was party-mode loud now and very unusual for the middle of the afternoon. She guided Kenny to the apartment door.

He looked up at her and asked, "Mom, is Uncle Zach having a party?"

"I don't know, sweetheart. I think we'll ring the bell so he'll know we're home." She retreated with second thoughts about going in, but it was too late. The door opened; Kenny grabbed Hassie's hand and moved closer to her body. Zelda stood in the doorway dressed in one of the long, slinky dresses that Hassie wore at the baths, a dark brown wig that flipped up at her shoulders, full makeup including red lips and several pieces of Hassie's rhinestone paste jewelry. It was as if she was staring at herself in some distorted mirror at a carnival sideshow. She was too shocked to speak and locked into a troubled gaze with Zach. Kenny broke the silence. "Uncle Zach, are you playing a game?"

Zach opened the door, ushering them inside. He walked over to lower the music and then said, "I'm rehearsing for a play I'm going to be in at a friend's birthday party."

"Why do you have to dress like a girl?" Kenny asked.

Hassie took hold of Kenny and said, "Let's get you into dry clothes before you catch cold." She glared at Zach, and he shrugged.

She returned a few minutes later without Kenny. Zach was on the telephone and ended the call when he saw her. She walked over, stood directly in his face and spoke in a low voice, "What the hell's the matter with you?"

He looked fairly unperturbed and said, "You told me that you were taking him out this afternoon."

"I didn't say we were never coming back. It started raining… and, anyway, it's four o'clock! You promised me you'd keep this— game of yours out of our house when there was a chance that Kenny would be here. What did you think you were doing?"

"A friend was coming over, but don't worry, it's been handled. Where's Kenny now?"

"In his room. I told him to work on his homework for a little while before dinner. He's horrified, Zach."

He walked Zelda over to the bar, slowly, with a decidedly effeminate gait. "Stop with the histrionics. I think I handled the whole thing rather well."

She stood beside him and said, "Maybe he bought your ridiculous little story, but *I* didn't. It's one thing to involve me in all of this but quite another to expose yourself to my son."

Zach threw his head back and laughed before he said, "I didn't *expose* myself to him, Hass. He's nowhere near ready for that—"

She slapped his face. Her hand stung and then started to shake. Zach looked at her like he wanted to slap her back. "You'll regret that," he said and then turned away to make a drink.

She took several shallow breaths and then said, "I'm sorry. I shouldn't have hit you, but I don't understand what you're doing."

"What don't you understand? I thought we agreed I could be myself."

"Yes. With *me*. In private and never when Kenny was around. It was one of the terms of our marriage."

"Do you want a drink?"

"No, I don't, and please change out of those clothes."

As he left the room, she stared after him. His beard pushed through the foundation; the exaggerated eye makeup and thick red lips disgusted her. She walked over to sit on the sofa. So many things were wrong right now. It seemed that their passion had reached its peak just after they were married, which by most people's standard was outrageous and totally unacceptable. But it seemed to die down as quickly as it got there, and she honestly understood why. The apartment was small, and Kenny's presence limited their time to be alone. Before they were married, Zach bought expensive silk panties and bras, garter belts, bustiers—sheer teddies and stockings. He made a big fuss over her when she'd wear the lingerie, and for a while, it was fun and exhilarating and kept everything alive and sexy. She knew of his proclivity for wearing her underwear, and they'd worked through the initial discomfort of all that. But then he became obsessed with wearing the things he claimed to have bought for her and started acting out fantasies. They both knew that it had escalated but avoided talking about it.

Do I Know You?

The day he brought home the strange looking apparatus had shocked her to the point of tears. Even now to think about it… to imagine what he'd wanted her to do. Did he not know her at all? Did he really think that she would just take that… *strapadicktome* and pretend that everything was normal. She grimaced with thoughts of the night that he talked her into trying it on and then chased her around the apartment. But that night hadn't ended well, and things hadn't been good between them for a while. She'd never been married and didn't know what was considered to be *normal* intimacy after a while. But she knew that she was unhappy with the perversity that Zach imposed and that he didn't seem to care how she felt.

She walked down the short hallway to check on her son. He was asleep on his bed, his small body wrapped around a furry, stuffed toy Saint Bernard Clay had given him when they left Reno. She gently pulled the door closed and walked to their bedroom where she heard Zach in the shower. She changed out of her damp clothes into a pair of lightweight slacks and a cotton blouse and then pulled her hair into a ponytail. As she sat at the dressing table mirror—her eyes puffy and tired—she realized that she had such a grip on her hairbrush her knuckles were taut white. She was tense and fraught with regret— her marriage to Zach wasn't going so well. And now she'd lost the only job that she'd really cared about since she left Las Vegas. She dabbed a bit of powder on her face and looked at the photo of Barbara propped against the mirror. Maybe she should take a week off from Rosenblum's and go over for a visit before she started looking for another job, which she still needed to discuss with Zach.

He opened the bathroom door, and the smells of his après-shower anointment wafted through the bedroom. He walked out in a silk-brocade dressing gown, every freshly groomed hair in place. There in the mirror stood the man she thought she loved—the beautiful, sensuous man whose wit and intellect charmed her over and over again… the same man whose dark, eccentric side was working hard to push her away. He watched her watching him until she said, "Feel better?"

"Where's Kenny?"

"He fell asleep." She turned to face him and continued, "Before I wake him for dinner, can I talk to you?"

He walked to his closet and removed a pair of trousers and a shirt. He took off the dressing gown and threw it on the bed. "No, Hassie. I do not want to hear anything else you have to say tonight. I'm going out, and you and Kenny can have the apartment to yourselves."

"Zach, please. It's important."

While pulling on his boxers, he said, "I'm sure it is. Everything you say and do is important. But I'm not in the mood for one of your lectures." He finished dressing, took his blazer off the wooden valet stand and walked to the door. "Enjoy your evening, and kiss Kenny goodnight for me."

She stood. "I was only trying to protect my son."

He sighed with resignation. "Hassie, relax. I just need some space."

He left. She walked into the living room and switched on the table lamps at either end of the sofa. It was such a beautiful room, and as she walked around in a large circle, it struck her that nothing in that room belonged to her. Although she had no specific knowledge of the value of antiques, she'd heard guests comment on some of the pieces—particularly the couple of fancy chests and the desk. She'd intended to show more interest and to perhaps read up on the various eras of Louis this and Louis that. Maybe she'd been so caught up in her own problems that she didn't care enough about the life that Zach had so willingly shared with her and her son. So what if her life wasn't perfect? It was a damn sight better than the one she'd recently left behind.

The rain pelted down, and the wind rattled the front windows. She'd been through enough summer storms to know that thunder and lightning were likely to follow, and Kenny would be frightened but pretend he wasn't. She'd stay home with him that night and wondered if Zach would come back.

She poured a short drink and thought again about her last conversation with Ruben. She knew that he'd been an accomplished musician in his life and was probably a better pianist than old Joe.

She'd also heard him talking to Zach about shows—both on and off Broadway—that he'd invested in or had some involvement with producing. His foray into the baths had strictly been an investment opportunity that he'd jumped on a year or so earlier. It wasn't surprising that he was ready for a new venture. It *was* surprising that he wanted her to be a part of it. But her pride wouldn't let her get anywhere near it. She took the recording of *Cabaret* off the turntable and replaced it with *Funny Girl*, wondering if she'd ever sing "People" again.

chapter seven

Warren rolled over and nuzzled into Andrew's side, breathing in traces of deodorant and musk. A pungent residue of tequila oozed from his pores; a carnal tang sent Warren thinking about the night before. He got out of bed and stood in the middle of the almost-but-not-quite-perfect-cube of a room, now in complete disarray after their bacchanalian party night. He slipped on a bathrobe and inventoried the wreckage—a pair of red stilettos and a black PVC mini dress in the style of a policeman's uniform laid strewn across the floor. A blonde wig in a pageboy cut perched on the bedpost like it was a Styrofoam wig head.

Andrew was the *straightest* gay man Warren had ever known. In the six months they'd been seeing each other, Warren had only dressed as Zelda a handful of times. It took him a while to even suggest the possibility. Warren preferred Zelda, the classy socialite, dressed in haute couture or beaded décolleté gowns. But Andrew had only shown interest in the blue-collar, costumed look—the naughty cop or French maid or nurse. If that's what it took to keep Andrew interested in Zelda, what did it matter? Warren picked up the cap with a badge on the front of it and left the room while Andrew lightly snored, one of a set of handcuffs still clamped around his wrist.

Most gay or bisexual men Warren knew were thin as rails, perpetual users of amphetamines to stay that way and as vain as Hollywood heartthrobs. Andrew was naturally thin and very comfortable with his body and had no patience with the "pretty boys" who went out of their way to get noticed. Maybe it was his age or the fact that he constantly dealt with so many different people. Despite his insouciant nature, he was probably the most confident person Warren had ever known, and he liked calling the shots, which meant Andrew decided when Zelda was allowed in the room.

Warren had met him earlier in the year at the opening of a gallery on 57th Street. Andrew had arrived with a leggy blonde woman; heads turned from every direction. Warren had had a brief conversation with Andrew, and they'd exchanged cards. Warren was certain he got a vibe from him, but he'd made that mistake before and decided to wait for Andrew to make the first move. He'd just met Hassie and was equally taken with her. She was accessible, Andrew less so.

Warren had learned that Andrew was a blue blood from old Connecticut money, which explained his impressive apartment on lower Fifth Avenue just shy of Washington Square. It was technically the edge of Greenwich Village, but one only had to announce the building's address for any knowledgeable New Yorker to know that it had nothing to do with the seedier part of the West Village. In fact, Warren had lusted after an apartment in the pre-war Art Deco tower prior to buying his place on 12th Street. He couldn't quite swing the expense at the time and settled for what he could afford, which was only four blocks away—technically, the same neighborhood. Andrew's tenth-floor apartment faced downtown with a spectacular view of the harbor, Ellis and Liberty Islands. On Warren's first visit to Andrew's home, he was as heavily seduced by that view as by Andrew's intoxicating presence. When he commented about it, Andrew wasted no time pointing out the two monstrous steel towers that were under construction at the tip of Manhattan, moaning that it was just his luck that the two tallest buildings in the world were now the dead center of his million-dollar view. He'd then walked Warren around the apartment pointing out key pieces of his art collection: a Lichtenstein, a Hockney, a de Kooning and the pièce de résistance—a portrait of Andrew in the iconic style of Andy Warhol.

He'd mentioned it rather nonchalantly by saying, "It was a gift."

The apartment itself was an eclectic gathering of odd pieces that individually were spectacular and no doubt ridiculously expensive. His taste in pulling them all together was questionable to Warren. But besides the extraordinary works of art on the walls, Andrew had an eye for color and loved glass sculptures—the more impressive pieces were acquired in Italy and Czechoslovakia. His wardrobe was much the same as his furnishings—*au courant* fashion. No color was taboo and on that body of his… everything looked great. He was impossibly handsome, teeming with style and panache. His hair was his trademark—a thick curly mess of dark hair being overtaken by gray. Thanks to the time he spent on Fire Island, he appeared perpetually suntanned. He'd been featured in *Esquire* and *Town and Country* magazines. Warren was only barely in his league.

When Andrew finally called him a few weeks after they first met, it was so out of the blue Warren sputtered some gibberish and hung up thinking he'd blown it. A month later, they met again and had lunch and then lunch again and then dinner and then…

"What's goin' on?"

Warren wheeled around to see a naked Andrew standing in the doorway, yawning and pulling on his robe, the handcuff dangling from his wrist.

"Good morning. I was just—rather Zelda was just thinking about our little sexcapade last night."

"You know, I don't really like it when you talk about Zelda like you're her or she's you." He lifted his arm and said, "Get rid of this, please."

Warren walked over and tugged at the clasp, which popped open as he said, "It's just a toy, Drew."

Andrew walked toward the kitchen. "Did you make coffee?"

"Not yet. I wanted it to be fresh when you got up." Warren followed him into the kitchen, picked a can of Maxwell House coffee from the cabinet and spooned it into the percolator basket. "I thought you had fun last night."

Andrew opened the fridge and stared inside. "Yeah. It was fun."

He took out a carton of orange juice and then shut the door and looked at Warren, broke into his lopsided, sensuous smile and said, "According to my aching body, it was a *lot* of fun."

Warren filled the percolator with water and plugged it in.

Andrew poured some juice and sat down at the small table. He yawned again and asked, "What got you out of bed so early?"

"I don't know. Traffic noise, I guess."

"You should be used to it by now."

"I know. I *should* be used to it. I've definitely spent more nights here than—"

"Than at home with your wife? I'm very well aware of that." His tone was slightly playful.

Warren took a grapefruit from a bowl on the counter and cut it in half. "So what do you want to do today?"

"I'm working, like I do most Fridays."

Warren turned to face him, tightened the sash on his robe and leaned against the counter. "I took the day off so we could spend it together. We talked about going to the Whitney and lunching *al fresco* on Madison."

Andrew looked at him like he spoke Swahili and said, "No can do. Got a big client in from Nice. We have a full day of viewing, and I'll probably take her to dinner. I thought I told you."

Warren dug the sections out of the grapefruit and dropped them in a bowl. "No, you didn't tell me, and you certainly didn't tell me that your client was a *her*." He squeezed the juice from the hull and put a spoon in the bowl. "Here, have some grapefruit," he said and then walked into the living room. There was no way that he'd have known and forgotten that Andrew was not intending to spend the day with him. That was the main reason they'd had a bit of a party the night before—like coming down from a big week on Friday night. They'd had a lot of drinks out at a couple of bars and then come home and gotten high right before Andrew suggested a romp with Zelda.

Warren put the shiny cop hat on and went back to the kitchen door. Andrew was sitting at the dinette table, thumbing through a magazine, drumming his fingers on the table. This was a typical scenario the morning after—Andrew acting like he merely tolerated their games with Zelda and that he actually didn't give two shits about what Warren thought. Warren walked around and stood behind him, moving his hands down Andrew's chest to where their heads rested side by side. He whispered in his ear, "Is there anything I can do to change your mind?"

Andrew reached up and stroked Warren's arm as he said, "Save it for later, honey."

"You just told me you're busy tonight and that I'm not invited."

"I didn't say you weren't invited. I said I have an important client, and I might have to take her to dinner. Let me see how the afternoon goes and if I think she would enjoy the company of my sexy lawyer."

Warren served them both coffee and then sat down across from Andrew. "Is there any chance you might want to take her out on your own? Are you attracted to her?"

Andrew slurped the coffee. "No, Warren. I'm not you. I don't need to have a woman tucked away to wheel out when I think it's appropriate. That doesn't mean I don't like to socialize with women or can't enjoy a woman's company over a meal. And would you please take that stupid hat off?"

Warren removed the cap and laid it on the table, then coyly said, "That's not what you said last night."

"Well, it's what I'm saying now. And I need some time on my own this morning. Are you going to work?"

"I might as well." He stood up and took the percolator to pour more coffee for Andrew, who took hold of his wrist and said, "You know you're very important to me, and there's nobody else I'd rather have dinner with—any time."

"I wish I believed you." He set the percolator next to the sink along with the empty bowl. His emotions seemed to bounce around like one of those balls with a weight in it that never quite lands where you aim it. He was becoming obsessed with Andrew, and the thought that he could push the guy away by being needy or downright stupid made him get a grip. He turned to face Andrew and said, "I hope you have a successful day and sell the bitch everything you've got. And if you do and there's something to celebrate, I'd love to be there."

Andrew smiled. "I do love you when you're all gorgeous and vulnerable."

"Your wish is my command."

"Oh, yeah? Then give me a little care from Nurse Nancy—make that Nurse *Warren*—before you go."

* * *

No one expected Warren to be in the office, so he sorted through the various documents on his desk that needed his sanction before being filed away. His mind frequently wandered, imagining how things were going with Andrew and *her*. He'd find himself staring out into space, thinking of the two of them mindlessly flirting over a bottle of Dom Perignon. Andrew could be a bit of a shameless tease when it came to selling his wares. When Warren had finally had enough and he hadn't heard from Andrew about dinner, he packed up and left early. It was cocktail hour at the baths. But since Andrew had come into his life, he hadn't had the desire to hang around a bunch of young studs and hope he got lucky. He decided to go home. Maybe he'd have the apartment to himself and could quietly get drunk.

* * *

He opened the door to Hassie standing in the middle of the living room—her arms akimbo—having sent her son to his room. He set his briefcase on the floor by the antique French commode. Hassie walked toward the bar and asked, "What are you doing here?"

He took off his jacket and placed it on the back of a chair. "I live here. What's going on with our boy?"

"Can I make you a drink?"

"Martini, please. Olives, very dry."

"I haven't forgotten how you like your martinis, Zach."

He sat in his wingback chair, and she took the drink to him. She didn't sit and Warren asked, "What's wrong with Kenny?"

"He lied to me."

"He's six. How big a lie can he tell? Sit down."

She sat on the sofa. "If you were ever here, you'd know that he's decided that homework is not important, and he'll do just about anything to get out of doing it."

Warren breathed deeply. "Again. He's a six-year-old boy. How many kids his age enjoy doing homework?" He bit one of the olives off the toothpick. "How'd he lie?"

"He wanted to go to a pizza party last night. The idiot mother who planned a party on a school night needs her head examined. But he begged and promised that if I let him go, he'd do all his homework straight after getting home from school with Jacqui, and I'd never have to remind him to brush his teeth again."

Warren rolled his eyes and nodded. "He's tried that deal on me."

"He not only didn't do his homework, he swore to me that he did and then tried to hide the note from his teacher asking me to call her. After the little genius threw his dirty pants on the floor, I found the note in his pocket. I called her and found out that he had told her he couldn't do it because I took all his pencils away, and he didn't have anything to write with!"

Warren laughed and Hassie said, "Zach, it's not funny. I couldn't get home before he left for the party so I couldn't check up on him. Later I was just too tired to care. And anyway, Jacqui had already put him to bed."

"Why are you getting home so late?"

"Myron started keeping the store open until nine on Tuesday and Thursday nights about two months ago?"

He wrinkled his nose. "Sorry. I forgot."

"It doesn't matter. I'm about ready to quit that stupid job anyway. In fact, I'm about ready to quit my entire life."

"Ah, come on. It can't be that bad." He sat back in the chair, took a sip of his drink and asked, "Hass, what's going on? What's really upset you?"

She took a tissue from her pocket and rested her head in her hands. He moved over to sit beside her on the sofa. Her hair fell loosely around her face; he pushed it back and lifted her chin.

"Tell Uncle Zach what's wrong. I know you're not this upset

about Kenny going off for pizza without doing his homework."

She smiled sorrowfully and said, "Nothing's been the same since Ruben took my job away."

"I know. I tried strangling him but—well, you know what he's like."

"I can't seem to get past it, and it doesn't help that I can't get hired for another show in this entire city."

"Are you auditioning?"

"Of course. But the only jobs I've been offered are scraping the barrel, and the pay is hardly worth the trouble. My agent says it's just a sign of the times, but I know plenty of other people working, and I can't be wrong for every single part that comes along."

"It's a fickle business, Hass. I've heard Ruben say that many times."

"That doesn't really help me, does it?"

"When did you get a new agent?"

She glared at him.

"You say that other people are working and there are plenty of shows going on. Why aren't you getting your fair shot? Is this agency any good?"

"I signed with them over a month ago, Zach. And I'm auditioning more than I did without an agent."

He swallowed the rest of his drink and asked, "Have you taken a close look at what you're being sent to audition for? Are they the right roles—roles that you really have a shot at?"

She looked at him like she'd just tasted something bitter. "What the hell does that mean? If you're trying to tell me that I'm no good at this business and should give it up, I've already come to that conclusion for myself." She hesitated and then said, "You think I'm too old, don't you?"

"I don't think any such thing." He took his glass to the bar. "You know, you're your own worst enemy. And I think you enjoy playing the victim, which is why you'd rather blame Ruben for replacing you at the baths than face the fact that there are other people that have talent just as good and better than yours. It's the way of the world, Hassie. Grow up and face it!" He turned away and emptied the martini shaker into his glass while wishing he could take back most of what he'd said. He walked back to his chair, sat down and said, "I'm sorry. I'm a little on edge. I shouldn't take it out on you."

"Why haven't you asked me if I'd like a drink?"

"I thought you were in control of the bar and… What would you like?"

She didn't respond and stared at nothing. "We used to be able to talk about anything and everything. We understood each other and cared about each other's feelings above all else." She looked at him. "What happened to us, Zach?"

He knew exactly what had happened but said, "I don't know, Hass. But it's not your fault."

She sat quietly for a moment and then asked, "Do you ever wonder what our lives would be like if Kenny wasn't here?"

"That's a very odd thing to say. He's your son. And he's just as important to me as you are."

"Then I guess we both cramp your style. You'd be better off without us."

He hated this tendency of hers toward martyrdom. And he should have heard from Andrew by now. "You're my family," he said softly.

"Then could I ask a huge favor? It's a lot to ask of you."

"Hassie, we're married, and occasionally we're nice to each other."

She grimaced. "That doesn't mean that you should be saddled with my problems."

He leaned forward, resting his elbows on his knees. "Try me. I'm really not a bad guy."

"I know you're not a bad guy, and I'm sorry that things are such a mess. But I need to make a trip to England, and even if I took Kenny out of school, it's not a good place for him to be right now."

"Is this to do with that woman you knew in Texas?"

She nodded. "Barbara. She's been ill for a few months, and when I called to check on her earlier this week, her housekeeper told me she'd just gotten home from the hospital and isn't doing well at all and—I think the family is preparing for the worst."

"You mean she's gonna die?"

Hassie sat frozen, trying to hold on to her emotions. "I've been promising to go over to see her for ages but for a dozen different reasons just haven't worked it out. I need to go now—before it's too late."

"For how long?"

She gazed out through squinty eyes like it was the first time she'd thought about it and then said, "I don't know—maybe a week?"

Warren raised his eyebrows but didn't respond.

"Kenny's in school most of the day. Jacqui will meet him to walk home as usual and stay with him until you get home." She stood up. "I need a drink now."

He jumped up. "I'll get it." He made another martini and then sat down beside her.

"Thanks," she said and took a big sip. "I do love you, Warren Zachary. And I don't want this to burden you. Will it be a problem for you to stay here so that Kenny can at least see you before he goes to school?"

He shook his head, thinking that he'd be giving up nights with Andrew and said, "We'll work it out, Hass. Go. Go see your friend. I'll help you with Kenny any way I can. I'll coordinate everything with Jacqui, and Kenny will be fine."

"Are you sure?"

"Yes, I'm sure. But what about your job?"

"Myron's used to my erratic scheduling requests. He calls me a flibbertigibbet and evidently, that's not Yiddish."

He laughed. "You know, you're adorable when you're feeling *farklempt*."

"Now, I know that's Yiddish. If you think you're smarter than me, you're *mishugina*."

They both laughed, and he leaned over and kissed her. "When are you planning to leave?"

"I'll get on to the plans tomorrow. Maybe I can leave by the weekend." She took his face in both hands and kissed him again. "Thank you. I hope you have better luck getting the little monster to do his homework than I do."

"He wouldn't dare lie to me."

She sipped her drink, sat pensively for a moment and then said, "Promise me that you won't play any dress-up games while Kenny's here."

"Give me a little credit, will you?"

"Sorry. But I just had to say it."

"Actually, you didn't have to say it, Hass. It was *one* time. And just because you think Kenny's been scarred for life doesn't mean you're right." He shook his head and mumbled, "Jesus. You either trust me to take care of him or you don't. I told you. I'll make sure he's well looked after. Speaking of which, are you planning to starve your child tonight as punishment?"

"Of course not. Will you have dinner with us?"

He checked his watch and then with a tight smile, said, "Sure."

"Great. I'll sort something out and then you can lecture Kenny about the evils of lying to his mother."

Warren stood up, loosened his tie and started back to the bedroom. Kenny stood at the entrance to the living room, looking sheepish and miserable. They briefly made eye contact before Kenny said, "Can I come out of my room now?"

Hassie looked at him and asked, "Uncle Zach, do you think Kenny should come out of his room?"

"I think this is between the two of you. I'm going to change my clothes." He walked into the bedroom and closed the door. Why hadn't he heard from Andrew? He knew that Warren was a little wigged out over losing his Friday with him to a client. He knew that Warren was waiting to be invited to join them for dinner. As he placed his dress slacks on a hanger and returned them to his closet, he felt irked and abused by Andrew's stultifying behavior. He picked up the phone and dialed Andrew's apartment, then quickly cut off the call before it could ring. What was he doing? He would sound pathetic and needy, which his gut told him would be the wrong follow-up to the morning's conversation. But he felt claustrophobic in his own home. And he couldn't stay there and play house with his wife and stepson. He wasn't in the mood to hang out at the baths or some testosterone-steeped bar. But he liked the idea that Andrew could wonder where he was. He dressed in a pair of casual gray slacks and a burgundy pullover sweater and grabbed his black leather jacket.

When he went back into the living room, Hassie had gathered the glasses and was tidying the bar. He watched her while putting on his jacket and then asked, "Where's Kenny?"

She looked at him, expressionless as she said, "Going somewhere?"

He nodded. "Change of plans."

She picked up the glasses and started to the kitchen. He held her arm. "Everything will be okay, Hass."

"No, Zach. Everything will not be okay. This is a real suck-ass way to live, and I'm sick of it. My six-year-old son just called me a bitch. You're out doing God knows what, and I have no life whatsoever. This is not a marriage, and my day-to-day existence is not a career."

He took the glasses from her, put them on a side table and then hugged her as he said, "Sort out this trip to England. Go and forget about everything here. I swear you don't have to worry about Kenny for a second. Take all the time you need and come back with that unflagging spirit you used to possess."

"That person doesn't exist any more. You said it yourself—I enjoy playing the victim, and I'm a useless no-talent." She pulled away from him. "Leave me alone." She took the glasses into the kitchen. He followed her, leaned against the doorjamb and said, "I really hate seeing you like this when I know what you're truly capable of."

"Then why don't you convince that son-of-a-bitch cousin of yours to give me back my job?"

"You know I can't do that." He walked closer to her and said, "Ask me to do something I *can* do."

She turned the faucet off, faced him and said, "Stay here with us tonight."

He looked into her eyes, the pain so deep and clear it made his gut ache. He had a hundred things to say and yet he had nothing to say. He kissed her face close to her ear, whispered, "I can't," and then turned and walked away.

She followed him to the door and said, "Zach. Please don't make a fool of me."

He put his hand on the doorknob, stopped for a moment and then said, "Goodnight, Hassie."

She flicked her wrist after him as if shooing him away and then just stood there for a long, sad moment before pulling the wedding band off her finger and flinging it at the door.

chapter eight

Hassie heard stirring in the kitchen and found Kenny standing on a step stool in front of the pantry. She stood at the door and watched him as he perched on his toes, intently scouring the shelves. When he seemed to have no luck finding whatever it was he wanted, she walked toward him and said, "Whatcha looking for?"

"Frosted Flakes. Uncle Zach hid them from me."

She laughed. "Why'd he do that?"

"He says I eat too much sugary crap."

She considered telling him not to say *crap* and then said, "I think he might be right. How about a scrambled egg and some juice?"

He made a funny face that basically said no to her healthier suggestion. She stood beside the stool and hugged him, savoring his soft warm breath as she asked, "Do you know how much I love you?"

He wriggled away from her. "I really need that cereal."

She located a box at the back of the top shelf and took it to the counter. While pouring it in a bowl, she said, "You can have a little bit but only if you'll have a banana as well."

He nodded and took a spoon from the utensil drawer, waited patiently while she sliced part of a banana on top of the cereal and then covered it with milk. She sat down at the table with him. There had been no sign of Zach since he'd left the night before—

not that she'd really expected it—and she realized that Kenny had stopped asking after Zach's whereabouts when he wasn't there in the morning. When he'd finished his breakfast, she dressed him in a pair of dungarees and a warm flannel shirt and then walked him around to the school playground for a regular outing with his friends. On the walk back, she rehashed some of the conversation she'd had with Zach the night before, but concerns about Barbara's ill health crept into her thoughts.

Back in the apartment, she made a piece of cheese toast and a cup of coffee and went into the living room. It was late afternoon in England... the best time to call. A woman answered Barbara's phone, asked who was calling and then put her on the line.

"Hello, dear. How nice to hear from you." She sounded weak. "Is everything all right?"

"I'm fine, Barbara. How are *you* feeling?"

"Pampered to bits. The family's keeping vigil like I'll be popping off any minute."

"You deserve to be pampered, and I'm sure they only mean to take good care of you."

"Yes, yes. How are you, love?"

"I'm very well, and I'm finally going to make good on my word and visit you in England."

"That's wonderful, dear." She was silent for a moment and then asked, "Will you think it terribly dramatic if I tell you that you shouldn't dawdle?"

Hassie could hear a muted muddle of voices, male and female. Someone took the phone from Barbara, covered the mouthpiece briefly and then a man's voice said, "Hello, Hassie?"

"Yes."

"I'm awfully sorry to interrupt, but the nurse is here to attend to Auntie's medication. It's no good if she get's off schedule."

He said shed-ule.

"Would it be better for me to call another time?"

He hesitated and covered the mouthpiece again. He had a pleasant voice, and his accent made him sound very grand. Was this the nephew that Barbara had mentioned in their conversations—the one who was in the navy?

The man came back on the line and said, "Please forgive me. This must all seem rude to you, and I know you're calling from America. I've just left the room so that we may speak more freely."

"That's fine. May I ask who I'm speaking with?"

"Sorry. The name's Charles Beauclerke, Barbara's nephew. My mother—her sister, Gwendolyn—and I spent the day with her. The night nurse just arrived and, I must say, it's not been a very good day."

"I'm so sorry to hear that, and I'm sorry for bothering her—and you—but since I have you on the phone, could I ask your opinion about something?"

"Of course."

"First of all, you're probably wondering who I am, calling out of the blue to ask about Barbara's condition."

"Actually, she's spoken of you several times. I've heard her say that you were a student of hers when she lived with Uncle Willis in Texas."

"That's right and well, I know that she's very ill, and I would like to see her face-to-face before she... in case she doesn't get well. But I don't want to intrude. I just want to see her again."

"I understand, Hassie, and I think it's a marvelous idea. But I do think you should make the trip sooner than later. Her pain is very intense at times, and the dose of morphine is increasing at regular intervals now."

"Charles, has the cancer gotten worse?"

"I'm afraid so. Unfortunately, it has spread and is slowly taking over her organs. There's no way for the doctor to know exactly how long she has, but the prognosis isn't good. Mind you, she's always been something of a fighter."

"Do you think I could speak with her again? Maybe I can call back?"

"I believe she's down for the night now—the drugs and all—so why not try calling a bit earlier tomorrow. Her housekeeper, Beryl, will be with her then."

"Okay, thanks, I will. In the meantime, I'll check into flights so that I can have something specific to report."

"Jolly good. Will this be your first visit to England?"

"Yes. I've been promising to visit for ages but with a small— well, you don't need to hear my excuses."

There was a brief silence before he said, "If I might, I would suggest that you fly directly into Gatwick Airport. It's an easy shot by train to Brighton from there, and then you can get a taxi to Rottingdean. I'd offer to collect you myself, but I'll be away for a few weeks."

"That's very kind, but I'm sure I'll manage."

"Then, bon voyage. I know my aunt will be delighted to see you."

She sat down at the desk and picked up the yellow pages. Zach had suggested she use a travel agent as she'd hardly been on an airplane, let alone flown across the ocean to a foreign country. While she scoured the ads for local agencies, the phone rang. "Hello," she said.

"Hello, beautiful stranger."

"Ruben, Zach's not here."

"I called to speak with you."

"What about?"

"I'd like to see you, Hassie. It's been much too long, and we need to have that conversation about my project."

"Ruben, I'm very busy right now, and I'm also planning a trip out of the country."

"Where to?"

"That's not important."

"Hassie, please come over to my office this afternoon. Give me one good chance to explain my ideas to you, and we'll discuss the timing as well. I think you might agree that your trip can wait a few days."

"Even if I wanted to, I can't leave here now. Kenny will be back in an hour or so, and there's no one to look after him."

"Then I'll come to you."

She sighed impatiently through her nose and said, "If you're planning to try to convince me to work with you on your idea for a musical, you're wasting your time. I didn't want to hear about it those weeks ago, and I still don't."

"Then please just remember how you used to feel about me when I was giving you a paycheck every week, and humor me for a minute. If you're truly not interested, I'll leave you alone."

"Oh, all right. I can do without the drama."

He coughed, said, "Scuse me a minute," and then made a horrendous noise like he was hacking up a lung. "Sorry. Um… where was I? Oh yeah. You ever heard of Jack Kingford or Jerry Schumfeld? Manny Horowitz or David Melville?"

"No."

"These guys have had, or currently have their fingers in many a Broadway production—and they're always looking for the next big hit."

"If you don't stop smoking, you're not going to be in any shape to give them one."

"Yeah, yeah. Anyway, I don't think you know much about the life I had before I dove head first into the baths—no pun intended. Hell, I lost two wives over those years and a bit of self-esteem here and there. But I never lost money. I grew up poor and without privilege, except that my parents worked like dogs to give me and my brother every possible chance at the American dream, including changing our Armenian surname—*Aslaynian*—to Layne. But because they couldn't afford much, they looked for all the free stuff—free piano lessons at the church, free lessons if I'd play in the school band—got stuck with the trumpet—yada yada. Now I know you're probably thinking *Oh, cry me a river, everybody's got a sad story*. But mine had a great ending, and after a few years of working with and learning from the masters—those guys I mentioned—I realized that I, too, had a nose for a good thing. I invested in a few shows—some were misses, but most were hits. And the rest, as they say, is history."

"That's a nice story, Ruben, but how does this concern me?"

"Turns out I also had a nose for the musical numbers that were stinkers and in danger of fucking up the show. Thing is—I could usually *fix* them—rewrite or rework them so they were a better fit. I got myself a real nice reputation as someone who could rescue potential disasters—it's called a *dramaturg*. I called it *dramaturd*." He laughed at himself and then said, "Anyway, that was all well and good, and my bank account kept getting fatter. But it made me realize that I'm as capable of putting a good show together as anybody."

She listened.

"Ya know. Everything's going real good here at the baths. I got some great managers. I've sorted out all the issues with the law and have a pretty damn good reputation. So, like I told you a while back, I wanna write that show. And I'm pretty sure I can raise the funds to get it on stage without having to put too much up myself. Now, I need a collaborator. I've always wanted that person to be you and… look, I know you're still mad at me because I let you go from the baths. But let me be the first to tell you that self-pity don't look so good on you. You're a pro and a damn good musician, and unless you're just gonna stay miserable and mope around in some utopian fantasy for the next who knows how many years, you need to pull on your big girl panties and get over it. Come work with me. At least give it a chance."

Her pulse raced and her ears were hot with anger, but she remained in control and casually asked, "How long did you practice that speech, Ruben?"

"I'll be over in half an hour."

chapter nine

Ruben had been taught at a very early age to go after whatever he wanted with all his guns loaded. So much so that by the time he reached young adulthood and was expected to make his own way, he wasn't equipped to take no for an answer. That resolute determination mostly worked in his favor but, from time to time, he got swatted about the face, knocked down a notch or two, metaphorically sent to his room without supper. Hassie had, at one time or another, done all those things to him when he'd attempted to seduce her. Sometimes she got angry, but mostly she laughed in his face. And it all took care of itself when Warren arrived on the scene and whisked her off to some never-never land that Ruben had no idea how to relate to. So as time passed, Ruben got over his lust for her—or mostly so—and focused on her talent, which he'd never believed to be extraordinary, but somewhere on the same plane as his own talents. Thus, it made sense that their collaboration *could* be extraordinary and was pretty confident that the old Ruben Layne magic would reel her in.

He rang the doorbell forcefully like it was a trumpet fanfare. She buzzed him in and waited for him at the door to the apartment. She'd gained some weight since he'd last seen her, which gave her a bit of curve in her tight pants and little sweater. He grinned at the sight of her and said, "God damn, you look good."

"Hello, Ruben. You're the last person I thought I'd be letting into the apartment today." She practically danced out of his way when he tried to hug her, so he backed off and then handed her a paper sack containing a bottle of chilled champagne.

She chuckled and then asked, "Shall I open this now?"

"It's for you. I got a bit of an ulcer situation going on right now. The booze sets my stomach on fire."

"Hmmm… must be all that clean living you do." She set the bottle on the bar. "I'll save it for later. Have a seat."

Ruben waited until Hassie sat on the sofa and then lowered himself into the wingback chair. He'd never been one to rehearse what he was going to say. He'd always believed he was most effective on the fly. But she exuded a Bolshie impenetrable shield of sorts that he quickly realized would be a challenge.

"So," she said, "you made it through the door."

"And I appreciate it. Let me get right to the point. I have a meeting in a few days to pitch my idea to these producers I mentioned, and believe me, it's like having an audience with the pope. I'd like you to be there, so just listen to me before turning me down."

"I don't see how you can pull some genius plot out of a hat in a few days."

"We don't have to have a finished product at this point." He sat up straight in his chair, focused and serious. "Remember the first time you sang that song you wrote out in Vegas about being hurt by that guy you loved a lot?"

"Yeah, and I also remember that it opened the floodgates to the story of my life at the Sands."

"I liked the song, but I was also strongly affected by your story—or at least the parts you told me. The more I think about it, the more I think we've got a significant plot line and basis for a show. And who's better equipped to write it than you—Hassie Calhoun in the flesh."

She wrinkled her nose and said, "I don't know, Ruben. I can't believe it's really all that interesting. Hasn't this same story been told a million times in a million different ways."

"Maybe. But here's where you gotta trust me and my instincts. And that's why it's critically important for you to help me sell the idea to my buddies. It's your story. You lived it, and you can tell it."

She gazed around the room, focusing on nothing. He knew from those couple of conversations they'd had that she was still pretty freaked out about certain aspects of that time, and she'd been known to shut it all down in mid-sentence. She then looked at Ruben and asked, "So exactly when's this meeting?"

"We're penciled in for Wednesday. I needed to confirm your availability before I set the time."

"Why now, Ruben? You've told me nothing that suggests this meeting is so urgent."

"Hassie, it's taken me months to get all these guys together on the same date and at the same place. The last meeting—the one where I tested the waters—was on your wedding day and that took equally as long to organize. If you really think about this, I'm sure you can understand. It's like trying to get several heads of state together when each of them thinks that his own life and schedule is most important."

She moved to the edge of the sofa, brushed her hair away from her face and said, "I heard what you said about my issue with self-pity. Zach's told me off a couple of times for being a self-wallowing brat."

"How does that make you feel?"

"Not great. But I don't argue with him, and now… you telling me the same thing? It must be true. But there's more to it than just the working side. It's my whole life. It's just a shitty, shitty situation."

Ruben stood, crept over to the bar and poured a scotch.

"That ulcer all better now?" she asked.

He forced a smile and said, "I know it's none of my business, and that's why I've stayed out of this so far." He swallowed half the drink and continued, "But it's time to ask. Do you and Warren have an open marriage?"

She gave him a knowing look but said nothing.

He took another pull on his drink. "Warren doesn't really live here with you and Kenny now, does he?"

She sat stone-faced.

"Hassie, Warren talks to me. I know he spends most of his time away from home. Where do you think he is?"

She pressed her lips together and crossed her legs. "Where do *you* think he is?"

"What does he tell you?"

"He tells me that I'm smothering him and that he needs space."

"Space to do what? Where does he say he's going?"

She shook her head. "I don't ask, and he doesn't tell me anything. *You* obviously know something. Why don't you tell me?"

"Remember the guy at your wedding—Andrew?"

"Mr. Gorgeous with the fancy clothes and expensive tie? Zach's been basically living with him, right?"

"So you've known about this—affair?"

She laughed, pitifully, and said, "I'd be a dimwit if I didn't know, wouldn't I?"

"And you're okay with it?"

"Of course I'm not okay." Her voice cracked, and she lowered her head. Ruben waited until she looked at him and said, "Our marriage is a joke, isn't it?"

"Honey, I really do think that Warren loves you and Kenny. I think he's a little mixed up right now."

"Mixed up? Is that what it's called? Do you have any idea how long it's been since he really touched me? Our life is about going through the motions. He pays the bills, and he shows up every now and then to *mix it up* with Kenny and make sure that everything's *okay*, and then he's gone again. If he doesn't want to be here with us, so be it. There's nothing I can do, and pushing him would make it worse. All I know is that we have a roof over our heads, and my son is safe."

Ruben swallowed the rest of his drink. "What the hell's going on here? Does Warren know that you know about his *other* life?"

"You know, if I'm honest, I knew the day we got married that I was competing with someone else. Was the fact that it was a *man* a surprise? Yes and no. You have to understand that nothing about our relationship has been what you would call conventional or *normal* and somehow it just seemed to work. He's a good man. When he's here and we're a family, I think about how much I wish things could be like that all the time. I miss that man. I miss his charm and his ability to make me feel special. It used to be good, Ruben. I swear. There was a time when I would do anything for him—and I did. I tried so hard. But it was never enough. I could never be the substitute for what he really wanted—which took a while to sink in but now makes so much sense to me."

"What's that?"

"He wanted a man. He wanted me, but he wanted me to be a man." She practically whispered, "And *he* wanted to be *me*." She sat for a moment, breathed deeply and said, "You once asked me about our sex life—if it was everything I needed. I know you're not really shockable, but I could—pardon my language here, but I could knock your dick in the dirt with stories of what Zach has put me through—what I've *allowed* for the sake of keeping him happy." She stared out at nothing for a moment and then continued, "I really tried to love him, and I genuinely wanted to have a good life with him and make a nice home for Kenny. I know you probably don't believe me but, honestly, I tried."

Ruben breathed deeply and then said, "You know, I hoped this moment would never come."

"What do you mean?"

"The moment when I had to say I told you so."

"God, Ruben, how is that helpful? Please say something useful."

He squinted as he considered his words and then pointedly asked, "Why don't you leave him?"

"And do what? I hardly make enough money to buy a pup tent. If it were just me I'd do whatever it took to get away. But…" She tried not to cry. "Kenny…"

Ruben stood and pulled her off the sofa, hugging her as he said, "Warren is very important to me. But so are you and Kenny. I despise what's going on here, and I sure hope you don't think that Kenny doesn't know that something's wrong. Kids aren't stupid."

"I know Kenny knows something's wrong, but he accepts the excuses I give him and loves the time that Zach's around."

"That's all well and good, but are you listening to yourself? I realize that I sound like the Grim Reaper here, but honey, this is really fucked up. You've got to get a grip and move on."

She nodded, her face contorted with emotion.

He tried to think of just the right, the perfect thing to say, but wasn't sure what was right or perfect in these circumstances. So he went straight for the issue at hand. "What would you do if you had the money to leave—to take Kenny, move into an equally nice apartment that wouldn't uproot anything about his friends or school?"

"I don't know. It's not been an option, so I haven't thought about it."

"Well, think about it. Think about how our success with your story and our show could set you free. Imagine that you have plenty of money. You can, on your own, give Kenny a safe, warm environment with all the proper care and plenty of time to do the things you love to do together. Just the two of you."

She stood up, paced a small area in front of the coffee table and then smiled at Ruben as she said, "Okay. I'll do it—I'll go to the meeting with you. But you've got to explain exactly what's in this for me. I've said things to you that I've never said to anyone. And I hope you know how hard all this is for me. Plus, I really need to visit a friend in England who's dying."

"I'm sorry to hear that, but we just need a few days. Come to the meeting with me and then you can go."

"Ruben, if I didn't know better, I'd think that you don't believe that you can land this big ole fish without me."

"Okay. You got me. I'm helpless without you. Now will you please have a drink?"

chapter ten

Hassie stood at the window with her second cup of coffee. One of the things she loved most about living in New York City was that there were four equal and distinct seasons. Her most vivid memories of her childhood in Texas were the long, hot summers, where the temperatures topped "a hundred and ten in the shade," as her daddy used to say, much like the time spent in Vegas and Reno. It occasionally snowed at home in Corsicana, and winter nights in the Mojave Desert could be downright cold, but those weather patterns could be sketchy—not like New York where July was going to be hot and humid and January meant snow and ice and April brought the rain that would usher in spring and October saw green leaves turning red and gold like the ones on the trees that lined the street outside their apartment.

Late morning was a quiet time on the street, the kids in school, the dog walking done with little else happening to disrupt her thoughts while waiting for Ruben to arrive. The first meeting with Ruben's *masterminds* had gone much better than either of them had expected; the second meeting was scheduled for two weeks after the first one. Ruben and Hassie were to present a complete synopsis of the show's story or *book*, which would serve as the basis for the script and lyrics, all needing further focus and Hassie's commitment to stay in town until it was done, which meant she had to postpone her trip to England.

She prayed that Barbara would hang on a while longer.

She heard the front door to the building open and shut as her neighbor, Mrs. Mickelson, emerged carrying her Persian cat down the steps. Ruben walked up and chatted with the woman, petting the cat's head, looking for every reason to keep dragging on his cigarette like it was the last one he'd ever smoke. If she had her way, she'd ban him from smoking altogether, but the best she could do was to enforce their policy for no smoking in the apartment.

Truth be known, there had been a time—not so many years ago—when she would've begged for a cigarette when faced with this upcoming discussion. She'd been forced to immerse herself in a time that had long passed—her life in Las Vegas and the people and places that had contributed to the story that was the basis of their script. She'd tried to suppress the part of the story that involved Jake Contrata—how he tried to control her and then abused her in just about every way possible and then killed her best friend. Why would she want to relive any of that time? It still haunted her. She still had dreams that Jake was back and that he promised his undying love and it was great and their passion exploded and then so did Jake's temper and he smashed her face and it was her fault. Nightmares. But she awoke, and she was safe. And she couldn't see an iota of sense in bringing that dreadful time in her life alive again.

She rapped her knuckles on the window. Ruben looked up, and she waved while he dropped the cigarette and stepped on it. She buzzed him in and waited for him to enter the apartment. He kissed her cheek as she asked, "You want to have our meeting outside?"

He brushed past her saying, "Just having a smoke. Last one for a while."

"You can take a break any time you like, Ruben. And thanks for coming here today."

"Kenny's sitter has the flu?"

She nodded. "I need to be here when he gets home from school."

"How old is he now?"

"Six." She walked toward the kitchen, and Ruben followed.

"Isn't that old enough to stay by himself? Hell, I think I started smoking around that age."

Hassie laughed and handed him a mug of coffee. "Well, call me old-fashioned, but I think a six-year-old needs looking after. So, again, thanks." She noticed that he'd arrived empty-handed. She led him to the dining room table and said, "I thought we could work here. Where are your notes?"

He took hold of her arm. "Let's sit in the living room."

Ruben sat in his usual armchair while Hassie sat on the sofa. She'd learned how to read him—his face a map of thoughts and emotions. He had an engaging smile that verged on lascivious when he was up to something that he hadn't yet shared with her. When he was deep in serious thought, his eyes narrowed—slits in the fleshy bags above his cheekbones. At that moment he was expressionless, which was rare and worrisome. She waited another few seconds and then asked, "Is everything all right?"

"Yeah. Everything's fine."

He sounded flat and distracted, which could have everything or nothing to do with her or their work. He slurped the coffee and then set the mug on the table and slunk down into the chair, resting his hands on his round stomach as he said, "Tell me about Jake Contrata."

"I've told you about him. He was the general manager of the Sands. He gave me a job in the Copa Room and then, well, we got involved."

"You loved him."

She nodded.

"And he loved you."

"Yes."

"Then why didn't you two live happily ever after?"

She cleared her throat and then sniffed. "Because he died."

She squirmed.

He said, "Don't you think it's time for you to tell me what happened? I don't mean to sound callous or stir up past feelings that upset you, but I need to hear the whole story. The way I figure, Jake was a pretty young man when you knew him. How'd he die? What happened?"

She breathed deeply with splinters of images that had never gone away. "There was this awful scene in the Copa Room one night. Jake was angry about a lot of things and there was a—fight. And my good friend, Julio, was hurt." She focused on the empty ashtray. "And then Julio died, and it was Jake's fault." She could feel Ruben's I'm-listening-but-tell-me-what-I-want-to-know stare. "He'd also taken a swing at Frank Sinatra, which was probably exaggerated in the full scheme of things but…" She paused, reminding herself to breathe. "Jake needed to lay low. He had some big bosses to answer to, and a lot of people were dodging bullets."

"So you didn't see him after that night?"

She shook her head. "I blocked it out. I went to a dark, lonely place and then President Kennedy was shot and then Clay told me that Jake was dead and took me away from Vegas."

"So, honey. How did Jake die?"

She fiddled her fingers. "Some guys found him in the desert. He'd been—decapitated."

Ruben picked up the mug as he stood and wore a path in front of the coffee table, an occasional pause punctuating his thoughts. Then she heard him laugh. She looked at him, and he laughed again. She looked away and he said, "Sorry. I suddenly saw gangsters with spats and violin cases. Are you saying that the Mafia was involved in Jake's death?"

She stood and took her mug to the kitchen. Ruben followed. She poured coffee in each mug and then relaxed against the countertop before saying, "Like I said, Jake had big bosses. Were they Mafia? Jake would never admit it, but I always thought so. I knew his boss at the Sands—a guy called Sid Casper—pretty well. I know these guys were unhappy with Jake, but I'm not saying they had him killed. Clay told me that his headless body was found in the desert, and that's all I've ever known."

"Did you see the body?"

"No. Clay came to identify it, but he wouldn't let me see. I was in pretty bad shape, living in a vodka and Valium haze. He took me to Reno, and that was the end of Vegas."

"And of Jake."

She nodded.

"Are you sure?"

She frowned and then looked away.

He led her back to the living room, asking, "Why did you leave Vegas the first time? When you went to Reno and met Jake's brother, Clay?"

They sat. She struggled with the tightness in her throat and said, "I told you about the night that Jake lost his temper and—sort of beat me up."

"He knocked you down and kicked you in the face, Hassie. That's a little more than *sort of* beating you up."

"Everything was wrong. My friends were nagging me to get away from Jake. I saw a chance to leave and took it."

"And was it the right thing to do?"

She shrugged. "I suppose so."

"But you went back."

She hesitated. "I didn't go back to the Sands. I got a job singing at the Tropicana. I did okay for myself, and my friends were happy and supportive that I'd left Jake behind."

"So where was Jake when you got back?"

"Still at the Sands."

"And he didn't try to see you or win you back?"

She shook her head, barely. "Not at first."

"And why was that?"

"He was involved with someone else."

Ruben stood up, ran his hands through his thinning hair and said, "Another woman? Are you kidding me? Why have you never mentioned this before?"

"Why would I mention her, Ruben? She was a witch. And a whore. She flung herself at Jake every chance she got and kept on until she landed him and made me look like a fool."

"But you'd gone to Reno. Did they get married?"

"She had his baby—a girl—so she told everyone they were married. But I found out later that Jake was only taking care of her— for the baby, I'm sure."

"Mister nice guy." Ruben moved a few steps away from her and then turned back and said, "Hassie, honey, this is fantastic!"

"What's fantastic, Ruben? That this woman humiliated me or that she had the life that *I* should have had with Jake?" She stood up to leave the room, but Ruben grabbed her, held her shoulders and said, "I swear I'm not trying to upset you, but you gotta understand what all this does for our story. We always had the Rat Pack and the sordid history of the mob in Vegas, but I've been kinda worried that it wasn't going anywhere. But now? There's a decapitation. And another woman. And a love child? Jesus, Hassie, this is gold!"

She pulled away from him and headed for her bedroom. She got as far as the dining room and collapsed in a chair. They say you can't remember pain, but she was certain that her heart was breaking all over again and that it must be visible to Ruben, who'd found some deranged pleasure in making her suffer. She felt his hand on her back and tensed with an instinct to ask him to leave. But the warmth from his hand was more than just transference of body heat.

She calmed down as Ruben sat beside her, took both of her hands in his and said, "I am such a fucking moron. Please forgive me for being so insensitive. Kick me or… cut my balls off, whatever makes you feel better."

She laughed and cried and wiped her face with her hands. "I hate dragging all this up again. I feel like such a fool."

He pulled a rumpled handkerchief from his pocket and dabbed it along her jaw line, shaking his head as he said, "You're a goddess."

She took the handkerchief from him and wiped her eyes.

"Do you know much about Greek mythology?" he asked.

"Not really. Why?"

"Listening to you talk about this Jake fella and the volatile relationship you had makes me think of the myth of Hades and Persephone. You know it?"

She shook her head, gripping the handkerchief.

"Hades was the god of the underworld."

"The devil?"

Ruben shrugged. "Persephone became the queen of the underworld after Hades kidnapped her from earth and dragged her down with him. Her mother, Demeter, tried to save her and convinced her father, Zeus, to let Persephone come back to earth. But she'd eaten the fruit of the pomegranate, which meant she must return to her captor each year as well. So now, the myth is associated with the coming of the seasons. When Persephone comes to earth, it's springtime. When she descends to Hades, it's winter."

Hassie listened with mild interest and then said, "So you're saying that Jake was Hades and I'm Persephone, and he dragged me down to this underworld of his."

"Can you see the parallels?"

"I guess so. A lot of people thought Jake was the devil incarnate."

"And the bigger point of this story, honey, is that Persephone always goes back to him. Despite the fact that he rapes her and drags her around by her hair, he also loves her. He hates letting her go, and she always goes back. That sound familiar?"

She forced herself to breathe and fought a dozen emotions as she asked, "Have you ever been physically damaged by someone who claimed to love you?"

He looked askance, like she'd asked him to reveal his deepest, darkest secret and then said, "No. No, I haven't."

"You know, I've never said this to anyone, but I've often wondered if one of the reasons I could never have a *real* relationship with Clay was because I subconsciously wondered if he would hurt me."

"Did he give you reason to think he might?"

"God, no. That's my point. I wasn't aware of it at the time, but I remembered later that my pulse would surge when I heard his footsteps. I'd stop and wait until I knew where he was. It was totally irrational, and I never seemed to relax while in that house with him. At the time I thought it was the drugs or my struggle with the infant Kenny. Clay did nothing but take care of me—of us. I had nothing to fear. But I was conditioned to stay on guard. I was jolted from my sleep many, many nights because a hard object slammed into the side of my face. I'm sure I cried out, but my room was far enough away from Clay's that I never believed he heard me. At least I hope he didn't."

Ruben held his hands together like he was praying, his fingertips touching and perched against his lips, mulling his thoughts. He pushed himself upright in the chair and said, "Clay sounds like a pretty special guy."

She nodded, tears running down her cheeks. "And I've been really shitty to him since we got to New York."

"How so?"

She wiped her face with Ruben's handkerchief, already streaked with her mascara, and said, "You know, he drove us out here—all the way from Reno. We could've come on the bus—I'd actually bought tickets. But he cashed them in, tucked the money in my suitcase and piled us in his car. It took two long days, and he paid for the entire journey. I knew that he was totally against the move—that losing us was killing him, but I let him do it because I had a single vision and that was to get us—me and Kenny—to New York City where I was sure we'd be welcomed with open arms, and I'd be the darling of Broadway and nothing that Clay feared for us would ever happen."

"But you stayed in touch with him? Didn't you get a job pretty soon after you got here?"

She nodded. "Yeah. We talked every few weeks for a while until…"

"Until what?"

"Until Zach came in the picture."

"You never told him about Warren?"

"No. And eventually I stopped being there for Clay's calls and never called him back, and then we moved in with Zach and the number Clay had for us was—dead."

"Are you saying that he doesn't know that you married Warren?"

She held the handkerchief to her mouth and nodded. "He doesn't know where we are. And he hasn't spoken to either of us since—"

"Hassie. This is your business. And I'm not going to tell you what to do. But I am going to keep my producer hat on right now and remind you that our story—our premise for this show needs Jake and that other woman—what's her name?"

"Natalie."

"And Natalie and that child, which by my estimation is Clay's niece. Right?"

"Yes. Norma. She's his niece just like Kenny's his nephew, and as best I know, they're his only real family."

"Then he probably knows where Norma is. And whether you like this suggestion or not, it's important that you connect with Norma. Sounds to me that Clay is your connector."

Hassie stood up. "Do you want more coffee or something to eat?"

Ruben patted his shirt pocket and said, "What I want is a cigarette. While I'm outside polluting your sidewalk, think about how you might approach Clay about all this. Maybe have a glass of wine and relax a little bit. I'll be back in a few minutes, and we'll brainstorm this whole idea some more."

Hassie took a bottle of wine out of the fridge, poured it in a juice glass and then went into the living room and checked the time. Kenny would be home within the hour and could be the perfect excuse to truncate the session with Ruben and put this whole issue with Jake and Clay and Norma off until another day. But that only pointed to how adept she'd become with procrastination—what was it that Zach called her—a *cunctator*? She walked to the window to check on Ruben but didn't see him. Maybe he'd gone for cigarettes or a walk around the block. It was late morning in Reno. Clay had cut back the hours he spent in his office a few years ago. Chances were good he'd be at home. She went to the telephone and dialed his number. It rang several times before he answered. She hesitated, searching for her nerve and then said, "Hi, Clay. It's me."

"Hassie?"

She swallowed hard. "Yes, hi. Please don't hang up."

He was quiet and then asked, "Where are you? Is Kenny okay?"

"I'm in New York, and Kenny's fine. Everything's fine."

"Then why are you calling? What do you need?"

"Clay, I am so sorry for hiding from you the way I did. It was wrong and selfish and, God, Kenny thinks you don't want to talk to him any more and I'm so, so sorry if I hurt you."

"*If* you hurt me? Do you know how long it's been since I've heard from you? Do you have any idea how worried I've been that something horrible happened to you?"

"I'm so sorry, Clay, but—"

"But what, Hassie? What possible excuse do you have for just shutting me out of your lives? It's unforgivable."

"Please don't say that. I know I was wrong, and whether you want to hear it or not, I do have my reasons. But I also know I was wrong."

"And you're calling now to ask me… what? Are you in some sort of mess again? Because if you are, I don't want to know. I've moved on with my life. I've met someone, and I'm happy."

"That's wonderful." She struggled to keep the tears out of her voice. "Are you married?"

"We're getting married on New Year's Eve—a small wedding with just a few friends and family."

"Do you still consider me and Kenny as friends?"

She could sense him smiling as he said, "Sounds like you're hawking for an invitation."

"You know we'd love to be there. Kenny would be so happy to see you again. We both would."

"I'd love to see you too. But I'm not sure that would work."

"Why not? We're way past due for a visit, and that timing would be good."

He hesitated. "How do I put this politely...? You've been on my shit list for a while and, well, Carolee doesn't really want to know you. In fact, it's a good thing she's not here right now or she'd be screaming for me to hang up."

"Wow. I don't know what to say. Except that I'll always be grateful to you, and I'll always care about you and—I'm sorry."

"You're always sorry, Hassie. But it's usually after the fact—a day late and a dollar short."

She needed to stay in control of her emotions and breathed deeply. She said, "I really am happy for you and hope you won't punish Kenny for my bad decisions. Remember, he really is your family."

"Hassie, you both are my family, and I've missed you, not to mention having been out of my mind with worry. Just give me a little time to deal with all this, and maybe we can work out a visit whether it's for the wedding or not."

"I'd love to meet the woman that got you to settle down." During a moment of silence between them, Hassie spotted Kenny walking up the steps to the building with Ruben. She perked up and said, "Clay, if you've got a minute, there's someone coming in who I know wants to say hello to you."

She laid the receiver on the desk and walked over to open the door, motioning for Ruben to give her a minute with Kenny. She led him over to the desk and said, "Uncle Clay's on the phone. He wants to talk to you."

Kenny took the phone from her and said, "Hullo."

Hassie waved Ruben over and whispered, "It's Clay."

"I guess so," Kenny said and then looked at Hassie. She motioned for him to keep talking, but he just listened and said the occasional, "Uh, huh." Ruben sat in the big armchair and waited. Kenny nodded. "Okay, here's Mom." He started to hand the phone to Hassie and then stopped and said, "Me too. Bye."

Hassie finished the conversation with Clay while Kenny went to change clothes. She took the juice glass of wine over to the sofa and sat down.

"So you called him?" Ruben asked.

She nodded. Her shoulders sagged with relief that wasn't warranted. "He's upset with me."

"Can you fix it?"

"I'll try."

chapter eleven

Before Warren met Hassie—and thereby, Kenny—he'd never thought what it might be like to have or raise a child. His own childhood had not exactly been dysfunctional, but it hadn't been storybook perfect either. So when it became apparent that he was going to look after Kenny while Hassie was in England, he pulled on the memory of his mother, which made him wonder if maybe Zelda was better equipped to take care of a six-year-old boy, despite Hassie's insistence that Zelda stay locked away while she was gone. At any rate, in order to get the little guy to bed so that he could have the apartment to himself, Warren let him select his dinner menu, which consisted of hot dogs smothered in ketchup and half a package of Chips Ahoy cookies. Warren let him watch television past the normally allotted time and, the biggest bribe of all, let him skip his bath. Hassie would throttle him if she found out, but it seemed worth the risk in order to get on with the evening that he'd planned for Andrew, who was due to arrive in just under half an hour.

He shut the door to Kenny's room and hurriedly changed into the African styled Dashiki pullover shirt and drawstring trousers. The ensemble had been a gift from a client Warren had helped through a dodgy investment in Kenya and though he liked the multi-colored tribal pattern—a yummy swirl of the colors of asparagus and pumpkin and mustard—and despite the fact that the look had become popular in certain ethnic circles, Warren had never imagined that he would wear it. Nothing about it was a look that he'd consider trying to pull off in either his business or social world. But something about the lightweight fabric and casual, flowing cut fit the type of evening he was expecting to have with Andrew.

He poured Aramis cologne into his palms and dabbed them over his days-growth of beard, checked his image in the mirror and then tied a yellowish-gold scarf around his neck. He'd combed his hair straight back after an earlier shower. In his mind the overall look was flamboyantly sexy—not exactly right for Zelda but sexy nonetheless. He returned to the living room, barefooted.

Andrew had introduced Warren to Cuban music, and he'd become addicted to Celia Cruz, whose salsa styling always put him in a good mood. He put one of Celia's recordings on the turntable, kept the volume low and immediately felt the beat in his hips and feet. He danced over to the bar and picked out two balloon wine glasses for the '61 Mouton Rothschild Bordeaux he'd planned to serve. It had been a wedding gift from one of the senior partners—one that he'd stocked away for just the right occasion. He opened the bottle to let it breathe. He had brought in Armenian food and returned to the kitchen to put the cheese pastries in the oven. They'd have them with the wine and then he'd set up the meal of salads and meat kebabs. He went in the dining room and stood in front of the china cabinet, the contagious salsa rhythm coursing through his body. He opened the left cabinet door and reached for the plates that belonged to his mother's heirloom pattern. He rarely had occasion to use them these days. On the odd night that he was home for dinner, the majority of their dishes and containers were either cardboard or Styrofoam. He picked out two salad and two dinner plates and set them on the table. The front doorbell chimed.

He checked his watch—nine o'clock. Andrew was on time for possibly the first time ever. Warren buzzed him in and then stood at the open door while Andrew stutter-walked along the corridor, having already had a few drinks. He was amorous in that sloppy, booze-driven way, which was a turn off to Warren, though he tried not to show it. Andrew walked deeper into the room, eyed Warren somewhat disapprovingly and then looked around as he said, "It's a lovely place you've got here. Very comfortable and—organized."

Warren laughed. "That sounds more like chastisement than praise. Have a seat. I'll get the wine."

He approximated a four-ounce pour in each glass and sat down beside Andrew on the sofa. They touched glasses, with flirty eye contact. Warren waited for Andrew to taste the wine before asking, "Do you like it?"

Andrew nodded and then leaned over to kiss Warren, who deftly turned his head, offering his cheek.

Andrew laughed. "What have I done?"

"First off, you're drunk, and you haven't said one nice thing about me or my home since you arrived."

Andrew swirled the wine in the glass. "I was always taught that if you can't say something nice, don't say anything at all."

The ill-mannered attitude stung more than the words, and Warren was off-footed in a way he hadn't experienced in all the months that he'd been subjected to Andrew's insensitive remarks. Warren looked at him, but before he could speak, Andrew touched his leg and said, "Relax, honey. Your apartment's beautiful." He rubbed his hand along Warren's thigh. "Very sexy. I didn't know I should have come dressed for bed."

Warren pushed his hand away and said, "If you're implying that I'm wearing pajamas, you're wrong."

Andrew chuckled, swigged the wine, and then stood up and walked over to the bookcase. He perused the shelves and picked up an Old Paris porcelain dish as he asked, "Is this an ashtray?"

"Hardly." Warren walked up and took the dish from him. "It's quite a rare piece of French china. Why do you want an ashtray?"

Andrew took a small plastic bag from his pocket that contained two joints. He dangled it in front of Warren's face. "Fancy a little smoke?"

"No, I do not. You know that Kenny is here, and I told you this was not allowed."

"Okay, okay. It's not mandatory. But it's good stuff. I thought it might help you relax, which you obviously need to do." He tucked the plastic bag in his pocket. He then pulled Warren into his chest and held him close, but said nothing. They held each other until Warren drew back from him and asked, "Is everything all right? You don't seem happy to be here at all."

Andrew's clear blue eyes seemed to cloud over. He took Warren's face in both hands, gave him a gentle but meaningful kiss and said, "It's been a rough few days."

"Then you should be happy to see me and to relax. I want you to enjoy being in *my* home, and I want to pamper you."

The oven timer dinged. Warren pulled away. "I'll be right back with tasty hors d'oeuvres," he said. "You must be ravenous."

"Actually, I had dinner."

Warren stopped. "You had dinner? Tonight?"

"Yes. We were meeting so late, I didn't think you'd want to be bothered."

"Drew, I told you I was having supper for us. And since when have you eaten before nine o'clock?"

"The opportunity arose, and I was hungry. It's not a big deal. But whatever you're cooking smells good. Go on. Bring it out. We'll nibble."

Warren went to the kitchen, took the pastries from the oven and considered dumping them in the garbage. Andrew was adept at egocentricity. Warren usually made allowances for him, believing that everything else about their relationship was worth the compromise. But this was the first time he'd seen his behavior verge on scurrilous. He put the pastries on a small platter and walked back to the living room. He heard Andrew talking to someone and thought he'd made a phone call. But when he reached the sofa, Kenny was sitting next to Andrew. He quickly set the platter down and said, "Hey, big guy. Why are you out of bed? Is the music too loud?"

"I heard talking. I thought Mommy was home."

Warren looked at Andrew, who was either pissed-off or amused. Either way, this was not a good scenario. He took hold of Kenny's arm. "Come on. Let's get you back to bed."

"But, Uncle Zach, I'm not sleepy."

"Let the boy stay up with us," Andrew slurred and then looked at Kenny. "Are you hungry? There are some delicious... things here." He picked up one of the pastries and said, "Uncle Zach, what are these called?"

Warren's eyes darted between Andrew and Kenny before he forced a smile and said, "Subereg. Kenny's had them before, haven't you?" He picked one up and took a small bite to make sure it wasn't too hot and then offered it to Kenny.

Kenny took a big bite and then looked at Warren and asked, "Why are you wearing pajamas?"

Andrew smirked and picked up his wine glass.

"Finish your snack, Kenny, and then it's off to bed."

Kenny looked at Andrew and asked, "What's your name?"

"Andrew. I'm a friend of your—uncle's."

Kenny said, "Oh," and took another bite.

"Andrew was there when your mom and I got married. Remember? He was my special friend like Mrs. Jordan was there for your mom."

Kenny nodded and with his mouth full asked, "Can I have another one?"

"One more and then you go back to bed."

Kenny took the pastry and then offered it to Andrew. "You want one?"

"You finish yours and then do as your uncle says and go back to bed. Don't you have to go to school tomorrow?"

"No, silly. It's Saturday."

"Oh, yes. Of course."

Warren stood next to Kenny. "Okay. Say nighty-night to Andrew, and let's go wash your hands."

Kenny brushed his hands together, scattering pastry crumbs on the sofa, then looked at Andrew and said, "Night."

"Good night, Kenny. It was very nice to meet you."

Warren said, "Pour more wine. I'll be right back."

When Warren returned, Andrew was standing at the desk holding the photo that he'd taken of Warren, Hassie and Kenny after the wedding ceremony. "So. It's Uncle Zach," he said.

Warren stood beside him. "Hassie calls me Zach. And anyway, he's not gonna call me *Dad*."

"Would you like it if he did?"

They'd never had a conversation about Kenny and what Warren's role really meant. Honestly, Andrew had never seemed remotely interested in anything to do with Kenny—or Hassie, for that matter. He led Andrew back to the sofa and said, "He's a great kid. His father died before he was born, and the men in his life have been substitutes."

"So he's had a lot of *uncles*?"

"Just his father's half-brother, who helped Hassie when Kenny was born, and now me. I'm not a blood uncle, but I'm married to his mother—which technically makes me his stepfather. But uncle is easier and nicer for him, we think. It's not a big deal, Drew."

Andrew poured the wine and said, "But it is a big deal, Warren. You should see yourself with that kid. I think you'd step out in front of a bus for him."

"Maybe. He's a great little boy, and he looks up to me. And let's face it, I'm never gonna have a kid any other way. Why not embrace what's right here in my lap?"

"I can't argue with you. I don't want to argue with you." Andrew sipped the wine.

"But…"

"But this isn't my life. It's been tolerable while these people lived elsewhere and nothing about my life was anything to do with them."

"These people?"

"Let me finish."

Warren gulped the wine.

"I know you're gay, and you know you're gay, but it's fairly obvious that you really don't want to be gay. You don't want anyone in your law firm to know, and you go to great lengths to keep it that way. Things have changed since the Stonewall riots, but you still don't want to embrace your sexuality. You live a double life, and for some reason that evidently only God knows, your wife shuts her eyes to that fact. But that doesn't stop you from wanting to be a father figure to that little boy, and I'm beginning to believe that it doesn't stop you from sleeping with your wife when you think that's the right thing to do as well."

"You're wrong about that. I swear to you, I haven't touched her—"

"You know what? It doesn't really matter. You're entitled to live your life however you want. You can be Hassie's husband or Kenny's father or Zelda or Godzilla. It doesn't matter because I can't do this any more."

"Drew, I'm the same guy here as when I'm out with you or in your apartment or on Fire Island. I just have a responsibility to Kenny when I'm here."

"Do you have more wine?"

Warren shook his head. "I want you to understand that you are the single most important person in my life. I'd do anything for you, and I know you know that."

"So if I asked you to, you'd divorce Hassie and never see Kenny again?"

The room felt airless. Warren asked, "Is that what you want?"

"That's not what I said. I merely asked if you'd do it—if I asked you to."

"Why would you ask me to do something so drastic? Are you saying that you want us to be committed to each other—exclusively? Is that what this is all about? Because if it is—" The look on Andrew's face stopped him. Warren wanted another drink, but he didn't want to serve Andrew anything more.

Andrew pulled his lips into a taut horizontal line and then said, "I'm going to be fifty this year. Part of me keeps saying to settle down—to enjoy life with a companion and to stop chasing the high life just for the sake of it. I've considered that that person could be you. You're smart and funny and handsome and sexy. At first, I wasn't so crazy about Zelda, but now she's an extension of you—a fun, little kinky way for you to keep things exciting between us. And I love you for that." He stopped and looked up at Warren. "And I'm going to miss it."

Warren wanted to touch him but somehow knew not to. "Why are you going to miss Zelda?"

Andrew inhaled like he was sucking in courage. "Like I said, I can't do this any more. I've been kidding myself for a while now, but every time I plan to break it off, you show up all sexy and full of life, and I'm weak. I want what I want. And you're always there. But this isn't what I want, honey. This is your life. Not ours."

"But we love each other."

Andrew looked away and said, "Love is a weakness."

Warren felt enveloped in an invisible bubble—sealed off from everything that he'd once shared with Andrew, who seemed completely unaffected by the gravity of their conversation. And then Andrew said, "If you won't let me smoke, can I please have a drink?"

Warren felt that if he moved, the bubble would burst, and he would break apart, and he couldn't let Andrew see him like that. He nodded toward the bar and said, "Help yourself."

Andrew returned with a glass of scotch and set it on the table without tasting it. He sat with his elbows on his knees, his head resting in his hands. After an uncomfortable silence he looked up and said, "I'm a real dick."

"What are you talking about?"

"I met someone else a few weeks ago. I knew right away that it was something special, but I wanted to be sure."

Warren stared at him, incredulous, and then curtly asked, "So are you sure now?"

Andrew shook his head. "I'm really sorry. I came here tonight to tell you about this and that it's over between you and me. And then that little boy appeared, and I saw a great opportunity to blame it all on you, which, by the way, I did mean a lot of what I said. Do yourself a favor and think about it."

Warren grabbed hold of his emotions and asked, "So how old's this guy? What does he do? Were you with him before you came here tonight? Is he going to move in with you?"

"Let's not talk about it now. I'm a little drunk, and you should probably take some time to think."

"Thanks for the half-assed advice, but you're the last person I need telling me what to do right now. But I am glad that you decided to be honest. And yes, you are a dick. Please leave." Warren stood and took the platter into the kitchen. The rest of the meal was cold and wilted. He heard Andrew let himself out of the apartment. He raked the food into the garbage, sat down at the kitchen table and cried.

He sat with his face in his hands until Kenny startled him. "Uncle Zach? Are you sick?"

Warren sat up, wiping his eyes and said, "Hey, big guy. I'm fine. Why aren't you asleep?"

"Where's Andrew?"

"He had to go home. Did you have a bad dream?"

Kenny shook his head. "I miss Mommy."

Warren reached out and pulled him onto his lap. "I miss her too."

He tucked Kenny back in bed and went to change his clothes. He stood at Hassie's dressing table and perused the many perfume bottles and jars of creams and makeup, some of which Zelda borrowed from time to time. He spotted the photo of Barbara and looked at it closely. The old woman had finally died, and Hassie hadn't gotten to her in time. Pity, but then she'd known that Barbara's time was limited, and she'd chosen to tempt fate. Warren didn't understand this trait of Hassie's—this propensity to believe that her life's schedule was the one that mattered—that others would adjust accordingly. This time, she'd been wrong. He'd offered to go with her—to see her through what would inevitably be a rough few days. But she'd insisted that she go alone. And as he turned to walk away from the dressing table, he noticed that his mother's wedding band he'd given Hassie on their wedding day lay inside a small china dish.

* * *

The rest of that night, into the next day was solitary torture, and for the first time in his life Warren thought about killing himself. He contemplated if he'd hang himself or take an overdose. Or maybe he'd do something shocking, like drown himself in the pool at the baths. He didn't want pain, and he didn't want to leave a mess for anyone to clean up. He simply didn't want to live without Andrew, and he didn't know what to do with his heart. And then he thought about Andrew's comment that love is a weakness. What did that mean? He had loved Andrew with reckless abandon, rarely stopping to consider the risks he was taking—the risk that he could be ostracized in his office or, worse, fired; the risk that Hassie would one day wake up and realize that their marriage was an atrocious lie that could land him in divorce court; the risk that he could lose all rights and privileges where his role as Kenny's stepfather was concerned. How could taking all of those potentially life-changing risks by loving Andrew be considered as being weak? Andrew left him feeling foolish and stupid and lost and in the kind of pain he'd known when his mother died. He hated himself like this, but it seemed out of his control. He'd had no warning and still didn't know when and why Andrew stopped caring about him. Five, six months wasn't a lifetime, but it had been a significant chunk of time out of their lives. And now, it was over, and Andrew had walked away from the relationship like it had never happened.

Despite his refusal to give in to his mawkish disposition, Warren had difficulty functioning as a sane, normal person. But he couldn't let Kenny see him that way. On Saturday afternoon, they took a Circle Line cruise around New York harbor. Kenny's genuine, wide-eyed amazement at the sights rejuvenated Warren, and he found himself thinking about the things Andrew had said to him and was able to seriously consider what he, Warren Zachary, wanted out of his life. Through extensive soul-searching, he dug deep into his youth. He recalled the horrendous scene, at age fourteen, after he'd been caught with his pants down in the neighbor's garage. He'd been seduced by his friend's older brother, whose mother had discovered them and run screaming to Warren's parents. His mother tried to chalk the incident up to the boys going through an experimental phase. But his father wouldn't hear her and didn't speak to Warren for days. And when he did speak he had told Warren that homosexuality was a disease and that, like many diseases, it could be cured. He'd said that a homosexual man could be saved by a woman and that they could "turn" straight and get married and have *normal* lives. Although at the time it had done nothing but create an irreparable schism between him and his father, he realized that those words had never really left his psyche.

Hassie would return from England the next night. Warren was hard pressed to decide what she was actually returning to. Their relationship had long passed strained, and he had no idea if anything about their marriage was salvageable—or if he even wanted it to be. But as he looked after Kenny and bonded with him in a way that took on new meaning, he thought about how different their lives might have been if he'd never gotten involved with Andrew—how different *his* life would be if he'd never given into the sybaritic lifestyle that his father had warned him against.

So, yes. He had been weak but not because he loved Andrew. He was weak because he let something as basic as… what was it the Armenian priest of his youth had said when speaking on the subject? He'd given in to the *sins of the flesh*—basic, carnal desire that some considered wrong and evil and for which he'd have much to atone. In reality, he'd never really been unconditionally happy in any relationship he'd had and nowhere, at any time, had he *known* that he was exactly where he should be. In essence, his life as a heterosexual man was a failure, and his life as a homosexual man had been a failure. Was he even capable of attaining—either physically or emotionally— that deep, profound love that one was supposed to experience in a lifetime? Maybe life with Hassie and her son was the best life that he could ever have. He loved Hassie on some level, and Andrew was right—he'd step out in front of a bus for Kenny. So maybe life with Hassie wasn't shambolic after all. Maybe that life as he'd imagined it wasn't such a bad thing—even if it meant that now he was *settling*. He hated that word, and he hated the thought, but the fact remained that Andrew Callegari had proven a big mistake, and despite the occasional one-sidedness of it all, it would be months before Warren, rightly or wrongly, would feel anything less than devastated at having lost the life and the love that he'd known with Andrew. Ultimately, Andrew had done Warren a favor. Now he just needed for his wife to come home.

part two

chapter twelve

As the crow flies, the coastal village of Rottingdean is located sixty miles directly due south of Charles Beauclerke's flat in North London. Charles set out almost half an hour later than he'd planned, knowing that traffic could easily add an hour to the two-hour journey. He'd had the call about his Aunt Barbara's death six days earlier and had yet to feel much in the way of grief. His opinion of her hadn't always been kind, and, unfairly or not, he'd too often considered her a nosey parker. Disrespectful, he knew, especially considering how she felt about him—like the son she never had—which she proved by leaving him the family house in Rottingdean and a healthy top-up of his bank account. But he could never seem to warm to her beyond the familial duty that his mother imposed. Her brother, his Uncle Teddy, warned him that she was prone to throwing about the money her late Texas oilman husband had left her—that she'd try to buy him—and to some extent it was true. But when all was said and done, she was his mother's only sister, and his mother would be furious when he turned up late.

He turned off the A27 onto Falmer Road and drove alongside the rolling green pastures and patches of ancient woodland, trying to focus on a childhood memory that would put him in the proper mindset for the service ahead. He'd been a spotty sixteen-year-old lad when his aunt moved back to England from Texas. He remembered being frog-marched to her house for Sunday lunch, which seemed interminably long at the time. She'd fuss over him and stand too close, emitting those perfumed "old lady" smells that made him sneeze. And now, the house with the smells and the piles of books and music, and the cats—those bloody cats—would soon belong to him; whatever he would do with it, he hadn't given it a thought. For today and the foreseeable future *he* belonged to Her Majesty's Royal Navy and since the first day of college, he'd had no desire to return to Rottingdean, full stop.

He reached the village green and parked near St. Margaret's Parish Church. A small group of mourners gathered in the cemetery. He remained in the background while a chilly sea breeze whipped around him beneath a blue-gray sky of diaphanous clouds. From that distance, it was difficult to tell exactly how many people were in attendance, but it looked to be no more than twenty-five or thirty. The vicar stood facing the attendees as they began to fill in the few rows of old wooden chairs. Most were bundled in coats or jackets, shawls or hats; the elderly hunched over walking sticks. Charles hung back and breathed in the sea air. Even as the sunshine occasionally broke through the clouds, the atmosphere was low, as though the shrubs and trees drooped in mourning. He suddenly felt displaced and foreign in a way that he'd heard naval colleagues talk about relative to changes in their lives once they'd had a taste of the rest of the world.

Barbara was to be buried next to his grandparents. He'd last been in this cemetery when his grandmother died almost ten years ago. He'd probably last been inside the fusty old church for his grandmother's funeral. What exactly that said about him he wasn't sure. The one thing he did know was that he'd jolly well planned to be absent on this day—off sailing the seas some place far away. Bad luck that he happened to be in London doing a course for the navy.

As he approached the graveside, he spotted Nigella standing at the front, greeting the mourners in her care-giving way. She was a good sister, of whom he was quite fond, but she'd have a right go at Charles for turning up late. His mother, Gwendolyn, sat in the middle of the front row. Two other ladies sat at the end of the row. One was bound to be Barbara's officious housekeeper and companion, Beryl. He wondered if she planned to stay on after he became lord of the manor. The other woman appeared younger with shoulder-length dark hair under a small black hat and sat at least a head taller than the woman beside her.

Nigella sat down beside Gwen. Charles preferred to remain in the back but supposed he should join them. He took a few steps closer. The vicar raised his hands in preparation to begin the service, noticed Charles and said, "Son, would you care to take your seat?"

He walked around to the front row and sat beside his mother, who stared straight ahead.

When Earth's last picture is painted and the tubes are twisted and dried,

When the oldest colours have faded, and the youngest critic has died,

We shall rest, and, faith, we shall need it—lie down for an aeon or two

Till the Master of All Good Workmen shall put us to work anew.

"It is befitting that Barbara Crumpler requested this Rudyard Kipling poem be read today. Kipling was a son of our village, and Barbara, a daughter who loved music and art and dedicated her life to sharing that love and to encouraging others to find an artistic canvas within themselves. A teacher, a mentor, a shining example of what it means to give of oneself. That was our sister, Barbara."

So now it was clear. Charles had officially annoyed his mother and was in for a day of it. He could always cut the weekend short and return to London that evening. Anything was tolerable for a few hours. Especially after they got to the pub. It was odd hearing his aunt being described as a stalwart of the arts scene in the area. He'd only ever known her to hole up in the front lounge that she had converted to what she referred to as her music *atelier,* which he thought was pretentious and a bit loopy. Especially after she installed the small grand piano she'd brought from Texas, which unapologetically consumed the entire room. The vicar suddenly raised his voice, pulling Charles from his wandering thoughts, and then focused on the dark-haired woman at the end of the row before saying, "We're joined today by one of Barbara's former students from the United States. Come, miss. I understand you've something to share with us."

The woman stood and slowly walked forward. She was tall and wore a black skirt and jacket that accentuated her small waist. The vicar leaned in to speak to her; she carefully turned to face the guests.

"Barbara Crumpler was more than a teacher and a mentor," she said almost inaudibly and then cleared her throat and raised her head. "She was my confidante, my conscience and my friend."

She had a tight grip on a white handkerchief in her left hand, which Charles noticed was devoid of rings.

She hesitated briefly and then continued, "I met her in Texas when I was a little girl. She implanted my love for music from those early days. She convinced me to believe in myself and that I could do anything I put my mind to. Her generous, selfless influence still lives within me." She stopped again and then with a weak smile continued, "I had no idea how heavy my heart would be today, but Barbara has done so much for me, I want to honor her the best way I know how."

The mourners remained quiet while she stood with head bowed, hands clasped at her waist. She lifted her chin and focused on the space just above the crowd. Beneath the brim of the hat was a beautiful face. Her voice broke through the silence with clear, controlled tones. The back of Charles's neck tingled, and goose flesh covered his arms. As he listened to the pleasant melody and Italian lyrics, he sensed his mother's restlessness. He had to believe that more feathers than just hers had been ruffled by this extraordinary departure from tradition where the Church of England was concerned—and by an *American,* no less. But, of course, she hadn't the foggiest idea that she'd committed such a faux pas, and something about the whole notion made him smile as he shamelessly ogled her.

When she finished singing, the vicar thanked her and said a few closing remarks before dismissing the attendees with a standard benediction. Charles stood to help his mother out of her chair. She ignored him and reached out to Nigella and said, "I must speak to the parishioners and then I'd like to go home."

Charles moved off to the side, catching Nigella's eye with a quick wink. He was much more interested in the movements of the beautiful American. She stood at the end of the first row talking with Beryl—a perfect time to speak to the nice, little woman. He started to step away when he felt a hand on his shoulder. He turned to be greeted by the vicar, who, through tobacco-stained teeth, said, "Charles Beauclerke. It's lovely to see you here today."

"Thank you, Father. Aunt Barbara was a special lady."

"Indeed she was and so very proud of you and your accomplishments. The Royal Navy, is it?"

"Yes, sir. Lieutenant now, sir."

"How marvelous," the vicar said while steering him toward his mother. "Dear Gwendolyn, you must be delighted that both your children are here with you today."

Through a tight-lipped smile, still refusing to look at Charles, she said, "It was a lovely service, Father. Although I'm not so sure the caterwauling in the midst of it all was such a good idea."

Charles cautiously spoke up, "I thought the song was lovely, and Auntie would have loved it, I'm sure."

Gwen ignored him, looked at the vicar and said, "Your words were so kind. My sister was very fond of you. Thank you again."

He reached out to her. "Could we have a quick word?"

Gwen walked away with the vicar, and Charles was left standing with his sister.

He kissed her cheek as she said, "It's lovely to see you, Charles, but you really should've tried to get here before the service. You know what Mummy's like."

"Yes, well, it couldn't be helped. And as far as I can see of our mother's concern, I might as well be a bloody lemon."

"Don't be silly. But you might want to keep your distance. You smell like a distillery."

Charles laughed. "How are you, Sis? And where's my favorite niece?"

"She's a bit young for this scene, eh?"

"Hmmm… what about the doting husband?" He looked back where he'd seen the American and spotted her walking with Beryl to the lynchgate entrance.

"Busy, busy in the City, but sends his regards."

"If you'll excuse me, I'd like to have a word with Beryl," Charles said. "See you in the pub?" He waved as he walked away, not bothering to look in his mother's direction. If she wanted to pretend that he didn't exist, so be it. Though it didn't escape his notice that she was possibly covering for her actual feelings about losing her only sister. The two women were barely two years apart in age and had always been close. The full impact of this void in Gwen's life was yet to be realized. When he was close enough to call out without seeming irreverent, he said, "Hello, Beryl?"

She turned as he approached, motioning the other woman to wait.

"Charles, 'ow nice to see ya. I thought you'd come by the 'ouse earlier this morning."

"Yes, I know. The traffic from London was diabolical. And then there were road works. I had quite a job to get here at all." He focused on the American and said, "Charles Beauclerke, Barbara's nephew."

She smiled and reached out to shake his hand. "Hello, Charles. I'm Hassie Calhoun. We spoke on the phone."

Charles shook her hand while their eyes locked into a saddened gaze. "It's nice to meet you. I enjoyed your song, though I wasn't familiar with it."

"It's an Italian art song… 'Lascia Ch'io Pianga.'"

"It was lovely and a thoughtful gesture—one that I know my aunt would have appreciated."

"I hope so. It's the first song she taught me when I started singing lessons. I'm actually surprised I remembered it. But then I guess some things you don't forget."

I won't forget you, he thought to himself and then casually said, "Would you care to join me at the pub for a memorial toast to Barbara?"

Hassie smiled uncomfortably. "Why don't you come back to Barbara's with us. Beryl's prepared a feast for the well-wishers stopping by. I think your mother and sister may be joining us."

Charles looked over his shoulder but saw no sign of them. "It's tradition to gather at the local pub after a burial—raise a glass or two in memory of the departed."

Hassie looked at Beryl as if asking her permission. Beryl smiled at Charles and said, "You go right ahead, Miss 'assie. Missus C woulda wanted ya to."

"Come with us, Beryl," Charles said, and led both women through the lynchgate.

Beryl shook her head and turned in the opposite direction. "You go on. I'll see ya later back at the 'ouse."

An awkward space of time passed between Charles and Hassie before he said, "Let's walk." They crossed the road and walked past the stone war memorial and along the edge of the duck pond toward the Plough Inn.

"It's very beautiful here," Hassie said. "Barbara mentioned the duck pond almost every time we discussed my promise to visit her. She talked about how I'd love the walk from her house to Sunday lunch in the pub and, afterwards, the stroll to commune with nature."

"So this is your first visit to England. You didn't make it over after we spoke in the summer?"

"Sadly, no. Between commitments with my—job and things, the time just got away."

They reached the entrance to the pub; Charles guided Hassie inside. He recognized a few people who'd attended Barbara's service and nodded as he led Hassie to the bar. "What'll you have?"

"What's appropriate?"

"I think a stiff gin and tonic is in order."

She nodded. "Sounds good."

He stood a head taller than the other patrons and quickly obtained two drinks. "I took the liberty of asking for yours with ice—a Yankee preference, I'm told."

She smiled. "Thanks. I'm told that ice is a luxury in this part of the world."

He moved her down the bar a few paces and said, "One could argue that ice reduces the effects of the alcohol." They exchanged smiles; Charles raised the glass and continued, "Anyway... cheers. To Auntie Barbara. May she rest in peace."

"Yes, cheers," Hassie said, and slowly swallowed the first sip.

Charles gave it a moment and then said, "So you've met my mother?"

Hassie nodded. "She and Nigella were at the house first thing this morning. She's quite a good organizer, isn't she?"

Charles laughed. "I suppose *organizer* is a bit kinder than rude, bossy cow."

Hassie sipped her drink.

"I apologize if she seemed overly tetchy," Charles said. "To be honest, I'm to blame."

"How so?"

"I'm assuming Barbara told you that I'm in the navy."

Hassie nodded. "She was very proud of your commitment to serving your country."

He chuckled. "That's an interesting way to put it—*serving* my country. So far, I've spent the time since I left college sailing around some rather exotic parts of the world."

"How long will you be in London?"

"Three months, give or take a week or two. Of course, there's some leave time in there as well. You can probably imagine what goes on when a load of sailors lets loose in town. But the course is also bloody hard work."

"In Greenwich, you say? That's part of London?"

"Hmmm," he nodded with a pull on his drink. "Southeast—on the Thames—specifically, the Royal Naval College. I'm undergoing a round of officer training."

Hassie smiled and pursed her lips before taking a sip.

"Did I say something amusing?"

"Not to be rude, but is everything in England *royal*?"

"Valid question. And, yes. It is." He smiled and continued, "And last night was one of our royal, pardon my language, *piss-ups* as they're called for a birthday celebration. If you can believe it, there are twin brothers from a different unit on this course. Yesterday was their thirtieth birthday. Suffice to say that the party went on until the wee hours, and, well, I did well to make it here at all." Charles downed the rest of his drink and motioned to the barman for another while saying, "Never mind all that. I should be asking about you and how *you* are feeling about all this."

"You mean Barbara's death?"

"Yes, and being in England for the first time to attend a bloody funeral."

"A little numb, I suppose."

Charles teasingly said, "Mightn't that be the effects of the gin?"

Hassie smiled and then hesitated, her demeanor turning to melancholy as she continued, "I'll always regret not having visited Barbara before she died—especially after you told me how sick she was."

Her voice had a sort of ring to it that, coupled with her accent, made her even more attractive. She was sad and subdued, which was completely understandable, but he somehow knew that her laugh would be just as alluring—one of those infectious laughs that Americans were known for and from which the English were discouraged from birth. And the eyes—those greenish gold, sensuous eyes. When he caught himself staring at her, he said, "Right. I suppose I should initiate this little tribute." He took the drink and raised it above his head. He focused on the small gathering of friends and spoke fondly of his aunt, inviting others to do the same. He furtively watched Hassie as a few others spoke. Her face was an open book, the complexity of her feelings showing through ever so subtly. He couldn't immediately recall a time when he'd had such a strong attraction to a woman he'd just met.

The drinks continued to flow, the somber mood turning to merriment. But Hassie seemed distracted or preoccupied and only smiled when he caught her eye. He touched her arm and said, "You must be exhausted. How about we get some air?"

She nodded, and he saw that her eyes were on the verge of spilling tears. He gently held her elbow and walked out of the pub and onto the path leading back to the village green. She slipped her arm through his; neither of them spoke. When they reached the church grounds, Charles stopped and asked, "Would you do me a great favor and walk with me back to the cemetery? I'd like to pay my respects to my father. He's buried a few rows up from my grandparents and Barbara."

They walked through a rose garden to the far side of the cemetery. Charles found the headstone: "James Carroll Beauclerke, beloved husband and father," birth and death dates. He should have arrived in time to visit it with Gwen, whom he was certain had placed the fresh bouquet of lilies there earlier that day. After a bout of silence, he thanked Hassie and then guided her back to the lynchgate where she sat down on one of the benches, smoothing her skirt across her lap. She was reverently quiet. He sat beside her and asked, "Is it too cold for you?"

She shook her head and without looking at him, said, "I'm not sure I can go back."

"To New York?"

"Back to Barbara's house. I can't believe she's gone."

Charles put an arm around her shoulder. She pulled a handkerchief from her coat pocket. While wiping her eyes, she said, "Please forgive me."

"Nonsense. You're allowed to grieve, Hassie."

"I should've come to see her when I found out she was sick. And I shouldn't have wasted all those years—when I decided that I didn't need her or anyone to tell me how to live my life. I turned away from her—and I'm not sure she ever forgave me. And why should she have? She was right. I was selfish and caught up in my own pathetic little world. And now I'll never be able to make it up to her."

Charles reached inside his coat and took a packet of cigarettes from his jacket breast pocket. He held it up and asked, "Do you mind if I smoke?" She shook her head but didn't look at him. He hesitated and then asked, "Would you like one?"

"No, thanks. I quit years ago."

"If it bothers you, I won't."

She stopped and said, "You know, it does bother me. And the air here is so fresh. Since you asked, would you mind not smoking?"

He put the packet back in his coat pocket. "Of course not. It's a bad habit, and I really should give it up. But I'd like to know how you feel about the way things were left with Barbara. I got the impression that the two of you spoke rather often. Did you have any conversation with her that gave you closure? Do you think she knew how you felt?"

She paused and then said, "I honestly don't know. She seemed delighted that we'd reconnected and was interested in the goings on in my life. But then occasionally she would say things that were hurtful and bitter."

"What kind of things?" He touched her leg. "If you don't want to talk about it, don't feel obliged."

She shook her head. "It's okay. It'll probably do me good."

"You said earlier that you don't think she ever forgave you for turning away from her. Does that mean you think she blamed you for what happened between you?"

"Oh, she most definitely did, and even if it was the drugs talking, she let her feelings be known with comments like, 'It's always been about you, hasn't it' and 'you just don't want to bloody well listen— you put yourself ahead of others.'"

"I know that she treasured those phone calls, Hassie. The last time I spoke with her she'd just finished a call with you. Despite her pain, her spirits were high, and she talked about you like you were her daughter."

"Really?"

He nodded. "I didn't have the most graceful of last visits. I was on a short leave and knew from my mum's reports that my aunt didn't have much time left. I made that visit under severe coercion, but I'm glad I did. And indeed, it was the last time I saw her."

"Were you always close?"

He thoughtfully considered just how honest he should be. He finally looked at her and said, "She shamelessly favored me over the others. But I was an adolescent boy when she came back to England, off at boarding school much of the time. So I wasn't in the mood to be mollycoddled and fussed over." Hassie furrowed her brow, and he realized he must sound cold. "Don't get me wrong. She was a wonderful person—if a bit eccentric. What am I saying? She was a *lot* eccentric and seemingly off her rocker on occasion. But she was a very loving and giving companion for my mother, especially considering that the pair of them fell out with their younger brother, Trevor, and haven't spoken to any of his family for years."

"That explains why there's been no other family around."

"And then there's the older brother, Teddy, who has a debilitating disease and lives in a care home in north London. Mind you, he still owns a lovely flat in St. John's Wood. I realize you haven't any idea where that is, but it's a jolly nice part of north London, and the family have allowed me to live there when I'm not gallivanting around the world. His swank Jaguar was left in my safekeeping as well."

Hassie sat quietly while Charles reflected on all that he'd said, fighting the urge for that cigarette.

"So you see, it took me a few years to realize that it was okay that I didn't idolize my aunt in the way she envisioned and that the important thing was how much she really meant to my mother. By that time, I was off at university and my life in the navy."

"It sounds like you may have some regrets."

"Regrets? I don't think so. But if you knew how much I didn't want to be here today—well, let's just say that I'm glad I came. Otherwise, I wouldn't have met you." She smiled, and he casually put his hand atop hers and asked, "When do you leave for New York?"

"Day after tomorrow. Are you trying to get rid of me?"

"On the contrary. Just wanted to offer up my help should you need it."

"Don't you have to get back to your course?"

He nodded. "I considered going back this evening but..." He hesitated, trying to read her mood. "Can I see you again before you leave?"

She nodded and said, "Better make it soon."

"Then pray for a sunny day tomorrow, and we'll go for a walk along the cliffs and have a nice meal. How does that sound?"

She hesitated and then smiled at him. "It sounds great. I haven't had a chance to really see much of this place that Barbara loved so much."

"You're in for a treat, my dear. I happen to be a real expert round these parts."

"Then I look forward to it." She started to stand. "And, Charles? Thanks."

"My pleasure." He stood, then helped her to her feet. "Let's get you back to Beryl. She'll be dying to fatten you up." He pointed and said, "The car's just there."

She hooked her arm through his. "I'd like to walk."

They walked along the path back to Barbara's house. After a brief silence, Hassie said, "I really don't know what I would have done without Beryl these last couple of days. She's told me practically every move to make."

"She's a family treasure." It was slowly sinking in that he would soon own Barbara's house. Perhaps he'd been a little hasty in thinking that he'd never want to spend time there. Perhaps it had been his aunt's way of pointing him toward a potentially happy life with his own family and his own need for Beryl. He covered Hassie's hand with his own and turned left on Northfield Road.

chapter **thirteen**

Charles parked in front of the two-story, red brick house that had originally belonged to his grandparents. As he stood on the pavement before it, he thought the house looked different—smaller and much less impressive. Or maybe he'd never really looked at it. In a sweeping survey of the unpretentious façade, he wondered if the bare shrubs were the same ones that he'd helped his grandmother tend as a boy and whose beds were bursting with daffodils at the first sign of spring. For a moment he was caught in another time—a young, sandy-haired boy with gangly arms and legs that took him a while to grow into and for which his grandfather loved to tease him. The wood trim could use a new coat of paint, and a dozen or so roof tiles needed adjusting. Twiggy, leafless branches hugged the red brick surrounding the windows in need of a gardener's care. The news that his aunt had left the house to him had, at the time, seemed more of a curse than a blessing. But now, as he pictured Hassie on the other side of the door, readying herself for his arrival, a desire for domestic normality set in, and he strangely felt quite the proud homeowner.

He leapt up the front steps, reverently observed the wreath of white flowers hanging on the door and then rang the bell. He expected to be greeted by Beryl, but Hassie opened the door. She wore dark-green, wide-legged trousers and a beige tunic top that looked a size too big for her slight physique. Her hair fell to her shoulders, perfectly framing her face. She appeared shorter than he remembered until he realized that she was standing in her stocking feet.

"Good morning," she said and motioned him in.

"I'm a bit early. Shall I leave and come back?"

"No, it's fine—if you don't mind that I'm not quite ready." She walked ahead of him through the front lounge, past the grand piano and down the narrow hall toward the kitchen. "It looks like that nice day you were hoping for."

They entered the kitchen; it was all familiar—glossy white cabinets, blue and white tiles, a row of flowering potted plants on the sill over the sink and the neatly turned out housekeeper in her crisp housedress and pinafore apron. "Good morning, Beryl."

"Mornin', Charles. I 'ave a fresh pot of Earl Grey. Would you like a cup?"

"That would be just the ticket. It's unseasonably warm today but still a bit nippy when out of direct sunlight." He sat down at the small dining table and was immediately joined by a well-fed black cat. "Well, hello there little puss whose name I don't remember."

"That's Beethoven," Beryl said. "'e's gettin' on a bit, but 'e seems to remember you."

"Ah, yes, Beethoven." He reached down to stroke the cat's head. "And where's your mate—what's his name?"

"You're thinkin' of Figaro. Sadly, 'e died a few years back now. I reckon ole Beethoven'll be right behind him now that Missus C's gone."

"Do you think he really knows that his mistress isn't coming back?"

She nodded. "Cats are clever. And this one slept at the foot of Missus C's bed 'til her last breath."

"Charles, do you still want to take that walk you talked about?" Hassie asked while tying a sash around her waist.

"Very much so. You'll want to wear a couple of layers—a jumper and maybe a jacket. Even on a lovely day like today, the wind by the sea can be rather brutal." She started to speak, but he jumped ahead of her saying, "Oh, and you'll want something for your head—some sort of scarf that will protect you from the bluster."

Beryl set the cup of tea in front of Charles. "'ere ya go. 'ow about a nice 'ot cross bun, fresh from the bakery?"

"That's very tempting, Beryl." He focused on Hassie and said, "If you want to finish getting ready, I'm in good hands here. Take your time."

"I'll be right back." Hassie left the room and then quickly reappeared. "You say I should take a *jumper*?"

Charles smiled. "I think you lot call it a sweater."

"Oh. I didn't bring one."

Beryl spoke up, "Don't worry, Miss 'assie. I'll find something for you. You just finish up." She stared after Hassie with an expression that Charles couldn't quite decipher. He gave it a moment and then asked, "How are you getting on without my aunt?"

"It's 'ard, Charles. Even with all the time I 'ad to prepare. It's 'ard."

"I'm sure it is. You've been a part of this family for a long time, haven't you?"

"Twenty-nine years next month. Blimey. I remember when you was born. And your sister too." She poured the tea through the strainer into another cup and said, "I can't 'ardly remember a time when I didn't come to work in this 'ouse. It's gonna be..." She stopped and busied herself with cleaning the teapot, then wiped her eyes with her apron and said, "If you don't mind, I'll go and get that jumper."

"Go right ahead." She started out of the room. Charles said, "Oh, and Beryl? Check with Hassie about her shoes. Maybe she'll need to borrow a pair of boots as well?" Beryl nodded and then hurried away. It hadn't occurred to Charles that she was a casualty with the loss of his aunt. But then, why should it have? He hadn't lived in the house, nor had he visited more than once a year—twice at the most.

Hassie returned wearing a heavy burgundy cardigan over her blouse and a patterned silk scarf around her neck, having tied her hair back. "How's this?" she asked.

"Perfect," he said. He glanced at her feet. "Will you be all right on the beach in those shoes?"

Hassie nodded. "They're my walking shoes. I don't think a little sand will hurt them."

* * *

As they walked along the village green and on to the high street, Charles said, "So, you arrived on Thursday?"

"Yes. I got the call on Tuesday and was able to sort things out to leave pretty quickly. I was on a plane the next night, which meant I arrived Thursday morning. So, between helping Beryl tend to those stopping by to pay their respects and trying to get a little rest, I've only had glimpses of the sea on the drive to Barbara's house."

They crossed the main highway and walked to the top of the walkway that led down to the rocky seafront. Charles pointed to the buttery-colored building to their right and said, "That's the White Horse, a popular watering hole and seaside inn. Aunt Barbara was known to stop in for a snort or two after a brisk walk along the cliffs."

Hassie stared out into the sea, silently surveying the area before saying, "There must be lots of history here."

Charles pointed to a spot at the base of a stone staircase. "There's a famous photo of Rudyard Kipling sitting right there on the beach with his beloved auntie, Georgiana Burne-Jones." He nodded toward a modern brick and stucco building on their left and continued, "That's Highcliff Court—obviously a new development, which caused quite a stir when it replaced a series of cliff dwelling houses a few years ago. Shall we walk?"

They meandered down to the craggy path below the cliffs. The wind blew briskly from the sea, but the sun momentarily beat down through a gathering of cumulous clouds. "We may have struck lucky with the weather," Charles said, breathing in the brackish air. "It doesn't look like rain at all. Mind you, I probably shouldn't have said that. The skies will open up any minute now."

Hassie giggled. "I'll pretend I didn't hear you." She looked up and said, "It's very peaceful and beautiful and—" A gust of wind caught her by surprise and knocked her unsteadily against Charles, who grabbed hold of her and said, "What's that you were saying?"

They laughed. Charles secured his arm around her shoulder and pointed her in a westerly direction. "Down there's the city of Brighton. It likes to refer to itself as 'London by the sea.' If you look far in the distance, you'll see the hint of a structure way off the shore."

She made a visor with her hand over her eyes and said, "I think I see something."

"It's the famous Palace Pier—a major focal point for the area. But that's for another time."

"Your mother lives in Brighton?"

"Yes. Well, actually she lives on the edge of Brighton where it's contiguous with a town called Hove."

They moved past an elderly gentleman out for a walk with a small black and white dog, who preferred running off into the shallow tide to keeping company with his master. Charles lightly saluted the old guy who, in turn, doffed his cap.

Hassie tied the scarf around her head while saying, "I thought I might get a chance to visit with Gwendolyn—get to know the sister that Barbara was so fond of. But she doesn't seem interested in knowing me at all."

"Never mind about Gwen. She's incredibly difficult at times and can be grossly myopic when it comes to her children. But she is my mother, and despite it all, she means well." He was ready to change the subject with thoughts of the miserable evening he'd had when he got to his mother's house after leaving Hassie the night before. She was determined to punish him for turning up late for the funeral, threatening to boot him out of her brother's London apartment and sell the Jaguar.

They walked in silence for a short distance until half a dozen gulls swooped down from above, apparently diving for something in the sand that they'd spotted all at once. The noise was disruptive and unexpected, and Hassie flinched.

"One gets used to these seaside noises and smells after a while."

"We have all this in New York."

"Of course, Manhattan is an island. How typical of me to assume that the entire area is tall buildings and pavement."

"You have to get away from Manhattan to really experience the beaches—you've probably heard of Staten Island, Coney Island, Long Island? Have you ever been to New York?"

"I have not." The wind picked up again, and Charles tightened his embrace around Hassie's shoulder. "I've yet to sail the waters of the Atlantic between England and the States. I'm sure it'll happen one day." He stopped and pointed directly ahead of them to an endless stretch of ragged coastline and said, "Now you're going to see what I believe makes this part of my homeland very special. See what looks like a range of white mountains?"

She shielded her eyes again and said, "Yes. They're either not very big or they're miles away."

"That's the Seven Sisters. A series of chalk cliffs. You may have heard of the White Cliffs of Dover?"

"Yes, of course."

"Well, these are the white cliffs of East Sussex, and some people think they're more impressive than those in Dover." They continued to walk in the direction of the steep hills. "Don't worry, I'm not suggesting that we walk that far, but if you had more time, I'd be tempted to take you down to the country park. I dare say there's nothing quite like those cliffs in America."

"We do have this rather impressive hole in the ground called the Grand Canyon."

"Yes, but is it made of chalk?" he asked, earnestly.

Hassie laughed. "So the white of those cliffs is really chalk?"

"Indeed. I won't bore you with the geological mumbo-jumbo. And you can imagine how this rough sea weather is having a real go at them."

"You said that Barbara used to take walks along the cliffs. It must have felt very special to her after all those years in dry, flat Texas. Did you ever walk with her?"

He nodded. "Only a couple of times. And sadly, it was after she first learned she was sick, and I suppose I felt guilty for basically ignoring her after I went away to college." Charles took hold of Hassie's hand and said, "I picked up that scarf you're wearing in Hong Kong for her birthday—it's Hermés. Another gesture to deal with my guilt, I imagine."

She carefully fingered the scarf and said, "It's very beautiful."

"I think she would've wanted you to have it."

"Oh, I don't know."

Charles gave it a moment before he asked, "Hassie, what made you get in touch with Barbara again?"

"After I left home and went off on my own little adventure in Las Vegas, it became harder and harder to contact the people I'd turned my back on. Then my life took another drastic change of course, and the estrangement continued until my mother died, and I went back to Texas for her funeral. That's when I learned where Barbara was in England. Eventually, I wrote to her and we worked through an awkward time of getting reacquainted. We agreed that we'd speak regularly after that."

"But she didn't tell you she was sick until when?"

"About three months before she died."

"It's a shame you didn't make it over for a visit."

"I swear, I wanted to but..." She withdrew her hand from his and pulled the cardigan tighter against her neck.

They walked along in silence. Charles gazed at the offing with thoughts of where they would stop. As they were coming on to the village of Telscombe Cliffs, a low-hanging cloud cover rolled in temporarily eclipsing the sun, and the temperature plummeted. He led them in the direction of the path up to the top of the cliff and said, "I think it's time for a drink. You may have noticed that all roads—and paths—lead to a pub."

Hassie laughed. "I've noticed."

They entered the Telscombe Tavern and selected a table by the window. Charles removed his coat and placed it on the back of his chair. "I could murder a pint of lager right now. Can I get you a nice dry sherry?"

She looked a bit horrified at the suggestion and asked, "Could I have a glass of white wine?"

"Of course you can, but I wouldn't recommend it. If you don't fancy sherry, I'd go for gin and tonic or cider."

She sat down. "I've never had cider, but if you recommend it, I'll try it."

While at the bar, he stood amidst the clouds of cigarette smoke and wondered if he'd manage the willpower to keep his Dunhills in his pocket. With drinks in hand, he returned to the table and touched her glass with his. "Cheers." They maintained eye contact while taking the first sip after which Charles asked, "Do you like the cider?"

She nodded. "It's different than I expected, but I like it."

"Good." He set his glass on the table. "Yesterday you said that you used to smoke."

"I started when I went to Vegas where practically everyone smoked as a matter of course."

"And you were singing then?"

She nodded. "It didn't bother my voice—at least, not at first. But eventually it fell on the list of things I needed to give up and then... well, it got complicated."

"You've alluded a couple of times now to your life being complicated. Was Barbara aware of it all?"

She hesitated. "Yeah, mostly. I told her about how I screwed up my career in Vegas, which I'm sure she wasn't surprised to hear. How I left around the time that President Kennedy died, went to Reno with a friend and..."

"It's complicated?"

Hassie turned serious and said, "I barely know you, Charles. I feel like there should be much more conversation between us before the difficult things come tumbling out of the closet."

He placed his hand on top of her left hand, again taking notice that she didn't wear a ring. She was giving him mixed signals—one that said she was comfortable talking to him about personal issues and another that pushed him away. His better judgment warned him to back away, but he focused on her and quietly said, "I don't mean to be forward. I'm just aware that we don't have much time together, and, honestly, I'm desperate to get to know you. As far as I'm concerned, we should throw caution to the wind and say all the things we want to say."

He offered a comforting smile, encouraging her to relax, but she sat meditatively until she said, "You're very kind, but, like I said, I don't know you."

"Then let's get to know each other. From what you've said so far, you're carrying around a bit of a load. I'm a good listener."

She shifted her weight in the chair and then proceeded to tell him the story of when her mother had first taken her to Barbara's *Academies des Arts* for singing and dancing lessons. So talking about Barbara was safe territory—nothing too personal and nothing that would encourage him to ask about all these complications. They shared a few more stories about their youths where his aunt had been involved. He knew that she meant it as homage to Barbara. But the attempt at keeping the conversation light and relatively impersonal came through loud and clear.

When he returned from the bar with a second round of drinks, Charles said, "I've enjoyed hearing about your triumphs and travails where my aunt is concerned. But I'd like to know more about Hassie Calhoun after life in small town Texas."

She frowned a soft, playful frown and then said, "I'm not sure you'd like the Hassie that left Texas."

He raised his glass to her. "In my mind, you are the most perfect woman I've ever met, and right now I'm totally besotted with you. So if you don't want me to fall hopelessly in love with the wrong woman, I suggest you tell me about the *real* you. And I promise I'm not going to run away."

"Maybe that's the beer talking?"

"I hardly think so. It's me, Charles Beauclerke, asking what about your young life is so complicated that you can't talk about it."

She gazed out the window, her arms resting on the table. Eventually, she looked at him, took a shallow breath and said, "I have a six-year-old son. His name is Kenny. His father died before he was born."

Unsure what she expected him to say, Charles leaned back in the chair and gently said, "Well, I don't really consider that to be so complicated. And with you as his mother, I bet he's a charming little boy."

She nodded, and her eyes became glassy. He waited while she regained her composure before he said, "Hassie, Barbara told me about your son and his father during my last visit with her."

"Why would she have done that? It wasn't her place to tell you."

"She'd just come off a phone call with you, and she wanted to talk about it. Remember, she was on a lot of medication. I'm sure she meant no harm."

"Then why didn't you tell me you knew? Was it enjoyable to watch me squirm and worry about how you'd react?"

"Of course not, but you haven't exactly promoted conversation about anything to do with you or your life. I thought that if you wanted me to know about your son, you should tell me yourself."

"And so I did. What else did Barbara tell you that you want me to tell you myself?" She moved her chair back from the table and said, "Excuse me. I need the ladies' room."

She walked off, and Charles felt that he'd been punched in the gut. He'd made a wrong call in thinking that he should give her a chance to tell him what of her past she wanted him to know. On reflection, she seemed to have some sort of issue with most every topic of conversation he raised. He was simply trying to get to know her. Instead, he seemed to be pushing her away.

Hassie returned from the ladies and sat down without looking at him. She swallowed the last of her drink and eventually asked, "Can we start over?"

He sat straight-faced and said, "Miss Calhoun, I know absolutely nothing about you or any children that you may have had or men that you might have been involved with. Would you please tell me how you became such an incredible woman? And whilst doing so, would you please explain to me why you must go back to New York tomorrow? Because, personally, I would like for you to remain in England indefinitely."

She drew her mouth into an I'm-not-going-to-smile expression, and he sat quietly. Yesterday he'd felt that her face vividly conveyed her emotions. Today he couldn't tell if she was miserable or ecstatic. He waited a while longer and then asked, "Are you hungry?"

She nodded. "Do they serve food here?"

"Yes, but I think we can do better than pub grub. I suggest we go into Brighton to the quintessential fish restaurant in the area—one that my mother and Aunt Barbara frequented."

"I love doing things that Barbara enjoyed. It makes me feel as if I didn't totally miss out on her life here. How far is it to Brighton?"

"I'll ask the barman to call us a taxi, and we'll be there in fifteen, twenty minutes tops." He stood up and removed his coat from the back of the chair. She remained seated, watching him with the first real smile he'd seen since they'd sat down. He put on the coat as he said, "That's a jolly nice smile. What are you thinking?"

She tilted her head slightly to the right and asked, "Have you always been called Charles?"

"As opposed to…?"

"Charles is such a formal name. I mean, most men I've ever known named Charles had some kind of nickname—like Charlie or Chuck."

"Well, Chuck is bone fide American and Charlie is for little boys." He fidgeted with the collar on his coat and asked, "Why do you ask?"

"I've gotten to know you a little bit today, and I don't think the formality of Charles fits you. Are you sure you've never had a nickname?"

He walked around and pulled out her chair as he said, "Chaz."

She stood up, slipping on Barbara's cardigan. "Chaz?"

He nodded.

"I once knew a wonderful bass player named Chaz."

"It's a nickname that was bestowed on me at Dartmouth. I've never encouraged it, but if it makes you happy, you can call me Chaz."

"Chaz. That's better, don'tcha think?" She smiled, took his arm and said, "And it makes me happy."

"Good. Now let's go have a nice meal."

chapter fourteen

Charles finished his wine while Hassie took her last bite of fish. "How was the Dover sole?" he asked.

"Delicious. And I really enjoyed the oysters, considering I didn't think I'd like them." She sipped her wine and then took a long, scoping look around the room. "I just love this, Chaz."

"What? The food, the restaurant? My company?"

"All of the above. The place is just so…"

"*Quaint?*" He smiled and realized that she had relaxed.

"Traditional, charming… yes, quaint is the word. I'll remember to describe it that way when I get back to New York."

He waited while she folded the linen napkin and tucked it next to her plate before he said, "We made it through the entire meal without my mentioning this, but are you still determined to get on that airplane tomorrow?"

"I have to, Chaz. This is the first time Kenny and I have ever been apart—except for the odd sleepover at a friend's. He was so nervous when I left, not really knowing where I was going and flying over an ocean to get here."

"You've spoken with him since you've been here?"

"Of course. But he's a little young to understand how long four days is. And I do have other responsibilities besides my son."

He'd noticed that she never talked about any men in her life other than her son's father who had mysteriously died. He didn't believe that a woman like her would have escaped other relationships in the years since the man's death. But, as she'd repeatedly reminded him, he didn't know her well enough to pry into such personal concerns. It was moments like this that he cursed his *proper* English middle class upbringing.

The waiter came by with the dessert trolley. Charles looked at Hassie and said, "I think you should try the trifle or the treacle tart."

Hassie slowly shook her head like she was seriously considering the options and then said, "Nothing for me. I've already eaten twice as much as I usually do."

Charles asked the waiter for the bill and then leaned forward. "You realize that you simply can not leave tomorrow. I don't know how you're going to handle it, but I'm sorry. I can't let you go."

She relaxed in the chair and gave him a slow, cheeky smile. "With all due respect, I don't think there's anything you can do to stop me."

"Oh, I do love a good challenge, and I'm a very poor loser. I suggest that you give in now and agree to come back to London with me for a few days. You've never been there, and you're this close. You could go sightseeing and shopping while I'm busy during the day. I'd show you a hell of a good time in the evenings. It would be silly to waste the opportunity. What's another week away from home?"

"First it was a few days, and now it's a week? You're very good at this game."

"Seriously, Hassie. I have this terrible feeling that I'm never going to see you again, and I can't let that happen. If you want me to beg, I will."

She stared at her hands propped nervously on the table and then asked, "Could I have another glass of wine?"

"I'll get another bottle if you'll agree to stay."

She did that *almost frown* thing he'd seen a few times now and then finally said, "When I get back to Barbara's, I'll make a phone call."

"That's what I want to hear."

She raised her right index finger. "Don't get too excited just yet."

He sat back in his chair. "I'm sure there's wine at Barbara's. I'll take you back and leave you to sort things out."

When they stepped onto the pavement in front of the restaurant, Charles said, "We're standing at the entrance to what's known as 'The Lanes'—a famous part of Brighton. If you like, we can take a stroll through."

"That sounds nice, but I think I should get back and make that call. It's a good time to catch my friend who's looking after Kenny."

* * *

The threadbare panels of fabric covering the guest room window struggled to block out the dim morning light. Charles had no idea if it was six or ten o'clock. But as he lay propped on an elbow beside Hassie, watching her sleep while the rain tapped against the windows, it mattered not that beyond those faded curtains was an inclement, gray day. The scar above her left eyebrow drew him close, and as he touched it ever so gently, she stirred like she was caught in an early morning dream—her nose twitched, and she turned to rest her face against him. He carefully laid his arm across her, as if doing so anchored her to the bed. Feeling her breath on his chest, he thought about those few hours earlier when after she'd made the call to New York they'd had a couple of brandies, which led to a rambunctious conversation about why she should go to London with him, which led to more brandy, which led to a flirtatious romp across the sofa where she protested that his kisses were annoying, until he took the snifter from her, lifted her off the sofa and carried her to this bed, where she abandoned the protest and relaxed with him, and he lost himself in her and in them, and he would never be convinced that this irreversible space of time was just about sex.

Though tentative and a little shy at first, she'd eventually let herself go and in one forceful, determined move pinned him against the mattress, straddling his hips. She had the appearance of a light-boned woman with no discernible weight, but her body on top of his had been slightly heavy, and it felt good. In fact, it had never felt so right to be dominated by a woman. As he remembered the sweetness that infused their lovemaking, he pulled her closer to his body until she squirmed, releasing a low sensuous moan, pressing her cheek into his chest.

He hesitated in the moment before whispering, "Am I really waking up with you in my dead aunt's house?"

"I thought it was your house now," she said sleepily. He pushed her against the mattress, kissing her with an intensity that sunk deep into his core. He moved his hand to her breasts and carefully ran his fingers across her left nipple, slowly moving his hand down her torso toward her belly, his slightly calloused fingers gently touching velvet that was her skin. She tensed as his fingers traced the marks and imperfections—the evidence that she had given birth. He rested his hand on her abdomen and watched her—her eyes moist and slightly red—kissed her gently and said, "I want to meet your son."

"Well, wow." She pulled away, wriggling out of his arms and perched against the pillows.

He waited a moment and then asked, "Are you sorry I stayed the night? Was it too much, too soon?"

She smiled. "It's true what they say about British men."

"What's that?"

"Always the polite, proper gentleman."

"I wouldn't say *always*. Only when it's deserved." He kissed her breast. "You deserve it."

She took a slow, deep breath, noisily exhaling as she said, "I'll say it again. You barely know me. Yesterday and last night were wonderful, and I thank you for the beautiful walk and the amazing dinner—"

"And the better than average sex?"

She stifled a smile as she nodded. "And the better than average sex. But—"

He touched his finger to her lips and said, "No 'buts' today, please. Let's agree that we've had a very special time together in Sussex and move on to London."

Hassie laughed. "Did you not hear anything I said last night?"

"I heard a bit of rubbish about having to get back to New York, for which I still haven't heard a valid explanation."

She pulled the sheet up over her breasts, released an exasperated sigh and said, "I made the call as I said I would. But I also made a promise to my son. I said I'd be home tonight, and he expects to see me when he wakes up tomorrow morning."

"Do you think he's able to understand that you're ruining another person's life by cutting short an opportunity to spend more time with said person? Could I have a word with him please?"

She touched his face. "You'd actually figure out very quickly that you are no match for my adorable six-year-old. He'd put you in your place and then pull rank on you in a second."

"But I'm a lieutenant in the Royal Navy."

"And he is my son."

Charles sat up and scratched his head. "And what did his minder say about you extending your stay?"

"I have a feeling he's just bribed the sitter to be on call day and night, so it's not a real bother to him. It's Kenny that I'm concerned about."

"So the minder's a *he*?"

"Yes. I think I already mentioned that."

"No, you said that a *friend* was looking after your son."

"Am I not allowed to have male friends?"

Charles smiled, guardedly, and then said, "I'm going to go work out how to make coffee. Join me when you're ready, and let's have one last chat about today's plans. If I can't convince you to stay, I can take you to the airport."

"What about Beryl? Won't she be coming in soon?"

"It's Sunday. She's up north with her sister." He slipped on his trousers and grabbed his shirt, buttoning it while mouthing a kiss at her and then left her sitting cross-legged on the bed.

As he rummaged through the cupboards in the kitchen for the coffee-making device that he'd once seen, he felt he *had* lost rank to Hassie's son, and he selfishly debated whether it was endearing or annoying. Kenny was obviously the most important thing in her life, and putting him first was understandable. But then Kenny is the kid, and in Charles's estimation, Hassie, the mother, could just tell the kid that her plans had changed. He found a jar of Nescafe and filled the kettle with water as Hassie walked into the room. "Did you ever see Beryl make coffee?" he asked.

"No. She made pots of tea."

She'd pulled her hair back from her face and had put his gray woolly jumper on such that it fit her like an oversized dress. She reminded him of his sister as a girl, home from school, still a little sleepy but relaxed to be in familiar surroundings. He turned on the kettle.

Hassie sat at the table and asked, "Who's Gordon Bennett?"

Charles smiled, appreciating how adorable she was, trying to fit into this foreign world. "Where'd you hear that?"

"Beryl's said it a few times—under her breath or to the cat. One day she shouted it at the radio. I assume it's someone she's not very fond of."

"He was a real person, a long time ago—a 'kiss and tell' journalist that liked to shock his readers. Now, saying his name is a declaration of exasperation but really, for people like Beryl, I think it's a polite way to curse. She does have some funny old ways, our Beryl."

"I think she's entitled to a few eccentricities."

He walked over and held her face in his hands. "And I think you're entitled to stay with me in London." He kissed her gently on the lips. "Evidently, I need to spend more time with you in order for you to fall in love with me."

She pursed her lips like she was trying not to smile and then relaxed and said, "If I stay a few more days, what do I tell my son?"

"Tell him you've been invited to Buckingham Palace for tea with the queen—tell him anything. What does he know about London?"

"He knows about big, red double-decker buses. They were apparently mentioned at school, and he told me all about them like they were in the same class as flying saucers."

"Well, there you have it. You'll take him a model. There are dozens of options available to tourists. So that's settled then? You'll stay?"

She exhaled with resignation. "I'll need to call the airline and see what I can do with my ticket. It might not be changeable now."

"If it's not, I'll buy you a new one." He held both of her hands and said, "In fact, I'll buy a return ticket so you have to come back." The kettle whistled, and he ignored it while he breathed in her presence, mission accomplished.

* * *

Charles set Hassie's suitcase on the front porch as the rain continued. He went back in to close up the house. Hassie entered the lounge wearing a white, long-sleeved shirt tucked into black trousers, the Hermés scarf tied loosely around her neck. She'd brushed her hair down around her face, which looked either tired or worried. He walked over, put an arm around her and said, "Got everything?"

She nodded. "I packed in such a hurry, I didn't think about bringing a coat."

"Take Barbara's cardigan, and we may need to buy something waterproof in London. It looks like today's going to be one of those dreary ones for which this country's known."

"Are you sure it's okay for me to take the sweater?"

"Of course it is. I hardly think there's any use for it here now."

She looked around the room, pausing as she gazed at the piano before saying, "It's sad to leave this house. I wish more than ever I'd spent time here with Barbara over the years."

"I enjoyed hearing you play last night."

"I'm not very good at much other than my own compositions."

"I imagine you have one of these in New York?"

"I don't have room for anything like this where I live." She walked around to face the keyboard and closed the lid.

Charles said, "Well, if you ever decide you have room for this one, just say the word, and I'll have it sent over to you."

"Really, Chaz? Don't you think someone else in the family might like to have it?"

He shrugged. "Doesn't matter if they do. I think my aunt would've wanted you to have it." He reached out to her. "And I'd like you to have it. Shall we go?"

As they drove away from the house, Charles said, "We have a couple of options now. I need to stop by my mother's house to collect some things. You're more than welcome to come in with me. If she's speaking to me, she'll probably insist on my sitting down with her for a cup of tea whilst she tells me off once and for all. You could remain in the front lounge away from the line of fire. Alternatively—and this is my recommendation—there's a lovely tearoom at the bottom of her road. You can wait there—have a cup of tea and a bun, and I'll come for you when I'm done with Gwen, which I don't expect will take long at all. There's no doubt you would be more comfortable at the tearoom, but it's up to you."

"I feel guilty about keeping you from your mother so soon after Barbara's funeral. Maybe she should have you all to herself."

* * *

Charles parked halfway between the tearoom and his mother's house off Norfolk Square. As he walked in the front door, he heard her call out, "Nigella, is that you?"

"No, Mum, it's Charles. I'm heading back to London and came to say goodbye."

He stood at the kitchen entry while she carried on arranging an assortment of flowers in a vase and said, "Goodbye, then. I hope you enjoyed spending the day after your mother's sister's funeral with someone other than your mother. You've been about as useful as a window box on a submarine."

Charles stood with his hands in his pockets and said nothing. He could take the bait and defend his choice to spend the day with Hassie or he could simply agree with her, plead *mea culpa* and let her get it all out of her system. He took a couple of steps closer and said, "I'm sorry you feel that I deserted you. That was never my intention, and I'm sure you know that."

"I'm just very disappointed in your lack of judgment, Charles."

"Again, I'm sorry you feel that way."

"I don't think it showed much strength of character for you to take up with that woman who you just met and then display such poor judgment by staying the night with her in your auntie's own house— barely twenty-four hours after she's in the ground."

"All right, Mum. I'm not going to have this conversation with you, and I would prefer it if we could have a civil moment between us before I leave. I'm going upstairs to change jackets and get my things. If you'd like me to join you for a cup of tea, I'll be down in about ten minutes." He turned and walked away.

As he exchanged the Barbour wax coat for the tweed jacket he'd worn from London, he thought about his mother's comment concerning his staying the night in his aunt's house. Had she forgotten that the house now belonged to him? But the bigger issue was that for a reason that wasn't immediately obvious, his mother was downright dead set against anything to do with Hassie Calhoun. He went back downstairs, set his bag by the door and then entered the kitchen. His mother poured the boiling water into a teapot and ignored him.

"What can I do to help?" Charles asked.

She didn't answer but placed the teapot on the table and sat down. Neither spoke while Charles poured a dollop of milk into each cup. While waiting for the tea to steep, he laced his fingers and asked, "Why do you dislike Hassie?"

"I never said I don't like her."

"You may not have said the words, but you refer to her as *that woman* and don't even attempt to hide the disdain in your voice. Did Aunt Barbara tell you something about Hassie that's turned you against her?"

Gwen studied him for a moment and then quietly said, "I can see that you're very taken with her, and there's probably little I can say that will dissuade you from trotting along after her."

"Mother, I hardly *trot* after her. I simply enjoy being with her. Besides being very attractive, she's clever and charming, and we have loads of similar interests. You don't know her at all."

"I know what my sister told me about her, and I don't think she's the right kind of woman for you."

"What's that then? You really must clue me in here because, personally, except for the fact that she lives on another continent, I think she's perfect for me."

He poured the tea through the strainer into each cup and then sat while she slowly stirred sugar into hers before she said, "My darling son, women like Hassie are trouble. They use their looks and charm to get what they want regardless of whom they hurt or leave in their wake. Hassie has a checkered past, and despite all efforts to smooth over some dreadful mistakes, Barbara believed that she never learnt a lesson and is still the selfish, self-absorbed girl that Barbara thought she'd left behind. She was very hurt that Hassie never visited her before she… well, died—despite all her promises and so-called good intentions. She said it was 'typical Hassie Calhoun behavior' and then pretended that it ultimately didn't matter."

"That's only one side of the story, Mum. I've never known you to judge someone that you barely know so harshly."

He waited while his mother sipped her tea and then looked at him and asked, "And what about Margaret?"

"What about her?"

"Have you forgotten about your commitment to her?"

Charles looked away.

"Well, have you?"

"We've had this conversation many times. I'm very fond of Peggy, and we have a good time together. But I'm not looking to settle down anytime soon. I'm away from home far more than I'm here and will be for the foreseeable future."

His mother pursed her lips like she was stifling another comment, which Charles took advantage of by saying, "I think you should know that Hassie has decided to remain in Britain for another week, and she's coming with me to London."

Gwen looked like she'd sucked a lemon. She remained quiet for a moment, then stood up and left the room. Charles sat at the table until he heard a door firmly shut in the back of the house. He walked out and down the road to the tearoom. When he reached the small establishment, he stood outside the window and spotted Hassie sitting at a table in the far corner. She looked deep in thought—probably pondering what she would say to her son when she spoke with him later that day. His mother's words *checkered past* came to mind, and he quickly reviewed the bit of conversation he'd had with Hassie about her life. Either she'd opted not to tell him everything that his aunt had known—and, unfortunately, shared with his mother—or his mother was overreacting in an effort to put him off her. It was obvious that Hassie's son was the center of her world and that leaving him in New York had been torturous. But, on reflection, it hadn't been that difficult to convince her to stay with him in London. So this male *minder* that she'd entrusted to look after her son was undoubtedly more than just any old friend.

chapter fifteen

Perhaps it was the disorientation from sitting on the wrong side of the car or riding on the wrong side of the road. Either way, Hassie said very little through much of their journey, and as they approached Prince Albert Road in north London, Charles worried that he had pushed her too hard to stay with him. He'd kept the conversation light, sharing stories and anecdotes as they traveled through the outlying boroughs of the city. Although she smiled at his attempts to charm her, and occasionally seemed a little awed by something he said, there was pointed silence between them, and this puzzled him. When the view of the Thames Embankment as they crossed over Westminster Bridge, past Big Ben and the Houses of Parliament failed to evoke much comment, Charles concluded that she was simply tired.

He parked the car in a resident's bay on the street in front of the mansion block in St John's Wood. Hassie peered out the car window and asked, "Is this where you live?"

"This is it."

"It's very impressive."

"It's actually quite old and lack's a number of modern conveniences, but then that's part of London's charm. And, occasionally, it's home."

He helped her out of the car and took the bags from the boot. Walking up the pavement to the entrance she stopped and said, "This is an apartment building?"

"Yes, it's just that we usually call apartments *flats*, and now you're going to see one."

They took the lift to the second floor, and he fumbled to open both locks before they landed inside the dark room; he switched on the ceiling light. With Hassie by his side, it struck him that the décor was old fashioned and stuffy. For the most part, it was the way Uncle Teddy had left it. He opened a window while Hassie surveyed the rooms that could be seen from the lounge. She then looked at him and said, "Well, if this is an indication of the difference between an apartment and a flat..." She gestured broadly with both arms while saying, "It's huge."

He spotted an empty wine bottle on a side table as he said, "Thanks to Uncle Teddy. Most of my friends live in flats so small there's no room to swing a cat." She smiled, and he clasped his hands together. "I'm parched after that drive. Let's have a drink." He took the empty wine bottle into the kitchen.

Hassie walked toward the open window. "The evening air's nice. You're lucky you can open the windows without so much street noise. New York is impossible."

"It's Sunday, so it's fairly quiet," he called from the kitchen. "Lord's Cricket Ground's just around the corner. Come 'round on any given day when there's a match on, and you'll get plenty of noise."

"You'll have to tell me about this cricket game some time."

Blimey, was the near-empty fridge the epitome of a bachelor's existence. He spotted a bottle of the *vin de table* that Peggy referred to as "cheap and cheerful." With that reminder, he located the bottle of champagne that had been stowed on the bottom shelf for ages, waiting for that special occasion, which, sadly, hadn't happened until now. He peered out into the lounge, observing Hassie as she silently took note of the décor. She fingered the fringe on one of the lampshades and studied a large painting of a ship struggling through a dark, stormy sea. Her facial features seemed to have relaxed. Charles took that as a good sign. He joined her with the open bottle and glasses and set them on the coffee table. While Hassie studied a couple of framed photos, he spotted two dirty wine glasses from his last evening with Peggy on the mantel.

"Is this your Uncle Teddy in this photo of Barbara and Gwendolyn?" she asked.

"Yes, it is. Quite an old photo."

"Hmmm… I wondered. Barbara looks younger than I remember her in Texas. There's a striking family resemblance between her and Teddy."

Charles picked up the dirty glasses, thinking of his mother's reminder about his so-called commitment to Peggy. He'd considered telling Hassie about her on their drive back, but her subdued mood had put him off mentioning anything that might make her wish she'd gone back to New York with no intention of seeing him again. He couldn't help wondering if she felt as awkward in that moment as he did. "The cleaner hasn't been in for a while," he said. "Sorry. I hope this doesn't make you uncomfortable."

"What? To learn that a bachelor living on his own doesn't keep a perfectly neat apartment?"

He was relieved to hear lightness in her tone. She'd seemed so serious in the car, and considering how little time they'd actually spent together, he didn't yet know how to read her. He set the dirty glasses on the mantel and opened the champagne.

She took the freshly poured glass from him and said, "You're spoiling me with all this champagne."

He held his glass out to her. "This is going to be a week to remember—champagne, caviar, chocolates… whatever your heart desires. Cheers."

"Cheers." She swallowed the first sip and then asked, "Now, which room is mine?"

He hesitated in mid-sip. "Whichever one you like, really. I'll give you a tour in a few minutes, and you can pick for yourself. I want you to be comfortable."

She smiled, walked over and kissed him. "Relax. I'm teasing you. I'm feeling a little tired. Maybe the jet lag is catching up with me."

"Maybe you're a bit anxious about speaking with your son?"

She gently nodded. "That's very perceptive of you."

He kissed her and said, "I'm simply interested in everything to do with you. The sooner you realize and accept that, the nicer all of this will be." He swallowed a gulp of champagne. "When do you want to call him? I'm not trying to rush you. I just thought you might like to, well, get that conversation over with."

She checked her watch and said, "Kenny tends to go off with friends on Sunday. I guess I should try to reach him before he gets busy."

Charles pointed to a table in the opposite corner and said, "The phone's over there."

"Are you sure you don't mind if I make a long distance call on your phone. I'll be happy to pay you for it."

"Don't be silly, and take all the time you need. I'm going to do some tidying up."

He took the dirty wine glasses into the kitchen and set them next to the sink, which made him think of the last conversation he'd had with Peggy when she'd queried him about his intentions for their future. She'd be very hurt to know that he'd brought another woman home for an evening, never mind an entire week. But then they weren't that serious as far as he was concerned. He started back to the bedroom, picking up Hassie's firm, no-nonsense tone—"Yes, Zach. You heard me correctly, and the decision's been made. Now, please put Kenny on the phone."

She looked back at Charles. He smiled and then carried on toward the bedroom. "Hi, sweetie," she said, cheerily. "What've you been doing?... That sounds like fun... So you saw the Statue of Liberty?" She laughed. "I know... it's huge."

Charles stood inside his bedroom and focused on the state of it. The bed was a tussled mess, and one of his shirts lay puddled on the floor. He imagined the lingering scent of Peggy's perfume but couldn't immediately recall her having left any of her belongings in the flat. He hung the shirt in the wardrobe and neatened the duvet across the bed, noting that the sheets should be changed. Hassie raised her voice again, and he heard her say, "I'll call again tomorrow. Try not to make such a scene."

She said something else that he couldn't make out and then noisily put the phone down. He stood staring at the bed until Hassie came in behind him and said, "It's all okay."

"See. I told you he'd understand. Did you bribe him with the double-decker bus?"

"He's been invited to go to a friend's birthday slumber party. I think he was expecting that I wouldn't want him to go since I've been away. He's very excited, so my return can wait, and the bus will be a little surprise for him."

"I couldn't help overhearing a bit of tension in part of your conversation. Is everything all right?"

"Oh, it's just my—Zach being difficult. It seems he's more bothered by my extending the trip than my son."

"And Zach is your—friend?"

She looked at him and dryly said, "Yes, Chaz. I told you. He's a good friend—someone I've known since I moved to New York, and if he hadn't been able to look after Kenny, I wouldn't have been able to make this trip." She looked around the room and then said, "Is this your bedroom?"

He nodded. "Yes, it is. But we may be sleeping in a guest room tonight."

Her lips and brow tensed before she turned and walked back to the lounge.

He followed her, stopping to close the window and then topped up their glasses. He lifted her chin as he asked, "What's on your mind?"

"Not that it's really my business, but are you seriously involved with someone?"

"Why do you ask?"

"It's the only reason I can think that you wouldn't want me to sleep in your bed. It's her bed, too, and she's recently been here—the wine glasses..."

He pointed her to the sofa, sat down beside her and said, "Yes, and no. Yes, she's been here recently but no, we're not seriously involved.

We've known each other for a long time, and we see each other from time to time when I'm in town." He hesitated, deciding what to tell her and then said, "It was my birthday last week. We had a drink to celebrate."

"Ah, hah. An October boy. What day?"

"The tenth."

"That makes you a Libra. I suppose you could balance relationships with two women if you chose to."

Charles laughed and held her hand. "Hassie, my relationship with Peggy is not a problem for me and you. It's obviously not *that* important if I brought you to my flat, having made you my priority."

She stood and walked over to the telephone table, picked up a necklace with a small gold locket on it, held it up to him with a cheeky smile and asked, "Is this hers or yours?"

He walked up and took it from her. "Sorry."

"Chaz, it's your apartment and your life. I just don't want to spend this time with you this week and have you tell me that you're actually engaged to someone."

"I can assure you that I'm not engaged. I'll explain in more detail later, I promise." He put the necklace in his pocket. "And in the meantime, you have my permission to get rid of anything that makes you uncomfortable in any way you like."

"So you just had a birthday?"

He nodded, pulling her into his arms and kissing her neck. She pushed back from him and said, "Let me guess. You're… thirty."

He looked askance. "Do I really look that old?"

"*That* old," she said, slightly annoyed. "I'll be twenty-nine in a few weeks."

He dropped his hands to his side. "Good Lord. You're old enough to be my mother."

She giggled. "Well, not quite. So how old are you?"

He crinkled his nose as he said, "Twenty-seven."

"Really?"

"Really." He crossed his arms over his chest, saying, "I've never been with an—older woman."

"Hmmm… I find that hard to believe."

"What about you?"

"No, I've never been with an older woman either."

He laughed, grabbed hold of her again and pulled her close. "What about this Zach guy? Are you sure he's just a friend… you're not involved with him?"

She put her arms around his neck, kissed his chin and said, "Zach and I have a very unique relationship. But I promise you, we're not lovers."

He smiled, reluctantly. "So you have no one special bloke back in New York?"

She pulled back from him and said, "I can honestly say that there's only one special *bloke* in my life, and he's six years old."

"Okay. Now that's out of the way, we need to put some thought into this week's planning. Unfortunately, I must get out of here tomorrow morning well before you're going to want to know. In fact, you should probably have a good lie-in tomorrow—catch up on the sleep you've lost over the last few days."

"That sounds great. If I really want to enjoy London—and you," she said, kissing him, "I'll need some rest."

"Then that settles it. We'll save the rest of the champagne for later, and I'll take you to a local spot for a quiet dinner where we can chat about your visit. We'll come back—you can unpack, we won't have a late night, and you'll fall asleep in my arms. How does that sound?"

She kissed him again and then said, "Or we could make love now, and I don't care which bedroom or bed we do it in."

"For someone tired and jet-lagged, you're awfully randy."

She laughed, unbuckling his belt, and said, "If you mean horny, you actually have no idea."

"Well, darling, it looks like I'm about to find out."

"I love the way you say dah-ling."

chapter sixteen

The lectures on all things *naval* were more tedious than usual this week, Chaz's attention span that of a gnat. Hassie would be leaving in a couple of days, and he couldn't stand the thought of losing her. He cringed at the idea of public transport, splurged and took a cab to Piccadilly. The cab stopped at the top of Lower Regent Street, and he saw her standing beside the statue of Eros wearing the trench coat he'd bought her and Barbara's scarf. He paid the driver and hopped out, waving to her as he crossed over the road. Her dark hair blew in the breeze as she met him; her smile nearly broke his heart.

He grabbed her shoulders and kissed her.

"Fancy meeting you here," she said and giggled. "I've always wanted to say that."

He put his arm around her shoulder. "Are you warm enough? From a distance, you look cold."

"I'm better now," she said and kissed him.

As they walked, Hassie slipped her arm under his jacket and around his waist, hooking her finger through a belt loop. He asked, "Did you make it over to Harrod's?"

"I did. What an amazing place. I had lunch in the restaurant on the top floor and then took a taxi over to Madame Tussauds."

"That creepy, old wax museum?"

"Have you been there?"

"When I was a kid. You made for quite the splendid tourist today, didn't you? I'd hoped you'd get over to the National Portrait Gallery at some point. It's a favorite of mine and a place that should have been first on your list."

"I enjoyed everything I saw, Chaz. Maybe you should have mentioned that gallery sooner than my next to the last day here."

"I'm sure I mentioned it on that first night. Never mind, darling. I have a special evening planned and ready or not, you're going to meet a few of my mates."

"Really? So where are we going now?"

"Straight ahead is a good old London pub. I thought we could have a couple of drinks—we might see a few people I know—and then we'll make our way into Soho where we're having dinner and a surprise."

They crossed the road toward the pub in Glasshouse Street where Charles drank two pints of lager while Hassie nursed a gin and tonic. The smoky, airless room was noisy with laughter and chatter, but she seemed not to notice, appearing distracted, gazing pensively around the room, forcing a smile when their eyes met. Anyone walking past would think that she'd just lost her best friend—not that she was out in London with her new lover. He swallowed the last of the lager and stood, reaching for her to join him.

Outside the pub, she took his arm and asked, "Where to now?"

"We've a short walk to the restaurant and plenty of time to get there, so relax and enjoy the stroll."

She remained pensive and quiet. When he couldn't stand it any longer, he asked, "Are you fed up with London now?"

She hugged his arm and said, "How could you suggest such a thing? I'm madly in love with this city." She stopped, appearing a bit emotional before she said, "I know I've barely scratched the surface, but the history and the culture and the... well, just about everything is much more than I could ever have imagined. Shows me how little I really know about the world."

He put his arm around her shoulder and said, "England has been here for a long time... going nowhere anytime soon. There's much more to see and learn. And there's Paris and Rome and Amsterdam and Cairo and—"

"Okay, okay. I get the message."

He stopped and pointed down to a small black sign with red and green neon light and said, "Meanwhile, there's Ronnie Scott's. Reputed to be the best jazz club in London."

"Is that the surprise? I love jazz."

"I know you do." They turned in the opposite direction. He motioned toward the end of the block to their left and said, "And there's the restaurant."

They pushed through the entrance to Kettner's. The maitre d' looked up from a large journal, removed his glasses and said, "Ah, good evening, Messier Beauclerke."

"*Bon soir, Henri. C'est une belle Americaine de diner avec vous ce soir*," he said, in his best schoolboy French.

The well-turned-out gentleman, whose dramatic comb-over made him look like a buffoonish cartoon character, raised his eyebrows at Charles and said, "*Trés bon.*" He then took Hassie's hand and lightly kissed it before saying, "*Enchanté, Mademoiselle.*" He made a sweeping motion with his right arm, smirking at Charles as he said, "*On y va!* I'll show you to your table." They were seated in the front room and served champagne cocktails, compliments of Henri.

Charles raised his glass and said, "To you, my love."

She touched her glass to his. "Cheers." She took a sip and then said, "This was nice of Henri. Do you get this kind of attention in all restaurants in London?"

"Hardly. And don't let that phony French accent fool you. I'd bet a crumpet to a beignet his real name is Henry Smith, and he comes from Essex."

"Was his French as good as yours?" she asked.

He ignored her and said, "I can't abide his sort of pretentiousness, but it bodes well in a place like this. It's a Soho institution, and the food is worth it."

Hassie smiled, and for a brief moment he felt that she studied him adoringly.

He reached over to touch her arm. "I imagine I'll go through some sort of withdrawal after you've gone."

She smiled. "Your life will just go back to normal."

"My course instructor will be glad for it. I've been bloody useless this week—between the late nights and the fact that I can't get you out of my brain for a single second."

She put her hand on top of his. They sat with no need for words until Charles leaned back in his chair and said, "You must be thrilled to be going home to your son."

She nodded. "He'll be full of himself and will have eaten everything imaginable. It'll take a week to bring him down to earth and the rules of our house."

When she talked about Kenny she seemed to switch into another gear—a brighter, happier tone.

"You're a wonderful mother," he said.

"I'm not sure Kenny would agree. But he's my whole world, and I wish I could stop him growing up."

"I'd like to meet him." When she didn't respond and began to fidget with the cutlery, Charles focused on the menu with the odd furtive glance in her direction.

When they'd finished the meal and a bottle of wine, Charles observed that Hassie seemed more relaxed and so elegantly feminine. He waited a moment and then asked, "Do you think you'll miss me?"

She pondered the question, a faint smile on her face. "Yes, I think I will miss you a lot."

"Good. I'd hate to think that I'll be going through this withdrawal on my own."

"How long will you be in London, and where will you go next?"

"We're not yet halfway through the course, and rumor has it that we'll be back in the Far East for the rest of the year."

"Hmmm… that's a long way away from London."

"And New York." She moved uncomfortably, and he motioned for the bill. "You'll probably want the ladies here before we leave. I don't recommend spending much time in the loos at Ronnie Scott's."

"The jazz club."

He nodded. "The club itself is rather unimpressive and depending on the crowd can get a bit rough around the edges. But I think you'll enjoy the music—though I have no idea who's playing tonight."

The waiter brought the bill, and Hassie took Charles's advice and excused herself. It seemed odd to him that she never wanted to talk about anything to do with her life in New York outside of Kenny. She'd yet to admit whether or not she even had a job. He'd tried asking specific questions. But, despite her pointed attempts to deflect from her *real* life in New York, Hassie Calhoun was a mature, beautiful woman with a past—and a present—that much more closely defined who she really was than their intense yet short-lived week together. Should he just accept that they'd had one of those rare, intoxicating affairs that comes along when you least expect it and that it was unrealistic to think that he'd ever see her again? Or should he do everything in his power to ensure that she would leave knowing how and when they'd see each other again? Hell, he was falling for her, and he seemed to have lost a foothold on his emotions. But as he watched her walk toward the table, he somehow knew that she hadn't been completely honest with him. There was still the issue of this man in New York who looked after her son. He caught her eye, and she smiled. How could he finesse the truth from her without pushing her away?

* * *

It was not quite nine-thirty when they arrived at Ronnie Scott's. The hostess greeted Charles and then showed them to the table he'd reserved in the corner closest to the stage, which was probably meant for six people but had eight chairs crowded around it. He selected the two with the best view of the stage and pulled out a chair for Hassie. He watched as she took in the room while their eyes adjusted to the low light and then asked, "So, what do you think?"

"It's a typical jazz club, isn't it?"

"Like the ones you're used to in New York?"

"Pretty much." She gazed at the stage.

He put his arm around the back of her chair and said, "You once mentioned Greenwich Village. Did you ever sing in those clubs?"

161

"Not exactly. My jazz scene was when I lived in Reno—off and on for a few years."

"One of these days, you're going to have to tell me more about this glamorous life you've led."

She laughed. "It's a lot less glamorous than it sounds."

A muddle of familiar voices drew Charles's attention as a group of four guys and two women approached the table. As one of the men called out to him, he leaned into Hassie, kissed her cheek and said, "The troops have arrived, and they look rather merry." He stood up, his hand on her shoulder, and waited while the men fussed over where the two women would sit. The spectacle was highly amusing. Charles eventually said, "Gentlemen, there are too few lovely roses amongst you ghastly thorns."

Realizing that the men were taking no bloody notice of him, Charles observed that they had focused on Hassie. One of them said, "So, Chazzo, this is the beautiful American that has you walking into walls?"

The men laughed, and Hassie smiled. Charles sat down and said, "Gentlemen—and ladies—this is Hassie Calhoun. This is her first visit to England, so please don't embarrass the nation by being your usual selves."

The man sitting next to Hassie shook her hand and said, "I'm Gareth Mansfield, and that handsome guy over there is my twin brother, Geoffrey." He waved from across the table, and Hassie waved back, saying, "I believe the two of you just had a birthday?"

Charles said, "And apparently they're still celebrating." He pointed to the guy next to Gareth and continued, "That's Hamish MacWhirter."

"He's Scottish," the fourth man said. "We don't mind if he embarrasses *his* nation."

Charles looked at Hassie, who seemed to be enjoying the sophomoric revelry. He put his hand on hers, motioned across the table and said, "And Peter Coddington. His sister was once a student of Aunt Barbara's at the Rodean School for Girls. Remember, I pointed it out to you on the road from Rottingdean to Brighton?"

Hassie nodded as Peter said, "That's correct," and then motioned to the waitress walking past.

Charles realized that the two ladies had not been introduced and concluded that his dick-head friends didn't know their names. He looked over at the blonde and said, "Sorry about my rude mates. We didn't get your name."

She said, "Sophie" and then pointed at the other woman who waved and said, "Gemma."

While the drinks were being sorted, the club gradually filled, the air thickening with smoke.

"So, Hassie," Hamish shouted across the table. "How do you like London?"

"I've only seen a little bit of it. But what I've seen is wonderful."

Peter lit Sophie's cigarette as he said, "I'm sure Charles wouldn't mind if you stayed a while longer."

Charles put his hand on Hassie's back and said, "She can stay as long as she likes."

She focused on the stage where a quartet of musicians joined their instruments. They played a long set that had distinct flavors of Miles Davis and Sonny Rollins. Although Hassie was congenial and chatted as the conversation demanded, the music repeatedly drew her attention with particular interest in the piano player—a tall, thin guy with longish dark hair and a beard, whose age was difficult to determine. When the set ended, the band dispersed into the audience, and Hassie watched him move around the room.

At the appropriate moment, Charles said, "He's very good, isn't he?"

"Who?"

"The piano player. You seem quite taken with him."

"He *is* very good. He reminds me of someone I used to work with in New York—a younger version, but he really knows his stuff."

"Would you like to meet him?"

"Do you know him?"

"Not personally, but I'm friendly with the manager. I'm sure an introduction could be arranged."

She smiled, holding his arm as she said, "That's not necessary, Chaz. It's just been a while since I've been in a place like this with really good musicians. I hope they're coming back."

Charles looked up as the pianist walked in their direction. He motioned for the man to join them, which he did. Charles stood to greet him and said, "Great set, mate. I believe you've earned quite a fan here." He touched Hassie's shoulder and said, "This is Hassie Calhoun. She's visiting from New York City. She's a singer and says you're very good."

The man reached out to shake Hassie's hand and said, "Hi. I'm Derek Collins. Where do you sing in New York?"

He was decidedly American but with that mixed breed of accent to indicate that he'd spent a lot of time in the UK. Hassie asked, "You know Greenwich Village?"

"Of course. I saw Brubeck at the Village Gate and played with a group of friends at the Blue Note several times in the early sixties. Where might I have seen you?"

Gareth walked around to chat with Gemma, and Derek sat down beside Hassie.

"When's the last time you were there?" Hassie asked.

"Five or six years ago."

"Oh, well, I haven't been there that long, so you wouldn't have seen me anywhere."

It occurred to Charles that he knew almost nothing about Hassie's life as a singer—mainly because, once again, she'd never discussed it. But here she was, telling this Derek guy the story of her life and carrying on the conversation like Charles wasn't even there, until he saw the moment to chime in and said, "Hassie used to sing in Reno."

Derek and Hassie both looked at him. Derek said, "Really."

She nodded and said, "And in Vegas back in the days of the Rat Pack."

Derek, looking duly impressed, asked, "So did you meet Sinatra?"

"Meet him?" Charles said. "She worked with him, didn't you, darling."

Hassie gave Charles a *what-are-you-talking-about* look and then said to Derek, "I didn't exactly work *with* him but, yes, I did know him, and he once helped promote my career."

"That's very cool," Derek said. "Sounds like a good guy."

Charles leaned into the conversation and said, "Let me get you a drink, Derek. What's your poison?"

"Thanks, but I gave up the drink a while ago." He focused on Hassie and asked, "How long are you going to be in London?"

"She's leaving on Sunday," Charles said. Hassie furrowed her brow at him and then went back to Derek and asked, "Will you be playing in New York any time soon? I'd love to hear you again."

Derek crossed his arms over his chest, and said, "I'm pretty committed to my life in London right now. But I love New York, and my roots are in the States, so if you ever hear of anyone needing a roving pianist, I'd be glad to know about it."

"I'll keep that in mind," Hassie said. "It was a pleasure to meet you."

He stood up. "Same here. Enjoy the rest of the evening." He started to walk away and then turned to her and said, "Sinatra? Really?"

"Really," she said and flirtatiously wrinkled her nose.

"You know, I think he's doing a concert at the Royal Festival Hall sometime soon. Maybe you'll want to check it out."

"We'll do that," said Charles.

Derek walked away, and Hassie looked over and said, "Chaz, you were rude to him."

"I didn't mean to be rude. I just felt the need to remind him that I'm in the room."

Hassie didn't smile but quietly said, "I'm glad we came here tonight. And your friends are actually very nice."

"I suspect you're just humoring me, but I can tell they like you."

Derek came back to the table, approached Hassie and said, "Why don't you come up and sing with us? We know plenty of the old standards."

She seemed embarrassed and said, "I'm a little rusty but—well, why not?"

As she stood up Charles took hold of her arm and quietly said, "Darling, don't feel pressured if you don't want to do it."

"It's fine, Chaz."

She walked away with Derek, and the two of them chatted in close quarters before he introduced her to the other band members. Was this life with Hassie Calhoun? Would someone always be interested in something about her, making it impossible to ever feel secure with her regardless of what she said or did where he was concerned? And, despite her claim that her singing was rusty, he knew the opposite was true. Her song at his aunt's funeral was flawless, and he'd heard her let loose once in the bath. Protest if she must, but she knew exactly what she was doing. And she was doing it to impress Derek.

The band took their places on the stage and played for a few minutes before Derek introduced Hassie, and she joined them. As she stood at the microphone, the piano and bass giving her the lead into the song, the place got quiet for the first time that night—possibly *ever*. Charles looked around the smoky room—people of all sorts crowded around the smallish tables lining the two tiers of elevated space, the flicker of candles momentarily creating the sense of a sanctuary. The room that was usually filled with laughter and chatter between numbers became eerily quiet—the anticipation of what was about to happen captivated everyone. And happen it did.

Hassie stood behind the microphone as if she were a magnet drawing the audience into her world. The low, concentrated light caught the angles of her face, and as she sang the first line of the song, she appeared to transport herself to another place. He recognized the song, humming along in his head until she sang its title, "I Got it Bad and That Ain't Good." Her voice was clear and controlled as she swayed with the sultry movement of the music. His senses were heightened by every note, and he imagined her wearing a shimmering, sexy gown. As the song came to an end, his emotions lurched from pride to fear. For there had been such palpable chemistry between singer and piano player, that if Charles hadn't known better, he'd have sworn that Hassie and Derek had known each other and worked together for years.

She stepped aside while the band played out of the song. Charles heard the applause, cheers and whistles, but nothing else about that moment felt familiar or recognizable or even real, as if he were standing in the wings and not allowed inside the scene. Derek urged her to take a couple of bows, said something close to her ear and then went back to the piano and played another intro. She came alive as she started to sing *I got rhythm, I got music*... Charles listened and watched her and then looked around the room again, wondering where Ronnie Scott was in the midst of this impromptu happening. When she finished the song and recognized the applause, Derek whisked her off the stage into the room they'd emerged from earlier. Charles stood, keeping an eye on the door to that room. Gareth walked around the table and offered him a cigarette. He took it and waited for Gareth to light it.

"She's a damn fine singer," Gareth said. "Are you impressed?"

Charles nodded. "You want another drink?"

"It's Geoff's round."

"Thanks," Charles said and dragged on the cigarette.

"What does Peggy think about your being MIA this week?"

"She knows I'm busy."

Gareth lit another cigarette, saying, "Does she know *how* busy you are?"

"Leave it alone, Mansfield. It's under control."

Geoff approached them with three pints of lager. Charles took one, and Geoff said, "Great job with the songs, eh?"

Charles nodded again and asked, "What happened to Hamish and Peter?"

"The ladies had a different sort of evening in mind—some other club."

Charles raised his glass. "Cheers." He took a big pull on the drink and then said, "Thanks for coming tonight."

"She got under your skin, didn't she?" Gareth said.

Charles looked at the stage. "She's leaving in a couple of days."

"Is she coming back?"

The door to the back room opened. Hassie walked out, directly followed by Derek and Ronnie Scott. Charles watched as she shook each man's hand and then hurried over to their table. She was smiling but composed, and he assumed that she'd received high praise from the club's owner. He stubbed out the cigarette and then reached out to greet her and said, "Darling, that was smashing. Was Ronnie pleased?"

She took hold of his arm and said, "I think so. What did *you* think?"

"You were fantastic," Gareth said.

"Bloody marvelous," Charles said and kissed her cheek. "Can I get you a drink?"

She nodded. "A very dry martini, please."

He pulled out a chair at the table and as she sat, he motioned to the waitress. He ordered a martini and then sat down beside her as Ronnie Scott sat on her other side. Charles leaned over and asked, "Mr. Scott, what can I get you to drink?"

"The name's Ronnie, and I'm being looked after, thanks." He propped his elbows on the table, sat seemingly consumed by his own thoughts and then, with a jerk of his head, looked at Hassie and said, "You're good with Derek and the boys."

She smiled, a little too coquettishly, Charles thought, and then said, "They're excellent musicians. It's easy to be good with good musicians."

Ronnie went back to his own thoughts for a moment and then said, "This crowd liked you, and this is the crowd that sustains this place. It's easy to fill the room when a headliner's here. Of course, we never have schlock, if you know what I mean." He waved at the barman and then continued. "I'm all about what works. And this worked."

"I'm glad you think so," Hassie said.

"How'd you like to sit in with the band a few nights a week? Say for a month. I couldn't pay you much, and it would be off the books, but you'd get some great exposure and then—well, we'd see how it goes."

She looked at Charles who hadn't a clue what to say except that the idea that she would stay with him for another month set his senses on fire. He touched her arm and said, "Think about it, darling. It's a jolly good opportunity. I'm sure you can sort it out for a few more weeks."

Hassie sipped her drink, pondering it all, and then said, "Thank you, Ronnie. I'm very flattered and more than tempted. But I'll have to see if I can make some arrangements in New York before I can give you an answer. Is that okay?"

"Take your time. Meanwhile, have a chat with Derek. I ran the idea by him earlier, and he likes it... has some thoughts."

Charles had spotted Derek at the bar ensconced in conversation with a well-dressed redhead. *Derek already has some ideas about working with her, eh?* He watched Hassie for a moment, recalling her resistance to extend her stay after Barbara's funeral. He'd done a fair bit of begging and had no delusions that the fact she'd never been to London hadn't figured in to her final decision. If she decided to stay on now, it would have everything to do with the job she'd been offered and nothing to do with him. Of that he was fairly certain. *Stop it, Charles! Don't punch a gift horse in the snout.*

chapter seventeen

Hassie usually slept in after a late night at Ronnie Scott's. Charles's routine of getting out of bed early, having his first cup of coffee and reading the newspaper while waiting for her was the closest thing to perfection he'd ever known. But her stint at the club was coming to an end, and he was back in the despair he'd felt those weeks ago. He hated the thought that she wouldn't again perch on her stool at the high table—a "poseur table" he was told—which she'd convinced him to purchase for the dining area next to the double window that overlooked a heavily wooded park and ancient cemetery on the grounds of St John's Wood Church. She'd selected four black leather stools with comfortable backs and swiveling seats. Initially, he'd argued that the look was too modern and American for his uncle's traditionally English décor. But she'd sweetly countered saying, "We need the height to take full advantage of the beautiful view of the bird sanctuary, don'tcha think?" He simply couldn't imagine that table and stools without her.

He heard the toilet flush and knew she'd soon appear, yawning and moaning that she shouldn't have had that last drink while soliciting assurance that her performance was worthy of the audience's adoration—if, in fact, they did adore her, and she hadn't misinterpreted their enthusiastic reception.

When she appeared at the door from the hallway, Charles said, "Welcome to the world, darling. Did you sleep well?"

Do I Know You?

She tied the sash on Uncle Teddy's brocade dressing gown, looking nowhere near like she'd had a good night's sleep. She stretched and yawned and then said, "Your bed is so comfortable and warm, but I can't seem to get through an entire night lately without a bad dream or... *nightmare*."

"What sort of nightmare?"

"I can never remember exactly," she said. "But it's usually something about me needing to be somewhere to do something important, and then all sorts of things happen that prevent me from getting there—like I discover a missing tooth, or I can't find my clothes or the car leaves without me." She walked toward the kitchen saying, "I feel so anxious for a couple of hours."

He followed her, took a mug from the cupboard and, while pouring coffee, said, "Go in and sit. I'll bring your coffee and a bun." He joined her in the lounge. She'd sunk deep into the cushions and looked miserable. He put the mug and dish on the coffee table and then sat in his chair. "I thought things were going so well. What's got you so down all of a sudden?"

She sipped the coffee, and with a slight pout said, "I really love singing in that club."

Here we go, he thought. "I know you do. And the crowds love you, darling."

"You really think so?"

"Of course they do. I've been in that audience several times now, and it's complete magic. And, as much as I hate to say it, you and Derek are really good together—with the music, that is." He gave her his best cheeky smile so she wouldn't get defensive.

She took her mug over to his chair and sat on the ottoman, put her hand on his leg and said, "I don't want to leave."

"I know. You're desperate to stay with me, and I can't say that I blame you." He gestured toward the table and stools and continued, "I mean, who else would buy all *that* for someone who was going to pick up and leave in a few weeks."

"You love *all that* and you know it. But the real issue is that I *can't* stay, Chaz. I have to get back to Kenny and my life in New York.

By the time I get back, I'll have been gone six weeks. I can tell every time I talk to Kenny he hates me a little more."

"Poppycock. You're his mother, and he'll never hate you. Besides, I'm sure he understands that you've been working."

"He's only six, Chaz. I don't think he understands why I can't work in New York and be at home with him."

"But he's in good hands with—what's your friend's name?"

"Zach. Uncle Zach to Kenny."

"So he's in good hands with Uncle Zach?"

"That's not the point."

"Then what is the point, Hassie? You're miserable because you want to stay here and work at a job you love. Ronnie thinks you've been a great success. I'm sure he'll pay you to stay. We can sort something out with Kenny."

She sat pensively for a moment, seemingly focused on a painting on the opposite wall and then said, "There's also this little issue of my not being legally able to work in this country. Ya know, the reason I get an envelope of cash every week?"

"There's an easy solution to that as well."

"Yeah, what?"

He took the mug from her and set in on the floor, then held both of her hands as he said, "Marry me."

"Are you serious?"

"Of course I'm serious. I wouldn't joke about something like that. I love you, and you love me." When she didn't respond, he kept talking, "I haven't thought this through yet, but there's time to have a simple ceremony before—"

"Before you go back out to sea? Chaz, you've told me a dozen times—you're committed to a life in the navy."

"For now. And, so what? Half the sailors are married. Some even have kids. I'd only be gone a few months, which would give you time to go back to New York and make the necessary adjustments. We could spend Christmas together—with Kenny. I could meet you in New York after—"

She stood up from the ottoman and swiftly walked away saying, "Whoa. You've got to stop this. I can *not* marry you, and that's enough talk about something that can't happen."

172

Do I Know You?

He slumped against the back of the chair and stared at her, but she wouldn't look at him, nervously pacing in the space before him. After a few seconds of silence, he calmly asked, "Are you involved with Derek?"

She looked more defeated than shocked. "No. Of course not."

He stood up, shoved his hands in his pockets and said, "You've been noticeably cow-eyed over him since the moment you met him, and let's face it..." His shoulders went up and down with his exaggerated breath. "You spend more time with him than with me."

She walked over, stood directly in front of him and said, "First of all, Derek has a girlfriend. And secondly—and most importantly—I dont *sleep* with him, Chaz. I come home to our bed every night. I *gladly* come home to our bed every night, and I love *you*." She turned to walk away and then spun back toward him as she said, "I may never have loved anyone as much as I love you. This is bloody ridiculous, and you know it."

He grabbed hold of her shoulders. "Then marry me, Hassie. Be my wife. Have a life with me. We'll figure out how to make it work. I love you, and I'll love your son. Give me one *good* reason that we shouldn't be together for the rest of our lives."

She took short, shallow breaths before saying, "Because I... I'm..." She pulled away from him and turned away. "Because I just can't. It would never work. We come from two different worlds, and we barely know each other."

He followed her into the kitchen and said, "But we have the rest of our lives to sort it all out. Don't you think it could be exciting?" She stood at the sink, staring into the basin. He approached her and turned her to face him, pushing hair away from her eyes as he said, "You know I didn't intend this to be an ambush. It just seems an obvious solution to your problem—to stay in the country and all."

She tried to smile, though he could feel that she didn't want to talk about it. He waited until she finally said, "I'm flattered that you want me to be your wife. But—"

He put his finger to her lips and said, "Let's stop this conversation for now. Just do one thing for me?"

She nodded.

"Think about what I've said."

"Okay, but—"

"No buts. Just think. And in the meantime, I want to talk to you about an advert in today's paper for Sinatra's concert at the Royal Festival Hall. I remember Derek mentioning it that first night we met him."

"When is it?"

"Next Monday, the sixteenth, one night only. Do you want to go?"

She nodded. "It's my night off."

"Good."

"And that reminds me that Ronnie asked me to headline the nine thirty show next Thursday."

"That's terrific, darling. That means they'll put your name on the main board and—"

"Don't get carried away. It's just for that one night before I leave." She wrinkled her nose and said, "They probably had a cancellation or something." She remained quiet while rinsing the coffee cups and then said, "It would actually be kinda nice to see Frank again."

He leaned against the countertop and crossed his arms over his chest. "How long has it been?"

"Since he left the Sands—what? Eight or nine years ago now. He may not even remember me."

Charles harrumphed and said, "You underestimate the power of Hassie Calhoun. Anyone who's ever known you could never forget you."

She stood in front of him, rested her forehead on his chest for a moment and then looked up and said, "You're an amazing man, Charles Beauclerke, and I really do love you."

"And I adore you. Let's take the afternoon off from all this drama and go for a walk and a quiet little spot for tea."

She nodded and said, "Okay." She untied the sash on the dressing gown and guided his hands around to caress her bare buttocks, then kissed his chin as she said, "But you got out of bed so early I didn't have a chance to say a proper good morning."

Do I Know You?

He pulled her close, kissed her and then followed her into the bedroom.

* * *

Charles held the umbrella while Hassie climbed out of the taxi next to the Royal Festival Hall. Sinatra's concert had long been sold out, but Charles's brother-in-law pulled some strings in the city, and they ended up with enviable seats. They entered the contemporary foyer; Charles shook the rain from the brolly. When they were through the bulk of the crowd, he checked their coats and guided Hassie toward the bar while saying, "What a filthy night. This man had better be worth it."

"He will be. Do you ever listen to his music?"

"Not if I can help it."

She playfully slapped his arm. "Chaz. He's one of the greatest singers of this century."

"And someone you've known quite well. What would you like to drink?"

She gave him a quick look of dismissal before saying, "A shot of whiskey would warm the blood."

"Wait right here." Charles joined the queue at the bar, more than a little irked that he was bothered that Hassie had a past relationship with the great and powerful Frank Sinatra. But then, wouldn't any man feel that way? She'd never actually admitted to what degree she'd been involved with him, but when she talked about him, her body language spoke for her. He took two whiskies back to where he'd left her, but she wasn't there. He canvassed the area and spotted her standing in front of the poster with a photo of a tuxedoed Sinatra wearing the look that Charles felt certain was meant for every woman in the crowd. He approached Hassie and said, "There you are." He handed her the drink. "I thought you'd left."

"Don't be silly." She touched her glass to his. "Cheers. And thank you." She took a big sip of the drink. "This is a real treat."

He steered her away from the photo. "So you didn't stay in touch with him after all that time you were together?"

She waited a moment before saying, "We weren't *together* for long at all. It was a complex situation."

"Isn't everything you do complex?"

"That doesn't sound nice. Are you okay?"

"Drink up. We need to get to our seats soon. Did you know that the concert is being filmed for television?"

"How exciting." She swallowed the rest of the drink and handed the glass to Chaz. "Do we have good seats?"

"They're good enough."

The orchestra filled the stage while the last of the crowd took their seats. The house lights dimmed; a man's voice presented Princess Grace of Monaco, and the elegant blonde appeared on stage wearing a white evening gown trimmed in white feathers. She introduced Sinatra with great admiration as well as a bit of light ribbing over their work together on the film *High Society*. Hassie glanced toward the wings like doing so would make Frank appear. He finally joined the orchestra, greeted Princess Grace and the audience and then launched into "You Make Me Feel So Young." There was no doubt about it—the man's presence was electrifying, almost annoyingly so. Charles remembered his mother talking about how women swooned over the young man… "Old Blue Eyes," he'd heard her say. Even now as the older version of that heartthrob took control of the great hall, it wasn't difficult to believe that Sinatra had maintained quite a reputation with the ladies. And Hassie had been one of them. He was familiar with the first few songs, furtively observing her body language throughout.

When Sinatra paused to speak to the audience, he joked and cajoled and then said, "We shall call this next section 'songs for losers'—unrequited love, girls running away from home and all that kind of jazz."

Charles carefully looked at Hassie, whose expression was difficult to read. If she felt his gaze, she didn't acknowledge it, staring straight ahead and seemingly rapt in the song's intro. He wanted to hold her hand but thought better of it and just listened to the man croon the first line, *I get along without you very well*. Hassie sat perfectly still, and when he glanced at her, he saw that tears streaked her face.

In the moment, he felt helpless and insignificant in this world that had once belonged to her. By comparison, his life was an utter bore, and he wondered if that was a factor in her hesitancy to talk with him about marriage. Conversely, Peggy thought that his life was exotic and exciting, and he knew that she fancied herself as the wife of a naval officer. Before he met Hassie, he'd half believed that he would eventually settle down with Peggy. But now… now, that was doubtful.

As the applause ebbed and Sinatra continued his section for losers, Hassie reached over and took hold of Charles's hand. She didn't look at him or change her expression. She'd obviously been moved by the choice of song—or maybe it was something the man had said. Either way, she had turned to Charles for comfort, and that was something.

The show lasted a brief fifty minutes. When he'd sung the last note of "My Way," taken his final bow and said goodnight—the audience on their feet—Hassie held Charles's arm and asked, "Did you enjoy it?"

He hesitated slightly and then nodded. "Yes, I think I did."

"Good. I thought he was great. The voice and charisma are still as strong as I remember."

They slowly moved up the aisle with the crowd to the foyer. Hassie seemed in a less fragile state than during the performance, but he still thought carefully about what he'd say. "You seemed a little upset at times. Was it too difficult a reminder of your past?"

Her eyes were glassy with emotion, and he waited while she pondered the question. But by the time they reached the foyer, she seemed to have shaken it off and smiled as she said, "Thank you for coming with me. It was magical, and I'm so happy I got to be here with you."

"It was entirely my pleasure, Miss Calhoun. Now, can we go home?"

Charles collected their coats, and within a few minutes they were in a taxi, heading back across the Waterloo Bridge toward the Embankment. Hassie was quiet and then snuggled up to Charles and said, "I have a confession." She breathed deeply and then continued, "I spoke with Frank this afternoon."

Charles swallowed and gently said, "Did you, now? How did you manage that?"

"I phoned the hall this morning and finagled my way to a conversation with the guy on the stage door. I told him that I had worked with Frank in Vegas and that I'd like to leave a message for him. The guy told me that he could get a message to Frank's people and then it would be up to them to give it to him."

Several thoughts surfaced, but Charles pushed them aside and said, "So I guess he got the message."

"He called me late this afternoon. We had a brief chat, and he was thrilled that we were coming to the concert—said that if he'd known I was in London, he'd have made sure we got the best seats in the house."

"That's nice," Charles said. "So he knew you were coming with someone."

She smiled, laced her fingers through his and said, "I told him all about you. I gave him a quick version of how we met, why I'm here, about working at Ronnie Scott's. He was warm and seemed genuinely interested, so I told him about the show on Thursday night and invited him to come."

Charles was surprised and skeptical all at once but admired her— *confidence*, he supposed, and asked, "Well? What did he say?"

"His son, Frank, Jr., is traveling with him, and he'd see if they could make it. He knows Ronnie and said they'd check it all out and, I don't know, but it sounded like he'd like to be there and that they would try to make it."

She didn't sound like she quite believed what she was saying. Charles considered his words and then carefully asked, "Do you think he and his son will actually show up?"

She let go of his arm and stared straight ahead as she said, "I have no idea. But if he does, you'll get to meet one of the most famous men in the world. Most people would die for that opportunity."

"Well, I doubt I'll die, but, I do hope he comes."

She paused for a long moment and then softly said, "So do I."

chapter eighteen

Hassie spent the day on Thursday relaxing, having decided the weekend before to wear one of Nigella's evening gowns—a slinky, black sequined number that hugged every curve, exposing a perfectly formed bosom in the sexy décolletage. In the makeshift bolt-hole of a dressing room in the back of the club, Charles watched as Hassie studied her image in the full-length mirror propped against the wall. She gathered the bulk of her hair off her neck and pushed it loosely to the top of her head and said, "I know you think I should wear my hair down, but I think I'd like to put it up tonight."

Charles cocked his head from side to side and then said, "It's very sexy like that. Maybe a little bit *too* sexy?"

She let the hair fall to her shoulders. "You'd have me wear a potato sack and a bowler hat if you could."

He took hold of her shoulders, released a guttural growl and said, "Now *that* would be sexy."

"Seriously, Chaz. I've got half an hour to make myself presentable. You promised to help me stay calm."

Charles took a step back and said, "Right. In a minute, Poppy will bring you a cup of weak, lemony tea, and in twenty minutes, she'll bring you a whiskey." He took hold of her again and said, "Nobody cares about your hair, darling. You're ravishing whichever way you

179

wear it." He turned her to face the mirror, stood behind her and said, "You'll be brilliant. Just remember how much I love you and how wonderful it would be if you were my wife."

She looked into his eyes in the mirror and said, "You're not going to let that one go, are you?"

"I'm afraid not."

Ten minutes later, Charles entered the club and sat at the bar. The barman approached him and asked, "Are you sitting here tonight?"

"Maybe. Pint of Carlsburg, please." The barman brought the beer. The attractive redhead Charles had seen a few times before sat two stools down. He took a big pull on the beer as the barman said, "Nice to see you, Judith. Does Derek know you're here?"

Charles looked over at the mention of Derek's name. The woman smiled at him and said, "You're Hassie's guy."

He nodded. "Charles Beauclerke."

She smiled. "Judith McRaney."

"And you're Derek's—*gal*?"

She laughed. "Soon to be wife."

"I hadn't heard. Congratulations."

"Thanks. Looks like there's going to be a special audience for Hassie's show tonight."

"Really? How so?"

"Rumor has it that Frank Sinatra is coming in with his son."

It wasn't that Charles had forgotten that the Sinatras might make an appearance, but he'd considered it a long shot and was, honestly, more comfortable with the thought that he wouldn't be emasculated in the presence of the great man. He swigged the beer again and then said, "That's a real coup for this place, isn't it?"

"I suppose so," Judith said and focused on the front entrance. "Actually, he's been in a few times, usually with a woman or two. Looks like he's opted for the boys tonight." She slid off her stool, looking past Charles as she said, "Sorry. I'm being summoned. It was nice to meet you."

She walked away, and Charles watched as Ronnie Scott led Frank Sinatra, a man who was obviously his son and two other men to a table reserved in the front. Hassie had said that she'd told Frank about her relationship with Charles and that they would be attending the concert at the Royal Festival Hall together. Should he go over and speak to them? He watched the two Franks settle in and then the elder lit a cigarette. Maybe it would be a good icebreaker to ask the famous singer if he could bum a fag off him. He'd then introduce himself and pull up a chair to watch the show. Yeah, right.

Charles was used to men ogling Hassie when she was on stage, but he'd never dreamed that he'd vie for her attention from Frank Sinatra. And now, here he was, in all his starring glory, sitting right at her feet. Charles finished his beer and ordered another one, occasionally stealing looks at *the* table.

The lights dimmed, and while the musicians took their places Ronnie stepped up on the stage, took the microphone and said, "Ladies and gentlemen, welcome to Ronnie Scott's. If you've been in for our late show during the past few weeks, you've seen and heard Hassie Calhoun—who's visiting from New York City—singing with Derek and the boys. Tonight, she's taking the stage with her own show. I promise, you're going to love it." He then pointed to Frank's table. "And if that weren't enough, we have a very special guest in the house. Mr. Sinatra, would you please stand and take a bow?"

Frank stood up, faced out to the room and waved; the crowd applauded and whistled. After a moment, Frank motioned to his son to stand and called out, "And this is my chip off the old block, Frank, Jr."

The younger Sinatra waved, and Ronnie said, "Sorry, Frankie. Didn't mean to ignore you."

He offered a mock salute, and Frank applauded, very much the proud papa. The applause died, and Ronnie continued, "So, I give you Hassie Calhoun. Enjoy the show."

The band played a generic intro, and Hassie eventually appeared in the spotlight, jumping right into a medley of "You're the Top" and "I Get a Kick Out of You." She was a vision in the sequin gown, her red lips and dark eyes more alluring than Charles had imagined. And she'd been right to put her hair up. Though he knew it would be better not to do it, he looked at Frank, whose expression was lost in the dim light. When she finished the song, Frank whistled and applauded without taking his eyes off her. She winked at him and smiled before saying, "Good evening, everyone." The applause intensified along with whistles and cheers. "Wow," she said. She waited a few seconds and then said, "Jeez." When the crowd finally settled down, she said, "Wow. You've reduced me to one-word responses. Thank you so much. Before I get on with the program, I'd like to extend a special welcome to Mr. Sinatra and his son, Frank, Jr. If you were lucky enough to see Frank's show at the Royal Festival Hall a few nights ago, you know what truly great company we're in tonight." She looked directly at Frank and said, "You're a busy man, and I know you made an effort to be here tonight, and I'm very grateful."

Frank raised his glass while saying, "Sing for us, doll."

Hassie sat on a stool and said, "This segment is to pay homage to three of the greats in this business—Billie Holiday, Fats Waller and Sarah Vaughan."

She went straight into an upbeat version of "Love for Sale," followed by "Mean to Me" and then finished the trio of songs with Charles's favorite, "Body and Soul." As he listened and watched, he wondered if she was thinking about how he loved it when she sang that song to him sometimes when they were in bed—her lips caressing his body between lines of the song. He could sing it with her.

> You know I'm yours for just the taking,
> I'd gladly surrender myself to you
> Body and soul.

When she finished the song and the applause began, Charles debated whether or not to look at her for fear that she'd be rapt in something to do with Sinatra. He gave in and focused on her. She acknowledged the people to her left and then scanned the room to her right, where she caught Charles's eyes and mouthed a kiss. When she went back to the microphone stand, Charles looked at Sinatra's table and met the man's inquisitive stare. Charles stifled a smug expression and then gazed lovingly at Hassie.

She stood behind the microphone. With a rhythmic, Latin intro, the band led her into a jazzy, sexy "Besame Mucho," which seemed to relax her for the first time since she'd been on stage. Her dress shimmered in the light as she subtly moved with the bolero beat. She followed that with a section of more contemporary numbers, including the Beatles and Dusty Springfield. This was not an ordinary evening at Ronnie Scott's, and as far as Charles was concerned the Sinatras being there had little to do with it. This was Hassie in her element, and he wished he could know exactly what she was feeling.

It was Hassie's choice not to take a break. Her rapport with the audience was fresh and natural, the reception between numbers nothing short of the adoration she craved. When she finished simple arrangements of "I've Got a Crush on You" and "My Funny Valentine," she invited Ronnie to join her on stage. He accompanied her on what had become her signature song—"I Got It Bad and That Ain't Good." When he broke into the saxophone interlude, the heart and breath of the club that he'd founded filled the room and seemed to propel Hassie to an even higher level of performance. Charles felt the difference in her demeanor—her confidence and professionalism—and certainly in her voice. It was a palpable turning point, he believed, and one from which she should never go back.

She followed with an arrangement of "Summertime" that she and Derek had worked together and finished the show with a rousing version of "If My Friends Could See Me Now." Charles was happy and sad all at once. The atmosphere was rife with exhilaration, both ineffable and portentous. He felt it in his gut and witnessed it in the faces of others. There were calls for an encore, but Hassie took a final bow and left the stage.

Charles took his third beer over to the Sinatras' table, stood in front of the men and said, "Good evening, gentlemen. My name is Charles Beauclerke, and I'm, well, I'm Hassie's *beau.*"

Frank looked at him, hesitated and then said, "She mentioned you." His son stood up and reached over to shake Charles's hand, saying, "Frank, Jr. Nice to meet you."

Frank lit a cigarette, exhaled the first drag and said, "She was sensational."

His son echoed, "Yes, truly sensational."

"I assume she's coming out to speak to us," Frank said.

"Of course," Charles said. "She'll be jolly chuffed to see you."

"Chuffed?" Frank said. "I hope that's a good thing." He laughed and then said, "Pull up a chair."

Charles dragged a chair over as the waitress arrived with drinks, and Frank said, "So, James, Hassie told me she's going back to New York next week."

"It's Charles, and as of this moment, yes, she is."

"I can't believe you can let her go."

"It's not exactly up to me, sir," Charles said. "I'd love it if she stayed."

Frank focused on the spot on the stage where Hassie had stood, dragging on the cigarette. She soon walked into the room with Ronnie.

The odd cheer rang out, and Hassie graciously smiled and waved before turning her attention to their table. Charles stood and waited while she greeted the Sinatras. Frank embraced her, kissed her cheek and then whispered something in her ear. When it was Frank Jr.'s turn, he took her hand and kissed it and then said, "Congratulations. You brought the house down."

"Thank you," she said. "And thank you so much for coming."

Frank shook Ronnie's hand and said, "You're a lucky man."

While the two men chatted, Hassie made her way over to Charles and stood in front of him. He pulled her close and said, "You took my breath away."

She looked up at him. He kissed her, and she said, "Really? Was it okay?"

"Darling, it was not *okay*. It was bloody fantastic. Everyone loved it, and every man fell in love with you. You're a star, my love."

She hugged him and said, "That means so much to me. So much of that show was for you. And us."

"Okay, you two," Frank said. "Join the party. Hassie, come over here."

She walked over and sat on the other side of the table between Frank and Ronnie.

The waitress arrived with a bottle of champagne. Frank said, "I know how you love champagne."

She smiled. "Thanks. I might drink the whole bottle."

Frank rested both elbows on the table and said, "You look fantastic, doll."

She stole a quick look at Charles and then, seeming a little embarrassed, said, "It's great to see you, Frank. And to meet your son." She smiled at Frank, Jr. and then sipped the champagne.

"So this really is your last week working here?" the son asked.

Hassie took another sip and nodded, "It's time to go back to New York."

"That's a real shame," Frank said. "I've been around a lot of good singers, but you got something special. You had it in Vegas, and it's even better now. This audience loved you."

Ronnie leaned on the table and said, "I'd gladly have Hassie on the regular docket but, Frank, as I explained earlier, right now, I can't hire her to mop the floors. Not while she's here without a legal right to be. As is, she's had to swear that if the authorities come 'round she's not been paid a penny to get up on that stage."

"So she'll get legal," Frank said. "There's more than one way to skin a cat."

Ronnie stood and said, "There's no doubt that bringing Hassie in for the last few weeks—especially tonight—was a good move. But I think we've reached the limit on fudging her *sit-ins* as a tourist. If she makes it legal? That's a different conversation. Now, if you'll excuse me, I have to work the crowd." He put his hand on Frank's shoulder and said, "I'll see you on your way out."

Frank, Jr. said, "I think it's about time for us to call it a night. We have an early flight tomorrow and some strategizing to do before we sleep."

Frank stubbed out his cigarette, reached over and held Hassie's hand and said, "You were terrific, doll. I'm glad I came. Something tells me it's the beginning of great things for you. If I were you, I'd do whatever it takes to keep Ronnie happy and keep this little gig. And if you can make a success of it here, you can do the same thing in New York. If anyone asks, tell 'em I said so."

He stood up, straightened his jacket and said, "By the way, do you ever see that loser—what was his name—Contata, Contrata?"

Hassie frowned. "Do you mean Jake?"

"Yeah. Him. Where's he now?"

She hesitated, glancing away and then said, "He died. In the desert. I thought you'd know."

"Nah. I thought I'd heard something about him back on the east coast. But, hey. You're sure as hell better off without him." He looked at Charles and said, "Pleasure to meet you, young man. Get our girl home safely."

Charles stood and shook Frank Jr.'s hand while Frank kissed Hassie's cheek, a little too close to her mouth, Charles thought, and was glad when the two men were escorted away.

Hassie sat and drained her glass before she said, "A part of my past crept in here tonight, and then it crept right away again."

Charles refilled her glass. "Was it not nice to see Frank again?"

"Of course it was nice to see him. It was great to see him. But..."

"But what, darling? Did he upset you with the mention of the man that died in the desert?"

"No, Chaz. I'm not upset. It's just a little—*odd*—seeing him again and to recognize that we've all moved on from that magical time at the Sands."

Charles leaned over to kiss her forehead and said, "We can make our own magic, you know."

She nodded. "Yes, we can." She focused on nothing, her eyes glassy with emotion.

He gave it a moment and then asked, "What's going on in that beautiful head of yours?"

She smiled sweetly and then hesitated before she said, "You just might be the most wonderful man I've ever met. You've given me so much. You've let me complicate your life while you're trying to work and study, and you've stood by me through every little whim and every big event. And tonight you stood by calmly—like the gorgeous gentleman you are—and let another man laud his celebrity over you."

"Well, when you put it like that, I sound like a tosser."

She shook her head. "No, my love. You are a fine, sensitive, generous man, and if you really meant it when you asked me to marry you... the answer is yes."

He looked into her eyes where he saw her love the way he'd always hoped he would—love without the pain and without doubt.

"And I promise you, Chaz. I'm not just saying this so I can keep working here. Do I want to keep working here? Yes." She kissed him and said, "But I also want to stay in London with you, and I want us to get married, and I want us to have a life together."

The crowds were thinning, but there were a few hangers-on that apparently wanted to have a word with Hassie. Charles stood and pulled her out of her chair and close to him as he said, "You really want to do this? You're not going to think about Kenny and New York and change your mind?"

"I swear on my father's grave. I want to marry you. Everything in New York will be just fine."

"Then go sign a few autographs and then let's take this celebration home."

part three

chapter **nineteen**

Hassie had consciously married two men. What had she been thinking? First off, her marriage to Zach was a total sham. If she really wanted to put herself—and Kenny—through it, she could probably have that marriage annulled. Zach had married her under false pretenses, and the discovery that he was involved with and actually living with a man had caused her untold amounts of grief. She was the victim. She deserved to have a shot at happiness. Secondly. Well, technically, there was no *valid* secondly, despite the sad situation with Zach. The fact remained that she had married Chaz while she was married to Zach. And she still couldn't explain to herself or any damn body else why she didn't just tell Chaz that she was married and then sort it out like a sane human being.

It was all a bit blurry now, but her recollection of those first few days in Rottingdean was that they were never intended to mean anything. She went to a funeral. She met a man. She liked him. He treated her like royalty. He wore red socks and heavy twill trousers, and when he had to do his own laundry, he ironed the front of his shirts—the part that would be seen under his jacket. The knot in his tie was always crooked. He made her laugh when he was actually being serious. She loved him. She grew to believe that if she left him or let him leave her, she'd never meet or know anyone like him again. She simply wasn't willing to take that risk.

Their wedding had practically taken place overnight and, as she prepared to return to New York to spend Christmas with Kenny, the reality of what she'd done left her with many a sobering thought and a few nightmares. Then came the raw emotion she felt over having said goodbye to Chaz as he left for a tour of duty in Australia. She'd known of his movements for weeks, but still felt that he'd deserted her when he left, unable to tell her exactly when he would return. It had surprised her how much she missed him but, fortunately, she'd kept busy. Her work at Ronnie Scott's led to an agent, and she'd had a few auditions. That morning she'd been seen for a new production of *Jesus Christ Superstar*, opening the following year in the West End. She sang and then read for the lead role of Mary Magdalene. What a fantastic debut that would be! But she wouldn't know the producers' decision until after the holidays, which meant that she could focus on the task ahead of her in New York.

She'd spent the afternoon shopping for Christmas presents and sat on the underground with a big bag of toys for Kenny anchored between her knees. She'd been struggling to picture his sweet face recently. But when she thought of seeing him again, she could imagine his eyes wide with excitement when she gave him the presents. She'd had mixed feelings about going back to New York. Oh, she loved the city at Christmastime but felt that she would miss London, with or without Chaz. And she dreaded facing Zach and the charade that was their marriage—one that had to end.

On reflection, Zach had been uncharacteristically nice to her when she called to check in, seemingly supportive of her opportunity at Ronnie Scott's but still eager for her return. She'd ignored his attempts at a more personal exchange, insisting that her time and money were limited, and she was desperate to stay connected to Kenny. In her mind, he was happy for the unbridled freedom where his relationship with Andrew was concerned, and, despite the odd worrying thought, she knew that Kenny was being well looked after. She was slightly nervous about the reunion with Kenny. But that worry was overshadowed by the knowledge that she must return to London the wife of one man—the first man that she had truly loved since Jake. The issue of how she'd bring Kenny into her life would follow on naturally.

* * *

Hassie checked the post when she arrived at the flat. She'd been expecting a letter from Chaz for over a week—he'd been so good about writing every few days. But the post box only contained a couple of flyers and a bank statement. Inside the flat, she stowed the gifts for Kenny in the spare bedroom that she'd once commented would be a nice-sized closet in New York and changed into a comfortable pair of gabardine slacks and a soft wool sweater.

She'd planned a girl's night in with Nigella, who was not just her sister-in-law, but had become a friend—one of the few women friends she had—and kept Hassie from missing Chaz so much. She took out the crystal stemware and the dishes that they'd need for a takeaway meal. The front bell rang. She opened the door to a rather-a-bit-more-pregnant-than-she'd-expected Nigella and said, "You look amazing! Come in."

Hassie exchanged kisses with Nigella, who said, "Sorry I'm late. I'd arranged for Karina's grandmother to stay with her, who, of course, turned up late." Hassie took the small overnight bag to the hallway while Nigella continued, "You've never had the pleasure of meeting Stuart's mum, have you? And you haven't missed a thing. That precious lamb of a daughter of mine is genuinely fond of the old woman so what can I say? Anyway, how are you, my darling? You look gorgeous as always. How my dear brother can leave you here alone for such a long time, I'll never know."

Hassie smiled. "Give me your coat, and make yourself comfortable on the sofa. I'll put this away and get the first drinkies on the way."

Nigella placed her right hand on her round belly and said, "Can you believe how big I've got? This one must be a bloody football player."

"How far along are you now?"

"Six months, but Stuart says I look like I'm going to burst any second based on his recollection of my pregnancy with Karina."

"Well, you look healthy and full of motherhood. Let's relax and enjoy ourselves. It's the last time I'll see you before I'm off to New York."

"Yes, yes. And we must talk about this trip of yours."

Hassie put Nigella's coat in the guest room and returned to the lounge with the champagne and glasses.

"That looks to die for," Nigella said. "I haven't had a drink for weeks, and I adore champagne."

Hassie poured the two drinks, handed one to Nigella and said, "Cheers to you—a happy Christmas, a blessed new year and a wonderful new baby for the Bonhams."

"Cheers, darling. And safe travels." They sipped the champagne before Nigella said, "You are coming back, aren't you?"

"Of course I'm coming back. I'm hoping to get cast in a new show in the West End."

"Is it the one you mentioned when we last spoke—something about Jesus?"

Hassie laughed. "Yes, something about Jesus. At least I should know the verdict by the time Chaz returns."

"When's he due back?"

"It's all a bit cryptic at times, but I'm pretty sure I'll return from New York well before he's back."

"So are you missing him madly?"

Hassie swallowed a sip of the drink and nodded. "You have no idea. But at least I've been busy—between auditioning and a couple of nights a week at Ronnie Scott's, I really don't have a lot of time to myself, except late at night. I get lonely at night."

"You two hardly had any time together after the wedding, never mind a honeymoon."

"We barely had time for a wedding."

"That ceremony was divine. Whose idea was it to have it in that gorgeous chapel in the Royal Naval College?"

"Chaz, of course. I knew nothing about the place. It really was special, wasn't it?"

Nigella nodded while looking around the room. "Do you have any photographs?"

194

"Not yet. Someone from the chapel took a few shots, but Chaz needs to collect them when he's back."

Hassie set her glass on the coffee table. Nigella took hold of her wrist and said, "Let me get a closer look at that ring." She studied the simple setting of tiny pearls surrounding an oval-shaped sapphire. "It's very elegant. Very *you*."

Hassie smiled and said, "It's an antique. We found it in one of the shops in The Lanes in Brighton. Actually, we looked at dozens of rings. Chaz asked me to point out my top choices and then he surprised me later with this one. Very sweet, isn't it?"

Nigella nodded. "And perfect with the simple band. I never knew my brother was such a romantic. But then, you seem to have brought out all sorts of romantic notions in him." She leaned against the back cushion before saying, "I'd better take it easy with the champers. I'm not used to alcohol, and it's gone straight to my head."

"Yes, do take it easy. Are you happy to have an Indian take-away?"

She nodded. "Sounds wonderful." She rested her head on the back of the sofa and closed her eyes. Hassie worried that she shouldn't have had the champagne, but she sat quietly sipping hers until Nigella looked up and asked, "Can I tell you something that I've wanted to say for a while now?"

"Of course you can. Are you feeling okay?"

"The drink made me a little sleepy." She sat up, looked at Hassie and said, "When I saw you with my brother at Aunt Barbara's funeral, I knew you'd already captured his heart."

"We'd only just met."

"Okay, maybe I exaggerate a little bit, but I could see it in his face. He was smitten—or at least, *intrigued* by you. And I thought to myself, typical bloody man—sees a pretty face, long legs, nice figure and loses his mind."

Hassie laughed. "I think you exaggerate a lot and anyway, why are you telling me this?"

"How much has Charles told you about Peggy—assuming that he's told you about her at all?"

"He told me that he's known her for a long time—that your families have been friends for—what's that word he used? Yonks?"

Nigella nodded. "Means for as long as one can remember."

"They saw each other on and off for years between prep schools and college and such and that prior to meeting me, he saw her occasionally, but I never got the impression that it was very serious."

"Hmmm. Not surprised that dear brother would downplay the relationship considering he was falling for you."

Hassie refilled her glass and asked, "Are you saying that I *wrecked* their relationship?"

"Of course not. The only thing you did was to turn up looking like a Hollywood goddess and say hello to my brother."

"Nigella, I promise you. I knew nothing about Peggy until we came back to London after those few days in Rottingdean. He had to tell me about her because there was evidence of a woman having been here, and he made it all so uncomfortable to ignore. But, I swear, I never got any feeling that the relationship was—*hot*. He didn't call her or she didn't call him—at least not that I'm aware of. Everything seemed perfectly fine."

"Well, Peggy is very hurt by the whole thing and thinks Charles could have handled it all a lot better. He'd given her reason to believe that they could have a life together and well, frankly, I think she was counting on it. Mind you, I do believe that she genuinely loves Charles more than he did her."

"Then why would she think he was going to marry her? And how could I, or anyone, come along and change his mind? I mean, if he really loved her and wanted to marry her?" Hassie put her hand on her heart and said, "I promise. Chaz barely said ten words about her. It never occurred to me that there was anything as serious as marriage between them."

"I believe you. I'm glad to hear you say it, and I should also give you fair warning that my dear mother will probably never forgive you for disrupting this perfect union that she and Peggy's family had predetermined."

"Oh, dear. That explains Gwen's sudden illness on the day of the wedding. I know that she wishes Chaz had married anyone other than me, but I had no idea that the ideal wife was Peggy."

"I didn't say that she was the ideal wife. She's attractive enough, I suppose, though a bit severe at times. Honestly? I never really warmed to her."

"Why not?"

Nigella made a face and stared up at the ceiling while considering her words. "This is probably going to sound harsh, but I found Peggy to be rather coarse. And I didn't always appreciate the way she talked to my brother. I suppose I got to know her for Charles's sake. But that's all water under the bridge now, isn't it?" Nigella sat on the edge of the seat and picked up her glass. "Anyway, this night was supposed to be about us girls." She took a small sip and then said, "I imagine you're quite excited about seeing your little boy."

"I'll need an entire suitcase to hold all the things I bought for him at Hamley's today. Zach suggested that I might want to spoil Kenny after being away for so long."

"Zach? Is he another child you've got stashed in New York?"

"No, just the one. Zach's a friend who's been looking after Kenny while I've been away. There's a nanny involved as well and, of course, he's in school much of the time. According to Zach, Kenny has a busier social calendar than *he* does."

"I must be honest with you, darling. I don't know how you've been able to stay away from your child for all these weeks. You must love my brother very much."

"Yes, I do. But I've also been working—building my career, and I really love living in London."

"So are you going to bring Kenny back with you?"

"Well, yes—eventually. But we're trying to cause as little disruption to his life as possible. There's a lot to consider, and I need to take it a step at a time." She stood up. "Are you getting hungry? Shall I bring the menu?"

"Yes, I'm feeling a bit peckish. Or is it the champagne? Either way, a spicy meal sounds just the ticket." She pushed herself up off the sofa and said, "I must first visit the loo. And I'm warning you, this will be the first of many visits before this night is over."

Hassie walked over to Nigella, took hold of her hand and said, "Please don't think badly of me for leaving my son in the care of someone else for so long. I speak to him almost every day, and, like I said, he's a busy little boy."

"Hassie, I understand that you live a completely different life than I. In fact, I may even be a little envious of your glamorous existence while I carry on like a frumpy *hausfrau*."

"You could never be frumpy, and seeing you with Karina does make my heart ache. I just keep telling myself that everything will work out and that eventually I'll have a wonderful home with a wonderful husband and my own precious lamb of a child here with us."

"I hesitate to ask the obvious question here, but don't you and Charles want a child or two of your own? I mean, the thought of what the two of you could bring into this world—darling, it's a must."

Hassie dropped Nigella's hand and said, "Sorry, I'm keeping you from the loo. Go on, and I'll get dinner sorted."

She stared blankly at the menu realizing that she and Chaz had never once discussed having a child. She'd been too busy soft pedaling the subject of Kenny and uprooting lives in New York and trying not to focus on Zach. She daydreamed about the life that she and Chaz would eventually have—dividing their time between London and the beautiful English seaside. Kenny always figured into that scenario, though she hadn't a clue how bringing him into their lives in England would be achieved. There was simply no doubt that this was where she belonged—with her husband and son, all predicated on the belief that her marriage to Zach was finished. Surely he believed as she did—that they would both be better off divorced.

chapter twenty

New York City, December 1970

Hassie arrived to an empty apartment—one she could no longer call home. She knew that Kenny would be in school when she got in from the airport, but she'd expected to see Zach. He'd rattled on like an excited schoolboy when telling her about the holiday plans he'd made for the three of them, most of which she would muddle through for Kenny's sake. But first, she needed to settle back into the apartment—both logistically and emotionally. She put her things in the bedroom, remembering that Zach had been more or less living with Andrew when she left. He'd been forced to modify that behavior when Kenny was there. Thus, she assumed that he already had one foot out the door, returning to his life with Andrew.

Back in the living room, she was reminded how much she loved the apartment. Zach had outdone himself with the holiday décor— no doubt it was more for Kenny than for her. But as she studied the beautifully decorated tree, observing that the star adorning the top touched the ceiling, she was reminded of the things that had drawn her to Zach in the first place—his kindness and generosity, his attention to detail and his ability to make her laugh. However. Would they get through the next couple of weeks?

In their phone conversations, Zach had informed her of any business that needed her immediate attention, explaining that he would leave her mail in the desk for when she returned. She walked over to the great

Louis Quatorze *bureau,* as she'd so often been reminded, and opened the left-hand bottom drawer where she found a file marked "Hassie's stuff." She thumbed through the various bits and pieces, but nothing in particular caught her attention until she glanced at what looked to be a stack of Christmas cards on the desk. The envelope on the top was addressed to her—the handwriting looked familiar. She picked it up and saw that it had been opened. As she started to remove the paper inside, she saw her sapphire engagement ring on her right hand. She'd left the gold band in London, having decided that wearing the sapphire kept Chaz close to her while they were apart. If Zach noticed the ring, she'd tell him that it had belonged to Barbara and that the family had given it to her. She'd also realized that it had become a little too easy to lie when the need arose. But in the moment, she cared more about keeping Chaz close than worrying about right and wrong where Zach was concerned.

The front door opened with a flourish and a mighty "ho, ho, ho" from Zach. She dropped the letter on the desk and rushed over to greet Kenny, who'd positioned himself behind Zach as if intending to hide from her.

"You guys are a sight for sore eyes," Hassie said and hugged Zach.

"How long have you been here?" he asked.

"Not long." She peered around Zach and said, "Hi, sweetheart. Can I give you a big hug and kiss?"

"We've just come from Kenny's Christmas party at school— that great excuse to eat a mountain of sugar, to screw around in the classroom and still call it a school day."

Hassie smiled. "So today was your last day before Christmas?"

Zach pulled Kenny around to face his mother. "Go on. Give your ma a big hug. She hasn't seen you in such a long time." He looked at Hassie and said, "Can you tell he's grown?"

Hassie put both arms around Kenny and pulled him in close to her. He didn't exactly resist, but it was apparent that their reunion would not be a simple case of I'm-back-now-let's-pick-up-where-we-left-off. She stepped back and said, "I brought you lots of presents from London. I think you're going to love them."

Kenny looked up at her. "Can I have them now?"

"Whoa there, sport," Zach said. "First of all, we say thank you. And Christmas is not for a few more days." He looked at Hassie. "I'm assuming they're Christmas presents."

"They're just presents. We'll get into them later."

Kenny looked down and said, "I'm hungry."

"Hungry?" Zach asked. "You just ate enough junk to feed a small nation."

Hassie laughed, put her hand on Kenny's head and asked, "What would you like to eat?"

He looked at Zach and asked, "Can we go to that Korean place we like?"

Zach raised his eyebrows at Hassie and said, "Don't you think we should ask your mom what she'd like? Ya know, she traveled a long way to be here with you for Christmas."

Kenny made a face and then rushed down the corridor toward his room. Zach looked at Hassie and said, "He's excited to see you."

"Oh, really? He has a strange way of showing it." She sat on the sofa.

Zach paused and looked at Hassie like he wasn't sure he knew her. "How 'bout a little holiday cheer?" he said. "It's past cocktail time in London."

"Sure," she said, but was more concerned about how she could smooth over the rough bump she'd encountered with her son.

"Vodka or scotch?"

"Whatever you're having."

Zach set the two drinks on the coffee table, joined her on the sofa and then took hold of both of her hands, lingering over the left one before kissing it. "*I*—you're abandoned husband—am very happy to see you. Just give Kenny a little time to adjust. He's missed you so much, Hass. He's gotta work through those emotions."

She withdrew her hand from him, picked up the drink and took a sip, deciding how wise it would be to go to a nitpicking level on the subject and then said, "Then let's talk about you. How's Andrew?"

"Andrew who?"

"Seriously, Zach. You know I knew all about him before I left."

He sat back and said, "You never once asked me about anything to do with my life while you were away. And we talked what—a few dozen times."

"Before you go blaming me for everything that's gone wrong over these past few weeks, might I remind you that your *other* life was not something I felt at liberty to discuss, so why would I ask you about it?"

He stared straight ahead, slowly shaking his head and then said, "That piece of my life is history. It was a mistake, and now it's over. And you were gone for over two months."

"You know that I was working. We talked about what a great opportunity it was for me and that you'd help Kenny understand."

"Yes, but you were originally going to be gone for *one week*."

She sipped her drink, carefully picking her words. "How was I to know that things would happen the way they did and that I'd find such success and my career would take off?"

"So London was all about you and your need to prove that Ruben was wrong to let you go and that, generally, it was a big *fuck you* to New York City for never getting another job."

She smiled bitterly and said, "I know you're angry with me, and I'm sure you think I deserve for Kenny to never speak to me again. I'm sorry to say it… Actually, I'm not sorry to say it. I wouldn't change a thing that's happened over the last couple months, and I certainly wouldn't turn down the opportunity to work in one of the greatest cities in the world. There's much more to this life than New York City, whatever you think."

Zach slugged back the rest of the drink and then looked at her, hesitating before he said, "What's going on, Hass?"

"What do you mean?"

"You're different. I can't exactly put my finger on it, but something's changed. Yeah, so you're a little nervous but underneath it all, you seem—what's the word—content." He stood up with his empty glass and went to the bar. He'd always had good instincts where she and their lives were concerned. He brought the second drink back to the table, stood in front of her and asked, "Why did you leave your wedding ring here?"

She carefully turned the sapphire around to face her palm and said, "I don't know."

"Well, it tells me that you left here thinking that we were no longer married."

"I honestly don't remember what I was thinking. I was mostly concerned about Barbara having died before I got to her. And I was upset that you'd chosen to spend more time with Andrew than with me and Kenny. I guess I didn't really know what I felt about our marriage."

"And, now?"

She looked down, considering that she should just tell him that she wanted a divorce.

He took a deep breath and said, "Never mind about that now. Do you at least admit that you're living two lives?"

She couldn't look at him.

"I don't know what's going in *your* other life, but I do know that you've got two wounded soldiers on the ground here in New York. And if you think that you're going to waltz back into our lives for a couple of weeks, sing Christmas carols around a chestnut-roasting fire and then merrily wing your way back to London without addressing the real issues, then you should leave right now."

"Zach, why are you attacking me like this? I've barely spoken, and you've created your own story complete with threats and ultimatums."

"Then tell me I'm wrong. Tell me that you only stayed in London because you got a great opportunity to work for a few weeks. Tell me that that's over now and you've actually come home to stay."

She remained quiet. Zach set his drink on the table and said, "That's what I thought." He stared at the floor for a moment and then looked at her and asked, "What's his name?"

"Pardon?"

"What's the name of the guy that's pulled you away from your son and husband?"

Her face warmed, and the space around her felt tight. She took a few shallow breaths before saying, "I was in London to work, and that's what I did."

"Don't lie, Hass. Don't forget how well I know you. My guess is that you've met someone, fallen in love and have plans to live happily ever after." He picked up his drink and took a big pull on it. She had no idea that he'd be able to read her so easily. Should she just confess her love affair with Chaz and hope that Zach would kick her out?

He sat in his chair and waited for her to speak. She buried her face in her hands for a long moment and then looked up as she said, "What did you expect would happen when I got back?"

"In what way?"

"Did you think that I'd just fall through the door and jump into your arms? Did you think that things would immediately return to normal—not that I have the slightest clue what normal between us is any more. Zach, you left me and our marriage for a man."

"But I told you. It was a mistake, and it's over."

"That doesn't change the fact that you did it, and things can never be the same between us again."

"I think you're wrong about that. I think that we can work through this. Okay, so maybe we won't immediately fall into some sort of connubial bliss. But if I've learned anything from all this—and that includes your extended absence—I've learned that I really do love you, and I want us to be a family with Kenny."

"It's just not that simple. A lot of damage has been done, and I don't think it can be repaired."

"What damage?"

"Are you serious? First, it was everything you put me through with Zelda—don't think I've forgotten all that. And then you basically *left* me for Andrew and, believe me, you don't need to spell all that out—"

"Okay, okay. I know. I just needed... Hell, I don't know what I needed, but I'm done with all that now. I swear. I've had a lot of time to think about all this." He stared out into space and then said, "I think it's a matter of time. And I'm willing to give you all the time you need. I'll bunk in with Kenny for a while. I promise, I'll prove to you that I've changed. You don't need to punish me. I've punished myself enough."

"I'm not trying to punish you, and I'm sorry it didn't work out with Andrew. But do you really think that I should believe that you can just turn off your desire to be with men and be emotionally and physically content with me? I think you loved Andrew more than you ever loved me."

Regret and shame spread across his face as he quietly said, "That's not true." He dropped his chin to his chest, and for a moment she felt she might have gone too far. She went back to the bar and slowly poured more vodka while considering what she should do next. She felt him standing behind her and turned to face him. He gently held her shoulders and said, "I know it sounds impossible, but I'm asking you to give me a chance. The one good thing that's come from this separation is that I've done a lot of soul searching. And I've been to a psychiatrist."

"Really?"

"I made a terrible mistake, Hassie. I don't know why I thought I needed Andrew in my life. It feels like a bad dream now."

She looked at him through squinted eyes, dimly aware that he was trying to tell her that he wasn't and had possibly never been interested in men—that he wasn't gay. She quietly cleared her throat and then said, "I'm not sure what you're saying, Zach. None of this makes sense."

"I'm trying to say that I was wrong to... do... what I did with Andrew. The whole sordid mess was wrong. And I've figured out that I don't want him. I want you. We have something special. And important. You're my best friend—maybe my only friend."

She walked away from him, completely caught off guard and a little light-headed. She was probably jet-lagged, which meant that this was not the time to engage any further in this conversation. He followed her back to the sofa. They sat down as she said, "I need some time and space to think about all this. Let's try to enjoy the holiday break—if only for Kenny's sake—and, I promise, by the time I leave for London we'll know what we're going to do about us."

"So you're going back?"

"I have responsibilities at the jazz club, and I've also auditioned for a new show in the West End. I'm up for the lead, and if I get it, well, let's just see what happens."

He slowly shook his head and then gently held her left hand. "Please don't leave again. Please stay here and help us get our lives back on track."

"You've just dropped—a *bombshell* on me. And we need to talk about it some more later. But I'm asking you to do something for me as well. I'm asking you to try to understand everything I'm dealing with. Zach, you know me. You know what I've been through trying to make a name for myself in this business. You also know that it's hard and that I struggled here and—well, pretty much failed. But I'm not failing in London. I'm tasting success, and I like it. Please try to understand. The facts are plain and simple. Our lives have changed, and we're different people now. Just think about what I'm saying. Please."

* * *

Hassie gave one present to Kenny every day leading up to Christmas. Each afternoon, they had a little ritual where he dug into a big bag full of the gifts and pulled one out. She'd found a large model of the red double-decker bus, which he opened on the second day and triggered the turning point in their relationship. He hugged her for the first time since she'd arrived and then started firing questions at her about London, which dissolved the wall between them.

On the afternoon of Christmas Eve, Zach had gone to a party, and Hassie called Kenny into the living room. When he entered the room wearing a striped shirt that he'd halfway tucked into a nice pair of trousers, his dark hair washed and combed, Hassie's emotions swelled. Her son was still such a little boy, but at that moment he was the spitting image of his father—and not just in his looks. Totally unaware, she was sure, he possessed that Jake Contrata charm that drew people to him—that had drawn her to him those years ago and that had made it impossible to get him out of her heart and mind. Kenny had reminded her of Jake from the moment he was born. But it seemed the older he got, the more he seemed to *become* Jake, and that unnerved her. She held out her arms to him and said, "Come here. You are so handsome. I need a big hug."

He walked over and let her hug him, then looked up at her and asked, "Are we gonna do my present now?"

"Well, we could. But I have another idea. I'd like to take you to see the beautiful Christmas sights. We can bundle up and go out for a while, and if you're a good boy, we'll stop off for the best hot chocolate in the world. How does that sound?"

"Good, I guess. But when do I get my present?"

She hugged him again, brushing his thick hair back from his face and said, "As soon as we get back. Uncle Zach should be back as well, and we'll have a nice Christmas Eve together."

He nodded and ran off to get his coat and suddenly it was eleven years earlier, and she was in the Plaza Hotel looking down on Central Park and then staring into the windows along Fifth Avenue while waiting for Jake to take her shopping. She still had the fur coat he'd bought her on that trip. It was the one thing she'd held onto during all the ups and downs that had followed Jake's death.

Kenny bounded back into the room wearing a hooded wool jacket that looked a lot like the navy peacoat that was part of Chaz's uniform. "Is that a new coat?" she asked.

He nodded while fussing with the buttons. "Uncle Zach bought it for me."

She smiled. "He's bought you lots of nice things, hasn't he?"

He shrugged. "Mostly clothes. He says I'm a weed."

Hassie laughed and said, "He probably said that you're *growing* like a weed." She put her coat on and took gloves out of the pockets. "Do you have any gloves to keep your hands warm?"

"No, Mom. Gloves are for girls."

"Oh, I didn't know." She smiled and herded him through the front door. They took a taxi up to Macy's to see the decorative window displays and then worked their way along Fifth Avenue past Lord and Taylor and Saks, ending up at Central Park. It was one of those cold, crisp days with deep-blue, cloudless skies. The streets were packed with shoppers and tourists doing exactly what she'd planned for Kenny.

When they reached the fountain in front of the Plaza Hotel, Kenny spotted the horse-drawn carriages parked along the sidewalk outside Central Park. He pointed to them and said, "Uncle Zach told me that when it gets warm, we'll take one of those rides. They go all around the park, and you can ride as long as you want."

"So you've been to the park with Uncle Zach?"

"Not *inside*," he said. "We've driven by in a taxi when we were going to visit Uncle Ruben."

"I see. And did you do that often?"

He shrugged. "I don't know."

"You want to ride in one of the carriages now? They have blankets to keep us warm."

He pointed and said, "They tie sacks to the horse's butt so he doesn't poop on the street."

Hassie took hold of his hand and headed to the entrance of the Plaza. "Let's go get that hot chocolate and then we'll decide about the park." She had spoken with Ruben the day after she arrived, but he was busy with holiday functions and some "hot tamale" that he'd met from Ecuador. Refreshingly, nothing ever really changed where Ruben was concerned. But she hadn't been aware that Kenny had spent time with him. Something about the thought of Kenny being around Zach and Ruben—particularly at Ruben's apartment—niggled at her.

Their table in the Palm Court was situated midway along a windowed wall. Hassie watched people come and go, aware that most were tourists much like she'd been on that visit with Jake all those years ago. And now she sat with Jake's son contemplating what it might be like to take him to live with her and Chaz in London. She thought about the conversation she'd had with Nigella, who in her well-meaning way had chastised Hassie for leaving Kenny in New York. And what about having a family with Chaz? These were normal expectations, but Hassie wasn't used to normal, certainly not since she'd gone to England and met and married Charles. She admired the sapphire ring, reminding herself that she must leave New York knowing that her divorce from Zach was underway.

"Mom?" Kenny said, tapping her arm.

"Yes, sweetie."

"Could I have another hot chocolate?"

"Not without having something to eat. How about a hamburger or a sandwich?"

He shook his head and said, "Let's wait for Uncle Zach."

Hassie motioned for the check before saying, "You want to make a quick visit to wish Uncle Ruben a Merry Christmas?"

"Yeah, okay. Can we take a taxi?"

"Of course. I'll pay this nice man, and we'll get one right out front." He stood up to put on his coat, and she said, "Was I right? Was that the best hot chocolate you've ever had?"

"I guess so." He ran ahead of her saying, "We're going to Uncle Ruben's."

* * *

Ruben opened the door looking like he'd just gotten in from a three-day drunk. He threw open his arms and said, "Well, look who's here!" He grabbed Hassie and held her in a ponderous embrace before ruffling Kenny's hair and saying, "Hey, big guy. Where you been lately?"

Kenny shrugged and Hassie said, "We were out and about enjoying the decorations and thought we'd drop by to say Merry Christmas. Hope it's not a bad time."

"Hell, no. Come on in."

They followed him into the living room—a high-ceilinged salon containing a mass of expensive unmatched furniture that went beyond eclectic but exquisitely defined Ruben's personality. The saving grace design-wise was the magnificent Steinway grand piano that occupied the right rear corner and had served as the studio for Hassie and Ruben's work sessions.

Kenny ran over and sat on the piano bench, lifted the cover on the keyboard and said, "Mom, listen." He beat the keys for a wobbly version of "Chopsticks," after which he beamed up at Hassie, soliciting her approval.

"That's great, sweetie," she said, glancing at Ruben. "Where'd you learn to play like that?"

"Uncle Ruben taught me."

"And what else did Uncle Ruben teach you?" Ruben asked.

Kenny hesitated for a moment and then slid off the piano bench and faced Hassie, put his forearms across the front and back of his waistline and slowly bowed. Hassie smiled at Ruben and then they broke into enthusiastic applause.

Ruben walked over to him and said, "Good job. You wanna go watch TV?"

Kenny nodded and took off down the corridor. Ruben walked over to Hassie and hugged her again before saying, "You look great, honey."

"Thanks, Ruben. I'd say the same to you, but I'd be lying." She laughed. "Tis the season to be jolly, huh?"

"Is it that bad?"

"Just giving you a hard time. How are you?"

"Fan-fucking-tastic, and glad you're back."

She walked over to the nearest armchair and sat down.

"You *are* back, aren't you?" he asked. "We've got a lotta work to do."

"I know, and I'm eager to get into it with you, but I have to go back to London in another week."

"I thought you were coming back to work on *our* project, Hassie. You told me you were committed to it."

"I am committed to it. But I have an opportunity to be in a West End production."

He sat in a chair opposite her and asked, "So did you get a big starring role?"

"Not yet."

"Whadaya mean, *not yet*? You either did or you didn't."

"We're still in the auditioning stages, but I'm being seen for the lead. It's a big show, Ruben, and something I really want to do—if I get it. I just have to go back to London to find out."

He slumped down in the seat and rested his hands on his belly while silently watching her to a point of discomfort. She uncrossed and crossed her legs, trying not to look as distressed as she felt. He finally looked her in the eye and asked, "So what's going on?"

"What do you mean?"

"Cut the crap, Hassie. Why don't you really want to come back to New York? I'm sure I don't need to tell you what an unhappy little boy you left behind. From the looks of things, he's forgiven you for all that, and I'm sure he thinks you're back for good. How do you think he's gonna feel when you up and leave again?"

"Ruben, I came here today to wish you a happy holiday, not to get a tongue-lashing. Let me have a relaxed couple of days with my guys, and then I'm all yours. We'll talk and work and plan the way forward. I want to get back to our project. Working successfully in London has helped me focus on what's really important to me now. Give me a chance."

"Okay, but don't jerk me around. If you're gonna stay in London and have a career as a performer, so be it. Just be honest with me so I can move on."

She stood up and called out for Kenny. Ruben walked her to the door, took hold of her arm and said, "Don't hurt that little boy again."

She nodded. "I know."

He then spoke close to her ear. "And if you hurt Warren—you're dead to me."

chapter **twenty-one**

Christmas Day came and went with little fanfare. Kenny
opened the rest of his gifts from Hassie, and Zach gave him a
popular game he'd been talking about for months. Hassie gave Zach
a Burberry cashmere scarf, and he gave her a pair of simple diamond
earrings from Tiffany. Someone from the outside would think that
they were ideal candidates for a Rockwell family portrait, and, funny
enough, there was genuine warmth between Hassie and Zach, which
spilled over onto Kenny and made for a relaxed couple of days. But
despite Zach's revelation that his affair with Andrew had been a mere
aberration, his resolute desire for them to be a happy family was never
going to happen. Hassie held him to his word that he'd bunk in with
Kenny until she felt ready to share a bed with him again. Of course,
she had no intention of that ever happening and vehemently ignored
his advances when he'd had too much to drink and thought he could
seduce her. The day after Christmas, Zach went out to meet a client
for a drink and returned just before midnight. She was confused and
disgusted all at once. But she was now dead certain that he would
never touch her again.

She missed Chaz and everything about her *normal* life when
they were together. But this turmoil that Zach had inflicted on her—
his preposterous notion that she should just *forget* what he'd done to
her with Andrew and accept that he'd made a mistake and was over

it now—had messed unmercifully with her mind and emotions. And though it had made it easier to push any real thoughts of her intimacy with Chaz to the back of her mind, her intentions to start divorce proceedings while in New York were becoming increasingly more difficult to fathom, let alone impose.

She remembered that morning that she'd neglected to go back to the letter she'd discovered on her arrival, having been interrupted by the tense appearance of Zach and Kenny. But when she went to the desk, the pile of cards and letters was gone. She rummaged around the top drawer and looked through the file containing the collection of her old mail, but the envelope in question was nowhere to be found. Zach must have done something with it, which annoyed her as it was clearly addressed to her. She recalled that the handwriting had seemed familiar. The more she thought about it, the more anxious she became to find the missing envelope.

Zach had dropped Kenny off at a friend's house for a few hours of boys' rough and tumble. She heard the front door to the building open and close. When Zach opened the door to the apartment, she stood up from behind the desk and said, "Good. You're back."

Removing his overcoat, he said, "You missed me?"

"Hmmm… desperately." She smiled and then continued, "I'm looking for the mail that was on the desk last week. Do you know what happened to the envelope addressed to me?"

"I wondered when you were going to get around to discussing that with me."

"Zach, I never read the letter. You and Kenny came in before I could get the paper out of the envelope. I don't know what it's all about."

"I assumed you'd seen it, Hass. It stayed on the desk for days. Anyway, it was from the guy in Reno."

"Clay Cooper?" she asked. Zach nodded, and she continued, "What did he say?"

"Your ex—Kenny's father—had another child. A girl named Norma."

"Yes, I know. What about her?"

"Her mother's ill, possibly dying."

Hassie stared up at the ceiling and then looked at Zach and said, "And Clay thinks she could live with us?"

"There's no *us* with this, Hassie. I will not be saddled with *another* another man's child. Ain't gonna happen."

She agreed with him. She'd be going back to London in a few days, and it wasn't fair to expect Zach to have anything to do with Norma. For all sorts of reasons, she hadn't had a chance to speak with Clay again after the call she'd made in September. But the fact that he'd written to her about Norma meant that he'd possibly put aside some of his bad feeling toward her. She'd call him again—explain the issue of her work in London and that, despite the blood connection to Kenny, it would not work for Norma to become part of their family. Not now—not ever. She looked at Zach and said, "Don't worry. I'll sort this out with Clay."

"I hope so. But tell me why the hell Clay thinks you owe Jake's kid that's nothing to do with you a place to live. After everything you've told me about Jake—how badly he treated you and caused you so much grief—why would Clay think you'd even consider doing such a thing?" He sat on the sofa. "Is there something you're not telling me?"

She sat down next to him. "Jake and I split up after a year or so in Vegas, and I went to Reno for a while. That's where I met Clay—who, as I've mentioned before, was one of Jake's estranged half-brothers and helped me get established as a singer in Reno. While I was there, Jake had an affair with a woman named Natalie, and Norma was born out of that relationship. They never married, but Jake agreed to take care of Natalie and the child and did so until he died. By that time I was back in Vegas. I knew about the affair and the child, but that's it. I left Vegas after Jake died and never looked back."

"So, again. Why does Clay think you owe the poor little girl a home? And, by the way, how old is she?"

"She'd be about eight or nine now. So, she still needs a parent, and evidently Clay doesn't feel up to the task. He's getting married soon, and from the little he's told me, the new wife doesn't want to know anything or anyone from his life before her. But I need to hear the whole story from him."

"Hassie, you did hear what I said. I cannot take on another kid in this apartment. Especially if you're hell-bent on going back to London and coming back who knows when."

She nodded. "I understand. I'll deal with it." She started to stand. Zach held her arm and asked, "Are you still hell-bent on going back to London? Can't you see what leaving again will do to Kenny?"

"Zach, I've gone this far with the audition in London, and I have a job. I can't just walk away now. I'll never get hired again."

"What about your commitment to Kenny and to me? What about us, Hassie?"

She stood up, pulling away from him. "Don't you get it? There is no more *us*, Zach. Don't you think the best thing for both of us is to move on with our lives? We'll always have special meaning to each other, but come on. We need to let go. We need to get—"

"Don't you dare say we need to get divorced." He walked away and stood in front of the window. Hassie followed him saying, "Why not? I really don't believe you love me as your 'til-death-do-us-part' wife. I think you love the idea of being married and having a family. In fact, I think you probably love Kenny more than you love me."

He spun around to face her and said, "Don't bring Kenny into this. It's nothing to do with him. You married me, Hassie, when you were down and out and needed someone to take care of you and your son. We had an agreement. And you've done little to uphold your end of it lately because you decided that your life was better in London. Well, too bad. You're not going to get out of this marriage so easily. I don't care what's really going on over there. You made a commitment to me, and it's time you start living up to it. Is that clear?"

She stood silent for a moment and then calmly said, "I don't think you mean what you're saying. Do you really want to live in this sham of a marriage? Everyone can see through it, Zach. Despite your insistence that you're not gay, everyone knows you'd rather be with a man, and think about it. What'll happen when you meet someone you're interested in or say, you get back together with Andrew?

Are you going to carry on this charade at the expense of your own happiness? I really doubt it, and I don't understand why you would want to live like this indefinitely. It's not natural, and neither of us is getting any younger."

He stared at her for a moment, then crossed his arms over his chest and asked, "Why won't you at least give me a chance?"

"To do what?"

"To love you. To make love to you. To have a real marriage—a home for Kenny. We did it once. We can do it again. And, honestly... I know it now. I was wrong. What I did with Andrew was wrong."

She'd been exhausted by every conversation, and the entire issue was becoming a joke, but she still had a single mission to accomplish. "Okay. But, Zach, whatever you say, we can never have a real marriage. You shut me out when you fell in love with Andrew. I know I didn't say anything about it at the time, but how do you think that made me feel?" She stopped and swallowed her emotions. "I've had some low moments in my life, but everything you put me through while you were obsessed with Andrew... Do you have any idea how worthless and insignificant I felt?" He just looked at her, defiant and pathetic all at once. She held back tears and asked, "Did we ever really love each other?"

"I loved you."

"Did you? Or did you love the idea of me?"

"What does that mean... the *idea*?"

"You needed a wife—a woman on your arm. There were numerous reasons, and it was complicated, but I think you liked the fact that other people could see that you *succeeded* in the wife department."

"That's ludicrous. You think an awful lot of yourself. I never had to have a wife, and I certainly never had to marry you. I married you because I thought you and I made a great team, and I could offer you something that you needed. But I also loved you. And I still do."

"Then let me go, Zach. Let me get on with my life, and you should get on with yours. We had some fun, and yes, you helped me when I needed help with Kenny. And he loves you."

"But you don't love me."

She shook her head and said, "Please, let's do the adult thing and end this marriage. It's best for everyone."

His beautiful dark eyes filled with tears. He sat down, and his hands slightly shook as he clasped them together in an attempt to calm his nerves. She understood that he was lonely, unhappy and vulnerable. But even without Chaz, she'd had enough of the ruse, and she was running out of time. She sat beside him and said, "Ruben's worried about you."

"Don't bring him into this. He's got his own problems, and frankly, I'm a little fed up with him."

"Why?"

"Since his last wife hit the dusty trail, he's decided he's God's gift to women, which is hilarious. I mean, look at him. He's fat, unctuous, rude and disgusting when he wants to be and thinks that any woman over twenty is too old. He generally makes a big fool of himself and spends money like there's an endless supply."

"That doesn't much sound like the Ruben I know. He's been very focused and revved up about our musical. If anything, he seems to have gotten himself together pretty well, considering that last break-up."

Zach asked, "Hassie, why are we talking about Ruben?"

"He's worried about your frame of mind, and now I see what he's talking about. You miss Andrew, and for some reason you've decided that you'll dismiss that part of your life and that you want to live a lie—pretend that you have a happy marriage and a loving wife who's decided to do *you* wrong. It's bullshit, Zach. And you know it."

"I'll say this one more time. I am not going to give you a divorce. You are not going to divorce me because you have no legitimate right to do so. If anything, you are the bad guy. You deserted me and your son and ran off to another part of the world. You don't contribute a bean toward the upkeep of this apartment or the raising of your child. You have repeatedly promised to come back, giving him false hope and causing him untold amounts of anguish. He's basically functioning on a promise that you do not intend to keep, thus causing more grief and exacerbating his abandonment issues. And to add major fuel to the fire, whether you'll admit it or not, I think you have a serious relationship with another man while being married to me." He picked up her right hand, looked at the sapphire ring and then dropped it as he said, "That's called adultery, Hassie, and does not put you in any position to make demands on me. So, basically, you're fucked. You're married to me both now and for the foreseeable future. I suggest you deal with that and reconsider any thoughts you may have had about taking the issue of divorce into your own hands."

"I'm not interested in getting into a pissing contest with you, but even if I were involved with someone—and I'm not saying that I am, I think you're forgetting that you were first to cheat on this marriage, and you did so with a man."

"Let me stop you right there. What I really should have said is that you should remember what I do for a living. You should believe that I know every way in and out of the legal system, and what I don't know, some close friend or colleague of mine does. So don't start swinging dicks here because, I guarantee, mine's a helluva lot bigger than yours. Got it?"

She sat motionless, knowing she was no match for his legal prowess. They'd started the conversation with her believing that she held the upper hand. How could she have been so wrong? What made her think that she could show up, announce that the marriage was over and that divorce was the only answer? She was stuck—faced with her worst nightmare. She would go back to London having accomplished nothing where this marriage was concerned. She was a bona fide bigamist.

chapter twenty-two

London, January 1971

Hassie took the red-eye from New York to London intending to sleep a few hours. But the days of harrowing confrontation between her and Zach had edged her limits, her nerves shot. She was exhausted to the point that she was too tired to sleep, and she'd mistakenly thought that drinking the lethal concoction of vodka, Khalua and cream would knock her out. She remained awake for the entire seven-hour journey, with nothing to show for her efforts but a dull, thudding headache. Kenny's refusal to speak to her after she finally admitted—with shameless coercion from Zach—that she was going back to London broke her heart. She promised that she'd be back to visit before he had time to miss her and that after his school year ended, she'd bring him over for a visit at which time he could ride one of the big red buses and see all sorts of wonderful things. He simply couldn't be consoled, and she left feeling like the ugly monster that he obviously thought she was.

She felt an odd sense of comfort that Chaz would not be back for a few more weeks, as she fully believed that she'd never be able to hide the sheer terror that she currently felt over her failure to end her marriage to Zach. She'd even considered telling him that she'd married Chaz, begging him to take pity on her and gracefully step away. But his vehemence on the subject grew stronger and more determined. Like he'd said—she was fucked.

219

A dozen useless scenarios went through her mind on the flight. But after weary consideration of where each option fell short, she decided that the only way to do the right thing was to do the right thing—tell Chaz that she'd made a terrible mistake in marrying him and that they should have the marriage annulled or divorce or whatever they needed to do until she could end the marriage with Zach, which, despite everything he'd said, she was still convinced he would agree to as soon as he met some young, virile stud or resumed his love affair with Andrew.

An English woman with three young children stood in front of Hassie. The children were all under the age of seven, she guessed, and increasingly unhappy that they couldn't rush forward to meet their father. The eldest was a boy with black hair and dark eyes and the easiest temperament of the three. He reminded her of Kenny, and she teared up. She thought of that moment when Kenny's pain and resentment toward her seemed to dissolve and how he didn't mind when she hugged him in front of others or called him *sweetie* or held his hand when they were walking around New York. Before she'd proceeded to ruin everything that she'd accomplished during that visit by telling him she was going back to London, she'd had her son and they were, once again, the invincible team that had traveled across the country to make a new life in New York.

So what happened? How did she actually land in this dual existence as a doting mother married to a man she didn't love and a carefree demi-celebrity married to a second man that she would die for? Why couldn't she successfully mesh the two and have her son with her in London and part of the beautiful, loving relationship that was Mr. and Mrs. Charles Beauclerke? It was one of the scenarios she'd entertained on the flight and the one she still had the greatest desire to achieve. But the facts were stacked against her. And because she didn't dare tell a soul in New York that she was married to two men, she could only imagine the trouble she'd be in once the truth were known—and in two countries, no less.

There had to be some significance to Zach's infidelity with a man. Wasn't it illegal for two men to have sex? Of course, she couldn't prove that Zach and Andrew or any number of other men that Zach hung around with had actually had sexual relationships and, as Zach had already informed her, he'd use every available source to fight her should she try to push the issue. And the indisputable fact was that she had married Chaz knowing that she was legally married to Zach. Had the stress caused by Zach's cruel indiscretions caused her to lose touch with reality? Maybe she should plead temporary insanity.

The canvas tote bag that she'd overstuffed on the way over to New York now contained her notebooks and manuscripts from the work she'd done with Ruben on the musical. They'd only had a few afternoons together but had made the most of it. She'd intended to spend a little time during the flight on the revisions they'd agreed to, but the issue of how she'd fix this mess engulfed her thoughts, which eventually blurred amidst the vodka and Khalua. She slipped the bag off her shoulder and located the notebook that she'd been working with. She'd constructed a letter that she intended to mail to Chaz when she got back to London. The drafted letter looked like a madwoman's rantings with lines drawn through complete passages and scribbles that even *she* couldn't make out. But she knew what the message had to be. She reread a lengthy passage that had taken a big chunk of time to construct:

> You've heard me talk about my friend, Warren Zachary or "Zach" who has been my son's caretaker while I've been on this journey in London. What I didn't tell you—and I admit that I was completely wrong—was that I ~~was once~~ am married to him. I know that sounds ~~horrendous~~ unbelievable now and I wish there was an easy way to defend how I could have married you when I was already married to another man.
>
> I can explain everything, Chaz, and I know in my heart that you—being the ~~gorgeous human being~~ wonderful, caring man that you are—will understand my thinking and rationale and believe that *I* fully believed that the marriage with Zach was over and was simply waiting for a divorce to be activated—something that I intended to accomplish on this trip to New York.

You see, Zach is a very complex person who ~~prefers the company of men to women~~ is currently confused as to his sexual preference. This is not an excuse—it is a fact. He actually left me and our marriage for a man last year, which may explain why I was a bit elusive when we first met. It's all so sordid and wrong. Please believe that I had every intention of sorting it out before having to burden you ~~with such an ordeal~~.

The problem now is that he is adamant that he doesn't want our marriage to end and that he ~~insists that~~ wants me to remain his lawful wife. I have begged and pleaded with the decent man that I know he is. ~~Of course, I didn't think it wise to tell him of our marriage~~ He was simply unwilling to entertain the thought ~~that I have found someone that I love so very much and~~ that his doing the right thing would be to let me go.

So, I believe that the best way to handle this unfortunate situation in the interim is for our marriage to be annulled such that we are not legally married until I can ~~finish off things~~ finalize the divorce from Zach.

She made it through immigration and entered the baggage claim area, quickly spotting the big, blue suitcase that Barbara had given her when she left Corsicana for Las Vegas over thirteen years ago. So much had happened since that gray, autumn day—the *first* time she ran away from home to follow her dreams. All that mattered now was that she'd had an amazing ride with the first man she'd ever loved and that from that wild ride she had an extraordinary son. Yes, things were a mess, and she had no real idea how it would all sort out. But Kenny was her son. She couldn't—she wouldn't lose him, despite Zach's threats. He had no legal right to Kenny. No one else had legal right to her son, and Chaz was the man she belonged with. Could he be convinced that they could work everything out and should she truly expect him to forgive her?

She placed the big suitcase on a trolley, loading her handbag and canvas tote bag on as well. She cleared the final checkpoint and pushed through the double doors into the arrivals hall, which was teeming with people carrying signs—some welcoming loved ones, others there to collect their fares into London. Her vision was slightly blurred both from lack of sleep and a double dose of emotional turmoil where Zach and Kenny were concerned. She scoured the big hall for directions to the taxi ramp, headed for the exit and then heard someone call her name. She looked around but saw no one before a hand touched her shoulder. Startled, she turned around to see a smiling face. "Oh my God," she said. "You scared me."

"Is that the best way to greet the husband that you haven't seen for over a month?"

She threw her arms around his neck and held him tight. "I'm just so shocked—surprised to see you. What are you doing here?"

He held her in his arms, kissed her firmly and then said, "I got back a couple of days ago—got a few days of holiday leave, which I'm calling our honeymoon. I spoke with Nigella, who told me that you'd be coming back this morning. So I decided to surprise you." He kissed her again, and she pulled back from him as he said, "You look like you've seen a ghost, darling. Is everything all right?"

"I'm just tired. And I have a headache. Leaving Kenny was so emotional, and I couldn't sleep on the plane."

He took hold of the trolley and said, "I want to hear all about your trip. But mostly I want to get you home. And don't be surprised if I don't let you out of bed for a day or two."

They started to walk. She put her arm through his, stroking the soft leather bomber jacket that she'd always loved and said, "God, I've missed you. And I need you too—more than you know."

He laughed. "You'll need me a little less by the end of this day."

* * *

Back in the flat, she plopped on the sofa, kicking off her shoes, while Chaz put her suitcase in the bedroom. When he returned to the lounge, she asked, "Would you bring me a couple of those headache tablets from the bathroom?" He watched her for a moment and then did as she asked. He'd taken off his shirt, sat down beside her while she washed down the pills and then briskly rubbed her feet before saying, "There. All better now?"

She yawned. "That's so nice. I could fall asleep right here."

He stood up. "Oh, no, you don't. Maybe later." He pulled her off the sofa and into the bedroom. He slowly unbuttoned her blouse, pretending that he was being considerate, which made her laugh. She pulled the shirt over her head and said, "You're such the gentleman."

He kicked off his trousers and then pulled her down onto the bed and said, "Shut up." As they wrestled in each other's arms, she had an array of disturbing thoughts. One moment his kisses felt like the most natural, familiar part of being with him and that they'd only been apart for a few days. The next moment, his lips felt strange, and his tongue was too forceful, and she didn't recognize anything about this reunion. It was both eerie and exciting, and she wondered if she really was losing her mind—if maybe the ordeal she'd been through with Zach had damaged her ability to function properly—or maybe her attempts to stave off her own desires while she was away had settled in permanently?

If his kisses had been somewhat strange, his body was totally familiar. He'd gone a little crazy, and she loved the frenzy. He tried to talk to her and then dozed off, and she held on to him like doing so would negate all the problems she'd created. For to have him shut her out of his life seemed completely inconceivable. But did she honestly believe that everything this little snatch of time had rekindled between them would overpower the magnitude of her mistake?

They slept. When she awoke, Chaz held her. He brushed her hair away from her eyes and asked, "Are you hungry?"

She meant to nod but instead grabbed him, buried her face in his chest and cried. She wasn't ready to tell him the truth but wasn't sure she could successfully hide her feelings of doom.

He kissed the top of her head and cradled her in his arms until she finally pushed herself up to a sitting position and took a tissue from the bedside table. She blew her nose and wiped her eyes. He rested his hand on her leg and said, "I hope these are tears of joy to be together and to make love again. It's been too long."

She leaned over to kiss him, and he put his hand on the back of her head and pulled her face close to his. He kissed her several times and then said, "I still can't believe that you're my wife."

She pulled away and sat up, fighting back more tears and carefully said, "I don't deserve you."

"Bollocks. Why would you even think such a thing? You're a gorgeous, talented star in the making, and I'm just a ruddy old sailor whose most recent claim to fame is having climbed Ayers Rock."

"Really?" she said. "That's very impressive—at least to me. I don't know anyone else who's done that."

He rolled over onto his back and stared at the ceiling. He looked so young and happy—like he hadn't a care in the world that she was single-handedly getting ready to destroy. She moved in close to him and caressed his bicep. "What great big muscles you have, Mr. Sailor."

He pulled her over on top of him, holding her in a firm embrace. "The better to hold on to you, my love." He kissed her gently before saying, "You feel so thin, darling. Have you been eating properly?"

The honest answer was *No, I didn't have an appetite the entire time I was in New York trying to divorce my other husband.* She kissed his chin and said, "Kenny kept me busy, and let's face it, I'm not always that excited about his choice of menu."

He smiled and tightened his embrace. "So leaving Kenny was difficult?"

"It was torture, Chaz. He's still such a little boy, and no matter how much he and Zach get along without me, it's so very wrong of me to expect him to understand why I have to leave."

He stroked her face, a little lost in thought before asking, "So was Zach happy to see you?"

She rolled over, sitting beside him, and pulled her legs up in front of her, crossing her ankles and pressing her thighs to her chest. "I don't know if he was exactly *happy* to see me, but I'm sure he was glad to be a carefree bachelor again."

He studied her, and she knew that he was thinking something about Zach and that they were headed to that uncomfortable bit of conversation that she couldn't resolve to his satisfaction. She rested her chin on her knee and waited for him to speak.

"You know, I will never understand this *arrangement* you have with this man. Is he going to look after Kenny indefinitely? Like a foster parent or something?"

She hesitantly drawled, "Noooo. As I've explained before, Zach has known Kenny since we moved to New York. They have a special bond, and he loves him like a son."

"But Kenny's not his son."

"I know that, Chaz, and Zach knows it. It's just something that has evolved, and he's well equipped to give Kenny a place to live while he's looked after by his nanny and goes to school, which is only a couple of blocks away."

"Why don't you bring him to London. We do have schools in this country."

"I know, but I struggle with the idea of taking him away from the life he's comfortable with and dropping him in a completely different culture."

"It happens all the time, and the kids usually have a much easier time than the parents expect."

"I didn't know you were such an authority on the subject, and at the very least, I'd want to wait until the start of a new school year."

Chaz turned to face her and pushed himself up on one elbow. "Well, I can't argue with that logic, but I think we should do a little investigating. In fact, if you want to bring a real authority into the conversation, ask my sister. She makes anything to do with children her business and would be delighted to research and advise, I'm sure."

"That's not a bad idea." She kissed his hand and said, "Thanks. It's a tough situation, and I don't want to make matters worse. You know that having him around all the time would make you an instant father. Are you ready for that?"

He said nothing for a moment and then smiled at her and said, "Your son is my son. I'd like the chance to be a father to him as well. That is, if you think Zach will let him leave New York."

"Chaz, it's not up to Zach. Just remember that this is a temporary situation and that it is up to me as to when I'll uproot Kenny and subject him to a completely different life. I'm very grateful that I have someone like Zach to help us through this transition. At least I know he's in good hands and is happy. And anyway, Kenny's being here all the time will change our lives pretty dramatically."

"Don't forget that I'll be going back out to sea. Wouldn't you like to have him around when I'm away?"

"I hadn't really thought about that. But considering my work schedule and all, it might be more difficult for him."

"Well, think about it, and we don't have to rush anything." He sat up and held both her hands. "Besides, I intend to spoil you something chronic for the next few days. There'll be no time for anyone else, and that's a promise." He kissed her forehead. "In the meantime, let's get something to eat." He cupped her breasts with both hands, saying, "You really have lost weight. There's practically nothing left here."

She grimaced playfully. "There wasn't that much there to begin with."

He got up and went to the bathroom. The radiator clanged; the room was exceptionally warm. She was a little sweaty and smelled like sex, still so happy and in love. But she was also caught in the moment when Chaz had shown interest in having Kenny as part of their lives. What if she reversed the situation for Zach? What if she brought Kenny to live with her in London, thus nullifying Zach's claim that she'd deserted Kenny? Would he leave them alone and get on with his life, eventually accepting that their marriage and so-called life as a family was over?

Her next callback audition for *Jesus Christ Superstar* was in three days. Once she knew the outcome, she'd be able to work out the next visit to New York and time her communication with Zach accordingly. This plan of hers needed careful consideration, and she was determined to beat Zach at his own game.

So she'd tuck the letter to Chaz away for the time being. She'd speak with Nigella, learn about the options for school and match their circumstances to Kenny's. She'd promised to bring him over for a visit in the summer. That gave her plenty of time to organize a permanent move. Zach was forcing her to cut him out of their lives. But it was time for sober, realistic thinking about how Kenny could live with her in London. She needed to remain as calm and normal as possible. And she needed to understand exactly when Chaz would leave again and how long he'd be gone.

part four

chapter twenty-three

London, July 1973

Hassie held the phone away from her ear while Zach continued his rant. She'd just arrived home from the strangest day anyone working in the theater could imagine. She laid the receiver on the table while pouring a drink, took a sip and then picked up the phone and said, "Zach. You need to calm down."

"That's fucking well easy for you to say, Hassie. You're a million miles away, and I'm... stuck here running a home for wayward children. For Christ's sake, you need to get back here and sort this out."

"Okay, please calm down, and tell me exactly what happened."

"Exactly what happened is exactly what I told you could *not* happen. This indigent girl from Vegas showed up on my doorstep, complete with suitcases and a speech telling me that her Uncle Clay gave her this address. Is this where her half-brother, Kenny, lives? Dammit, Hassie! I thought you told Clay that we could not do this."

She took a big swig of the drink and said, "I never got a chance to speak with him about it. But I intimated in our last conversation—"

"*Intimated?* What about *our* last conversation about this didn't you get? And, more importantly, what are *you* gonna do about it?"

She had no idea what to do and was honestly more concerned that her career had just taken a cruel turn. She needed more time to process it all. She huffed and said, "Let me call Clay. He'll know what's going on. My guess is that he bought her a ticket—how did she get there?"

"On a bus. A friggin' Greyhound bus and then some asshole Good Samaritan took pity on her and brought her here in a taxi. Jesus."

Twice, Hassie had been a passenger on the silver behemoth. However, both times she'd been significantly older than Norma. And whether she liked it or not, she was actually now free to go over and handle the situation personally. She breathed deeply and said, "Okay."

"Okay, what?"

"I'll catch a flight and come over. I promise, you don't have to do anything except give me a little time and try not to traumatize the poor girl. Her mother died."

"What do you mean you'll come over? Aren't you still doing *Hair*?"

"I was until today."

"You get fired?"

"No. The roof collapsed on the theater last night. The show's on hold until further notice."

"Oh, crap. The roof collapsed? Are you okay? Was anyone hurt?"

"Thankfully, it happened overnight after everyone had gone home. We got called in today to a somber meeting with the producers. They have no choice. The theater's been shut down, and there's no idea when the show will reopen or *if* it will reopen."

"Sorry about that, but you had a pretty good run at it, didn't you?"

"A little over a year."

"I know, because you were supposed to take Kenny for a few weeks last summer and then reneged."

Her entire plan to bring Kenny to live with her in London and distance the two of them from Zach had gone on hold when she was cast in *Jesus Christ Superstar* and then in *Hair*. "I know, Zach. I'm a horrible mother, and you're a saint. But I'll be there within a day or so to deal with Norma. Can you please be civil to her until I get there?"

"Of course I'll be civil to her. It's Kenny who's not so thrilled with the situation."

It was a stinking hot July day, and Hassie just wanted to have a bath and drown her sorrows. "I'll sort out a flight and call you back."

"And give that jerk in Reno a call while you're at it. The nerve of him to just decide that the girl should come live here."

"Please don't take this out on Norma. She must be terrified."

He sniggered and said, "If you ask me, she's just a smartass kid who thinks somebody owes her something. And she's not the ideal influence for Kenny either."

"By the way, where is she sleeping?"

"I cleared out the back room and set up a cot I scrounged from a neighbor. It's delightful, and she's thrilled."

"Okay, I'm hanging up now. I'll call you back later."

Hassie topped up her drink, sat on the sofa and propped her feet on the coffee table. Man, oh man. Yesterday, she was happily and securely working in the ultra-successful production of *Hair*, dropping in at Ronnie Scott's when she had a chance and, generally, enjoying the life of a carefree performer. Chaz had been gone for months at a time over the past two and a half years that they'd been married. But they spoke once every two to three weeks and sent each other mushy love letters. So, basically, her existence was frozen in time—nothing accomplished where her bigamy status was concerned… and nothing accomplished with regard to Kenny. The guilt had consumed her, and at one point she'd decided to leave London and go back to New York. She'd even written a note to Chaz, confessing her sins so that he wouldn't come looking for her. But as much as that whole scenario would have hurt her, it would have hurt him more, and she loved him too much to make him another victim of her selfish wiles. He didn't deserve anything about what she'd done to him. And Kenny didn't deserve to have a mother who put everything else in the world above being at home with him. She simply had to fix the mess she'd made. At the very least, she would remain faithful to Chaz.

Early the next morning—she'd fallen asleep before she'd had a chance to focus on flights to New York—she made a strong cup of coffee and sat down to think. The phone rang. Had Zach stayed up half the night waiting to torment her? She answered with a defeated, "Hello."

"Hassie, it's your ace theatrical agent."

"Oh, hi, Mona. I guess you heard the news."

"Yes, my darling, a huge bit of bad luck. But. Never fear. I'm on the case, and you'll never believe it, but there was a call to recast a few roles in *Oh! Calcutta!* just two days ago. Of course, I didn't call you then because you were duly employed. Now? Well, they're interested to see you. Can you get over to the Royalty Theatre today?"

"Of course I can. Just tell me when and what to do. I'll be there."

She hung up the phone debating how to feel. First of all, in her mind, this was a sign that her career was the more important issue. She'd been known to handle worse situations with Zach and would figure this one out. She decided that she would go to the audition, wow them, and then tell them that she wasn't available for two weeks. If they really wanted her, they'd see this as a minor accommodation. First off, she needed to get the job. She probably needed more sleep—or more coffee—or both.

Mona told her to wear something that she could comfortably move around in. She'd be asked to sing, read and possibly work through a modern dance routine. It all sounded easy enough. She showed up at the Royalty Theatre a couple of hours later wearing black Lycra tights and a white cotton shirt, ballet flats and her hair in a ponytail. The theater was dark except for the stage and orchestra pit. Several people gathered on stage; someone spotted her and motioned her forward. A man swept past her, lightly bumping her, turned to her and said, "Sorry." He kept walking and then stopped and looked back at her. "Hassie?"

"Derek."

"What are you doing here?"

"I've come to audition. What are you doing here?"

He walked over and put his arm around her shoulder, hugging her. "I play rehearsal piano occasionally and got called in today to play for this audition." He watched her for a moment, smiled carefully and then said, "You do know what this show's about."

"I haven't seen it yet, but I know there's some nudity and—"

He laughed. "Uh, *some* nudity is an understatement. There's absolutely nothing left to the audience's imagination by the end of the first number."

"So? I just did about a year's worth of risqué in *Hair*."

"Honey, as someone says at the end, this show makes *Hair* look like *The Sound of Music*."

"So are you telling me I shouldn't be here? That I shouldn't do it?"

"I'm not saying that at all. I just wonder what your husband would say about his wife parading around in her birthday suit, night after night, while he's out on a big boat somewhere in the middle of the ocean. If it were me—and you being you—I wouldn't like it so much, and I'm a helluva lot more liberal-minded than he is."

"So you wouldn't let your wife do this show if she wanted to?"

"Thankfully, Judith has no interest in the theater other than watching it. But, no, I don't think I'd like her up there every night."

Hassie pulled her mouth into a straight line and looked around the stage. Derek held her arm and said, "Hey, it's none of my business what you do. You're an actress and a performer, and this show's hot right now. Do the audition, and then see what you think."

She nodded. "What should I sing?"

He chuckled. "They don't want to hear you sing. They want to see you move." He motioned to a skinny black guy with the biggest Afro she'd ever seen, who walked over and said, "Give us a few more minutes, Derek. We're waiting for Margo, and then we'll get started."

Derek held up a finger. "Is this going to be the standard audition?"

"Yep. Just play the opening as directed."

Derek crossed his arms over his chest, and Hassie asked, "What's the opening number?"

He looked at her. "You really should see this show before you decide you want to be in it."

"If I get offered the job and don't want to do it, I'll just turn it down."

"They're recasting three of the women and two of the men. Unless you fall down and break your leg, you're gonna get offered a part." He glanced at a few of the others waiting to audition and said, "I'd bet on it."

A woman wearing wide-striped bell-bottoms and a halter-top leapt on stage, clapped her hands three times and said, "Sorry to keep you waiting. Who's here to audition?"

Four women and six men raised their hands; she headed off stage saying, "Come with me."

* * *

Two hours later, Hassie walked out of the dressing room wondering what she'd just done. Derek was right. The director wasn't even there, and no one wanted to hear her sing. The woman, Margo, was the choreographer and one of the original cast members. She knew every move intimately and was mesmerizing to watch and work with. First off, the ten of them had been put in a dressing room and told to shed all their clothes and put on a long silky robe that was slit up both sides to the tops of their thighs and had no belt or tie of any sort. The women were thin but slightly curvy, and the men were muscular and fit. She was starting to get the picture and quickly got over the initial awkwardness.

They were then asked to form two lines parallel to the edge of the stage and to follow Margo's lead as Derek underscored. The dance moves weren't especially difficult, but, if done properly, the robe had a hard time staying on their naked bodies. They were each given a slightly different move to practice on their own, during which time Derek took a break. He moved away from the piano. Hassie twirled around. Her robe slid down her arms; she caught it at her waist, baring her breasts. She could feel Derek's eyes on her but avoided looking at him. There was something artistically thrilling about the freedom of expression that this dance evoked, and she somehow knew that the others felt it as well. After a few more minutes, Margo stopped them, asked Derek to play the number from the top and then walked them through the whole segment. They repeatedly performed the number so that Margo could focus on each of them. She then thanked them and said that someone would call them about the casting decision. They may need another callback, and those who were successful would need to start rehearsals immediately.

Hassie went back into the auditorium. Derek had gone. Margo sat in the front row of the audience, studying the headshots and talking to herself. She looked up as Hassie started down the steps from the stage, smiled and said, "It's Cassie, right?"

"Hassie. Hassie Calhoun."

Margo stood up, removing her oversized, black-framed glasses, and walked over to join her. "I know I said that someone would call you about the decision, but that's my way of not having to put anyone on the spot right here. I'd like you to join this cast, Hassie. It took you a little while to warm to the thought of what you were doing, but once you did, you had the look."

"The look?"

"It's hard to explain but easy to spot. Derek saw it as well."

Hassie's face flushed as she said, "So, this is a job offer?"

Margo nodded. "Our company manager will contact your agent and formalize the details, but, as far as I'm concerned, you're in."

"That's wonderful. But I may have a conflict with starting into rehearsals right away."

"Are you still in another show? Because if you are, your agent shouldn't have sent you, and you've wasted my time."

"No. It's a personal matter in the States. It would only take a couple of weeks—"

"Hassie, you have twenty-four hours to decide if you want to join this show. Please let me know your decision by this time tomorrow." She started to walk away and then turned back and said, "And if you take the job, you'll need to do a bit of *housekeeping* down there," she said as she pointed at Hassie's crotch.

By the time she got home it was going on noon in New York and although Zach should have been at work in his office, she expected the phone would be ringing when she walked through the door. She made a cup of tea and paced around the lounge and dining area, thinking of what Derek had said about how Chaz would feel about her doing something like this—what was it he'd said? *Parading around in her birthday suit?* They'd made a pact in the early days of their marriage never to succumb to the urge to doubt each other's fidelity. Their marriage was based on trust, and they were both intelligent enough to know that doubt and suspicion would tear them apart.

And then she thought about how comfortable she'd actually been on that stage knowing that Derek was watching her and imagined what it might feel like to have hundreds of eyes on her every night. And then reality slapped her in the face, and she remembered the predicament that Norma—actually, Clay had caused and her promise to Zach to sort it all out.

After a light supper of cold roast beef and salad, she took her third glass of wine and pulled the telephone over to the coffee table. It wasn't like Clay to do something like this without any warning. Maybe he didn't know how to reach her in London, but he certainly knew how to reach her through Zach in New York. She reached for the phone to call Clay just as it rang. She answered the call.

"Were you ever going to call me again?"

She rested her elbows on her knees and stared at the floor as she said, "Zach, I was just getting ready to call Clay."

"You were supposed to call me back last night. Or at least this morning. Why I am having to chase you, Hassie? Have you booked your flight?"

"Not yet. And before you go off like a lunatic, I have something else to tell you."

"What? And this better be good news for me."

"I got offered another job."

"In another show?"

"Yes. It's a good role and something I really want to do."

He was quiet for a moment and then calmly said, "Do you hear yourself? *I* got offered a job and it's something *I* really want to do. What about the rest of us? *I* was really hopeful that you were going to do the right thing this time, but I guess *I* was wrong."

"That's why I wanted to speak with Clay before I called you. He shouldn't have sent Norma to you without letting us know. It's not like him to do something like this, and I'm sure that he'll fix it once he knows the problem it's caused."

238

"So once again, you expect everyone else to deal with your problems."

"Zach, Norma is *not* my problem. I didn't give birth to her nor did I dump her on someone else to take care of. Clay's her uncle, for Christ's sake. I don't know why he decided that she should live with us—you, Kenny, whatever."

"Okay, then call him. But I really think you should come back to New York for a few weeks. Kenny hasn't seen you for months and now all this confusion is not good for any of us. Norma is obviously mad at the world, and her attitude is unhealthy for him."

"How so?"

"I heard her telling him that his mother obviously lives in another country to get away from him."

"Oh, God."

"Now do you understand the urgency here? You have enough problems with Kenny without his being poisoned by a punk bit of trailer trash."

She breathed deeply and then said, "Let me speak to Clay. I'll call you back."

chapter **twenty-four**

New York City, July 1973

From the bedroom, Hassie heard shouting, which she intended to ignore, and then the door to Kenny's room slammed shut with such ferocity she had to join the fray. She slipped a short cotton robe over her T-shirt and underwear, slid her feet into furry slippers and walked into the living room. Zach rested his butt against the edge of the desk, his arms folded across his chest, staring out into space. Norma sat slumped on the sofa.

"What's going on in here?" Hassie asked.

"Kenny's upset," Zach said.

"Yeah, I heard. In fact, the entire building heard."

Norma didn't look at either of them but said, "I know you people don't want me here. And I don't really care. I'm used to taking care of myself, and if I have to, I can live on the street." The girl was a mess. She was somewhere around twelve years old but was dressed and made up to look several years older. She was tall for her age with full hips and heavy thighs, which gave her a woman's curvy figure. Her chest was hidden under a rough black leather jacket. She wore tattered jeans and thick, clunky boots.

Hassie stood at the end of the sofa, waited a moment and then said, "I was a little jet-lagged last night when you all were telling me about how Norma got here, so please bear with me." She looked at

240

Norma. "I spoke to your Uncle Clay who said that he not only didn't buy your bus ticket, he didn't even know you're here."

"So? Who said he did?"

"Who's your guardian since your mother died?" Hassie asked.

"I don't have one."

"I doubt that's true, Norma. You're a minor, and your mother didn't die suddenly, so who did she intend to take care of you?"

"My grandmother."

"Your mother's mother?" Norma nodded, and Hassie continued, "So where does your grandmother think you are right now?"

"She doesn't care. She's dead."

Zach shifted his weight in his chair and said, "Your grandmother died *after* your mother died?"

"Are you people dense or do you just not understand English too good?"

Hassie sat at the end of the sofa, taking in the bizarre details and then said, "You have to admit that this whole situation is a little unusual. I think we're due a proper explanation, and if you're going to stay here—even temporarily—you need to respect the rest of this family. And that includes Kenny. In fact, you should respect him most of all. He's your own flesh and blood. The two of you have something in common, and you should appreciate that and embrace it."

"We have a dead father in common. Whoop-de-doo."

"What's wrong with Kenny?" Hassie asked.

"He just needs some space," Zach said.

"He's nine years old, Zach. I don't think he understands what *space* is."

Norma sniggered and said, "He's pissed off because he's had to share his precious life with me. He's a real little douchebag, you know. I would say a *momma's boy*, but then his momma doesn't even live here. So I guess he's *Uncle Zach's* boy. Pathetic."

Zach looked ready to unload on her as Hassie moved to the edge of her seat and said, "You know, I knew your mother."

"So?"

"So you're a lot like her."

"And?"

"And that's not such a good thing in my book."

Zach moved uneasily, and Hassie caught his eye while Norma pushed herself upright in the seat. "You got no right to talk bad about my mother."

"And you have no right to talk bad about my son." Norma fidgeted, and Hassie continued, "The way I see it, you're pretty damn lucky to even know Kenny let alone be related to him. But if you think it wise to antagonize and alienate him, then I'd say it's no great loss to him. He has a family who loves and takes care of him. So, regardless of your opinion of me, it seems that you would be a little more gracious about the living circumstances, considering that you just showed up unannounced, uninvited and probably missing in action from some welfare agency." Hassie stood and walked toward the windows and then turned to face Norma as she said, "In fact, why did you come here? What did you expect would happen?"

"Hassie," Zach said.

"No, I'm curious about this now. You said that, before she died, your mother told you that you have a half-brother and that you found some letters between her and your Uncle Clay telling her who that half-brother is, where he lives—the whole nine yards. So you took some money that your mother left and bought a bus ticket, turned up on perfect strangers' doorstep and announced that you needed a place to live. Is that correct?"

Norma narrowed her eyes, sneering at Hassie and finally said, "Like I said. I can take care of myself. So don't knock yourself out on my account." She stood up.

Hassie walked to the door and opened it. "Then it was nice to meet you. Good luck." Hassie looked at Zach, whose expression was one of either shock or pleasure. After all he'd said while coercing her to come back to deal with the situation, why was he now just sitting there like a knot on a log? Hassie stood at the open door, watching Norma, who looked at Zach and said, "I guess I'll get my things."

Zach nodded. "If you need help, let us know."

She left the room, and Hassie shut the door. She looked at Zach and asked, "Where were you during all of that? Where's all the anger and swearing and abuse you hurled at me over the telephone?"

"You were doing such a good job of humiliating her, I didn't feel the need to chime in."

"Zach, what do you want from me? Now that we know that Clay had nothing to do with this decision of Norma's to join this family, I can't really expect him to sort it out, can I? I assumed you wanted me to get rid of her."

He rolled his eyes and shook his head and then softly asked, "Did you take the part in the new show?"

"No."

"Just—no?"

"No, I didn't take the part. If I had, I wouldn't be here right now."

"Well, then I'm sorry."

"Sorry about what?"

"That you gave up an opportunity to work. Did you definitely have the job?"

She nodded. "If I'd accepted, I had to start right away, and they didn't want to hear about personal problems in New York."

"Does that mean you're back to stay?"

She actually didn't know what it meant. "I haven't had time to think about it. You insisted that I sort out this problem with Norma, and that's what I came to do."

"But you're telling me that you don't have a job in London now, which, according to my latest information, is why you've been living there. If you don't have a job, then why don't you do what you've been promising to do for months—make that years now, and come home?"

"Because I still don't have any confidence that I can work in New York. And, by the way, we still don't have a marriage, and we still need to get divorced."

"But you still have a son. A son that misses you so much, mentioning your name still hurts him."

"Then maybe he should go back to London with me."

"Now? You'd just jerk him away from his life here?"

"Which way do you want it, Zach? Do you want me to have him with me or not? And, anyway, taking him away from New York would negate the notion that Norma belongs here with her half-brother."

Zach's focus was drawn to the hallway. Norma walked into the room having removed her leather jacket and wearing a faded black T-shirt. She stood quietly; Hassie and Zach watched her. She took a couple of steps closer and mumbled, "I'm sorry."

Hassie looked at Zach from the corner of her eye and then asked, "What was that?"

Norma looked up. "I said, I'm sorry. I didn't mean to be disrespectful."

"So what do you mean to do, Norma?" Hassie asked.

"I don't have anywhere else to go."

Zach gave it a moment and then asked, "What about your Uncle Clay?"

"I don't know him."

"You didn't know us," Hassie said.

She stared at the floor. "I wanna know Kenny."

Hassie looked at Zach who seemed more annoyed than before and then said, "From what I hear, you haven't been very nice to him."

Norma nodded. "I know."

"First of all, we need the truth about where you're supposed to be right now. And *if* we let you stay," Hassie said, "You'll respect whatever Zach says, and you'll do your fair share of keeping the house tidy, and you'll apologize to Kenny, and you'll—"

"I'll do whatever you tell me to do. Just don't kick me out."

Hassie sent Norma to have a bath with instructions to wash her hair and scrub her face and then went to check on Kenny. He was watching television and didn't look up when she said, "Hey, you hungry?"

He shook his head and asked, "Is *she* in there?"

"No. Come talk to me and Uncle Zach for a minute."

"Is she gonna stay here?"

"Maybe."

"Why?"

"Because she doesn't have any parents. You—we—are the only family she has."

"Because her father and my father are the same guy?"

Hassie nodded.

"So did she know him?"

"I think a little bit. But she was pretty young when he died. So I doubt she remembers him." Hassie walked over to sit beside him, put her arm around his shoulder and said, "Isn't it kinda cool that you have a sister?"

He shrugged, looked at her and asked, "Are you gonna stay home now?"

Hassie hugged him. "I'm thinking about it."

"Really?"

She smiled. His vulnerability tugged at her heart, reminding her that she locked up her feelings when she was away from Kenny—a protectionist mode she'd adapted in the early days. She still hated her own mother for choosing a man over what was best for her children. How could she have allowed herself to do something much worse where her own child was concerned? She breathed deeply and said, "If I have to go back to England for a little while, would you like to come with me?"

"Is *she* gonna come?"

"No. Just you and me. I promise."

Hassie went back to talk to Zach, who sat waiting for her and asked, "So what did we accomplish here?"

"I'm not sure."

He took a deep, noisy breath and said, "I can't do this, Hassie."

"Do what?"

"Raise another kid while you live your own life thousands of miles away and phone in every so often."

She sat down. "You know you can get out of this."

"Get out of what?"

"Any responsibility to me, Kenny and certainly to Norma."

"You can't put Norma in this equation. And for the fiftieth time, I don't want a divorce. You're my wife, and Kenny is my son. I'm sorry.

That's the way I see it, and that's the way I feel. And I know you're not stupid enough to argue against the fact that I have a stronger, more significant place in Kenny's life than you do right now."

"I wouldn't be so sure about that if I were you."

He looked like he might break down. "Hassie, he's *your* kid. I have no delusions that I can take your place, nor am I interested in doing so. I've simply been the surrogate parent while you've... been away."

"Zach, you're more than a surrogate parent, and you know it. But maybe it's time for Kenny to live with me."

"In London?"

"Maybe. Or maybe I'll come back to New York. But, Zach, I'll only do one or the other if we get a divorce. Think about Kenny. Think about what's best for him. And if you want Norma to leave, then she'll leave."

His eyes were those of someone who'd been defeated. She smiled gently and said, "Here's what I think we should do. I'll call Clay and tell him all that's happened. If Norma truly doesn't have an option outside of government welfare, maybe he and his wife wouldn't mind taking in his brother's daughter. They don't have children and—I don't know—maybe that would work. And then I'll take Kenny to London with me. I've checked out schools for him, and I think it's time he and I have some time in my world. It's not a bad place or a bad idea. Actually, I think it'd be great for him, and I'd love it. That means you can have your life back—a clean slate. Do whatever you want to do with no encumbrance from anyone. I'm sure if you give it a chance, you'll find someone over the age of nine that you want to spend time with. And then I'm sure you'll do the sensible thing and let us both get on with our lives."

He became very emotional and didn't look at her. She waited, not interested in pushing him but determined she'd offered a reasonable solution. Chaz had encouraged her to bring Kenny into their lives, and she had no reason to believe that he hadn't meant what he'd said. But at this moment, her concern wasn't for Chaz or Zach or the fact that she was a bigamist and had made a mess of her life. Her concern was for

Kenny and how she could begin to rectify the near mess she'd made of his life before it was too late. The issue with Norma was another story.

She heard someone in the kitchen and said, "Think about it. I'll be right back." Kenny stood with the fridge door open, peering inside. Hassie walked closer and said, "I thought you weren't hungry."

He shrugged, looked at her and asked, "Can you make me French toast?"

She smiled. "Of course I can."

"Do they have French toast in England?"

"I'm pretty sure they do."

"Cool. Can I have grape jelly on it?"

"If that's what you want."

He didn't look at her and left the room.

She took milk and eggs from the fridge and closed the door. Zach approached the doorway and said, "There's a call for you—somebody named Mona?"

Hassie laid everything on the counter and hurried to the phone. "Mona. What's up?"

"Have you finished your business in New York?"

"I think so. Why?"

"I had a call from the company manager at *Oh! Calcutta!*. They still want you to join the cast. When can you get back to London?"

"When do they need me?"

"Yesterday."

"Okay. Leave it with me for a little while. I'll get back to you."

She hung up the phone and turned to see Zach standing on the other side of the room, his arms folded across his chest with a benign expression that she knew very well.

"So you got the job after all," he said.

She nodded.

"Still want Kenny to move to London with you?"

"Of course I do." She paced the space in front of the coffee table. "It won't be easy, but I'll figure something out."

Zach walked toward her and said, "Kenny belongs here. If you let him stay, I'll let Norma stay as well."

"What does that mean?"

"It means... it means that I'm feeling sorry for Norma now. Like you've said repeatedly, this situation isn't her fault. But I'll only let her stay if Kenny stays here as well."

Hassie sat down, feigning concern over a hangnail. Zach was a master manipulator where her life was concerned, and this was a big issue. If she took Kenny to London, she'd basically be throwing Norma out into the big, bad world. Of course, Zach knew this, and he was betting that she was more concerned about her career in London than her responsibility to her son or Norma. And why shouldn't he? She looked up at him, took a couple of shallow breaths and said, "I think Kenny should come back with me. Like I said, I'll call Clay and plead with him to take Norma in. After all, as best I know, he's her next of kin, and we all need to address the issue of legal guardianship."

Zach sat down beside her. Neither spoke for a long moment. He finally put his hand on her leg and said, "Can you really see Kenny in your life in London? Won't he cramp your style?"

She took hold of his hand. "I know you love him, and it's generous and unselfish of you to agree to take care of both him and Norma—especially after you swore that the latter could never happen."

"Yeah, well, if you won't live here with us, I'd still like to try to keep the family together."

"It probably is the best thing for Kenny. At least until I sort out the routine of working in *Oh! Calcutta!*."

"Then consider that you'd be doing the best thing for these kids. But you gotta drop the issue of divorce—if you want me to leave you alone while you carry on with your life in London, you'll leave things just the way they are."

She pulled away from him, shaking her head as she said, "I should've known that this wasn't about Kenny or Norma or even me. It's about you and your sick determination to live in this—I can't even say the word."

"What? Marriage? You can't say *marriage*? Because, Hassie, my love, we're still very much married, and if you think differently, you've made an astounding error in judgment."

248

She stood up, turned toward the hallway and shouted, "Kenny? Sweetie, come here, please."

"Don't be so dramatic, Hass. We both know that Kenny's not going anywhere."

chapter twenty-five

London, July 1974

⬤   In the year since Hassie left Norma to settle into the apartment in New York with Zach and Kenny, she'd spent ten months in the production of *Oh! Calcutta!*, jetting off a couple of times to New York and taking time after she left the production to have a holiday with Chaz in Bali. Of course, Zach had accused her of forcing the brief visits with Kenny and then spending the bulk of the time she was in New York working with Ruben. But Kenny and Norma had learned to like each other's company, and Hassie bribed Kenny with an impending trip to London. Now she was unemployed—except for the occasional gig at Ronnie Scott's—and Chaz was out at sea. The kids were on summer vacation, and Zach had been the one to suggest—rather forcefully—that it was time for Kenny to make that visit Hassie had promised.

    The morning after Kenny arrived, Hassie lay in bed with her eyes closed in that unidentifiable place between dreams and reality, her last conversation with Chaz cradling her thoughts while the space beside her remained empty. She burrowed deeper under the duvet, listening for signs that Kenny was awake, though she hoped he'd sleep late into the morning. He'd been a cranky little malcontent from the moment they landed at Heathrow, tired and fussy from the flight, and the long taxi ride to St. John's Wood hadn't helped. He seemed to have grown overnight from the slight, sensitive child to a ten-year-old, solid, clever, spitting image of his father, which she'd previously recognized and prayed he'd outgrow.

However. According to Zach, Kenny was regularly called out for misbehaving in school—everything from hurling racial slurs to taunting the girls. His grades were better than average, but his teachers knew that he barely applied himself. He breezed along, doing well enough to keep everyone off his back academically, but fell short socially. As Zach boiled it down, Kenny didn't really give a shit. The thought that the Jake Contrata gene could be taking hold made her squirm. She threw the duvet to the vacant side of the bed and sat up.

Zach had also expressed concern that Norma's attitude and undisciplined approach to things was a bad influence on Kenny and that Hassie should be a little tough on him while she was in control. Despite her worries that Jake's personality might be rearing its head, Hassie chose to believe that Kenny was just being a prepubescent boy. And she was determined to let him be that little boy on vacation while they were together, having promised him rides on double-decker buses and fish and chips and soldiers in bearskin hats while educating him on London's great history and culture. If he fell in love with the city, it would be that much easier to talk him into a permanent move—whenever that time came.

She grabbed Uncle Teddy's dressing gown and padded into the kitchen, turned on the kettle and took the jar of Nescafé from the cupboard. July was a lovely time in this part of London—the density of birds in the gardens of St. John's Wood Church seemed to overpower the leafy green bushes and trees. She'd spent hours crossing Primrose Hill on her way to Regent's Park, which reminded her of similar walks through Central Park in New York with so many of the same sights—dog owners walking their pets (or vice versa), families or nannies out with children, joggers, the elderly, the infirm. The soundtrack was the same, only with different accents. Would Kenny like the idea of calling her *Mummy*, and would Chaz eventually become another *uncle*?

Hassie took her coffee into the lounge just as the phone rang. She hoped for a call from Chaz.

"Hello," she said, cheerily.

"Hassie, it's Gwendolyn."

"Oh, hello. It's nice to—"

"I understand that your son is coming to visit."

She'd give anything if Chaz hadn't told his mother that she had a son, which had evoked a nosey barrage of questions at one of their insufferable dinners. "Yes. He arrived yesterday," she said.

"I see." There was a long pause, and Hassie wondered if Gwen had hung up or possibly fainted. "I would like to invite the two of you to visit me in Brighton. The boy would have a jolly good time at the shore and on the pier. I think he should see this part of England whilst he's here."

"That's very kind of you, Gwen. *The boy's* name is Kenny, and I'm sure he'd be delighted to meet his—you." She'd considered saying grandmother and then thought better of it, knowing how Gwen felt about being related to her. Besides, Gwen barely tolerated being a grandmother to her own grandchildren.

"Do you have a specific day and time in mind?" Gwen asked.

"Well, no. Is there a time that you would prefer we make the visit—that is, if we can work it out?"

"How long is the boy going to be here?"

Hassie sighed. "Kenny will be here for a little over two weeks and then I'll take him back to New York."

"I see." Gwen had a habit of sucking her teeth when she was thinking, which was another thing that drove Hassie crazy when she had to deal with the woman. Gwen finally sighed and said, "Well then, might I suggest that you come down on the Friday before you leave for New York? Plan to stay the night."

Hassie strongly suspected that the only reason they'd been invited was due to some guilt-ridden coaxing from Chaz. But at the moment, Kenny could know nothing about Gwen or any other member of Charles's family. She'd play along for now and then gracefully bow out closer to the time. "As I said, I'll have a look at our schedule and get back to you to confirm."

There was another bit of teeth sucking until Gwen said, "Don't keep it too late, dear. I'm quite a busy woman, you know."

"Yes, of course."

Hassie hung up, thinking that it would be nice if just once Gwen had something positive to say to her. She turned back to the sofa to see Kenny standing in the hallway at the edge of the room. She walked over to him and said, "Good morning, sweetie." She hugged him. "Did you sleep well?"

He shrugged. "I'm hungry."

She guided him toward the kitchen. "We're gonna have a fun breakfast." She poured orange juice for him and took two eggs from the fridge. Kenny watched her and asked, "Can I have some cereal?"

"You can, but I want to make you something that we like to eat in London." He frowned and slurped the juice. She took a loaf of bread from the cupboard and filled a small pot with water. "You know how you like to eat those fried eggs that Uncle Zach makes for you?"

He nodded. "The ones with the runny yellow?"

"That's it. Give me a few minutes to cook and then we'll sit down together."

He ran off to the bathroom, and the pot containing the eggs started to boil. She set the poseur table for the two of them, dropped two pieces of bread in the toaster and then waited for the egg timer to ring. Kenny climbed up on a stool and watched as Hassie set a plate containing an egg in a cup in front of each of them. "Mom, you didn't take the shell part off."

"I know. Just wait. I'm going to show you how to eat this." She'd cut the pieces of toast into thin strips and placed them on a plate between them. She then cut the top off the egg in his cup and said, "See. Here's that yummy yolk you like." She took a piece of the toast, dipped it in the egg and held out it to him saying, "It's called boiled egg and soldiers. You dip the toast in the yolk and take a bite and then dip again until all the yolk is gone. Then you can eat the rest of the egg with this little spoon."

He looked at the yellow-tipped piece of toast and then took it from her and bit off the yolk-soaked end. He dipped the toast again and then again and she asked, "Do you like it?"

He nodded, took the last bite and asked, "Can I have another one?"

She cut the top off the second egg and put it front of him. If only everything new and different for him in this country could be so easy.

* * *

So Hassie's two lives had become her normal existence. For one thing, it seemed to work. Though Zach insisted on moaning about it, she believed that he was actually enjoying having Kenny and Norma to look after, and the fact that she'd been busy in London had kept her away from that scene. And whether Chaz was there or not, her life was about working. She'd achieved reasonable success in the West End and had become an occasional headliner at Ronnie Scott's. She'd yet to land that leading role—though she'd gotten close a couple of times and had understudied a few, including *Jesus Christ Superstar*, for which she received high praise. Then she had the longish run in *Oh! Calcutta!*, which had been great fun but had come close to driving a nasty wedge between her and Chaz. She didn't tell him much about the show for a while until he announced he'd be home for a short break and, of course, wanted to see it. Since Derek and Judith had married, as far as Chaz was concerned, Hassie could spend as much time with Derek as she liked. So Hassie asked Derek and Judith to go with Chaz to see the show, during which time Derek explained that Hassie had quite a stern reputation for being totally professional and completely untouchable as far as the rest of the cast were concerned. She never really knew if Chaz believed Derek, but after a mild rant about the nudity Chaz simply thought the show was silly, and his only real concern was that his mother never found out about that one.

So this was the first time that her two lives had overlapped. Kenny's presence meant that New York had come to London. Of course, he was too young to have any curiosity about how she lived in this nicely fitted out flat and so far, she'd had reasonable answers to all his questions about her life in this foreign country. She kept him so busy with bus rides and sightseeing and a cruise on the River Thames that he fell asleep early and slept late, which gave her time to recharge and reflect on what might happen next.

First and foremost, she could not take Kenny to visit Chaz's mother. She'd phoned Gwen a couple of days after her gratuitous invitation and concocted some story about being unable to get away from London after all. She'd probably regret that decision the rest of her life, but such a meeting could not take place. However, ten days into his stay, and with less than a week left, Hassie realized that she'd forgotten how active a kid Kenny's age needed to be, which meant they'd worked through her agenda faster than she'd expected. So she considered taking Kenny to the East Sussex coast on that last weekend and, if the weather cooperated, spend a couple of days outdoors. She'd run him ragged on the rocky shores and the steep, grassy downs and then stuff him with fish and chips and all the sugary sweets he could stand while he buried himself in the arcade games on the grand pier in Brighton.

Hassie carefully considered how they would show up in Rottingdean and remain incognito while in the area. After Beethoven, the cat, died, Beryl semi-retired and basically lived up north with her sister. Charles asked her to look in on the house once a month, and so Beryl tended to stay there during the last week of the month. Thus, Hassie deduced that the house would be empty on the coming weekend, and she couldn't imagine that Gwen would be anywhere near the attractions that would most interest Kenny. It was a calculated risk, but one Hassie thought worth taking.

Friday morning, they took the train to Brighton and then a taxi over to the house in Rottingdean. It was a mild, sunny day. The taxi driver set their bags on the front stoop. Kenny hung back like he'd been faced with entering a creepy, haunted mansion.

"Come on, sweetie," she said, motioning him to follow her. "Let's get settled in and then we'll have some lunch."

He hesitantly joined her on the porch and then asked, "Mom, whose house is this?"

"It belonged to Aunt Barbara—remember, my teacher from Texas who died a few years ago?"

He bobbled his head as if to say *I guess so.*

"Now it belongs to her family."

He looked around the porch and then softly said, "It's kinda old."

She unlocked the front door. "Uh, huh. Remember how we talked about how old the entire country of England is and how—?"

"Oh, Miss 'assie. You gave me such a fright!"

"Beryl, I'm so sorry. I didn't think you'd be here this weekend."

She stood in the entrance to the lounge with her arms akimbo studying Kenny as she said, "Family wedding changed my schedule this month, dear. And who's this 'andsome fella?"

Hassie put her arm around Kenny's shoulder, moving him deeper into the room. "This is Kenny." She looked at him and said, "Kenny, say hello to Miss Beryl."

Kenny stood silent and fluttered his fingers.

Beryl approached them, focusing on him and said, "Is this the lit'le lad you spoke about with Missus C?"

Hassie nodded and smiled uncomfortably.

"Well, I reckon you're a might peckish after that journey from London." She reached out to him. "Come with me to the kitchen, poppet, and we'll find ya somethin' to eat."

Kenny hesitated; Hassie gently pushed him forward while saying, "Go with Beryl while I unpack our bags. She has the best goodies you'll ever see."

Kenny looked up at her and then reluctantly followed Beryl. How was she going to handle the situation now that they were stuck with Beryl? Her first instinct was to tell Beryl the truth—that they'd turned down Gwen's invitation and that she couldn't know that they'd made the trip. But Hassie had never been sure about Beryl's allegiance to Gwen. When she joined them in the kitchen, Kenny sat perched on a stool next to the counter. Beryl had given him a small square cake with chocolate icing.

"You're going to turn into a sack of sugar," Hassie said, gently hugging him. She then looked at Beryl and said, "How about one of your delicious meat and potato pies?"

"Ah was just thinking 'bout that. Maybe a nice cot'age pie with a lit'le extra cheese?"

"Sounds wonderful," Hassie said. "But please don't go to too much trouble, Beryl. I have lots of plans for Kenny this weekend, and you're not meant to be a slave to us."

"Never you mind, Miss 'assie. It's been ever such a long time since I had a lit'le one to look after."

Later that afternoon, Kenny nestled into the big sofa in the study and fell asleep. Hassie found Beryl in the garden and asked if they could have tea. She sat at the kitchen table, mulling over the various bits of conversation that had crossed her mind since they'd arrived. When Beryl brought the teapot to the table, Hassie asked, "How've you been, Beryl?"

"All right, I s'pose," she said as she sat. "'ow's Mister Charles and where's 'e now?"

"Finishing up a tour somewhere out in the Indian Ocean. I haven't spoken with him in a couple of weeks, but his letters sound the same— he's ready to come back to London. Ready for a change of scenery."

"Hmmm. I bet 'e misses ya somethin' rotten." She smiled while pouring the tea. "And now with this lit'le fella. Does he feel like he's got his own lit'le son?"

"He hasn't actually met Kenny yet." She waited for some sort of reaction and then continued, "Beryl, would you think it strange if I asked you not to tell Gwendolyn or Nigella that Kenny and I were here this weekend?"

Beryl peered up from her teacup. "You never did warm to the old missus, did ya?"

"It's more that she never warmed to me. She phoned me a couple of weeks ago and invited us to visit her this weekend. But the invitation was forced and insincere. I'm sure Charles was behind it, and honestly, I don't think I could have stood two days in her presence, never mind subjecting my son to her. Do you understand?"

"Course I do. And I can see no reason to say a word. Just enjoy the visit with your boy. He's a gorgeous lit'le thing."

Hassie placed her hand on top of Beryl's and said, "Thank you. And thank you for looking after us. But please don't spoil Kenny. He's got to go back to real life in New York next week, and I know what you're like."

Beryl smiled. "'ave a good time, and let me know when you need somethin'." She stood up from the table and took the teapot to the sink. Hassie took her cup into the garden for a bit of quiet time while Kenny napped. Once again, she was hit square in the face with her dual-life dilemma and was already worried about what Kenny would tell Zach and Norma about this house she'd taken him to with this odd little woman fussing over him. She moved around the grassy yard, surveying the various beds of flowers and bushes, which reminded her of the garden in Texas that Barbara had always tended like the plants were her precious pets. Here, spiky white flowers blossomed on dense, leafy shrubs while a tiny, blue flower pushed from the earth surrounding a slight, elegant tree. She smelled magnolia and something a little more pungent and missed Barbara and Chaz all at once. This was the life she loved. This was where she belonged.

Saturday was a gloriously sunny day by the sea, and Kenny ran along the shore and chased after the diving gulls, guided by the wind and drawn in by the sea. The more swept up he became with the sights and sounds, the happier Hassie was they'd made the trip. Sunday saw a bit of cloud cover, which meant cooler temperatures. Hassie felt that Kenny had had enough of the sea but loved the fact that he took to the various aspects of the countryside like the proverbial duck to water. They had one of Beryl's great "fry-ups" for breakfast and then set out to hike up the South Downs Way—a national park that Chaz had introduced Hassie to.

"Are you warm enough?" she asked Kenny as she wrapped the woolen scarf they'd borrowed from Beryl around his neck.

"Yes, Mom. It's summer." He pulled the scarf away from his neck and trudged up a hill to an open field that actually took her breath away. He threw the scarf on the ground and took off running, spreading his arms like the wings of a great bird, the wind against his face while the sun struggled to peek through the clouds. Hassie watched him, momentarily sensing the grassy plains outside of Vegas, and as Kenny ran toward her, she saw the little boy back in Reno who never left her sight and loved life with his Uncle Clay in his great ranchero spread. When she thought about it, it would be a slight miracle for her son to grow up unscathed by the life she'd subjected him to. But then she'd believed for a long time that being *normal* was overrated and that he'd lived a much more interesting life than many of his friends. Was this a bit of guilt-ridden rationale? Probably. But he was happy in the moment, and that was more than she'd witnessed or been party to in an entire year.

As Kenny neared her, she called out, "I think we should move on."

His cheeks were rosy red, his thick, dark eyelashes fluttering against the wind. "Can we go back to the pier now?"

"The pier? I thought you played every arcade game a dozen times last night." She held his head and ran her fingers through his tussled hair.

"I just wanna go back. Pleeease."

She pulled him close to her body and held him tight. This visit had brought new meaning to her role as Kenny's mother. She was glad that she was going back to New York with him. She also knew that this time, she wouldn't be able to leave him behind.

chapter twenty-six

Charles's ship had been stationed in the Arabian Sea not far off the coast of India when the call came in from Nigella. He'd immediately assumed something had happened to his mother and was relieved to hear that all was well in Brighton and that the urgent business was to do with Hassie. Evidently—and unbeknownst to Gwen or Nigella—she'd taken her son to stay in Rottingdean the weekend before. And, most probably unbeknownst to Hassie, dear old Beryl had taken it upon herself to inform Gwen that not only had Hassie visited the coastal region with her son, the charming little boy had delighted in telling Beryl about his *stepfather*—the man in New York that was married to his mother. In a little over twenty-four hours, Hassie and Kenny would be on a flight back to New York. Charles reported a family emergency and arrived in London earlier that morning. And now he was in a taxi on the way to his flat in St. John's Wood, where he'd make sure she got on that airplane and left his life for good.

The taxi turned into St. John's Wood High Street, and Charles debated the wisdom of springing himself on Hassie by simply walking into the apartment. Considering that the boy was likely to be there with her, he decided to do the more civilized thing and announce his arrival. He rang the flat from the building entrance. She answered cheerfully and his heart sank. "Hassie, it's Charles. Please let me in."

The intercom buzzed, unlatching the front door lock. Hassie said nothing. His habit was to take the stairs to the second floor. As he rounded the corner at the end of the corridor opposite his flat, he spotted her standing just outside the open door. She appeared terrified, barely able to smile. He approached the door, consciously avoiding eye contact as she said, "Darling, I didn't know you were coming home today." She reached out to him, but he brushed past her and entered the flat.

A small boy sat on a stool at the poseur table, wearing shorts and a Derby County football jersey. He looked over at Charles who smiled and said, "You must be Kenny."

The boy nodded. Charles laid his cap on the other side of the table and placed his uniform jacket around the back of one of the other stools as Hassie said, "Can I get you a cup of coffee?"

"Yes, please." He stayed focused on Kenny. "That breakfast looks mighty good."

Kenny nodded and stuffed another piece of toast in his mouth as he asked, "Have you ever had eggs and soldiers?"

"I most certainly have. I'd say it's one of my most favorite things."

Kenny grinned, and Hassie returned from the kitchen with a mug of coffee. As he reached to take it from her, the buzzer rang, and Charles walked toward the intercom saying, "That'll be Nigella. She's come to take Kenny to the zoo so that we can have a chat."

A minute or so later, Charles stood in the dining area alone with Hassie, having sent Nigella off with Kenny and two of his nieces, Karina and Molly. He said very little to Nigella but knew that she understood the urgency of his being left alone to speak with his wife.

Charles took the coffee over to sit in his leather armchair as he said, "We need to talk."

Hassie stood at the table and asked, "Can I get you something to eat?"

He shook his head. "Sit down."

She sat on the edge of the sofa, holding her coffee cup with both hands. "I had no idea that we'd get to see you." She took a clasp out of her hair and let it fall to her shoulders as she said, "I wish I'd known you were coming. I must look—"

"Hassie, be quiet."

She set the cup on the table and pushed back in the seat. He still hadn't made direct eye contact, which was the best way he knew to keep his temper intact. He finally looked at her and asked, "Did you and Kenny enjoy your weekend in Brighton?"

He watched her as she physically faltered but then somehow managed to remain calm as she said, "Yes, we did. It was a last-minute decision. Kenny was getting bored with London. He loved the sea and the food and the games on the pier, and he ate so much sugar. Beryl was there, spoiling him."

Charles held up his hand to stop her talking, stared at her with a bleak expression of disgust and then said, "My mother was very disappointed that you didn't take Kenny 'round to see her. Especially after she'd invited you to spend a couple of days with her and let *her* spoil Kenny."

"I'm sorry, darling. I shouldn't have declined Gwen's invitation, but you know how much she dislikes me. I didn't think it would be a healthy or fun atmosphere for Kenny. But I'm sorry if I upset her. I'll try to make it up to her." She appeared to perk up a bit and moved to the edge of her seat. "Are you sure I can't get something for you?" she asked. "A piece of toast? Or maybe you need something more substantial. How about a chicken sandwich?"

He inhaled from deep within his body, feeling on the verge of some sort of breakdown. His back stiffened, he grasped hold of the arms on the chair and with an icy stare said, "Hassie, I do not want anything but to know why you married me while you are married to another man."

She gripped the sofa cushion on either side of her body, steeling herself as she started to shake. She appeared faint and avoided looking at him while he watched her pathetic reaction. She closed her eyes and sat still. When she finally looked at him, tears ran down her face as she cried. "I'm sorry. I'm so sorry. But please don't hurt me."

He'd had many thoughts in reaction to this news but had never considered doing anything to physically hurt her and didn't know why she would have thought that he would. He remained quiet until she wiped the tears from her eyes and cheeks and then looked at him and said, "I need a minute and then I'll tell you everything." She stood and left the room, unsteady on her feet, and he honestly pitied her. Since the moment he'd found out that she was a bigamist, it had taken him a while to actually use the word. Since that moment, he'd tried to imagine how or why she would have done such a thing. Why didn't she just tell him that she was married when she met him? She hadn't minded telling him that she had a son and that the boy's father had died before he was born. Wouldn't it have been just as easy to tell him that she had a husband in New York? Even if the marriage was a dire failure and she had every intention of ending it, wouldn't it have been far easier to deal with the situation back then before they got so involved and certainly before she agreed to marry him? He hadn't had time to process the big picture and, sitting there with her now, felt nothing but disdain for her having landed him in this position.

She emerged from the bathroom, stopping in the kitchen for a glass of orange juice, which he assumed she'd laced with vodka. She sat on the sofa, having put the clasp back in her hair. Charles remained quiet in his chair, but they finally met each other's eyes, and Hassie took a deep breath before sipping the drink and asking, "How'd you find out?"

"If it's important to you to know, your son is to blame."

"Kenny?"

"He got quite friendly with Beryl—telling her about his life in New York and about his Uncle Zach who's actually not his uncle at all because he's married to his mother, which makes him his stepfather. Evidently Kenny's quite proud of the fact that he has a stepdad. And that the three of you—when you're not working in London—live together in a cozy little flat in some sort of village and, well, it's just one happy little family."

Hassie looked down; he expected that she would fall apart again. But she dabbed a tissue under her eyes and then looked up at him and said, "So Kenny told Beryl and Beryl told Gwen?"

"Something like that. Suffice to say that my mother found out and enlisted Nigella to track me down. Also understand that it is of utmost interest to my mother and sister that this marriage is—done away with and never spoken of again. I'm here to ensure that this is your last visit to this country. Your return ticket should be canceled, refunded— whatever it takes to get it out of your duplicitous, deceitful hands."

"I'm sorry that this had to involve your mother and Nigella."

"You mean you're sorry you got caught."

She sipped her drink and then proceeded to tell Charles the whole story of her marriage to Zach, his affair with some man before Barbara died, her efforts to undo that marriage and the complications that ensued. Charles listened, but he couldn't have been less interested to hear her sorry tale and was on the verge of telling her to shut up when she started to cry as she said, "I'm actually glad this is all out in the open now. It's been a terrible burden for all these years and all the more so because I love you so much. I don't regret the time we've had together. I'll never regret having been your wife. But I gravely regret having hurt you." She stopped to collect herself and sipped the drink, then took a ragged breath before she asked, "Is there any way that you can forgive me? Can you find a way to understand that I did what I did because I truly believed my marriage to Zach was over and that I loved you too much to leave here without being your wife?"

He studied her, his emotions roiling through his system, and then gently shook his head as he said, "Hassie, you are the most magnificent woman I've ever known. Do you have any idea how much I loved you and how proud I was to be your husband?"

"Please don't use the past tense."

"But you have reduced all that we ever meant to each other and all that our life could have been to one selfish bit of bad judgment. Please do the kindest thing you can for me and get the hell out of my life."

She stared into her drink and then softly said, "What do you want me to do?"

"Get on the airplane as planned. Take your son and go home. But I'm very serious when I say you should never come back."

"I'll need to let Derek and Ronnie Scott know. And my agent."

"You can do that with a few phone calls."

"And what will you do about the—?"

"Divorce?"

She nodded.

"I'll take care of it and inform you accordingly. You just worry about getting your life in order in New York."

She pulled herself together and said, "At least you got to meet Kenny."

"Yes, poor boy." He walked over and took a packet of cigarettes from his jacket pocket, lit one and asked, "By the way, does he have any idea who I am?"

"He saw a photograph of you in Rottingdean. I told him that you are Barbara's nephew and that you have been kind enough to let me stay in your flat while you are out at sea."

He stared at her. "You just lie as a matter of course, don't you?"

"Chaz, that's not a lie."

"It's also not the truth. But it doesn't really matter now." He dragged on the cigarette and then walked over to the telephone table and picked up an ashtray, took it back to his chair and sat. Without looking at her, he asked, "Would you please bring me a whiskey?"

She stood and took her empty glass to the kitchen, quickly returning with two drinks. She handed him the whiskey and asked, "How did you get back to London so fast?"

"It doesn't matter. It was mandatory that I saw you before you left for New York."

"I'm glad you did."

"Don't be too glad. I meant it when I said that this will be the last time I'll ever see you and the last time you will visit this country to my knowledge. You do understand what I'm saying?"

Her eyes filled with tears, and she nodded.

"Good." He ground out the cigarette and then swigged back the drink before walking over to get his jacket and cap.

Hassie rose, wiped her eyes, and said, "You're not leaving, are you?"

"There's no reason to stay."

"I can't just let you walk out the door."

"I'm afraid you don't have a choice."

"But this is your flat. I'll take Kenny to a hotel. We're leaving tomorrow morning. We can stay at the airport. Please, Chaz. Please don't make me feel worse than I already do."

He put the jacket on. "I'll take a room in the Naval Club. There's no reason to upset your son at the end of his holiday."

There was a knock on the door. Hassie opened it and was met with Nigella carrying her toddler, with Karina and Kenny in tow.

Nigella forced a smile and said, "The doorman let us in. I'm afraid our little outing isn't going to happen. Molly's got a dodgy tummy."

Kenny ran past Hassie toward the table where he'd left his breakfast.

Hassie looked at Nigella, who stood in the corridor and curtly said, "You look terrible."

Feeling embarrassed, Hassie looked away and asked, "Is there something we can do for Molly?"

"No, thanks. We're better off getting her home." She took hold of Karina's hand and said, "Speak to you later, Charles."

"Thanks, Sis. Hope Molly feels better." Hassie closed the door and then walked over to Kenny and said, "Sorry you didn't get to the zoo, sweetie."

He shrugged and then pointed at Charles. "Are you a sailor?"

"Yes, I am."

"Is that a real sailor uniform?"

"It is," Chaz said.

Kenny cocked his head. "One of my friends has a sailor suit, but it looks different than yours."

"There are many kinds of sailor suits—different ones for different events."

"What's that one for?"

"Hmmm. Hassie, what event would you say this suit is for?"

Her shoulders sagged, and she put her arm around Kenny as she asked, "Are you hungry? You didn't finish your breakfast."

"Can I have a sandwich?"

"Sure. Chaz, will you join us for a quick bite before you leave?"

"Thanks, but I must make a move." He reached out to shake Kenny's hand and said, "It was a pleasure to meet you, young man. I hope you enjoyed your visit to England."

Kenny shook his hand. "It was real fun."

Charles looked at Hassie. "I'm sure you'll take care of those things we discussed before you leave."

She nodded and walked toward the door. Charles waved to Kenny and then followed her. She opened the door, looked at him, her emotion welling again as she quietly said, "Please forgive me."

He paused for a few seconds and then walked out. He'd been so angry when he heard the news of her bigamy that the sooner this loathsome task was dealt with the easier it would be for him to forget about their marriage and move on. What he'd neglected to take into consideration was the fact that he loved her deeply, which meant it was unlikely that he would forget about Hassie Calhoun for a very long time to come. It was a blessing that there would soon be an ocean between them.

He stood on the pavement in front of the building, waiting for a taxi to pass by. He'd often struggled to feel that his uncle's flat actually belonged to him and that he wasn't just a visitor when he lived there. He hesitantly turned back toward the building, focusing on the window from his lounge—the room that Hassie had changed and turned into his home. The face in the window was that of her son's. He waved and Charles turned away, his chest heavy with sorrow. He'd felt bitter and vindictive when he'd arrived. But he would leave unbearably sad—his heart was simply worn out.

part five

chapter twenty-seven

New York City. 1982

Ruben's apartment in The Dakota had become Hassie's second home in New York City. Before John Lennon was killed outside the building, she occasionally saw him and Yoko Ono. Sometimes she chatted with them—John was a talker. Now, almost two years after his death, she occasionally met Yoko in the lobby for an exchange of smiles and a silent ride on the elevator.

Hassie probably knew her way around Ruben's fourth-floor apartment better than he did. He'd breezed in only minutes earlier and immediately escaped to his bedroom to shower and change. She made sure the decanters were full and the glasses at the bar were clean—something she would never depend on Ruben to do—and checked the wine and champagne in the fridge. Despite the swarm of butterflies in her tummy, she decided against a quick snort of vodka. They could be in for a long, intense evening; she'd best keep her wits about her. Since the moment they began working on the musical about her young life in Vegas—some twelve years earlier—they'd spent hours behind Ruben's piano or planted on his leather sofa and chairs creating, debating, laughing, crying. They'd only recently reached the point where they could see the musical on stage, thus the hunt for funding was officially on. A handful of potential investors were expected within the hour.

Ruben entered the room buttoning a shirt, what little hair he had wet and slicked back. He stopped and eyed her up and down before asking, "Who you out to impress?"

She'd decided against wearing her standard business attire of black skirt and white blouse, opting for a red-belted, crepe wool dress that hit just above the knee. "Just felt like changing it up a bit tonight."

He poured himself a shot of scotch and said, "Well, you look great." He faced her. "Have a seat, and I'll tell you more about our guests."

"Anybody I know?" she asked as she sat on the sofa.

He sat in his leather armchair. "You remember Jack Kingford?"

"Of course. He was part of that first group of producers we met way back when. I'm surprised he's still around."

"Yeah, he's around—still loves betting on the underdog and knows my reputation for success. Between you and me, he's got an ego the size of Wyoming and an overblown idea of his importance. But, hell, as long as he writes that check, he can sit on whatever throne he wants."

"What about the others?"

"I haven't met them in person, but I've had several conversations with the guy I think of as the kingpin."

"A New Yorker?"

His head lightly bobbled. "I'm not exactly sure where he comes from, but I'm told he has a pot load of money and could be interested in off-loading a big chunk of it in our direction."

"How'd you meet him?"

"Friend of a friend. You know, all these money guys know each other. They're in their own world. I've been there. It's never as simple as it seems, but I don't care what their motivation is as long as we get what we need."

"Does this *kingpin* have a name?"

"John Champion. You'll have to wait 'til he gets here to find out anything more."

"And the other guys?"

"Acquaintances of Champion's and, best I understand it, not from around here." He lit a cigarette. "This meeting's our chance to answer their questions and ask a few of our own. So you'll be the hostess with the mostess and serve 'em drinks and whatever while I get the conversation going. Then we'll just let it rip and see where we end up."

She half-smiled, considering her response before saying, "You're lucky I'm feeling generous tonight or I'd tell you what you can do with your *hostess with the mostess* idea."

"Pardon me, *Mizz* Steinem. Just giving you a chance to turn on your considerable charm with these guys."

"Yeah, right." She laughed and then said, "So is this where I finally learn how much money we're looking for? Do *you* even know how much we need?"

He dragged on the cigarette. "Course I do. But I'm not asking for a nickel 'til I see what cards these guys are playing. And I expect there'll be plenty of discussion before we can begin to talk about money."

"But they all do know why they're here tonight?"

"If they don't, they're lug nuts, and we don't need 'em."

"Okay," she said. "You're the boss."

* * *

Half an hour later, Hassie opened the door to three men. The one in front said, "Hello, Hassie." She took a step backward before he proffered his hand and said, "John Champion."

She felt that the air had been sucked out of the room, and as she carefully shook his hand an eerie shudder traveled down her spine. She eventually said, "Sorry. Please, come in."

Ruben walked up to join them and shook the man's hand. "It's nice to finally meet you, John." He shook hands with the other two men who introduced themselves as Marcus Fratelli and Jeremy Glass.

Hassie moved away from the men. From the moment she opened the door, John Champion's swarthy appearance grabbed her, uncomfortably so, and then his voice was so familiar it occurred to her that if she didn't know better, she was standing in the room with Jake Contrata.

Ruben faced her with a look of *what's going on here?* and said, "And that's my partner in crime, Hassie Calhoun."

Her adrenaline kicked in; she rushed forward. "Can I take your coats?" She was unsteady on her feet, and Ruben continued with the strange looks. Was it obvious to the others that she'd been completely broadsided by this man's appearance? Maybe she should make light of the fact—*ha ha ha, he looks like someone I used to know*. She took the coats into the guest room. Ruben met her coming back and quietly said, "What's the matter with you? You're acting strange."

She wanted to shriek but calmly said, "Nothing. I'm fine." The doorbell rang again; she moved swiftly ahead of Ruben and let Jack Kingford in. He kissed her cheek. The men stood as if needing instruction on what to do next. She tried to smile and addressed them all: "What can I get you to drink? We have a bull far—I mean full bar." She laughed an unnatural laugh, staring at her feet. "Or wine, champagne, cola, coffee. Whatever you'd like."

Ruben invited the men to sit. Hassie took their drink requests and went to the kitchen to get ice. When she shut the freezer door, John Champion stood next to the sink. Her nerves spasmed, and while she shakily transferred the loose ice cubes into a stainless-steel container, he said, "You always did look good in red." She knocked over the bucket of ice, scattering it across the counter and onto the floor. She stooped to pick up the cubes; Champion knelt beside her. When she looked at him, he touched the scar over her eye and said, "I'll never forgive myself for hurting you. I'm sorry there's a scar, but you're still as beautiful as I remember."

She stood up and threw the dirty ice cubes in the sink. She was overly warm and dizzy and couldn't speak and for a few seconds felt as if she were standing outside her own body. This man was trying to tell her that he *was* Jake Contrata, which meant that he—Jake—was alive. She picked up the half-empty ice bucket and said, "Excuse me." He followed her into the living room and sat down. She served the drinks two at a time and then sat in the chair next to Ruben with a large shot of vodka. Ruben watched her, bemusedly, and then focused on the group and said, "Cheers. Or as we say where I come from, Genatset!"

The men raised their glasses. Marcus mumbled something that was meant to mimic Ruben. But John Champion focused on Hassie and said, "Cheers."

She looked at no one and sipped her drink, convinced that the others could hear the pounding in her chest. She sensed that Ruben was waiting for her to say something, but she continued to focus on nothing. He finally said, "So, gentlemen—"

"And lady," John said, still watching her.

"And lady," Ruben said, sounding annoyed. "Shall we begin?"

"I understand you're putting together a showcase," said Jeremy.

Ruben nodded and looked at Hassie. "That's your cue."

She crossed her legs, reminding herself to breathe, her temples throbbing as she said, "We've, uh, amassed, uh, a terrific group of performers who've been rehearsing for, uh, several weeks." She took a deep breath, looked in Ruben's direction and said, "Ruben's canvassing potential investors now..." *What had she intended to say?* "...with the hopes of presenting the showcase very soon."

"September fourteenth," Ruben said. "If most people can make that date, we're on."

"You can count me in," Marcus said. "How much of the show are we going to see?"

Ruben continued, "You'll get a full synopsis of the book—and by that we mean the story, the plot, and a good taste of the music."

Bile crept into Hassie's throat. She felt sweat on her upper lip, which she gently blotted with her cocktail napkin and then breathed as deeply as she could before she said, "There's a good variety of style and, uh, enough of it all so you'll walk away humming the tunes—um, we hope." She tried to smile, her face tight like she wore a mask, and focused anywhere except in the direction of John Champion, where she could feel his steely gaze and imagined what he was thinking or remembering or—worst thought of all—conjuring.

"So are you funding the showcase, Ruben?" Jack asked.

"Unless you guys want to do it." He pointed to an ashtray on the coffee table and said, "Feel free to have a smoke if you're so inclined."

John sat back in his chair, focused on Hassie and asked, "Are you singing in the showcase?"

She looked in his direction, her stomach knotting as she said, "Yes. One of the lead roles."

"The young girl who goes to Vegas and meets a handsome, powerful man?"

She gave Ruben a tight look of displeasure. "I didn't know you'd already been talking about the plot."

Ruben didn't comment, and Hassie said, "Ruben?"

He shot Champion a quick look and then said, "I didn't realize I'd said anything about it."

"And are you planning to perform the role if it makes it to Broadway?" John asked, still holding her with his eyes.

Ruben stood up with his glass and said, "All that's up to the director, which, by the way, we still don't have."

"Do you have someone in mind?" Marcus asked.

Ruben walked toward the bar, and Hassie meant to speak, but a wave of nausea rolled through her stomach, and she was afraid if she moved or spoke she would be sick. Thankfully, Ruben turned toward them and said, "We have a couple of people in mind. Once we know we have the money we need, we can start that process. Anyone need a refill?"

Hassie stood and excused herself while Ruben accepted Jack's empty glass. She went to the powder room and locked the door. She stood at the vanity and observed her flushed face in the mirror. Why was there no air in this apartment? She was aware of how every muscle and tendon was attached to her skeleton as she ached and shook and wished that she would vomit and that doing so would rid her of this deep, disturbing feeling of impending disaster. She turned on the cold water and splashed it on her cheeks. She had absolutely no doubt that the man calling himself John Champion was Jake Contrata, and despite her efforts to block it out, she saw fists flying and glass breaking and women screaming and blood spattering and men struggling to stop a melee brought on by temper and ego and actions so severely inflicted that someone died. The image was crisp and three-dimensional, and she wanted to cry out. But then she remembered where she was and what was happening on the other side of the door.

She turned off the water and dried her face with the hand towel, wiping the smeared makeup from under her eyes. She lowered the lid on the toilet and sat down, taking long, deep breaths. Though it had been almost twenty years since Jake had disappeared into the night and been reported dead, she had the feeling that she'd just been given the news. Only this time, she knew better than to believe he'd actually died. This time she jumped to the perfectly logical conclusion that the local mob boss, Sid Casper, had seen to it that Jake was taken away from the Sands after the unfortunate incident when Julio had died and—well, she didn't know what they might have done with him, but it made perfect sense that he was still alive. The thought terrified her because now she knew what she'd always suspected—despite his attempts to deny it, Jake Contrata was part of the mob. And then it struck her that her concern wasn't that Jake was supposed to be dead but that she was worried for Ruben. He had high hopes for this man's financial contribution to their production, and she had a sick feeling that this revelation... this revelation could wreck it all.

Ruben rapped on the door, startling her as he asked, "You okay in there?"

She flushed the toilet and called out, "Yeah. Be right there." She looked in the mirror again. Her face was pale and drawn, but she breathed a little easier. She pinched her cheeks to return some color and then smoothed her dress over her thighs and opened the door. She walked toward the men with what she hoped was a confident stride but feared that she looked as bad and off-kilter as she felt. She smiled and asked, "Has Ruben answered all your questions?"

The men stared at her like she'd returned to the room with two heads. Marcus finally cleared his throat and said, "Miss Calhoun, we've heard all about Ruben's track record in this business but—and I mean no disrespect here—but could you maybe fill us in on your background... your qualifications?"

She walked back to her chair, nodding congenially and thinking this was her chance to rectify her iffy behavior. She started to speak when John said, "That won't be necessary. I happen to know Miss Calhoun's got a pretty decent pedigree." He looked at her and said, "Didn't Sinatra record one of the songs you wrote?"

Her nerve momentarily steeled as she asked, "Do you know something I don't know?"

"Well, if he didn't he should have. That's a nice piano, Ruben. Are you going to give us a preview of some of the new songs? Like maybe the ones that Nia Jackson sings?"

Hassie sat still, her head ready to explode with the desire to stand up, get right in this guy's face and demand that he leave and never contact her or Ruben again. Instead, she looked in his direction and casually said, "If I didn't know better, Mr. Champion, I'd think you'd seen a script."

He smiled. "Call me John."

There was silence all around before Jeremy said, "Sounds like we all need to be brought up to speed here."

Hassie felt a burst of anguish and fatigue that so thoroughly enervated her she ignored Jake's comments and said, "Gentlemen, we seem to have gotten off track. Ruben has a nice speech prepared that I expect wraps everything up." She nodded at him. "That's *your* cue."

She sat down, and Ruben took over the conversation. The men listened, seeming only mildly interested with the occasional interruption to ask a question. Champion remained quiet until Ruben expounded on the plot and the underlying message of domestic abuse. He then shifted his weight in his chair and said, "That sounds like a pretty serious message for a musical."

"It is a serious message," Ruben said. "Just wait until you see our treatment. We expect it'll have some significant impact."

"I see," John said, while Hassie physically strained to avoid looking at him, struggling to hide her uneasiness. In the moment, she willed them all to leave.

"So," Ruben finally said. "That's the basis of this meeting. Any more questions?"

John shifted in his chair again and asked, "Are we going to hear the music now?"

Ruben started to speak, but Hassie firmly said, "We should save the music for the showcase. It's the best way to hear it—with all the voices and a bit of staging."

"That's very disappointing, Hassie," John said. "This domestic abuse issue has piqued our interest, hasn't it, gentlemen?"

Before anyone could respond, Ruben said, "Hassie's right. The showcase is just around the corner, and the music'll have much more impact hearing it there for the first time."

John stood, set his empty glass on the coffee table and said, "This has been very enlightening." He walked over to Hassie and reached for her hand, which she tucked behind her. He smiled a nefarious I'll-get-you-later smile, stepped back and said, "Thank you for your hospitality. I hope we can continue our conversation another time."

She ignored him and went to get the coats.

Ruben closed the door behind the last man to leave. He wheeled around to face her and said, "What the hell was that all about?"

She shrugged and with the intention of avoiding the inevitable, said, "I need to go home, Ruben. I'm exhausted and Zach—"

"Zach can wait. Sit down. You hardly touched your drink."

"No. I'm going home. We'll talk tomorrow."

He helped her with her coat and said, "Just answer one question. Why did John Champion make you nervous?"

"He didn't. Good night, Ruben."

* * *

When she was safely in a taxi, the driver asked, "You wanna go through the park?"

"Just take the quickest route to Twelfth Street between Fifth and Sixth."

The driver was young and aggressive, and she knew he'd get her home pretty fast. What was she going to say to Zach? He knew as much about Jake as Ruben did. The main thing they both knew was that Jake had been killed before Kenny was born. She was still debating why she felt the need to protect Ruben from the truth, but Zach had enough on his plate right now. The last thing he needed was to be bombarded with more of her problems. But she needed to say some of what she was thinking out loud, and Zach was usually the voice of reason.

When she opened the apartment door, Zach was sitting in his chair, wrapped in a heavy sweater, reading. The room was quiet and unusually warm. She sensed an air of doom and stopped to consider if it emanated from Zach or from her. He looked up at her, expressionless, and asked, "How'd it go?"

"Are you cold?" She moved closer to him and realized that he had almost no color in his face or hands.

"I'm fine," he said.

She sat on the sofa. "I'm going with you to the doctor tomorrow. Despite everything else going on right now, you and your health are my priority."

"That's nice, but what do you want to talk to me about?"

"You know me very well." She stared at her hands, studying her nails, searching for words. She finally looked at him and said, "Remember a long time ago—after we first got together—when you asked me about Kenny's father, and I told you a little bit about him?"

"And he's a character in your show now—Jake somebody."

She nodded. "Do you also remember that I told you he was dead? That he was killed before Kenny was born?"

"Yes, of course. What does he have to do with your meeting?"

"This is going to sound insane." She breathed deeply. "Ruben told me a while ago that he'd met some guys—one in particular— that were interested to invest in our show and that's what this meeting tonight was about—meeting these guys, giving them a private view into what's required, and now I get it that Ruben's looking for a commitment that'll at least secure the theatre and—"

"Hassie, what does dead Jake have to do with all this?"

She peered out into the room and then said, "Jake is one of these investors. He's alive, Zach. He talked to me—apologized for leaving me with this scar. It's crazy."

Warren said nothing.

She stood up and walked toward the window, eventually facing him to say, "I can't explain it, but, despite the fact that he looks different, I knew it was Jake from the moment I saw him and heard his voice. And then as the night went on and he practically undressed me with his eyes…" She leapt toward Zach's chair. "I realized that he's just a thug who took advantage of me when I was too young to know better and then thought absolutely nothing of making me believe that he'd been decapitated in the desert. Who does that, Zach?" She ran her hands through her hair. "Who treats someone that they supposedly love with such little regard for what something so horrible might do to them?" She manically paced in front of the coffee table, flicking her wrists like she was trying to rid her hands of something nasty. Zach started to speak until she blurted, "I'll tell you who does something like that. The guys in the mob. Those heartless beasts. And believe me, I know all about this."

"Hassie, please sit down. You're making me dizzy."

She sat on the sofa and put her face in her hands. "Sorry. I'd really just like to kill him."

"So I'm guessing that Ruben doesn't know any of this."

She shook her head. "And that's really what bothers me about recognizing that Jake is—by the way, he calls himself John Champion." She stopped and breathed. "I don't think Ruben realizes who he's dealing with. And I don't know how to tell him, because if he finds out that this is the guy who did all the things that Ruben knows Jake did to me, he won't want his money, and he'll get rid of him."

"So? He'll get somebody else's money."

She took a deep, noisy breath. "I know that sounds like an easy option, but I'm not sure it is. I think Ruben is really counting on Jake… John's money, and anyway, he brought a couple of other guys with him whose money we'd lose as well. I really don't know what to do."

Warren was quiet for a moment and then said, "I know Ruben loves you and wouldn't like dealing with someone who treated you badly. But he's a wise old guy, and he won't do anything stupid with regard to you or your show. I think you should tell him."

chapter twenty-eight

At least once a week, Warren dreamed of his mother. Sometimes she was young and vibrant, beautiful and full of grace. Other times, she was old and ill and woeful, and words couldn't comfort her. She'd been gone for almost twenty years and, though it wouldn't be honest to say that he thought about her every day, he guessed it was true that one never stops needing one's mother when in pain—whether from a broken heart that's never been understood or from a disease that's breaking the body down, making every step of every day a little more difficult. The silver-topped cane that had belonged to Ruben's father had now become a necessity for Warren to walk farther than from the bed to the toilet.

In the absence of his own family—except for Ruben—Warren was grateful for the one he'd inherited. Hassie was busy with the musical that she and Ruben had finally completed. Norma and Kenny were both taking classes at NYU—Kenny lived at home; Norma stayed on campus. So Warren spent lots of time alone, especially since he could no longer go into his office. He had good days and bad days, but he'd learned to cope—as long as his family eventually came home.

As he waited for Hassie to take him to his doctor, he took the cane over to the bookcase and perused the shelves. He was in the mood for a Mozart symphony. The tragic, passionate tone of No. 40 in G minor felt right in the moment. He placed the LP on the turntable and set the volume to fill the room. The phone rang, annoying him as he hobbled his way toward the desk.

"This better be important," he said as he answered.

"Zach, it's me. I just have a second, but I wanted to let you know that I can't get home to take you to Dr. Metcalf this afternoon. Kenny will go with you. He'll be home soon."

"You chickened out."

"No, I didn't. We had the first real run-through of the show this morning. It's kicking my ass, and the cast is freaking out about the state of things here. It's..." She covered the mouthpiece and then came back and said, "Kenny will look after you, and I'll be home by the time you get back. Gotta go."

He hung up and stood behind the desk, disappointed that, despite her claim that he was her priority, she'd once again put everything else in her life above anything to do with him. He spotted the telegram that had arrived for her earlier that morning. His name was nowhere on the envelope, but he rationalized that it might be urgent news and sat down to open it. He read the brief message once and heard the front door slam. Kenny entered the apartment, stood at the door glaring at the bookcase and said, "Isn't that... whatever you're playing a little loud?"

"That *whatever* is the penultimate of Mr. Mozart's great symphonies and one of his more popular ones, familiar to dilettantes and lovers of classical music alike."

Kenny stared at him. "I didn't understand a word you just said."

Warren focused on the bookcase and said, "Listen. *Da-da dum, da-da dum, da-da da, dum. Da-da dum, da-da dum, da-da dum.* That's the main motive of the first movement. You'll always remember it if you sing it like this—*Mo-zart's in the pan-try, let him out, let him out, let him out.*"

Kenny giggled and rolled his eyes. "Man, you are so weird."

"Says the guy who's dressed like a plumber with bad taste. But, seriously. Remember that little ditty—Mozart's 40th Symphony in G minor. You never know when that knowledge will come in handy."

"How much you wanna bet that's something I *don't* need to know?"

Warren ignored him, folded the telegram and said, "I hear you're taking me to the doctor."

"Yep. You ready to go?"

"You know I can go by myself. I know how to hail a taxi."

Kenny walked toward Warren, saying, "I'm sure you do, but I'm going with you, so let's go."

Warren held up the telegram. "This came for your mother from someone on a ship—HMS something or other. Read it."

Kenny read the message and then threw it on the desk. "It must be from that guy in England."

Warren leaned back in the chair. "What guy?" he said, knowing exactly whom Kenny meant.

"Remember that teacher of Mom's who lived in England and died and—"

"Yeah, yeah, and Hassie went over to her funeral. What does that have to do with this guy?"

"He was her nephew. I met him when I went to London that summer. In fact, Mom stayed in his apartment while he was out at sea. I gotta get something from my room, and then we need to leave."

Warren felt weak and nauseated all at once. Hassie had come home to stay after Kenny's visit that summer, but he'd always wondered if she and the Englishman had continued their love affair through letters and phone calls. Perhaps Ruben had let her use his address, and she certainly spent enough time at his apartment to take any number of calls. If that were the case, why did this guy—Charles—find it necessary to send her a telegram to let her know that he would be in the city and needed to see her? If she'd gone to so much trouble to keep him away from Warren, it didn't make sense that she would have given him this address.

Kenny came back toting his leather jacket. "Ready?" he said.

Warren didn't look up. "What do you remember about this British fellow?"

"He was tall. He was in the navy and stayed out on the ocean on those big ships like you see in the movies."

"Uh, huh. And what else?"

Kenny shrugged. "I only met him once and just for a minute. Some lady was gonna take me and a couple of little girls to the zoo while he visited with Mom. But one of the girls got sick and we never got there."

Warren shook his head as he imagined the handsome sailor tearing Hassie's clothes off and carrying her to his bed where they tousled passionately between the sheets while her son was out feeding the monkeys.

"Why are you asking me all this now?" Kenny asked.

Warren waved the telegram at him and said, "He's in town for a few days? Navy business or something, but he asked to meet with your mother."

"Oh, yeah. You think he's coming here?"

"No, I don't think he's coming here." He dropped the telegram on the desk. "But Hassie and I have a few things to discuss when she gets home."

Kenny turned the stereo off and said, "Okay. I just let Mozart out of the pantry. Let's go!"

* * *

Dr. Metcalf examined Warren and then allowed Kenny to sit with him on the Naugahyde loveseat in his office. He shuffled through some papers before removing his glasses and focusing on the two of them. "The short story here is that we've done all we can to stop this disease from breaking down your bodily functions. The basic problem, as I've explained before, is that your immune system has stopped working, leaving you unable to fight off infections that have led to more serious problems. We've tried to isolate each problem as it occurs and treat it like we would any other time. But your body isn't responding to these treatments—in fact, the opposite seems to be happening in that you're getting worse, and I'm very sorry, but I don't think there's anything else we can do."

Kenny frowned and said, "What do you mean there's nothing else you can do? He's sick. You're a doctor."

Zach held his hand up to Kenny and said, "It's okay, Doc. I know that you've tried, and I have to say that I'm getting a little tired of being poked and prodded only to be told that you don't know what's wrong with me. I guess I'm just some sort of freak—maybe I should be studied like a lab rat."

Kenny avoided looking at Warren as he said, "So it's definitely not cancer?"

The doctor shook his head. "There were some cancer-like symptoms in the beginning, but there are no tumors."

"What about those patches on his skin? Aren't they a type of skin cancer?"

"Not really. Again, the lesions are symptomatic of the failing immune system." Dr. Metcalf stood and walked behind his desk. He thumbed through a pile of magazines and pulled out one with a dog-eared page. He skimmed over it for a moment and then said, "There have been some similar cases reported in the more recent medical journals, and a bit of research has gone on in Europe. It's being described as an auto-immune deficiency disease, which is basically what I've already spelled out. The real problem is that there is no cure."

Warren couldn't speak.

"So I'm afraid that I have no good news for you, and the best I can do is tell you to think seriously about getting your affairs in order."

"How long do I have?"

"It's hard to know for sure, but based on the recent deterioration of your liver, bladder and bowels, I'd say two to three months." The doctor remained focused on his file.

"So what do we do?" Kenny finally asked. "I mean—can he stay at home?"

"Yes. Warren, you can do anything you like for as long as you're able. The pain will gradually worsen, but we can control that. And you should think about eventually going into hospice where you'll get all the best care."

Two to three months meant that it was unlikely he'd make it to Christmas. Warren felt that he might vomit and seemed to weaken as he sat there. The doctor observed him for a moment and then asked, "Would you like some water?"

He nodded. "And a Valium?"

"I'll prescribe something for you." He looked at Kenny and asked, "Do you have any questions?"

Kenny looked at his hands, his fingers nervously entwined.

The doctor asked Warren, "Any more questions?"

Warren stared at an elegantly framed diploma hanging on the wall and then said, "What did I do to deserve this?"

"We don't know. It's a medical conundrum right now, and I'm sorry it caught you. I'll do everything I can to make you comfortable, and I'll ask the nurse to give you some information on hospice care."

* * *

In the taxi going home, Kenny stared out the window, and neither of them spoke until Warren put his hand on Kenny's leg and said, "It'll be okay."

Kenny looked at him, his eyes glassy. "What're you gonna tell Mom?"

"The truth."

"She should've gone with you."

"She's busy. And I'm not dead yet."

Kenny dropped Warren at the apartment and carried on with the taxi to a late afternoon class. Warren opened the apartment door and heard Hassie call out, "Zach? Is that you?"

He walked toward his armchair saying, "No. It's Western Union."

She entered the room in her underwear, pulling on a long silk robe. "How was the doctor? And what are you talking about—Western Union?"

"The doctor was fabulous, and go look on the desk."

She rushed past him as he sat down. His back was to her as she read the telegram. She tucked it in the pocket of her robe, smiled uncomfortably and said, "Tell me what Dr. Metcalf said."

"I'm going to die."

"We're all going to die, Zach. What exactly did he say?"

"They've done all they can do. They'll make me comfortable with drugs, and don't count on me for Christmas."

"What do you mean they've done all they can do? That's insane! They've done nothing in my opinion."

"Hassie, please sit down."

She sat on the edge of the seat and quietly said, "I should've been with you." She looked down for a moment and then sniffed as she focused on him. "Where's Kenny?"

"He had a class."

She stood up, tightening the sash on her robe. "I'm going to call the doctor. I can *not* accept this." She then stopped and looked at him. "Really, Zach, are you telling me the truth? Did Dr. Metcalf really say that you only have… a few months to live?"

"Why would I lie about that, Hassie? Look at me. I'm a wreck. I might as well be dead." He looked down, the intense shock of it all shattering his nerves until he lost control. He tried to stop, but the deep sorrow boiled over, and he heard himself sob and then wail and then he felt Hassie's arms around his head, gently holding him while he let it all out. He held on to her and tried to calm down. They stayed still and quiet until he cleared the emotion from his throat and said, "Please don't go back to him until I'm dead."

She walked around to face him and sat on the sofa. "You read the telegram?"

He nodded.

"I swear to you. I don't know what he wants. We haven't seen each other since I left London. He's coming on navy business, and I think he's just being cordial."

"After all this time?"

She seemed genuinely unaware, and he wished he knew what she was thinking. He took a handkerchief from his pocket and wiped his face before asking, "Are you going to meet him?"

"I don't know. You have to believe that I knew nothing about this until now. And, as you know, the showcase is the most important issue in my life right now."

"Thanks. Glad to know it."

"You know what I mean. Until the showcase is done, I'm not planning to see anyone or anything outside that rehearsal space and this apartment." She tried to smile, but her emotions took over, and she started to cry as she said, "You can't leave me, Zach."

"I fully understand that, because you're completely hopeless when I'm not around."

She laughed through the tears and stood up. "Enough of my moaning. You must be exhausted. What can I do to help you relax?"

* * *

Warren walked into the bathroom and carefully removed his undershorts before stepping into the shower stall. As he adjusted the water temperature, the room filled with steam, and Hassie stepped in to join him like an angel pushing through a cloud. They stood face to face; she ran her right forefinger down the left side of his face, along the line of his jaw and said, "You are such a beautiful man."

"If you can look at me now, and still say that..."

She put her finger on his lips and said, "Shhh. Let's pretend." She took a can of shaving cream from the wire shelf and motioned for him to turn around. "Let's pretend that Zelda is going out for a big night on the town, and she's going to wear a sexy, low-cut dress."

"Halston."

"Okay, Halston, and her body must be nice and smooth." She gently rubbed her finger across one of the dark, oblong spots as she said, "Does it hurt?"

He shook his head and asked, "Are you sure you want to do this?"

She slathered the foamy cream over his chest and arms. With a razor from the same shelf, she carefully shaved his entire upper body and legs, one part at a time—carefully avoiding the dark patches— until she had rendered his back, chest and limbs hairless. His legs were weak, and he had to steady himself by holding onto the wall, but the first downward stroke of the razor along his back sent a shocking sensation through him, and for a moment he was thrust back to a completely different time and place. What once would have excited him and undoubtedly led to an hour of playful ecstasy with Hassie, now only made him deeply remorseful for what he'd done to her when he left her for Andrew, letting her know that his life with her had been a lie.

As he rinsed the shaving cream off his body, Hassie massaged his shoulders with a loofah, gently stroking his buttocks. He turned and put his arms around her; the water streaming over his face masked tears. They held each other before she said, "Please, believe that I am here for you... that I'll do anything I can to keep you comfortable and that I will never leave you."

He turned off the water; she opened the shower door, grabbed a plush white towel and handed it to him. He put the towel around her, pulled her close to his body and said, "I believe you." He kissed her gently and asked, "Do you believe that I love you?"

She nodded, her lips quivering.

"Then believe that everything will be fine."

She nodded again—her attempt at bravery touched him deeply. But her eyes told him differently. She was scared.

chapter twenty-nine

On September fourteenth, Hassie arrived at the rehearsal space ahead of the others. The rectangular room was flanked by a row of small windows on one side and ceiling-to-floor mirrors on the other. There was no stage, per se. The set consisted of half a dozen platforms of varying heights to lift the performers off the floor and create focal points. Two black flats or partitions were erected at the back of the space as a point of entrance and exit between numbers. For the most part, the dance movement was simple, though some numbers were choreographed for dramatic effect. Primarily a musical showcase, the songs had to sell the show, and the singers had to sell the songs. As best as Hassie could get out of Ruben, and in addition to the four men she'd already met, there were thirty-to-forty potential investors attending. There was ample seating for this audience, comfortably arranged on three rows of risers against the back wall. The most nerve-wracking part of this sort of arrangement was the lack of distance between the performers and the audience and, of course, there were no lights. If everything went well today, they'd get their chance to fully realize the dream. For now, the pressure was on Hassie and her cast to knock the socks off a room full of conservative business people and entice them to write checks with the understanding that there could be no guarantee of return.

When Ruben first suggested they write a musical about her time in Vegas, he'd made it sound glamorous and entertaining—the glory of the Rat Pack days at the Sands. "Imagine a Copa Room set, a big band on stage playing the occasional old standard to set the mood," he'd said. Hassie's own struggle to become a star was the dream of many a young girl and the subject of numerous stories, films and shows. But Ruben was convinced that the presence of a charismatic, flawed antagonist like Jake Montana gave their show an edge that would set it apart from today's average, run-of-the-mill musical—more reminiscent of the powerful story lines from the likes of Rogers and Hammerstein or Bernstein or Gershwin. And now it appeared that Jake Contrata would be there to witness this reenactment of their time in Vegas, complete with the terrifying scene when he attacked her and left the permanent reminder of his violent temper over her eye. The thought unhinged her, making her doubt that she could actually go through with the number as they'd planned and rehearsed. Would the showcase really suffer if she decided to take it out? And could she do so without telling Ruben?

She walked over to the baby grand piano that they'd borrowed. They'd adapted to the old space in every other way, but the ancient upright piano—no doubt some dead patron of the arts' castoff—was not acceptable. She'd gone to her former boss, Myron Rosenblum, and asked a favor. He'd agreed to lend them a piano with the understanding that he and his wife could attend the workshop. Small price to pay for a brand-new Steinway. Plus, he probably still had the first dime he'd ever made. If he liked what he saw, maybe she could pry a bit of money out of his liver-spotted hands.

She sat behind the keyboard and rolled out a few chords, and for a moment she was sitting on the stage in the Copa Room, sharing the piano bench with her friend and virtuoso, Julio Villanueva, while he listened patiently to the song that she'd been writing since she left Texas. He'd helped her with the sonorities and chord progressions and made sure that she finished it. More than anything, he'd given her the *confidence* to finish it, to believe that it was a good song and then to perform it and record it. If she hadn't been such a fool, it might have given her career the professional boost it needed. It pained her to think about it now—having completely lost the rights to the song for a while, which was one more thing Clay Cooper had done for her. He'd somehow paid her debt to the guys who'd laid claim to the song. It belonged to her again, and now it was part of the show.

"Trying to take my job?"

She turned to see Derek Collins walking toward her. "Hey. What do you think about this?" Hassie asked, gesturing across the keyboard.

He looked at the piano and said, "Nice. She looks brand-new." He sat behind the keyboard and ran through an etude of scales that sounded like Horowitz warming up at Carnegie Hall. Derek's masterful professionalism filled the room, and she relaxed. She'd once postulated that he'd followed her back to New York, teasing him with accusations that he couldn't make a go of it in London without her. Now he was a godsend as a member of the team that put the showcase together.

She moved to the bow of the piano. "Would you warm me up, please?"

"Aren't you glad I talked you into singing the lead role today—what's her name?"

"Nia. Nia Jackson." Her nerves threatened to overtake her as she said, "Yeah, I guess so."

He rolled out a few chords. "What do you want to warm up with?"

Would she really be able to sing this song with Jake in the room? She took a deep breath and said, "'I Just Can't Figure It Out.'"

Derek played the intro that Ruben had written to more seamlessly work with the underscoring that preceded the song in the show. But she still heard Julio's haunting arrangement with muted horns and double bass. The song still set her back in Vegas—the Copa Room, the Tropicana, Jake's suite at the Sands, her hospital room. She ran her finger across the faded scar and then looked at Derek and began to sing. She got about halfway through and then motioned for him to stop. He waited and then asked, "Everything okay?"

She simply said, "Let's get ready for the run-through."

Derek stood up and cracked his knuckles. "How are you feeling about all this now?"

She couldn't let him or anyone know how anxious she really felt. Because, in reality, it had nothing to do with the material or the performers and everything to do with Jake. The cast, which seemed to travel as an inseparable pack, entered the room, chatting and laughing. Hassie looked at Derek and said, "Guess this is my cue to get it together." She hugged him. "If I haven't told you how much I appreciate all you've done to help get this damn thing off the ground—"

"Just go get ready to wow these people. You'll be brilliant." She started to walk away, and he said, "Oh, and Judith's coming. Knowing her, she'll be late, but she'll be here."

Hassie smiled and waved and then approached the cast as she asked, "Ready for the final run-through?"

Heads nodded as they mumbled and changed their shoes. The men wore black trousers and black T-shirts; the ladies wore black chiffon wrap skirts over flesh-colored leotards and tights. Hassie wore simple black capri pants over a black, long-sleeved leotard and her nearly worn out tan character shoes. The youngest was nineteen, the oldest— not counting Hassie—was thirty. The run-through was solid, and now the reaction from the potential investors was in the hands of the gods.

Ruben arrived with Zach, Kenny and Norma. From a distance, Zach looked about half his normal size. She'd been so caught up in the rehearsals she hadn't noticed how much he'd deteriorated. She joined them and hugged Kenny while saying, "I'm glad you guys are here, but you're gonna make me extra nervous."

As Zach lowered himself into a seat on the front row, he said, "Just do that thing where you picture everybody in the audience naked." He wore heavy makeup to camouflage the dark spots on his face and neck.

Kenny wrinkled his nose. "That's gross."

Norma laughed, appearing to be the only one of them who was somewhat relaxed.

Hassie lightly stroked Ruben's worn corduroy jacket as she said to the kids, "I better make myself scarce before our audience arrives." She then looked at Ruben. "Can I talk to you for a minute?"

They started to walk away and Hassie said, "Enjoy the show and remember—applause! Applause! See you later."

"Break a leg," Zach called out. She waved and winked at Kenny.

When they were out in the anteroom, Ruben asked, "What's up?"

"I'd like to cut the scene where Jake hurts Nia—the scene and the song."

He crossed his arms over his chest. "What the hell are you talking about?"

"I don't want to do that song today. It's practically pulled out of context and may just be too melodramatic. Plus, we have the fight scene in the Copa Room later. I think that's enough violence."

He took hold of her arm and led her deeper into the anteroom. "I don't know what's brought all this on, but you've lost your mind. How the hell will my narrative concerning domestic abuse make any sense if we cut the damn scene that conveys that point?"

"You can still talk about it, Ruben. We're not doing every number that you have some reference to in the narrative."

He took a shallow, huffy breath and said, "No, Hassie. We're not cutting that number. Now I gotta go greet these people, and you need to relax. Go have a sip of something." He looked at his watch. "We can't change a word or a note of this now, so get yourself together." He kissed her cheek and then walked back into the room.

She closed her eyes and breathed deeply, trying to block Jake's face from her mind, the sickening image messing with her nerves. But the inevitable moment had come, and it was hard for her to concentrate on the real reason she was there, which meant that there was simply no place for her personal feelings, legitimate or otherwise. Jake Contrata had imposed himself on her life again, and this went much deeper than any mundane involvement with her theater production.

She walked over to the small window into the main room and spotted Ruben talking to Jake, whose back was to her. He had straight, black, shoulder-length hair and stood slightly hunched. She recalled that his full moustache and beard were heavy with gray. Maybe he dyed his hair. That would befit the Jake she'd known—vain and suave and sure of himself. He'd be in his early sixties now, which made her think of Sid Casper and the hell he'd put her through after Jake disappeared. And to now know that Sid knew all along that Jake was alive. And that now Jake was Sid—the *kingpin* as Ruben had called him. The boss. The mob boss.

As she watched the two men chat, it occurred to her that she actually felt calm, and she thought it strange. She was certain that this man was her son's father—the man that she thought had been killed... the man who'd tried to ruin her young life and contributed to the deterioration of her mental health. She should emotionally and mentally be unable to be anywhere near him now, never mind in the same room. But she realized that all she really wanted was for the showcase to be a success, and that obtaining the funding they needed was the only thing that concerned her—whether with Jake Contrata's money or not. Life had moved on, and eventually she'd be forced to face the reality that Jake's presence inured. For now, she had a job to do, and it was time to get started.

When Ruben took control of the room, she called the cast in from the dressing room. With everyone seated, there were only a few empty chairs. Ruben stood comfortably before the audience, pushed his hands deep into his baggy trouser pockets and said, "Dear distinguished guests, thank you all for taking time out of your busy schedules to be here. You're going to see a sampling of a work in progress—a first look at a new Broadway show written by yours truly and Hassie Calhoun."

One by one, the cast joined Hassie, whispering the requisite *break a leg*. She motioned for them to stay quiet and listened as Ruben continued, "Our story is about a young girl who leaves her home in Texas and goes to Las Vegas where she meets the handsome and powerful Jake Montana. Her youth and looks get her a long way. She meets a famous headliner in the Sands Hotel and eventually gets pulled between the two men, which ultimately results in disaster. If this plot sounds familiar, it's because, although it's loosely based on the actual life of our protagonist, there are many elements to the story that we all run up against at various times in our lives, whether dealing with troublesome social issues or relating to the mythological aspects of life. You may recall the underlying messages of physical abuse and domestic violence in shows like *Carousel* and *Porgy and Bess*. These shows, among others, are just as relevant today as they were decades ago, and we've worked hard to ensure our take on the subject will carry significance in the theater world long into the years ahead of us.

"So, without further ado, I am pleased to present Hassie Calhoun and the showcase players. Please cast your mind back to the heyday of Las Vegas, the Sands Hotel and the Rat Pack. Enjoy."

Derek played an overture while the cast entered the room and took their places. The opening number set the stage for a typical night in the Copa Room and a young girl's arrival at the Sands. The ensemble number showed her being pulled in different directions and ending up in the company of the powerful, debonair manager, Jake, and for the first time possibly ever, Hassie actually felt the power that had drawn her to him. She floated between the various characters vying for her attention and instinctively pulled away with determined grace when Jake reached for her. It was 1959 all over again, and this new world was exciting and tantalizing. She moved easily into the duet between the young girl, Nia, and the manager's young assistant—her new best friend. Their Sinatraesque crooner performed in the Copa Room, the music strong and evocative of the era even without the full house band. It was thrilling, and Hassie relaxed as she led the small ensemble number in a montage of songs that captured her new life in Vegas, including a flirtatious dance with the Copa Room's famous headliner, which left her breathless and emotionally charged as she landed in Jake's arms, struggling with her feelings for him but ultimately breaking away and slipping behind the back partition.

Her adrenalin surged as she thought ahead to the next number. She could do it. She had to do it. The underscoring moved them along. Hassie slowly reemerged, tentatively at first, but as the music kicked into the chaotic rhythm of the fiery scene, choreographed to portray her fear, she ran toward Jake and then away from him and then he caught her, and she struggled in his arms until he threw her forcefully onto the floor, repeatedly kicking her while she covered her face and cried out for help. The music swelled while sirens were heard in the distance, and Jake walked away while others sought to help her. She lay on the floor, helpless, sobbing and unable to move, the fear she'd experienced on that night so many years ago coursing through her body. Several of the cast tried to help her up, but she pushed them away and lay curled up in a tight ball, wishing she could disappear as a mist in the night. The music stopped. Arms reached for her, lifting her off the floor and carrying her out of the room, the applause roaring in her head.

As she sat alone in the anteroom, barely able to recognize what had just happened, she heard Ruben talking but couldn't make out what he was saying. Within a minute, the intro to the fight scene in the Copa Room began, and the cast performed the intense ensemble number, which eventually would be choreographed to steal the show. Jake's untimely death came next, and Hassie found a moment to return to the stage. Derek picked up with the intro to the penultimate number showing Nia vulnerable and devastated. Hassie performed the show-stopping ballad with depth that she'd never before felt. She stayed with the cast for the finale, which was both poignant and uplifting— the young girl will go on with her life having lived, loved, lost and survived.

The audience was slow to react, which worried Hassie until, one by one, they started to stand, their applause weighted with appreciation. Hassie asked each of the cast members and Derek to take a bow, after which Ruben motioned for her to join him and called out, "Ladies and gentlemen, the incomparable Hassie Calhoun." She and Ruben took a bow. He put his arm around her waist and held her so tightly she could barely breathe. Finally, Ruben gestured for the cast to leave the room.

As the applause died, Ruben said, "Hassie and I are here to answer your questions. There's an assortment of drinks in the anteroom. Please help yourself and stick around. We'd love to have your feedback or discuss any specific thoughts about going forward."

Hassie took hold of Ruben's arm and said, "Most of all, thank you for coming. I hope you could see how committed we all are to making this show a success. But without the support of people like you, it can never happen. As Ruben says, we're happy to talk about it."

A woman in the back row raised her hand and asked, "What's the show going to be called?"

"Good question," said Ruben. "We've kicked around a few ideas. I personally like 'Persephone Rising,' but we've settled on the working title 'Sands of Time.' If you have any other suggestions, we'd be glad to hear them." Through a low murmur of comments, Ruben leaned into Hassie and asked, "Are you okay?" She nodded, and he said, "That was some performance you gave."

A man in the front row called out, "Which theater are you looking to go into?"

Hassie saw Derek's wife, Judith, standing by the door. While Ruben addressed the question, Hassie walked over to meet her and said, "You're not leaving, are you?"

"No, no. Just waiting for Derek." She leaned in to hug Hassie and asked, "How the hell are you, darling? We haven't seen you for ages."

Hassie made a sweeping gesture around the room. "This has pretty much been my life since I got back from London. What did you think?"

"It's great. Very powerful and a thrill to hear you sing again."

"Thanks. I hope a few of these moneyed folks agree with you. And we couldn't have done it without Derek."

"Here's our superstar now," Judith said and smiled as Derek walked toward them.

He kissed his wife.

Hassie asked, "Well? What did you think? Did we get the job done?"

He nodded. "I think it went really well despite those couple of challenges you threw at me. But, hey, that's live theatre, isn't it? You really nailed Nia emotionally."

She smiled. "Thanks again for all your hard work. You two gonna stick around? Get a drink."

"Thanks," Derek said. "But I have another rehearsal in a couple of hours, and I'm going to have an early dinner with my wife."

"We miss seeing you, Hassie," Judith said. "I'll call you for lunch, and I don't want any excuses about having to work."

"It's a deal," Hassie said. "And, again, thanks for coming."

Derek kissed her cheek. "Good job. See you soon."

They left, and as Hassie faced the room, Jake walked toward her. As he got closer, her heart raced. She tried to move, but her legs didn't cooperate.

He stopped in front of her, proffered his hand and said, "Congratulations."

His voice cut through her like a Samurai sword. She hesitated, then shook his hand and said, "Thanks."

He smiled, her hand clasped in his. "You were right to make us wait to hear the music."

Her pulse quickened, her heartbeat strong and intense. She pulled her hand away and managed to say, "So you liked what you heard?"

He nodded. "And what I saw. You have a riveting presence up there. I'd forgotten how beguiling you can be."

"Riveting. Beguiling. My, my." She looked away, the bloody image of the bandages and the pain that Jake's violence had inflicted first on her and then... poor Julio. She took a shallow breath and said, "You'll have to excuse me. I need to speak to a few people who're leaving."

She calmly walked over to Zach and the kids, hoping she looked more normal than she felt.

Kenny hugged her and said, "You're shaking."

"Nerves. Norma, would you be a doll and get me some white wine?" She felt her face burning; sweat beaded on her upper lip. Her hands were cold and clammy, and her stomach flipped and flopped. But, ultimately, she felt strong and had survived a major catharsis.

"It was sensational, Hass, but you look ill," Zach said. "Has all this finally gotten to you?"

Norma handed Hassie a plastic cup of wine, which she downed in one big gulp and then looked at Zach. "I'm fine. How are you holding up?"

"I'm getting tired, but it's been a hell of an emotional ride. You and that Jake character were really something."

"Nia and Jake, Zach. Not me and Jake." She looked around for Ruben. "I'm taking the cast to Joe Allen's for a meal after everyone leaves. You guys want to join us?"

Zach looked at Kenny and said, "I think I should go home, but you two can go."

"And how will you get home?" Kenny asked.

"In a taxi. I'm not an invalid."

"I've got other stuff to do now," Norma said. "But, Hassie, who knew you were so talented? Damn. That was fantastic!"

"Thanks, Norma. I'm glad you decided to come."

Kenny helped Zach stand, saying, "Come on, old man. I'm taking you home, and that's the end of the conversation."

Zach looked at Hassie. "Mr. bossy boots here is getting more like you every day."

Hassie kissed his cheek. "Thanks for coming, and Kenny's right. Go home and rest. I'll see you later."

She'd spotted Myron and Gilda Rosenblum earlier and looked for them again. When she turned to walk away, she bumped into Ruben. She crossed her arms over her chest, still a little shaky, and asked, "Are you pleased?"

He nodded. "I don't know what was going on with you out there—the cast is a little flummoxed right now. But your performance probably sealed the deal with our angels, producers—hell, probably a few passersby as well."

She smiled. "We're a team, Ruben. And we're gonna do this, aren't we?"

"Go get yourself a drink. You deserve it. And then get ready to kick some butt all over Broadway."

She walked away, desperately wanting to be alone. She needed to cry—a great big, blubbering, feel good cry that would release everything she'd pent up to deliver that performance and to prove to herself and everyone else that she could leave Nia Jackson on that stage.

CHAPTER THIRTY

As the deputy executive officer with a navigation specialty, Charles Beauclerke occupied a watchstation on the HMS *Ark Royal*, making her way through the Atlantic Ocean. It was the first time he'd sailed the waters between Southampton and New York and his first visit to America's great city. Having only recently returned to England from the conflict in the Falkland Islands, he'd volunteered for this diplomatic journey on behalf of Her Majesty the Queen. The flagship moved with elegant stealth through the calm waters, and Charles thought of that last battle in the South Atlantic Ocean, when his ship was bombed, leaving dozens dead—the moment when he was certain he'd never leave the ship alive. But he had lived and emerged a different man. It was correct to say that the Falklands War had changed his life.

Charles was joined by the operations officer, wearing a dark-blue "woolly pullie," who pointed straight ahead and asked, "Do you know what that is, sir?"

"Yes, Johnstone, it's a bridge," Charles replied.

"The Verrazano-Narrows Bridge, to be exact." He pointed to the left and followed the span of the bridge with his finger as he said, "It connects Staten Island with Brooklyn and marks the entrance to the New York harbor, Forts Hamilton and Wadsworth starboard and portside, respectively."

Do I Know You?

"You've done this before."

He nodded. "A few times. This your first?"

"That it is, and I'm ready."

A certain reverence hung in the stillness of the morning as the sun steadily crept above the horizon. The men remained quiet as they neared the bridge until Johnstone said, "So, sir, is it true you'll be retiring this year?"

Charles nodded. "Done my twenty years, mate. Time to move on."

"That business in the Falklands changed a fair lot of us, eh?"

"I suppose it did."

"You were on the *Argent*?"

Charles breathed deeply and then said, "One of the lucky ones." His injuries would forever be reminders of his attempt to assist his comrades that had been hit. The inhalation of the noxious smoke that engulfed the ship badly damaged his lungs, and he'd be vulnerable to lung-related illness for the rest of his life.

"So what now? Time to do the proverbial settle-down—get married, take a job in the City? Have a couple of little Beauclerkes?"

"There'll be time for all that," Charles said, knowing that all of the above was imminent.

They stood silent as they passed under the Verrazano Bridge, past Fort Hamilton, and moved through the shipping lane toward Liberty Island, arguably one of the more impressive sights of Charles's naval career. The vibration of the engines traveled up his legs as the ship slowed to turn astarboard, giving them a clear, portside view of the torch-bearing statue. The rich mixture of the ocean's salt, the dewy atmosphere of the early morning and the olio of smells from the city's industrial sites were temporarily eclipsed by the engines' marine-diesel exhaust. Nonetheless, Charles's senses were dulled with thoughts of Hassie—bad memories, which had led him to embark on a life of escapism in its most basic form.

"She's a real beauty, eh?" Johnstone called out.

Charles looked at him quizzically and asked, "Who?"

"Lady Liberty," he replied, looking straight ahead. "I trust the Stars and Stripes have been properly rigged for our arrival pierside."

Charles nodded in agreement and then focused on the great statue, now in clear view. They sailed past Ellis Island, through the mouth of the Hudson River, where the steel-structured twin towers of the World Trade Center stood directly to their right. As he scanned the height of the mammoth buildings, Charles wondered if London would ever allow such architecture amongst its historic institutions and landmarks. He studied the imposing towers a while longer, recalling an incident some ten years earlier when a Frenchman had walked a tightrope between the two buildings. Imagining the height at which the stunt occurred, it was difficult to fathom what that must have been like—for the man making the walk as well as the onlookers from below. The Empire State Building loomed large in the near distance. What must it feel like to stand at the base of these buildings and look up? He couldn't help wondering where Hassie might be in the midst of it all.

She'd sent greeting cards and a few letters over the years. Her return address was West 12th Street. According to Charles's research, the ships' terminals were located between West 46th and 52nd Streets. When he decided that he would meet her, he'd sent a telegram telling her his arrival and departure dates, asking her to pick a place and time to meet and to answer by return telegram. He recalled her message: "Meet me at the cafe on the lower plaza of the Rockefeller Center—the 50th Street side of the block—at noon on Friday. Look forward to seeing you, H."

Charles recognized Governor's Island from maps he'd seen. He lightly punched Johnstone's arm and said, "Time to join the captain." They made their way to the pilot house where the captain, junior officers and watchstanders readied the ship for docking, the atmosphere thick with concentration intensified by the inherent danger that mounted as they approached the port. Everyone had a task, whether poring over charts, studying equipment or bearing responsibility to the books and logs. The focus was to safely moor the ship—something that Charles had done innumerable times without incident—something that continued to test his nerve until the captain's address confirming a successful detail came over the loudspeaker.

Do I Know You?

As the ship pushed toward its berth, he tried to remember Hassie on that last day he'd seen her. He'd spent so much time over the past years trying *not* to remember her, he could only recall certain traits: her almost but not quite black hair, the odd green, gold and brown marbled color of her eyes, the thick, rich pout to her lips—that one he'd worked very hard to forget. But with these thoughts came the image of her as he'd last seen her—sad and contrite in having to face him under such unmentionable circumstances, begging him to forgive her but fully aware she'd broken his heart. He wondered if she was still married to Zach and if maybe they'd had a child.

Through the ruckus of shouts and cheers, Charles looked out to see the FDNY fireboats he'd heard about spouting showers of water in the direction of the ship's berth. This welcoming ritual had a calming effect on him, and he felt relieved to have arrived at the famous port, where the simple fact of the matter was that in order to move on with his life, he needed to shut the door on his past with Hassie. They were once again in the same city where everything could be brought to a civilized conclusion. And Charles would put that part of his life behind him.

* * *

Two days later, Charles walked the distance from the ship's dock to the block-wide concourse of Rockefeller Center, arriving almost an hour before the designated time to meet Hassie. After a cool, rainy start to the day, the skies had brightened with early autumn warmth under the sun. He roamed around the open space until he came upon the large bronze sculpture of Atlas carrying a replica of the world on his shoulders. He stopped and studied the brawny, god-like specimen, at once identifying with the suggestion that no matter how strong the man might be, the weight of the world can be an awesome load.

He found the cafe that Hassie had suggested, which was located on the lower level of the plaza. He took the elevator down and decided to wait for her there with a cup of coffee. About half an hour later, he felt someone approach the table and looked up to see Hassie standing opposite him.

"Hello, Chaz," she said. "I hope you haven't been waiting long."

He stood up, gently shook her hand and said, "Hassie. It's been a long time. Please, have a seat."

She placed her coat and bag on the chair beside her. A corner of the silk scarf that had belonged to Barbara trailed from the coat pocket. As she sat across from him, she said, "I seem to have brought you to the busiest spot in Manhattan."

"Not to worry. I had a bit of a wander around the area this morning—had a chance to read a little history of this place and actually sat down earlier for a coffee."

"Well, good for you. And good for us." After a moment's gap in the conversation she smiled at him. "You look wonderful—so healthy and... well, strong."

He laughed, happy to see her beautiful smile again. "The navy is good for all that. Though I must admit I'm not the tough young buck anymore. It's not as easy as it used to be."

She gave him a cheeky look and said, "Don't forget, I'm older than you."

"Well, you don't look a day older than the last time I saw you. I hope life is being good to you."

Her expression was difficult to read. "I was just going to say the same thing to you. Shouldn't you be an admiral or something by now?"

"Not quite. I'm actually getting ready to retire."

"Already?"

He nodded and sipped his water. "I've done twenty years of service and decided to go out with a bang—literally."

"You haven't been injured, I hope."

He hesitated before saying, "I won't bore you with navy talk, but I've had reason to think twice about how I want to live the rest of my life."

"I see. And this trip to New York is for pleasure?"

"It's actually a chance for Britain to wine and dine a select number of the city's important people—to say thanks for being our ally and friend and to represent the queen in the jolliest way."

"Sounds like pleasure to me. How do you like New York so far?"

"I must admit, I thought I knew exactly what it would be like, but it's surpassed all my expectations. And if last night's reception at the National Art Club is any indication of the city's society, it's quite impressive."

"That sounds wonderful." She looked around, uncomfortably, and then said, "It's turned into a nice October day."

He nodded. "I went out for an early constitutional and got caught in a bit of rain. But, yes, it's lovely now. But I didn't come here to talk about the weather."

She tried to smile and said, "You're right. And I've got to get back to work soon. Shall we order some lunch?"

"Coffee's good for me. But, please, order something for yourself."

She motioned to the waiter. "I may be in for a long afternoon, so I think I'd better eat something." She ordered a tuna salad sandwich and a Diet Coke and then focused on Chaz. "So you're thinking about the rest of your life? Any conclusions yet?"

He contemplated for a moment how much of this conversation he really wanted to have and then said, "I've had quite an exciting time sailing around the world and since you… left London, I've been on a bit of a wild ride where my personal life was concerned."

"I can imagine." An awkward silence passed between them before she said, "So, Chaz, I'm just going to be very American and ask why you never sent the divorce papers. Is it done?"

He shifted his weight and cautiously said, "There will be no divorce. I only need apply for an annulment in order to erase the unfortunate incident from my life."

She raised her eyebrows, and her face slightly flushed. "I see. Then why did you want to see me?"

"I didn't particularly *want* to see you. I needed to."

She sat still, nonplussed, while he continued.

"Firstly, if you don't mind my asking, what have you done to dissolve the marriage from your side?"

The waiter set the cold drink in front of Hassie. She took a sip and then said, "Nothing. You emphatically told me that you would take care of it and that I should—I believe your words were *to get the hell out of your life and never step foot in your country again.*"

Aware that patrons at nearby tables were eavesdropping, he leaned into her as he asked, "Did it ever occur to you that you could contact me about what was going on?"

"Chaz, I did contact you."

"You sent sentimental holiday wishes."

Her eyes darted to the next table. She lowered her voice and said, "And letters."

She sat back in her chair, and Charles took a deep breath. "Hassie, this is not the way I wanted this meeting to go. Please. I know it's been a long time, but can we talk sensibly now?"

She nodded, staring at her hands, and then looked up at him. "You obviously didn't read the letters I sent you."

He gave it a moment. "I'm assuming you never told your… husband about us."

She shook her head. "I never told Zach anything about our marriage. He knows that we had an affair while I was in London and that I loved you." She sipped the cola again. "But he seemed to forget all of that when I came back to New York. And we have continued on with our lives as if nothing happened."

"So you're still married to him?"

"Yes."

"And it never concerned you that you were living as a bigamist?"

"Of course it concerned me, but, again, you told me you'd handle everything and, honestly, it would have been difficult for me to do it from here without—"

"Without letting people know you'd committed a crime?" They sat quietly until Charles said, "Look. In reality, it's none of my business how you handle this as far as your own situation goes. But do you understand that choosing to ignore what you did could land you in prison?"

She fiddled with her fingers and took shallow breaths and then quietly said, "I thought you'd taken care of it—like you told me you would—and that you just didn't want to ever have anything to do with me again, so you just… got on with your life."

He was uncomfortably aware that there was some truth to what she said. He'd not wanted to contact her again, and for a long time he didn't mind if she'd actually suffered a bit. He pitied her in the moment and said, "I need to file a petition for the annulment, which will name you as the *respondant*. Once received, you'll have thirty-one days to respond. This includes the opportunity to disagree with the petition, which I can't imagine you would attempt to do, bearing in mind that bigamy is a criminal offense in the UK and carries a penalty of up to seven years imprisonment or a fine or both."

"But I don't live in England now, and I'm not a British citizen. And it's been so many years—"

"There's no statute of limitations. You committed a crime in England, and I'm advised that it wouldn't be difficult to convince a judge that you did so to obtain a marital visa."

She covered her mouth with her right hand, and he noticed that she wore the sapphire engagement ring he'd given her. He waited and then asked, "Hassie, do you understand how serious this is?"

She nodded and struggled to keep her emotions intact. The waiter brought the sandwich, which she ignored. She finally took a deep, slow breath and asked, "Why didn't you file the petition years ago? Why, now?"

"I've been busy, out at sea much of the time. It made better sense to immerse myself in my career than to worry about anything to do with you or us." He hesitated, deciding whether or not to continue with the real reason he was forcing the issue and eventually said, "I'm engaged to be married. The annulment will void our marriage, and I'll be free to marry again." He knew he sounded cold, but he wanted to shake the emotion from the conversation.

She picked up half of the sandwich. "Engaged? That's wonderful. I'm surprised it took you so long."

"Like I said, I've been busy. Settling down was the last thing on my mind. Besides, I tried that once, and it didn't work out so well."

She laid the sandwich down and stared at her plate, but when she looked up, their eyes locked into a sad, pain-filled gaze that got right into his gut. She broke the silence. "I know I was wrong to marry you when I was already married."

"We've already had this conversation, and it doesn't really matter now."

She leaned it to him. "It matters to me."

"Why?"

"It matters to me because I really loved you, and I'm so ashamed of how much I hurt you."

He rested his hands on the table and took a couple of shallow breaths, unsure that he should try to speak.

She tapped the top of his hand and said, "And you are the only man that I've ever been completely faithful to."

"Even when you were cavorting around a stage naked much of the time and sharing dressing rooms with naked men?"

"Especially then. And if you'd like some specific examples—"

"That won't be necessary. And thank you for saying this. One doesn't expect a bigamist to be chaste as well."

Hassie laughed. "And what about you, oh-mister-sailor-in-a-foreign-port?"

"That's different," he said, unable to keep a straight face. "But, seriously, I was a one-woman man when I was with you. And if you don't believe me, ask the number of my mates that ribbed me unmercifully and called me 'Chazzo, the homo.'"

"That's very rude." She laughed and then fanned her blushing face as she said, "They obviously know not of what they speak."

He laughed out loud and then gently said, "If it helps you feel any better, I do know that you're sorry for what you did, and I suppose I've forgiven you. But you must accept that my fiancée has helped. She dotes on and caters to me, and I've probably never been so well looked after."

Hassie furrowed her brow and pulled her lips into a tense straight line. "She's a lucky woman, and I hope you'll be happy."

He half-smiled at her attempt at sincerity. "Is something wrong with your food?"

"I'm not so hungry any more. Anyway, before I have to leave, tell me about this woman who looks after you so well."

He narrowed his eyes and asked, "Do you really want to know?"

She nodded.

"Her name is Margaret—Peggy. She and I have known each other for a very long time."

"You were seeing her when I met you."

"That's correct, and although we went our separate ways after you and I married, she came back into my life recently, and, well, we've decided to have a life together."

She avoided looking at him, gazing around at nothing in particular before asking, "Do you love her?"

"Sorry?"

"Forgive me, but I need to hear you say it. Do you love her?"

"Hassie, the only conversation we should have about this is that I'm going to petition the annulment now—when I get back to London. I'd like your word that you will agree to the petition, sign the papers accordingly and return them to the courts as soon as possible."

She sat firm, watching him and then said, "Okay, if that's what you want. Have you set a date for your wedding?"

"Not exactly. But if you give me your word that you'll return the papers soon after you receive them, I'll feel much happier about letting Peggy get on with the plans. Lord knows she's waited a long time for this, and I promised I would help move things along."

Hassie nodded. "I won't cause you any more anguish and..." She looked down taking shallow breaths and then focused on him and continued, "I really do want you to be happy. And I hope there'll be a couple of little ones too. You'll be a great father."

His shoulders sagged, and he motioned to the waiter for more coffee. "How's Kenny? He must be a young man now."

She wiped her nose with her napkin. "He's eighteen and believe me, we never thought he'd get there. We've been through a few major upheavals, which I won't bore you with. But basically, life has carried on, and the only reason I'm still sane through it all is that I've been consumed by a musical project that I started working on right before I met you. I mentioned it to you a few times."

He nodded. "Yes, I remember. I'm happy it's working out."

"We still have a way to go, but the hard work's done, and now we're trying to raise the money to put it on a Broadway stage."

"That sounds very exciting. Well done."

"Thanks. We're hopeful."

He took a deep breath. "And you and… Zach never had a child?"

She shook her head. "That wasn't in the cards." The waiter refilled Charles's cup, and Hassie said, "I'm going to have to go soon."

Charles asked for the check and then looked at her. "Thank you for meeting me. And I apologize for my contribution to this uncomfortable mess. But, seriously, an annulment in England may not preclude any action that you should take to protect yourself. So do yourself a favor, and take some proper advice. I don't think you'd enjoy spending time in prison."

She nodded while resting her forearms on the table and then calmly said, "I wish…" She stopped to gather her emotions. "I wish you well, and I hope that your new marriage will be everything that you want."

He looked past her, pursing his lips. "Thank you. And I wish you great success with your show." He laid some cash on top of the check and then smiled as he said, "Perhaps it will transfer to London."

She tried to smile. "Thanks for lunch."

They stood, and she picked up her coat and bag. He offered to walk out with her, following her to the entrance. When they were back out on the street, she turned to him and said, "Enjoy the rest of your time in the city. Hope you're getting to see the sights."

"Yes, I'm logging my fair share of time as a tourist."

She pulled a calling card from her bag. "Take this, and if you need anything or just want some friendly advice, call this number. It's the studio where I spend most of my time. And if you really get stuck and can't reach me, try this one. It's my home number."

"Thank you. I'm sure I'll be fine."

"So. I guess this is goodbye," Hassie said.

She stuck out her right hand, which he held while he said, "Goodbye, Hassie. You are still such a beautiful, charming woman." He pulled her hand up to his lips, kissed it and then stopped as he said, "You're still wearing my ring."

She nodded. "I should've given it back to you. I thought about sending it to you several times but…" She shrugged.

He said, "It's yours now. Wear it in good health."

chapter **thirty-one**

No one could accuse Ruben Layne of being the understanding type. He had three ex-wives and a string of disastrous relationships to prove it. Nevertheless, Hassie thought his ear was worth chewing over just about everything to do with her life, which—let's face it—involved almost nothing other than the theater and Warren's illness. She had dissected the showcase so many times that Ruben was starting to abhor mention of the damn show. But he still received a call from her about every other day, convinced that it was all headed to the toilet. They'd rewritten parts of the songs so many times he'd lost the plot. But, ultimately, her dedication to their success was much greater than he'd ever have the patience for. The least he could do was lend a sympathetic ear, help her rewrite something that she was sure was a dud and then agree with her when she went back to the original version. When he opened the door, all cocked and loaded to give her a hard time about needing his help *again*, she brushed past him, saying, "Give me a drink. I'm here to fall apart."

He chuckled to himself, watched while she threw her trench coat into a nearby chair and then said, "Nice to see you too."

"Ruben, I'm serious. Vodka, please."

He gestured for her to be patient and went to the bar.

She sat on the sofa that seemed to swallow people her size, patted the space beside her and said, "Sit down. I need to talk to someone, and you're it."

He handed her the drink before sitting in his leather armchair. "I'm gonna sit right here. What's wrong?"

She took a sip and then set the drink on the table beside her. After a couple of deep breaths, she buried her face in both hands and cried. Ruben sat quietly until she looked up, wiped her cheeks and then tucked her feet underneath her, her creamy-white thighs sticking out from under her dress. "Sorry about that," she said. "I promised myself I wasn't going to cry."

He waited.

She sat for a moment and then looked past him and said, "I don't know how much you know about this, but I had a serious relationship while I was in London."

"Warren mentioned—hell, he told me all about that affair. He knew that you were pretty besotted with the guy. He also knew that's why you stayed in London for—however the hell long you were there."

She had a look that said she might have changed her mind about talking to him about this guy and then blurted, "I just saw him."

"Who? The limey?"

She nodded.

"You just ran into him on the street?"

"He came to town with the navy and contacted me. I haven't seen him in eight years." She released a sigh weighted with anxiety and then looked at him with such sad eyes he didn't think it wise to push her. She bit her lip and then said, "I made a terrible mistake."

"I gather that."

She sipped the drink, focused on the coffee table and said, "I married him." She looked up at Ruben. "Chaz. The limey. I married him."

Ruben's instinct was to jump up, grab her by the shoulders and shake her brains back into place, but he simply said, "So that explains why you basically moved to London, huh?"

"I never meant for it to happen, Ruben. We met at Barbara's funeral and..." She stared into space. "There's no other way to say it. We fell deeply in love. And remember, Zach was involved with Andrew when I went over to Barbara's funeral. I really thought I could end the marriage with Zach, and no one would have to know—"

"That you're a bigamist?" He stood up and walked away from her, debating whether to be understanding or berate her. He faced her. "So you're still married to him?"

She nodded.

"You've been married to two men for eight years?"

"Twelve."

"Christ, Hassie. I don't know whether to be appalled by your stupidity or worship you for pulling off such an incredible—*crime*. It's still a crime to be married to two people at the same time, isn't it?"

She sipped the vodka. "I still love him. He's the best thing that ever happened to me, and I completely screwed it up."

Ruben sat down in the armchair. First off, he had to wonder about this guy. What kind of guy stays married to a bigamist? And why didn't he go after her legally? He reached over to pick up his drink and said, "I suppose the Brit... what's his name?"

"Charles."

"I suppose Charles found out about Warren and sent you back to New York."

She filled him in on the story of Kenny's visit and the spilling of the beans where Warren was concerned.

"So are you gonna get a divorce?" he asked.

She nodded. "That's why he contacted me—to let me know that he'll be filing for an annulment in England. It should've happened years ago, but just didn't for all sorts of reasons."

He studied her for a minute. He'd never seen her so intensely overwrought by another person. She'd been on the proverbial emotional roller coaster with Warren but had never displayed such genuine love—something that he'd fantasized about more than once over the years. She finally relaxed. Ruben carefully asked, "When you met him, you didn't—sleep with him or anything?"

"No, of course not. We sat across the table from each other in a crowded room for all of forty minutes."

"Who else knows about this?"

"His mother and sister found out when Kenny told the housekeeper. But I never told Zach. Chaz—I call him Chaz—told me he'd take care of the divorce and just send me the papers. I kept expecting to receive them every week for a while. I even wrote to him about it, but he never responded, so I just kinda put it to the back of my mind."

"Really? You put the marriage to a man you married while you were married to Warren to the back of your mind... the man that—your words—was the best thing that ever happened to you?"

She held her head in her hands for a moment and then huffed as she looked at him and said, "Ruben, my plate's been kinda full, don'tcha think?"

"I don't know what I think about this, Hassie. It doesn't make sense."

"What doesn't make sense?"

"You married a man in England while you were married to a man in New York. The Brit found out, sent you away and you just put it all outta your mind? Again. Really?"

"I told you. He told me to get the hell out of his life. Told me never to contact him again and that he would take care of the divorce. What do you think I should've done?"

Ruben stood up. He reached into a wooden box on the coffee table and pulled out a package of Marlboros. Hassie said, "I thought you quit smoking. Again."

He waved a cigarette around. "And I'll quit again tomorrow."

She tried not to laugh as she said, "I don't care if you smoke, Ruben. In fact—"

He joined in, "I don't care if you burn!"

They laughed. He lit the cigarette and then propped himself on the edge of a Biedermeier table across from the sofa. He gave it a moment and then said, "You wanted to divorce Warren while you were basically living in London. Now I know why."

"Ruben, if you're honest, you know that Warren and I should've divorced a long time ago. Hell, according to you, we should never have gotten married and then after all that—crap—with Andrew? Do you think I should've just stayed in that ridiculous excuse for a marriage and given up the only real happiness I'd ever known?"

He took a deep drag on the cigarette, exhaling before saying, "Regardless of all that—and you're not wrong in what you've said. But, regardless of all that, you shouldn't have married another man without a divorce from Warren being final. Right?"

She nodded. "Yeah, yeah. I know. And believe me, I've paid for that mistake, and I'm still paying for it. But I really did expect Chaz to handle everything and then I was thrust full throttle back into life here. Norma, Kenny, our show and then Zach got sick. Do I really need to spell all this out to you?"

He stubbed out the cigarette and went back to his chair. "No. You don't have to spell it out, but maybe you should've come to me earlier. Maybe I could've helped."

"God knows, I thought about it. But you're Zach's family, and he was determined that Andrew was a mistake and that our marriage was what mattered, especially after all he'd done for me and Kenny. And then Norma came along, and he was so good about accommodating that fiasco. I couldn't be that big a monster to push him out of my life. He's right. I owe him a lot."

"There was more to his wanting you to remain his wife than just your debt to him or even keeping up the appearances, Hassie. Warren really does love you, and he's petrified of losing you—especially now. And he knows how much you loved the limey."

She looked like she might cry again. "Why didn't you tell me that Warren had told you all about Chaz?"

"Some things are meant to be kept between cousins. You know what I mean?"

She nodded and focused on nothing.

"You can't let Warren know that you saw Charles today, and you can't let him see how deeply this has affected you," Ruben said and sat on the opposite end of the sofa. "If you're still married to Charles and you still love him so much, why didn't you tell him that Warren is dying?"

She lowered her head. "I thought about it. But that would've been a pretty shitty thing to do. I mean, it's like saying, hey, give it a few more months and the other husband'll be dead. I couldn't do that, Ruben. Not now. Not after everything we've been through." She spoke *sotto voce*, like there was a sleeping child in the room that she didn't want to wake.

"So what're you gonna do?" Ruben asked.

"Nothing. I'm going to stay focused on the show and make sure that Zach is taken care of. And then one day, I'll get the annulment papers from London, and that'll be that. Anyway, Chaz is engaged now and wants to wrap this up so he can remarry."

"So that's it. The guy's officially off the market so you can never get him back. Can you put this behind you now, honey?"

"I have to." Her voice quivered, and she cleared her throat. "I wasn't prepared for it to hit me so hard."

"Sounds to me like you've kept all of this pent up inside for so long, it's spewing out like goddamn Vesuvius. You're only human, ya know."

She smiled at him. "I'm not used to this softer, caring side of you, Ruben. I like it. You should try it more often."

He grumbled, "Yeah well, it's just for you. And don't tell anybody." He stood up, pulled her off the sofa again and then put his arms around her. He pulled back, took hold of her shoulders and asked, "You okay now?"

She nodded, then kissed him gently. "Thank you. I do feel better for telling you about all this. But Zach can never find out."

"I'll be the last person to tell him. And I'm truly sorry for your pain." He let go of her and said, "Dammit. There I go being a nice guy again." He walked toward the piano and said, "Come over here for a minute." She followed him. He sat on the piano bench, flipped through the score until he located the number he had in mind and played the intro. She hummed along until he said, "Pick it up with the verse."

She leaned against the bow of the piano, waited for her cue and then sang.

> Do I know you? Were you there when the world was fading?
>
> Were you with me? Did you know what was going on?

Do I Know You?

Do I know you? Have you always been there waiting to
be with me?

Now the reason is all wrong.

Through miles and years of dark and light

The greener grass, the deeper sea

There's no more reason for the fight.

Your head knows where your heart should be.

Do I know you? Were you there when I lost my footing?

Were you with me? Did you tell me how I was wrong?

Do I know you? Were you ever there to help me?

Were you with me? Now that time of life is gone.

Ruben played the instrumental interlude, mesmerized by the
emotion in her voice. From the first day this song started to materialize,
he'd known that the lyrics came from way down deep, and she'd
practically written them in one session. It was the song itself—the
melodic line, the choice of a minor key and the structure that had taken
weeks to perfect. She knew what this song had to represent and convey
and, for once, he'd let her drive their collaborative process. As the
interlude came to an end, she didn't look up, but he felt her breathe
with him as they continued.

Through miles and years of dark and light

The greener grass, the deeper sea

There's no more reason for the fight,

My heart is where my heart should be.

Do you know me? Were you there when my world was
fading?

Were you with me? Did you tell me to stay strong?

Do you know me? Were you always there to help me?

Were you with me when I faltered?

Were you with me when I fell?

Were you with me when I triumphed?

When I fought my way through hell?

Yes, you know me

And you know me very well.

As he brought the song to its conclusion, he knew that she was going to be all right. The song and the music had had the effect on her that he had hoped for. He wouldn't want to be in her shoes right now, but he believed she was a pro, and her performance of that song had given him the reassurance he needed.

They walked away from the piano. He put his arm around her shoulder and asked, "Have you heard from John Champion?"

She abruptly stopped. "No. I hope I never do."

"He asked me for your phone number."

"Did you give it to him?"

"Sure."

"I wish you hadn't done that."

"He wants to take you to dinner."

She walked over to get her coat and then looked at Ruben and said, "I don't like him."

"You only met him once. Did you even speak to him at the showcase?"

She slipped on the coat, nodding. "He spoke to me afterwards. And he seemed pleased with what he saw. Isn't that good enough?"

"You know his investment could make or break our ability to get the show on stage."

"I thought you said he'd already committed that money."

"He hasn't written the check yet. He just wants to take you to dinner, which would be a great opportunity for you to talk with him about the show. I think you can help him understand more about the process and what he can expect in the coming months—especially if the previews are successful."

"Why me, Ruben? There are dozens of people involved that know a lot more about all this than I do."

He exhaled a deep breath and said, "He's a man, Hassie. A well-traveled, interesting man who would rather discuss business in the company of a good-looking woman than a bunch of boring old farts."

"Like you?"

"Yeah, like me. How bad can one dinner be?"

With total lack of emotion, she said, "I can't, and I think it's wrong of you to ask me."

"What's the big deal? You've done just about everything else under the sun—that's legal—to get this show on stage. And don't tell me that you're a married woman and don't go out with other men because we both know that's not true."

She made the exasperated face that let him know she couldn't argue with him and then asked, "One dinner?"

Ruben nodded.

"Give me his number, and I'll call him."

"I'm sure he's gonna call you."

"Give me his number, Ruben."

He found Champion's card and copied the number that he'd written on the back.

She took the piece of paper from him and stared at it before saying, "If this is some sort of sick plot of his to seduce me, I'll never let you forget it."

He started to open the door and then stopped. "Have dinner with Champion, and get him to write that check, and I'll do something for you."

"What?"

"Do you have any idea what kind of trouble you're in with this bigamy situation?"

"Not really. Chaz said that I could go to jail, and that I should take legal advice for myself."

"Chaz is right."

"But, Ruben, I don't want anyone else in New York to know about this. Not yet."

"Let me speak to my attorney who's helped me with my divorces. I won't tell him your name at this point, and anyway, I'll be asking for legitimate advice that I'll pay for. He'll be bound to keep it all between me and him."

She suddenly appeared scared. He held her by her shoulders and said, "Don't worry until we know what we're dealing with here. And I'll be by your side all the way."

chapter **thirty-two**

It was macabre and she knew it, but it had recently occurred to Hassie that she didn't own a decent black dress other than an evening gown. So when she saw a worsted wool fitted dress with a scoop neck, long sleeves and belt in Macy's window, she ducked in to try it on, took it home and hung it in the back of her closet. On the evening of her dinner with John Champion—who was she kidding? She was having dinner with Jake. She rifled through her closet searching for the right thing to wear. After vetoing everything else, she pulled out the new dress and decided that it would be perfect—elegant but not sexy. She'd recently had her hair cut into a chin-length bob. She wore sheer black pantyhose and low-heeled pumps, kept her makeup to a minimum and dabbed on pale coral lipstick. There would be no mixed signals coming off her tonight.

While sifting through her jewelry box looking for the diamond earrings that Zach had given her, she came across his mother's platinum and diamond wedding band. She'd never worn the ring again after she returned from England. She wore Chaz's ring on her right hand every day. But she wanted to remind Jake that she was married, and she slipped the diamond band on her left ring finger. She held both hands out, studying the indisputable evidence that she was married to two men, which sent her thinking about the conversation she'd had with Ruben's lawyer— Hassie is the sole guilty party, and until a divorce

323

was granted or at the very least the marriage annulled in the United States and England, she's a criminal, having committed a felony in the US and liable for a fine or up to five years in prison or both. It made no difference that she and Chaz had lived apart and in different countries for the better part of eight years… that is, there is no statute of limitations. Thus, she's a bigamist until the marriage is legally nullified in the United States and technically, Charles, as the victim, could seek criminal charges against her if he wanted to.

How could she have let so many years pass without addressing the severity of what she'd done? It was as if she'd believed that ignoring the situation would make it go away, especially given the belief that Chaz was handling the "undoing" of what she'd consciously done to both of them. It was a mess, and, whether she liked it or not, she had a grave responsibility to herself and to Chaz to set everything right and, in doing so, hope that she didn't end up in prison.

Tonight was a completely different state of affairs, and she needed to get her head on straight. She took both rings off and laid them on the dressing table. Zach had long since given up caring about what went on in Hassie's personal life. Chaz was waiting to marry another woman. She looked at her image in the mirror—a forlorn, rueful woman who'd possibly never truly been happy. But then she knew that wasn't the case and smiled with fleeting thoughts of better days. She put the diamond band on her left hand.

When she'd called Jake to arrange the evening, she'd maintained a businesslike tone, which he seemed determined to break down by being much too familiar, and she'd been tempted to call the whole thing off. But, remembering how important the relationship with this man was to Ruben and feeling guilty that she still hadn't told him that John was actually Jake, she suggested that they meet at La Grenouille—one of New York's finer restaurants that wasn't too intimate. He said he preferred the Four Seasons and offered to pick her up from home in a taxi. But she wanted him nowhere near her private life and insisted that she'd meet him there.

She arrived at the restaurant at eight o'clock. The maitre d' whisked her through the dramatic two-level space past the square wooden bar, which was surrounded by a variety of movers and shakers—tall, reedy girls flicking their hair while laughing and being charmed by a disproportionate number of men in suits. A chandelier-like sculpture made from hundreds of suspended bronze rods glistened above them. It was modern and anachronistic all at once, and for a moment she was back in the lobby at the Sands hotel among a cast of glamorous patrons who'd come to gamble, dine and be entertained, where Jake Contrata was the majordomo, the ringmaster, the fixer.

Jake was waiting for her at a table in a private dining room in the far-right corner of the restaurant. At a first, quick glance at him, she questioned if this man was really Jake. He was bigger than she remembered Jake being, his nose was wrong and the long hair, mustache and goatee were not a look that she could imagine him wearing. He stood up, thanked the maitre d' and then took her hand and kissed it. She pulled away and sat down.

"You've had your hair cut," he said. "I like it."

"Thanks."

"Martini or champagne?"

She stared at him for a moment, then asked, "What are you having?"

"I'd like champagne."

The sound of his voice drove her crazy. She preferred not to look him in the eye and quietly said, "Then champagne it is." While he discussed the menu with the waiter, she observed the décor of the intimate room. The tall windows were covered with shimmering chains that draped over each long panel of glass like waterfall curtains. High above them, random pinhole ceiling lights emulated a starlit sky. It was elegant and romantic—just the kind of place that would draw Jake Contrata's attention.

He focused on her and said, "I've asked the kitchen to send out a selection of their more popular dishes. And they have an excellent vintage of Cristal."

"You're determined to call the shots tonight, aren't you?"

He put his hand on top of hers. "I always loved taking care of you. Old habits die hard."

She pulled her hand away. Her heart beat strong—like she'd seen or heard something frightening. She took short, shallow breaths and said, "Ruben tells me that you want to know more about producing a Broadway show."

He slightly cocked his head to the right. "Where'd you meet this Ruben guy?"

"That's not relevant to this conversation."

He shrugged. "I understand he didn't always treat you so good when you worked in his club."

The waiter arrived with the champagne, which he presented for approval and then opened and poured.

Jake lifted his glass to her. "To you, Hassie Calhoun, and to new beginnings. Cheers."

She took a sip, waited a moment and then asked, "Why are you so interested in this production? And why would you want to invest money in something that you know nothing about?"

"Are you saying that I know nothing about theater?"

She tried not to stare at him, but there were moments when a little alarm went off in her head, warning her to be careful that she wasn't being conned. She couldn't put her finger on the things that made her doubt what he was saying. Something was different, and she didn't know how to make sense of it all.

And then he smiled that verging on sinister smile that she'd never been comfortable with and said, "Do you still doubt that I'm the guy you knew in Vegas?"

She swallowed and said nothing.

"Okay, let's do this your way." He took a slow, deep breath. "Hassie Calhoun, my name is Jake Contrata. I ran the biggest, most important venue in Las Vegas for a few years during the time of the Rat Pack and just about every other name that mattered in the entertainment world between LA and New York. I was also responsible for giving a certain ingénue from Texas a job as a waitress in the Copa Room, and I protected her from the piranhas and lechers." He watched her like he dared her to say something and then continued, "And then I fell in love with her and was desperate that no one hurt her or lure her into the darker, seedier side of Vegas. She wanted to sing and to write songs and Julio Villanueva became her mentor, and Frank Sinatra stroked her ego because he'd decided that he wanted her for himself."

She looked away from him and said, "Don't do this now."

"Then when can we do it?" She didn't respond and he continued, "I didn't intend to dredge up the past or to hash through painful memories. But you gotta believe me, and I know you want an explanation about my—disappearance. I'll tell you everything." He removed a package of cigarettes from his breast pocket, shook one loose and offered it to her.

She shook her head. "I quit a long time ago."

"Good for you." He pulled a cigarette out of the pack with his teeth and lit it. "I'd like to be courteous, but good champagne calls for a smoke."

She watched him exhale and realized that in mere minutes he'd taken control of the evening, had decided what she would eat and drink and generally treated her like she was eighteen again. It almost felt normal, and it scared her. She took a sip of champagne and then asked, "Why the long hair and beard?"

He dragged on the cigarette. "You don't like it?"

"Not really. And you're still smoking and drinking like a—"

"Like a what?"

She wanted to say *like a gangster* but looked away from him and said, "Never mind. Just tell me what happened in Vegas when I thought you'd been killed."

He sat back, giving away nothing and then looked directly at her. "First of all, I hope you believe that I never intended for Julio to get hurt. I made a grave mistake letting Sinatra get so deeply under my skin. I couldn't accept that I'd lost you and certainly not to him."

"There was never anything serious between me and Frank. I told you that a hundred times. He enjoyed taunting you, and you took the bait every time."

He nodded, almost imperceptibly. "Yeah, well, that was my undoing."

"How so?"

"If you recall—that night in the Copa Room when Julio got... hurt, I was so angry. I attacked Frank, and if his goons hadn't taken him outta there, I might have pounded his fucking head in. Of course, Sid Casper was nearby, heard a major bunch of noise from the bosses in New York, who'd had an earful from Sinatra's cronies, and they decided I needed to be taken off the front line for a while." He stopped, breathed deeply and then said, "I've changed my mind. I don't want to talk about this right now. I'd rather focus on you and on us."

"There is no *us*."

He leaned over and kissed her gently on the lips. She pulled away and said, "Jake."

He smiled at the mention of his name. "Sorry, but I've wanted to do that since I first laid eyes on you again." He touched her hand. "I've missed you."

She didn't look at him. "I... can't."

He sat quietly, his eyes holding her. After an uncomfortable moment, he reached over and touched the scar above her eye. "I'm not the same man you knew in Vegas. I've been to hell and back, but the important thing is that I'm back. I've been given another chance, and I won't make the same mistakes—ever." He took a long drag on the cigarette and then ground it out.

She hated the way he got to her, and her brain was telling her to get the hell out before another word was spoken.

The waiter entered the room with a serving cart containing several dishes, explained in flowery detail what they were being served and then left them to enjoy the meal. Jake spread *foie gras paté* on a piece of toast and offered it to her. She took it from him and put it on her plate. "How long have you been in New York City?"

"That's another part of my story—one that I'll tell you another time." He washed a bite of the paté down with the champagne, then took hold of her arm and said, "There's only one thing you need to know right now. I've never stopped loving you. And, although I doubt you'll admit it, I believe you still love me. Why can't we just be together and just—let things happen?"

Her hands shook as she twisted the ring around her finger before saying, "For one thing, I'm married."

He steadied her hands with his. "And your husband is going to die."

The words landed on her ears like they'd been blasted from a boombox. "How do you know that?"

"I saw him at the workshop. He obviously wasn't well. I asked Ruben."

"What else do you know?"

"You mean did I see the young man and woman that were with him at the workshop?"

She sighed, frustrated by the range of emotions he'd put her through since they sat down at that fancy little table. He put a crab cake on her plate and said, "Try this. You'll love it."

"What do you know about them, Jake?"

He put some beef Carpaccio and salad on her plate. "I know they're my children. I knew Norma as a little girl—was sorry to hear about Natalie's passing. I only recently found out about Kenny."

She pushed the food around with her fork. "Did Ruben tell you about him as well?"

"No."

"Your brother?"

"Who, Clay? No, and he could've." He laid his fork down and sat back. "Were *you* ever going to tell me about Kenny?"

She didn't know what to say.

"He's my son, Hassie. *Our* son. Don't you think that if I'd been able, I'd have gone to you and married you and taken care of my family?"

"You didn't marry Natalie."

"I didn't love Natalie, and I did take care of her and Norma."

She nodded. "When Norma came to live with us, I could see right away that it meant a lot to both her and Kenny to have found each other. They painfully shared the knowledge of a father they never knew. It's a noticeable bond between them now." She hesitated and sipped the champagne. "He's so much like you."

"How so?"

"First of all, you should've noticed that he's the spitting image of you physically—dark hair and eyes and a bit of a swagger that he knows how to use. He's charming and witty and has a great, big heart." Jake smiled and took another bite of the crab cake. "And you should see how he takes care of Zach. He's very tenderhearted as well. I think he'll be devastated when Zach… goes."

"I think the kind-heartedness comes from your side of the family."

"Maybe. But there's no doubt he's your son."

"And Norma?"

"There's a lot of you in her as well. She's stubborn and a bit crass at times, which reminds me of Natalie. But she's tenacious and works hard." She hesitated and shook her head. "I thought we'd never live through those first couple of years with her. She was one angry adolescent and did her best to convert Kenny to her jaded way of thinking. We had a helluva time."

"But you coped."

"Thanks to Zach. He was amazing. You know, he's—was—a lawyer and a damn good one. He has terrific insight into people, and he instinctively knew how to handle her. While I was losing my rag and threatening to throw her out into the street, he just dealt with it." She stopped and took a bite of the Carpaccio. It tasted good, and she realized that although Jake had not been there to physically influence those kids, his spirit lived in them, and she saw that every day of their lives.

Jake took a piece of the crab cake and put it to her lips. She took the bite off the fork and slowly chewed it. "More?" he asked. She nodded and took another bite and then another until the whole thing was gone. He laid the fork beside the plate. "See. I knew you were hungry."

The waiter came in to pour the champagne. He cleared the plates and asked, "How was everything?"

"Delicious," Hassie said.

"Would you like dessert now?"

"Give us a few minutes," Jake said. He studied her for a moment. "Did you even mourn my death?"

She pursed her lips, thinking how much she wanted him to know. "Things were a mess after you and Julio died. I couldn't cope, and without Clay's help I don't know what would've happened to me."

"My brother was just a knight in shining armor, huh?"

She ignored him and continued, "Before Kenny was born, I was clinically depressed, but the doctors were careful about giving me drugs because of the pregnancy. I had a terrible time. And, yes, Clay was my savior. The man deserves a special place in heaven for everything I put him through. He was kind and giving and took untold amounts of abuse from me. After Kenny was born, I became even more depressed and really scared Clay. He'd stayed in touch with Henry Berman, who was still involved with managing the Sands. One day Henry turned up to visit, claiming that he wanted to see the baby and to see how I was doing. The next thing I knew, he was lobbying to have Kenny taken away from me. Seems he knew a couple that was looking for a child to adopt. The whole incident put me over the edge, and somehow Clay got rid of Henry, and it was never talked about again."

Jake clenched his jaw and mumbled, "That little faggot weasel. And to think that you once hung onto every word he said."

She breathed deeply. "So, yes. I mourned your death. But from the moment I held Kenny in my arms, I felt that you were still there. Of course, he looked like you, and that wrenched my heart. But it also had a calming effect, which eventually gave me strength."

"Why did you name him Kenny?"

She smiled, remembering the animated debate she'd had with Clay while deciding on a name. "I wanted to name him Julian—after Julio. Clay didn't think that name fit him, and we kicked around some other ideas. Of course, Clay suggested naming him after you, which I considered but decided it would be too painful. I thought about my father—Jackson—but that didn't seem to fit either. One afternoon I was watching television, and there was a report following Jack Ruby's conviction for killing Lee Harvey Oswald. I had such a vivid memory of the day that President Kennedy died. It was right after I learned that you died. So many things were wrong with my life, and it's the only time I ever actually contemplated what it might be like to die."

"Remember the night you met Jack Kennedy in the Copa Room?"

She nodded. "I'll never forget it. I'll never forget that amazing smile and how he made me feel so special. It had been only a few months since his death—the shock and horror of it all still stung. I decided that afternoon to name my baby Julian Kennedy Calhoun and to call him Kenny. Kenny Calhoun."

"Kenny Calhoun Contrata."

"He'll always be Kenny Calhoun, Jake. Anyway, I thought your name was Champion now."

Jake sat back in his chair and asked, "When am I going to meet him?"

She interlocked her fingers and rested her hands on the table. "I won't upset Zach."

"How much longer do you think he'll hang on?"

It was an awful question and sounded very cold. "I don't know, Jake. We certainly aren't sitting there willing him to die."

"Of course you aren't. I didn't mean to be unkind. But if you need some help getting rid of him…"

"Jake! Don't even joke about that."

"Relax. Just a little levity."

She sat back and calmly said, "I want Kenny and Norma to know you. But I won't subject them to anything that could cause them more grief. It's way too soon to know when the time will be right."

Jake looked past her and said nothing. The waiter came in with a plate heaped with something white and frothy. He set it on the table between them and said, "The chef's favorite—Baked Alaska." He took out a lighter and held the flame next to the small mound until it caught fire.

"Thank you," Jake said. "And thank Jean-Luc. It looks great." The waiter poured the rest of the champagne and left the room. Jake blew out the flame, looked at Hassie and said, "This has been a helluva night, and I don't want it to end."

"It has to end, and I don't think I should see you like this again."

He sat back in his chair, frowning. "Why not?"

"I promised Ruben that I'd have one dinner with you. We came here tonight to talk about your investment in our show. We shouldn't have gotten off that track, and that's the only thing that we can discuss going forward."

He watched her. "Well, like it or not, there is more between us than business. And I'm not just talking about those two kids."

She sat quietly before saying, "If you truly are the Jake that I knew—"

"And loved."

"If you really are the Jake that I knew, then you are also the man that scarred me both physically and emotionally. You killed one of my dearest friends and sent me toward a nervous breakdown, which pretty much finished my career in Vegas. So your looks might have changed, but people don't usually change that much, and I don't believe that you've really changed at all."

"And you have changed?"

She hesitated and then said, "Maybe I have and maybe I haven't, but I'm smart enough to know that getting involved with you again would be a big mistake."

"You obviously need more time."

"I'd like to go home now."

They left the restaurant and stood on the sidewalk. He waited a moment and then asked, "Will you let me drop you off?"

"Thanks, but no."

"Okay." He looked up the street and waved at a taxi approaching from the next block. "When can I see you again?"

She looked at him, straight-faced, without emotion and said, "You still owe me an explanation of where you've been all these years."

He nodded. "And you owe me the chance to prove to you that we belong together—you, me, Kenny. And Norma."

"Can I ask you something?"

"Sure."

"Are you still in touch with Sid Casper?"

"Why do you ask?"

"Never mind." She took a deep breath. "I think our next meeting should be with Ruben. I'll have him call you to arrange a time."

The taxi stopped at the curb beside them. Hassie offered a weak smile and said, "Thank you for dinner. It was a good choice."

He kissed her cheek.

"I meant what I said about Kenny and Norma. You'll get to know them when the time's right. Meanwhile, let's talk about our show. If you think you can stick to the business, I'd be grateful for you to be involved."

"You mean you'd be grateful to have my money."

She drew her mouth into a straight line. "I sincerely hope your interest in this production has nothing to do with our private lives—past or present." His smile sent a shiver through her; she turned away from him as she said, "Goodnight, Jake."

She sat in the back of the taxi and stared out the window, considering the suggestion that they could be one big happy family. It seemed preposterous, but she knew all too well how persuasive Jake could be. And then she thought about Ruben's insistence that she was like the Greek goddess, Persephone, and that Jake, as Hades, would drag her back to his hell. She shuddered, put the thought out of her mind and watched as the lights from the city she loved at night went by in a blur.

chapter thirty-three

A forty-three-year-old man never expects to learn that he can no longer take care of himself on his own. A healthy forty-three-year-old takes the simple things for granted—things like making a pot of coffee or collecting the mail from the box in the lobby or taking a shower or getting out of bed. Warren had come to the conclusion earlier in the week that the walking cane was no longer enough when he went out. And though he'd fought it at the time and still didn't want to face it, unless he intended to live out his days housebound, he'd have to start using the wheelchair the doctor had prescribed on his last visit.

Kenny arrived home from school about the time Warren sat down with the pamphlet about hospice care. He slammed the front door and walked into the apartment carrying two loaded canvas bags. He stopped when he saw Warren and said, "Hey, old man. What's happening?"

Warren squinted at the sight of him and said, "What on earth are you wearing?"

Kenny glanced down toward his feet. "Which part?"

"Those jeans." Warren gave them a closer look. "They look like you fell in a vat of Clorox."

Kenny laid the bags on the wingback chair and said, "These are my favorite jeans, man. They're the bomb."

"Well, they look like they belong in the garbage."

Kenny laughed, removing his black leather jacket. "You wanna go for a walk? It's awesome out there."

"If you mean go out and put one foot in front of the other, I don't think that's gonna happen today."

"Why not? I'll go with you. We can walk up to the corner and back."

"What's in your bags?" Warren asked.

"Books. What else?"

"That's quite a load."

Kenny walked closer to Warren. "You're pale. Let's go out in the sunshine."

Warren waited, took a deep breath and said, "Then go get my wheelchair."

"You have a wheelchair?"

Warren nodded. "In your bedroom. In the closet I used to use. Folded up against the wall."

Kenny slung his jacket over his shoulder and left the room. It was probably the effects of the drugs, but the strangest thoughts crossed Warren's mind these days. His day in and day out existence—such that it was—forced all sorts of emotions and questions, and top of the list was the inevitable *Why me?* Was he being punished for his lifestyle choices—his *sins*? For hurting Hassie the way he did and for forcing a life between them that was a lie? His parents were dead, and his brother might as well be, and Ruben came around less and less often—said he didn't do well with sick people. Who does? And despite the family that Hassie, Kenny and Norma had become, their presence oftentimes felt strange, causing him to question why they were there. As he sat around, his body deteriorating, he recognized that he was on this final journey on his own. The reality was that he preferred it that way. After all, no one would really care that he died. Which meant that no one really cared that he had lived.

Kenny came racing down the hall with the wheelchair, singing, "Rol-lin', rol-lin', rollin' down the hall-way," like Tina Turner singing "Proud Mary."

"Must you be such a moron?"

"This is fun."

Warren slowly stood. "Take the chair to the bottom of the stairs. I'll walk that far and then you can take over."

Kenny watched him try to stand and then asked, "Are you sure?"

"No, I'm not sure, but..." He fell back down in the chair. Kenny stood by, looking frightened and helpless and then walked over and put Warren's arms around his neck and pulled him up out of the chair. Without a word, Kenny picked him up, cradling him by the crook of his knees, carried him over to the wheelchair and gently sat him down. He then wheeled him through the apartment door and down the short corridor into the small entrance lobby. As they neared the front door, Kenny stopped and said, "I'm going to carry you down the steps. Is that okay?"

Warren nodded. They went through the door onto the front stoop. Kenny walked around and lifted him from underneath his armpits, pulled him up from the chair and guided him over to the brick post.

Kenny stood beside him for a moment and then asked, "You okay to stand here?"

"Yeah, yeah," Warren said and adjusted his position.

Then, as if it were made out of balsa wood, Kenny carted the wheelchair down the steps and left it on the sidewalk at the bottom. He raced back up the stairs, stood in front of Warren and said, "I'm going to pick you up and walk down to the chair."

"If you drop me, I'll sue you."

Kenny pushed the chair down the sidewalk toward Fifth Avenue. Warren took a minute to regain strength and then said, "Let's go into the church garden."

They rolled along the craggy path and then stopped next to the bench situated in a wooded area beside the church's side entry.

"Sit down," Warren said. It was cool underneath the trees, and Warren suddenly felt weightless. For a moment he thought this might be the place where he'd take his last breath. He wiped his brow and asked, "What has your mother told you about your father?"

Kenny looked away, focused on an old oak. "He died before I was born. And that she loved him a lot."

Warren nodded. "Do you ever think about him?"

"In what way?"

"Do you ever wonder what it might have been like to know him?"

"I used to. But not any more."

Warren looked around the peaceful patch of greenery and then sighed as he asked, "Do you ever think of me as a sort of... father figure?"

Kenny smiled. "You're the only father I've known."

"What about your Uncle Clay?"

"I haven't seen him since I was five."

"Your mother would do anything for you."

Kenny watched him and then nodded before saying, "You know, we're going to take care of you. You don't have to go through this alone."

A gust of wind blew through the trees, and Warren felt weight in his lungs. He coughed and Kenny asked, "You wanna go back?"

Warren gazed up at a patch of blue sky. "If it were up to me, I'd never go back."

Kenny walked over to the wheelchair, preparing to take him home. Warren touched his arm and said, "I'm sorry."

Kenny patted Warren's hand. "What are you sorry for? This isn't your fault."

* * *

Kenny opened the door to the apartment and pushed the wheelchair inside. Hassie and Norma sat on the sofa. As Kenny helped Warren out of the chair, Norma jumped up, picked up the silver-topped cane from beside the desk and took it over to him. Hassie stood up, smiling through an expression of surprise as she asked, "How was your... outing?"

"Just dandy," Warren said as he walked over to his chair. "My driver needs a little practice, but we made it." He sat down, looked at Norma and asked, "To what do we owe the pleasure of your company today?"

"Evidently, we're going to have a family chat," Norma said, while Hassie motioned for her and Kenny to sit.

"Oh, yeah?" Warren said. "Wouldn't happen to be about me, would it?"

Hassie took a couple of steps like she intended to pace while she thought what to say. She then focused on Warren and said, "I talked to Dr. Metcalf this morning. And before you get hysterical, he called me. He wanted to know how you were doing and if you were using the wheelchair. I told him no because I didn't know you were."

Kenny crossed his arms over his chest and took a deep, noisy breath before asking, "What else did he say?"

She picked up the pamphlet about hospice care off the coffee table, but before she could speak, Kenny grabbed it out of her hand. "He's not going to any strange place, Mom. He's gonna stay right here and *we'll* take care of him."

"Sweetie, that's been fine so far, but the doctor said—"

"I don't care what the fucking doctor said. He's gonna stay here. We'll figure it out." He got up and went to the kitchen and slammed around. He broke a glass and screamed, "Shit!"

Hassie looked at Norma and said, "I know this is upsetting, but we have to do what's best for Zach."

"Zach's still in the room," he said, wiping a tear from his cheek. "Zach still has a say in all this."

"Of course you do. I'm sorry. I just want what's best for all of us."

Kenny came back with two beers, handed one to Norma, and then looked at Hassie and asked, "Do you want one?"

She sat down, shaking her head.

Norma moved to the edge of the seat. "Am I allowed to speak?"

"Of course you are," Hassie said.

"When my mom was sick, I was too young to really help her. She had a couple of friends who came around for a while, but then she got too sick to do much of anything for herself. We had a nurse come to our house. She gave her the medication and took care of all the stuff they'd do in a hospital. Then we had another woman who came to clean her up and look after the house. Maybe we could get some people like that to help us here."

"For sure," Kenny said. "We'll get a nurse to deal with all the medical stuff, and the three of us can look after everything else."

"I don't think you know what you're talking about," Warren said.

"We'll make some calls and find out what the options are for home care," Hassie said. "But I think we should also take the doctor's advice."

Kenny jumped to the edge of his seat and then pointed at Warren and said, "I'm kinda liking the thought of bossing *you* around for a while."

Warren shook his head. "Don't even dream about it. I'll be kickin' your butt 'til they close the lid."

Hassie smiled uncomfortably and then stood up. "I'm going to make coffee. And then we're going to finish this conversation."

Kenny stood, crossed his arms over his chest and asked, "Are you seriously thinking about putting him in a hospital… place?"

"I think it's something that we have to seriously consider. I know we all want him to have what's best for *him*, don't we?"

Kenny's mouth tightened, his eyes glassy, as he glared at Hassie. "How do you know what I want for him? You don't even know how I feel."

She reached for him. "Of course I know how you feel."

He backed away. "No, Mom. You don't. While you were off doing whatever the hell you did in London, Uncle Zach took care of me. He helped me with my homework. He took me to the park and to the playground with my friends. He took me to all kinds of restaurants and taught me about different kinds of foods. He took me to the doctor when I had a fever or sprained my wrist, and he even bought me new shoes when the ones I had wouldn't fit my feet any more. Where were you when he was doing all these things?"

"Kenny, I— "

"You. Weren't. Here. You weren't my mother." He pointed at Zach. "That man took better care of me than you ever did. And I intend to take care of him. So forget about sending him away."

Hassie started to speak. Kenny took a step closer to her and raised his voice. "Forget about it." He looked at Norma. "Let's go."

Do I Know You?

Norma stood. "Whoa, dude. Where're we goin'?"

"To get some food. There's nothing to eat here." He focused on Warren. "Can we bring something back for you?"

Warren looked at Hassie and then back at Kenny and shook his head.

"See you later."

"Let's go to that funky Lebanese place on Seventh Avenue," Norma said.

"You always want to go there."

"No, I don't, and anyway, what's your big idea?"

They left, and Hassie sat down next to Warren. Her hands shook as she said, "I'm sorry you had to witness that." She took a tissue from her pocket and blew her nose. "Why is he so angry with me?"

"Hassie, he's been angry with you for fifteen years. Have you really been so caught up in your own world that you didn't notice?"

"I thought we got past all that."

Warren looked away from her and neither spoke for an agonizing moment until he focused on her and said, "You're his mother. He loves you in spite of it all. But you hurt him very deeply, and all I can say is that you are one lucky woman that he has the capacity to forgive you and the maturity to let bygones be. But he's still a kid in so many ways, and most of all he's a human being with feelings and some deep wounds. I can't believe that you don't understand what's going on here."

"I know he's going to miss you terribly. I can't stand to think about it. I don't want to think about it."

"That's too bad, because if you really want to help him and truly atone for your sins where he's concerned, you'll get your head in the right place." She started to interrupt him, but his piercing glare dared her to speak while he continued, "I know you have your own rationale, and I could probably write the damn script. But for once in your selfish life, will you shut up and listen to me. You need to put Kenny's and Norma's feelings well above yours. Do what Kenny needs you to do for him."

Hassie touched Warren's arm as she nodded and said, "I hear you, Zach. You're right. I'm going to do everything I can to keep things as normal as possible for as long as possible. And I promise, I won't push Kenny. I'll talk to him, and he and Norma will figure into every decision we make."

"Okay."

"You look exhausted."

He nodded. "I think I'd like to lie down for a little while."

"Then let's get you in bed."

"I've been waiting to hear you say that for months."

She laughed.

* * *

She helped him undress and pulled the bedcovers back and then said, "Get some rest, and then I'll make you some scrambled eggs."

He kissed her forehead. "Will you do something else for me?"

"Sure, what?"

"Lie down with me for a few minutes. Just until I relax and maybe fall asleep."

She hesitated and then said, "Don't you dare start any hanky-panky." She looked into his sad, wet eyes, grabbed hold of him and buried her face in his neck.

He cleared the emotion from his throat and said, "Hassie, honey, it's going to be okay. Kenny will be fine, and you guys need to be strong for each other."

She pulled back from him, wiping his tears from her cheek. "He's my whole world. I never meant to hurt him."

"Just let him do whatever he wants—even if he gets it wrong. I want to leave him feeling that he did well by someone. It would be just as important to me as to him. He still has a chance. I don't."

"When did you become so wise?"

"Ramblings of a dying man."

"Ramblings of a wise old queen."

He laughed and then cried a little bit.

She helped him get into bed and then crawled in beside him. They stayed quiet, and he felt her relax. He wished he had more time with her like that.

chapter thirty-four

Ruben hadn't had a drink during the day for several weeks. It was one of his deals with the devil that if the necessary funding came through to at least get *Sands of Time* into previews, he'd stay off the hooch until the day's work was done. But as he hung up from the phone conversation with the mouthpiece for the show's production team, he seriously doubted he'd uphold his end of the deal that day. He lit a cigarette and paced the area around the piano. If they'd already reached a verdict on Hassie's audition for the part of Nia Jackson, then the audition must have been over for a while. And whether Hassie was delighted or devastated over her performance, he should've heard from her by now. Since the day of the workshop, she'd been convinced that she was the only actress and singer who could effectively play the role. Ruben's debates concerning the age of the character fell on deaf ears, and he finally gave up trying to talk to her about it. Warren was too sick to draw into the mix. And anyway, it was debatable how much influence he actually had.

The phone rang. When he answered, Hassie said, "Oh, good. You're home."

"I was just thinking that I hadn't heard from you. How'd it go?"

"I'll tell you when I get there. I'm on my way."

She hung up and, knowing that the inevitable was getting ready to happen, he walked over to the bar and muttered, "I'm already going

343

to hell." He ground out the cigarette, poured a stiff drink of scotch and gulped it. He'd been a big player in the theater world at one point and knew very well how ruthless and cruel it could be for the sake of the almighty dollar. He'd opted to stay out of the production side of this show. He and Hassie had a massive responsibility to the creative side of it all, which he'd decided was exactly where he wanted to remain. He paced around, fighting the urge for another drink in the space of twenty minutes. The doorbell rang. When he opened the door, she stood smiling, looking radiant, and his heart sank. He showed her through the door.

She loosened the belt on her trench coat, unbuttoning it while saying, "What a day it's been. I'm pooped."

"What time was your audition?" he asked, on his way to the bar.

She laid her coat across the back of a chair. "Two o'clock—just after lunch."

He joined her on the sofa and handed her a shot of vodka. "*Genatset*."

She looked at the glass, suspiciously. "What? No champagne?"

He touched her glass with his and then asked, "Who all was there from the production team?"

"Everyone. Chris and Paula, Jarred, James, Constance, Ben, Alan—and a couple of investors whose names I can never remember. I sang the first ballad and then one of the duets with James. They had me read several passages including the one where Nia gets beaten up by Jake. That was a piece of cake. I'd like to see anyone else capture the sheer terror of that moment."

Ruben set his drink on the coffee table, leaned in to touch her leg and said, "Honey, they loved your audition, but you didn't get the part."

"How do you know?"

"George Jenkins called me a little while ago after they'd made the decision. They thought you should know sooner than later."

"Who the hell's George Jenkins, and what does he know about it?"

"He's one of the producers."

"So you've been having all this conversation behind my back? Did you just agree with them and that's that?"

He took his drink and walked away from her. "You know, I tried to talk to you about this a dozen times. I thought you understood the issue with your age and this role."

"First of all, actresses play roles both younger and older than their official age all the time. It's called *act-ing*, and that's what makeup and costumes are for. Judy Garland was sixteen when she played Dorothy, who was supposed to be a schoolgirl of ten or twelve. They made that ugly blue gingham dress to camouflage her young figure." Ruben started to speak, and she continued, "And secondly, you said that my performance at the showcase was brilliant. *Perfect* was your word, I think. What changed?"

Ruben approached her slowly and said, "It's a done deal, honey. You're not going to be in the show. But you have a much more important role as the writer, co-composer and lyricist. You are the heart and soul of this production, Hassie. You and I are slated for some big things to come."

"Like what?"

She wouldn't look at him. He sat down beside her. "You've been so caught up in the audition and your plans to be in the show that you haven't been paying attention to the buzz and the hype. There's a lot of interest, Hassie. We're on our way to being the next great team of Broadway writers."

She looked at him, hurt and skeptical. "I sincerely doubt that. What's there to talk about? They haven't even announced the cast yet."

"Well, now that you're out of the running, you can help with the final vetting. That is, if you think you can be objective."

She emptied her glass. "So, you're telling me to buck up and swallow my pride and just accept the fact that I'm never going to have a starring role on Broadway—not even when the role is *me*?"

"Think about it. You are now *most* qualified to cast the role of Nia, and the team wants your input."

She stared pensively toward the piano and said, "They obviously want a big name. Do they have anyone in mind?"

"It's a tough role to cast, and they're scouring agents' books. It's probably gonna be an unknown, and you gotta help find that someone."

She stood up and paced around. He probably should have been firmer with her over the whole audition thing, but when he saw how determined she was to take on the role, he knew that getting in her way would ultimately drive a nasty wedge between them.

She walked toward the piano. Ruben followed her and said, "Hey. You're a pro and deep down, I think you know this is the right decision."

"Yeah, I guess." She stood in the bow of the piano and faced him. "I also came to talk to you about something else."

"Okay. Shoot."

"Zach is getting worse. We have full-time hospice care now, which has taken a lot of pressure off the kids. We brought in a hospital bed, which Zach insisted on placing in the living room so that he can be in the middle of everything. It's generally a shitty, shitty situation, and I'm glad I've had a legitimate reason to be away a lot."

"How's Kenny holding up?"

"Amazingly well. He's going to school part-time, so he's there most afternoons and evenings. For a while, when the weather was good, he took Zach out in his wheelchair. They'd go up to the Presbyterian Church on the corner. There's a peaceful little garden there, and they'd hang out and talk. Zach's pretty much bed-ridden now. But they still drive each other crazy. Zach won't let him get away with anything." She stifled the urge to cry and continued, "Norma's great too. She comes around most days and brings little treats. Occasionally she convinces Kenny to go out for a break."

"This is a tough question and probably unfair of me to ask, but what's your gut feeling about the time he has left?"

"It's been a little over six weeks since the doctor told him he has two to three months. Of course, none of that is an exact science, but, well, I guess, if I had to say… I think it'll be a miracle if he's here at Christmas."

Ruben raised his eyebrows. "Really. That soon."

Hassie nodded. "You need to visit him more often."

"I know."

She leaned on the piano. "I don't think I've ever felt as empty as I do right now. I've lost or am losing so much of what has meant anything to me for the last ten years."

"Have you heard from the limey about the divorce?"

"Please... his name is Charles. And he's going for an annulment."

"Have you heard from Charles about the annulment?"

"Not yet. But I expect that envelope every day."

"So what have you done to sort yourself out legally?"

She walked away and sat on the sofa, slumping down in the seat. She stared straight ahead and then said, "I decided a few weeks ago that I need to give my full attention to Zach right now. And I don't want to take any chances that he might get wind of a divorce or annulment or whatever I've got to do to rectify that—mistake."

"And that's all you're concerned about?"

"Until I receive those papers..." She paused, lost in thought, and then said, "I promised Chaz I would sign and return the papers as soon as I received them. Your lawyer says that having proof that the marriage has been annulled in England will help my case here. I guess I'm thinking that having those papers in hand will kick-start the process here. Meanwhile, I don't have to risk Zach having any exposure to this whole nasty mess."

"Have you considered calling Charles and asking what's going on?"

Her face displayed pain but she didn't look at Ruben as she said, "I don't know exactly where he is now. He's out of the navy and could be anywhere."

"I bet he's right where you left him in London. It couldn't hurt to try."

She sighed and then nodded as she stood up. "Right now, I think I should go home and check on Zach."

He motioned for her to stay put. "Not yet. Since we're gettin' everything out in the open, there's one more thing I need to talk about."

She sat down. "If you're going to get into more conversation about John Champion, don't."

"I don't want to play games with you about this."

She squinted her displeasure and asked, "About what?"

"Warren told me that John Champion is actually Jake Contrata—the real flesh and blood, which explains why you were so freaked out at that first meeting."

"Zach shouldn't have done that."

"And I understand why you didn't want me to know. You're afraid that, knowing what I know about how he treated you, I wouldn't want him involved in our production."

She nodded. "At first, I was more afraid that you didn't know what you were getting into with him. He has a very sketchy past, and I'm almost positive he's involved with the mob."

"I don't care if he farts rainbows for a living. How can I take money from a guy that practically destroyed you?"

"Because we need his money. Don't be an idiot and let all that history keep us from putting the show on stage. I'm over it now."

"Are you going to let him back in your life?"

She tucked her legs underneath her and said, "I have no intention of having a relationship of any kind with him. But I do want Kenny and Norma to know him... eventually." Ruben said nothing. She laughed and asked, "What happened, Ruben? Did someone appoint you as Hassie's guardian angel?"

He half-smiled. "I don't think you always look after yourself so good. I don't want to see you make more mistakes."

"Don't worry. I have no desire to go backwards. But we need his backing, Ruben. I'm trying not to let my feelings about him get in the way of his involvement in the show. Plus, I don't want him around while Zach's alive, and I haven't decided how I'm going to tell the kids about him. There's still a whole lot I don't know about him and, although I know he's on his best behavior right now, I haven't forgotten how manipulative he can be. In fact, I'm convinced more than ever that he's hiding something."

"How so?"

"For one thing, he's altered his looks. His nose is different. When I look at him in the scruffy beard and long hair, I can't help but believe it's meant to be a disguise. He's hiding. I'm sure of it."

"That's an interesting theory. Why don't you ask him?"

"I will, eventually. Right now, I want to keep distance between us. He's smart enough to know that it'll be much easier to do this my way."

Ruben rubbed his chin, considering his words before saying, "You're probably gonna slap me now, but has it occurred to you that in the not too distant future you'll be a widow *and* a divorcee?"

"Uh, yeah. After all this bigamy drama and the horror of Zach's illness, I'll be single. Single, Ruben, and I'm sure you think I'll be vulnerable and stupid, and Jake will be standing right there like the big bad wolf ready to pounce."

"Actually, that's a pretty good analogy. I can just picture you in Red Riding Hood's cape with the wolf threatening to eat you."

She stifled a laugh. "Oh, please. That's a disgusting image."

He guffawed, walking away from her. "How about another drink?"

She shook her head. "I need to go home."

"Okay, but give me a few more minutes while all this is on my mind." He poured a large shot of scotch and then sat in his chair. "I've given this a lot of thought. And—after Warren's gone—I don't think you should tempt fate with Jake being in such close proximity and all." He swigged the drink and then continued, "I think you should just go ahead and do the most obvious next best thing."

"And what would that be?"

"Settle down with me. You know I'd take good care of you."

"That's very sweet, but I'm not a charity case. To be honest, I think it'll be nice to be on my own for a while. And losing Zach is going to be tough. I'm going to need some time."

"Sure. I'm not doubting that. And I don't think you're a charity case. I just don't want you to be one of those women who rationalizes her way back to the guy that's not good for her and is gonna screw her up all over again. You know what I'm sayin'?"

She smiled. "Yes, I do, Ruben. And I love you too." She stood up and went to get her coat. Ruben walked toward the door. She followed him, pulling the coat on as she said, "Don't forget what I've said about Zach. Come over and see him as often as you can. They've stopped most of the serious drugs that never seemed to do anything to help. He's on a high dose of morphine now and sleeps a lot, but he still tunes in when he's awake, so I'm sure he's aware of your absence."

Ruben tightened the belt on her coat and said, "I'll be over soon. Meanwhile, put your bruised ego aside and think about how you're going to get involved in casting Nia Jackson. Call Charlotte about the auditions. Please go help 'em out—for the sake of the show."

"Okay, okay. I'll do it tomorrow."

He kissed her cheek and quietly said, "And, by the way, you may have lost Charles, and you may be losing Warren. But you'll never lose me. Understood?"

She nodded and gently kissed his lips.

Ruben closed the door behind her, feeling like a puppy that she'd patted on the head and called a "good boy." And despite what she'd said, he didn't trust that she wouldn't fall right back into suave, lover-boy Jake's arms. The fact that she didn't want *his* arms around her was a blow—one that he should've expected, and he guessed it was time to move on. But, whether she liked it or not, he'd never stop caring about her, and he'd never stop trying to keep the big bad wolf away from her door.

chapter thirty-five

The ceiling appeared to move—swirling arcs of motion that Warren had never before noticed. If he could reach it, it would be like whipped cream or marshmallows, and he'd be able to poke his finger into its softness. If he could move, he'd sit up and look out the front window at the dawn of a new day. He'd fussed with Kenny about positioning his bed so that he could see out that window. Now, when he opened his eyes, it was like looking through a fine metal screen or a kaleidoscope—the images unidentifiable and beautiful all at once. He was almost blind. But he'd memorized the faces. When Kenny, Hassie, Norma or Ruben spoke to him, his mind's eye conjured an indelible image.

He heard Hassie and Kenny talking by the bookcase. "No whispering," he said. His voice sounded strange in his head—like it was pitched too high and he'd lost all power to project.

Hassie walked over to stand beside him and said, "Sorry, sweetie. We thought you were asleep." She tucked the blanket in tighter around the mattress. "How's it today?"

"Swell."

"Pain under control?"

"There's a faucet of morphine running through my veins."

"It's just a drip, Zach. The nurse is monitoring the dosage."

"Hmmm… the nurse." He'd asked for a male nurse and had been rather rude about the appearance of this middle-aged woman shaped like Humpty-Dumpty. Why couldn't he have a gorgeous young hunk of a thing as his dying wish—one last fantasy?

He heard Kenny clattering around and asked, "What's that moron up to in the kitchen?" He longed for the time when the smell of coffee didn't turn his stomach and when counting calories and watching his waistline was a tedious task.

Hassie sat down beside the bed. "He's making breakfast. Ruben's stopping by soon."

"Hope he arrives before Humpty-Dumpty gets here."

"Zach, one of these days you're going to call her that when she's in the room."

"So? Raise my head a little bit."

The phone rang. Norma, who'd taken on the responsibility of gatekeeper, scurried to answer it. The doorbell rang, and Hassie let Ruben in. It was highly amusing when he tried to be quiet or reverent.

"I'm not dead yet," Warren said.

They approached Warren's bedside, and Ruben touched Warren's leg. "Hey, man."

"What brings you out at this time of day?"

"Can't a guy visit his cousin?"

"I've never seen you before cocktail time."

"Well, I'm here now, and I need to talk to you about something."

"I knew it. You want me to leave you Zelda's wardrobe."

Ruben laughed. Hassie walked away.

Warren had moments when it felt like a baby hippo sat on his chest. He needed to cough but knew it would hurt. He stayed quiet for a moment and then sputtered before asking, "What's on your mind?"

"Are you sure you're up for this? Maybe you should rest."

Kenny came in with a cup of coffee for Ruben and then stopped beside Warren and said, "You want some tea?"

He shook his head. "Have your breakfast."

Kenny walked away, and Ruben said, "He's a good boy."

"Yeah, he's an angel. What did you come to tell me?"

"Your brother called, and he wants to see you."

"I don't have a brother."

"Yeah, you do, and he's in the city for a few days. He just wants to stop by to say hello."

"You mean goodbye."

"Warren, I told him that I'd give you the message but that it was completely up to you whether or not you'd see him."

"He didn't want to see me when my father disowned me because my lifestyle made him angry. He wouldn't even speak to me at our father's funeral. Why the fuck would I want to see him now?" He started to cough, and it wracked his chest with such pain that he cried out.

Hassie ran into the room and yelled for someone to bring a warm cloth. She said something to Ruben and then put her hand on Warren's forehead before she said, "You need to rest. The conversation can wait."

Warren imagined her giving Ruben a dirty look and said, "Don't blame Ruben."

She put the warm cloth on his forehead. "Then stop talking and rest for a while. Ruben, go join the kids for breakfast. Kenny made pancakes."

Hassie walked to the far corner of the room and returned with the portable oxygen tank that Warren had nicknamed Gomer. She put the mask over his mouth and nose and said, "Gomer's here. Breathe easy. Relax."

He tried to look at her—imagining her beautiful, kind face. She stood beside him, fiddling with gauges and monitoring his movements. She'd barely left his side since he'd become bed-ridden. And when she did, Kenny was there. They were the family he'd lost a long time ago. The idea that his brother wanted to see him now was insulting. If he ever saw him again, it would be in hell.

* * *

He awoke to the sound of someone humming in the background. It wasn't a voice he recognized, nor did he know the melody. But something about it sounded familiar, and he wanted to hum along. Maybe Hassie was singing. He tried to speak, but the mask covered his mouth. He tried to remove it but his arms were too weak, and he realized that tears were streaming from the corners of his eyes. He was ready for all of this to end, but he still had some things to say.

The telephone rang. Norma answered it quickly and said she'd take a message. She hung up, and Hassie came into the room. They talked too softly for him to hear what was being said. Hassie joined him and removed the oxygen mask, wiped his face with a warm cloth and said, "Sorry if the phone woke you."

He took a shallow breath, stayed quiet for a little while and then had an overwhelming feeling of remorse. "I'm sorry I ruined your life."

She stood beside him, lightly rubbing his arm. "Let's not have this conversation now."

He looked in her direction and said, "I should've let you go."

She sighed. "You didn't hold a gun to my head."

He softly sniggered. "Everything but."

He wanted her to tell him that it was all right and that she wouldn't really have left him if he'd told her to. But she remained quiet except for an intermittent clearing of her throat, which he suspected was her effort to stave off emotion. A sensation of exhaustion waved through his body, and he knew that he'd soon be asleep. He reached for Hassie and said, "Promise me that you'll get married again."

"Shhhh."

"Promise me that you'll marry someone you really love, who can give you everything you need and deserve." She took a tissue from her pocket and blew her nose as he continued, "Please don't get to the end of your life with regrets."

There was pointed silence before she said, "Do you have regrets now... about how you chose to live your life?" She took a slow, sorrow-laden breath. "Do you regret not trying to work things out with Andrew?"

"Why would you ask me that now?"

"Because I've always believed that Andrew was the true love of your life. And I could never understand why you sacrificed... why you never fought to have a life with him."

Tears streamed from Zach's eyes, and it took him a moment to compose himself before he said, "I've told you many times, Hass. It was wrong..." He broke down, images of the days with Andrew that he'd pushed to the back of his heart and mind for such a long time flashing before him. Hassie held his bony hand with both of hers, sitting quietly while he struggled to regain his composure before he finally said, "I once believed I'd grow old with him. But he hurt me so much."

She waited for him to calm down and then said, "Do you want me to try to find him?"

"No."

"Don't you think he'll want to know?"

"He can read the obituary."

"Well, let's say that I hear from him. Is there anything you'd like me to say to him?"

He felt the hippo on his chest again, sapping his strength and intensifying the pain. He considered her question and then slowly, with heartbreaking resolve, said, "Tell him that love is not a weakness. He'll know what you mean." He had no more energy to talk and closed his eyes.

* * *

He was awakened by a tug on his hand and winced in discomfort.

"It's just me, Warren," the nurse said. She fiddled around with the IV and disconnected the tube from the cannula. "I need to irrigate this today."

"You're poisoning me."

"It's saline solution. We need to keep the passage into your bloodstream clear and clean."

He closed his eyes and waited for the nurse to carry out the simple procedure. The rush of the cool saline had a strangely calming effect, and he dozed off again. When he awoke, the nurse was gone, the morphine had been reconnected and his body felt tightly wrapped within his skin but nearly pain-free.

Kenny stood at the side of the bed to his right. Warren took a moment to try to focus on him and then asked, "Are you stalking me?"

"You want some jello?"

"Come near me with that congealed piss—" He coughed for a few seconds and then continued, "…and I'll sue you." He fought for shallow breath and then said, "I'm a lawyer, you know."

Kenny stood by quietly and then carefully asked, "Can I talk to you about something?"

"Yes, you *may*."

"So you know how we talked about the music for your—service?"

Warren nodded.

"I got the organist at the church to help me, and I think it's everything you like."

"So there's none of the head-banging crap you and your sister listen to?"

"Nope. It's all like church music or opera—pretty boring if you ask me, but I think it's what you want." He then leaned down close to Warren's ear and softly began to sing, "Mo-zart's in the pan-try, let him out, let him out, let him out."

Warren smiled and then fought his emotion before saying, "There's hope for you yet. Where's your Uncle Ruben?"

"He left when you went to sleep. He said to tell you that he'll take care of everything you talked about, and he'll be back later."

"Go get your mother. And you and Norma go out for a while." As Kenny started to walk away, Warren said, "Wait a minute."

Kenny stood beside the bed, his hand resting on the side rail. Warren reached up to touch him and said, "Take care of your mother. Make her have a real life."

"You know I can't make her do anything."

"You know what I mean. And you—get serious about school, and figure out what you want to do."

"I'm working on it."

"Good. Now take your sister out for a beer."

Do I Know You?

Kenny's hand trembled as he touched Zach's arm. He sniffed back tears, and Warren was tempted to say something to taunt him and make him laugh. But he remained quiet until Kenny walked away. Maybe it was time to stop joking.

He was used to the place the morphine sent him. It was both indescribable and exact, and it regularly gave him the sensation of having left his body. He'd done his fair share of mind-altering drugs during his days of hard partying with Andrew. But there was something uniquely different about getting high—losing your inhibitions for the sake of a good time—and knowing that if you didn't have the drugs, you'd beg someone to kill you.

The front door buzzed, and Kenny tended to it, calling out, "Mom, you need to sign for something." Hassie went to the door. Kenny and Norma left.

She spoke *sotto voce* and then closed the door and walked over to the desk. After another minute, Warren looked toward her and said, "Something important?"

She walked to him and said, "Nothing that can't wait."

"Well then, will you do something for me?"

"Sure."

"Lay with me."

She sighed before saying, "I don't know, Zach. I don't think it would be very comfortable for you."

"There's plenty of room. I'm the size of a twig now. I just want to be close to you one more time." She was quiet. He reached out to her and said, "Hass... please."

She carefully lowered the side rail and sat down. He patted the space beside him. She stretched out next to him and took hold of his arm, resting her head against his shoulder as he asked, "Am I... okay? Are you—?"

"Shhhh. I'm fine." They lay still for a moment. Her body next to his was the most natural thing he'd ever known—her warmth radiating the comfort of a soft blanket. He had an evanescent sensation that he was falling off to sleep but believed he was awake. He moved just enough to kiss her head before saying, "You know Ruben would do anything for you."

"I know."

"And Kenny, and Norma. They'll all look after you."

"We'll look after each other."

"I'm worried about Kenny."

"Me too. He loves you so much."

"He's been a great son."

"You mean a lot to Norma as well. I hope one day she'll understand what an unselfish and kind thing you did taking her into our lives."

"It wasn't any picnic for you either."

"I know. But because of her connection with Kenny..." She stopped, and her body tensed.

"It's okay, Hass."

"Ruben says your brother wants to see you. How do you feel about that?"

"No." He felt ill and sad and said, "Don't want him at my funeral."

She patted his chest. "Ruben will handle it."

He had the sensation again that he was floating somewhere out in the room. He concentrated on feeling Hassie next to him and said, "Sing to me."

She sniffed and said, "What?"

"Judy Garland. 'Get Happy.'"

Hassie started to cry, and Warren breathed as deeply as he could and said, "If you don't sing, I will."

She laughed, kissed his shoulder and took a minute to regain her composure before starting the first verse.

> Forget your troubles
> Come on get happy
> You better chase all your cares away.

Even through her emotion, her voice was the purest sound he'd ever heard. He closed his eyes and relaxed.

> Sing hallelujah
> Come on get happy
> Get ready for the judgment day.

Do I Know You?

Zelda stood in front of the full-length mirror. She'd decided on the fiery magenta, orange and red Valentino cocktail dress. The décolletage was shallow with three-quarter-length sleeves. She'd always looked good in those colors. Where were the deep red *peau de soie* pumps?

> The sun is shining
> Come on get happy
> The Lord is waiting to take your hand.

Her body was smooth. Her eyes were beautifully lined, her lips luscious red.

> Shout hallelujah
> Come on get happy
> We're going to the Promised Land.

The door to the wigs cabinet stood ajar. Zelda walked over and opened it and removed her favorite. She held the Styrofoam head and studied the dark brunette hairpiece. It needed brushing. She removed it from the stand and placed it on her head. The straight, dark locks fell just above her shoulders and framed her face in long, soft arcs. Hassie stood behind her in the mirror. She reached down to adjust the wig and then touched Zelda's shoulder and said, "You look beautiful."

part six

chapter thirty-six

When Hassie had learned of Jake's death, her shattered heart left her feeling numb and hollow and lost to a world in which she'd never really belonged. The day Chaz walked out of her life, she was overwhelmed by the sheer sadness of the moment—the result of her own mistakes and bad judgment. Zach's death had simply brought down the curtain—the weight of her grief lay in the recognition that, despite the length of time that Zach was ill, and despite the knowledge that the end was near, Kenny had been inconsolable. It was difficult to watch him struggle to function, but she felt it best to let him work through it all in his own time. And it was uplifting to observe the solace that Kenny and Norma provided each other.

The apartment was quiet. In the kitchen, a knife lay on the counter, caked with butter and strawberry jam. Since the day Zach died, Kenny had gone out in the mornings before Hassie emerged from her room. She assumed that he went up to the garden on the grounds of the church where he had taken Zach in his wheelchair. He grieved; the pain on his face tugged deeply at her heart. She encouraged him to talk to her, but he seemed to pull further and further away, which petrified her.

She heard the door to the apartment open and shut and called out, "Kenny?"

"Yeah, hey. Can you come in here, please?"

She entered the living room; Kenny stood at the bar. "Isn't it a little early to be hitting the booze?"

He turned and said, "I got his ashes."

Hassie walked closer to see a bronze urn sitting next to the decanters of vodka and scotch. Her first instinct was to walk away. She hadn't considered that they'd keep Zach's ashes in the apartment. As she neared the bar, Kenny reached out and put his arm around her shoulder. She stood beside him, silently, and then in little more than a whisper, said, "That's the perfect place."

"I know, right?" Kenny said.

Hassie touched the urn. "Did he ever tell you what he wanted us to do with—this?"

Kenny nodded. "We talked about it a couple of times. But in the end, he left it up to us."

Hassie slipped her arm around his waist and said, "I'll always be grateful that you insisted we take care of him here."

"There was never an option. I could never have stood to just visit him and then leave him with strangers. And it was best that he died right here with us." She nodded. After a moment's silence he said, "It must've been tough for you when he asked you to sing to him."

"It was. But it's the last thing he ever asked of me. He drifted off while I was singing, and I was sure he was gone."

"Nah. He waited for me. Guess he knew that I'd sit with him all night." He paused, taking short, shallow breaths. "He didn't wake up again, but I'm sure he knew I stayed with him until..."

"You know, he left the apartment to me and you."

"Yeah, but I don't want to stay here."

"Why?"

He walked over to sit on the sofa and then said, "It's not my home without Uncle Zach."

Hassie took a tissue from the box on the desk and then sat down beside him. "After my father died, I missed him so much I couldn't stand going home knowing that he wouldn't be coming back. I hated my mother for still being there—mind you, that was a complicated story in itself. I hated our house without him in it, and

I eventually left, so I understand what you're saying. But my real point is that my father was always in my thoughts and my heart, and he still is. Rarely a day goes by that I don't think of something that he told me or that we did together. I hear a song that reminds me of him or see someone who makes me remember his kind face and his gentle, loving way."

"I still think that it would be easier if I lived in a dorm or some other apartment."

Hassie sat reflectively for a moment, wondering if knowing that his natural father was alive would help him through this. "So it really bothers you to be here without him?"

He shrugged. "It hurts. I want him to walk through that door and make a martini and sit in his chair and call me a moron. But I want the healthy version of him." He looked at his hands, tightly clasped in his lap. "And there's something else."

"What's that?"

"The apartment doesn't smell right. It smells like... it smells like death."

She knew what he meant, but she also knew that it was more likely that these *smells* were residual memories of the many months of caring for Zach in that room. She started to address his comments when the phone rang. Hassie didn't move, and Kenny said, "Do you want me to get it?"

She shook her head, walked to the desk and answered the call.

Silence and then breathing and then a voice said, "Hassie? It's Charles."

"Oh, hello. I wasn't expecting to hear from you."

"I'm sorry to bother you. Is this a bad time?"

She took a deep breath and said, "Zach died. His service was a few days ago."

"Oh, my God. I'm so sorry for you. I didn't know."

"Of course you didn't know." She couldn't fall apart now. She took another breath and said, "Anyway, I'm sure you want to know if I've signed and returned the papers."

"I—"

"I'm sorry. I received them…" She paused, pulling herself together. "I received them last week—actually on the day that Zach died so—"

"Hassie, please don't worry. I just wanted to make sure you'd received the papers. You have plenty of time to sign and return them."

"I promised you I'd deal with it right away."

"Yes, but I think you have a perfectly valid excuse for the delay. Is there anything I can do for you?"

"Are you calling from London?"

"Actually, I'm here—in New York. I had to come over for orientation at Goldman Sachs. Apparently, my years of traveling the world qualify me for their international relations division, and now I must become an expert on the overall operations."

"That's wonderful and so exciting for you. I'm sure Peggy is thrilled."

"Yes, you could say that." He hesitated and then said, "Anyway, I thought I could take the papers back to London with me—that is if you hadn't already sent them. But I can see that the timing is terrible."

"How long are you here?"

"Not exactly sure, but a couple more days, at least. And I really don't want to burden you. If you're not ready to deal with all this before I leave, you can always post them as per the court's instruction."

"I'm sure I can get them back to you before you leave." She dabbed her runny nose with a tissue and then asked, "Where are you staying?"

"The Algonquin. Do you know it?"

"Of course." She realized that Kenny was listening to her and quietly said, "I'll take care of this before you leave."

"Don't forget that they'll need to be witnessed. If it's awkward for you to sort that out at home, I'm sure the concierge at the hotel will be happy to oblige. I'll have a word with him."

"Thanks."

The silence between them hurt.

"Thank you, Hassie. And, again, I'm very sorry for your loss. Did he die suddenly?"

"No. He'd been sick for a while—some disease that the doctors couldn't pinpoint—or cure. It's been a terrible time. He suffered too much."

"I hate to hear that. And forgive me for saying this, but I can't help realizing that you're no longer married to two men."

The thought had loomed heavy more than once since Zach died but had yet to really mean anything. "My life is getting ready to change in many ways."

"I'm sure."

Silence again and then she said, "It's been nice talking to you. I hope your stay in New York is successful. Do you like becoming a world-class banker?"

"It's a bit daunting at times, but I'll get the hang of it. I'll let you get on with your day now."

"Goodbye, Chaz. And good luck."

She stood at the desk for a moment, staring at the telephone and wishing she'd said things a little differently. Kenny broke the silence as he asked, "Was that the sailor from England?"

She turned to face him. "Why would you think that?"

"Your voice was different."

She laughed, nervously dabbing her eyes with the tissue, wishing she'd suggested that she meet Chaz to sign the papers. He was right. She was only married to one man. She walked back to the sofa thinking *don't be silly, Hassie*, and then sat beside Kenny.

"You didn't answer my question. Was that the sailor from England? What'd you call him—*Chaz*?"

"Yes, it was. His name is Charles. He's starting to work for an American bank in London, and they've sent him here for training."

"So why did he call you?"

"Just to say hello."

They heard the front door to the building shut. Kenny looked at his watch. "That's probably Stormin' Norma. She was supposed to go with me to get the ashes but got *detained*," he said, making quote signs in the air.

Norma entered the apartment wearing a short black skirt and a white blouse with big, puffy sleeves and white, high-top sneakers. Kenny whistled and said, "So you really do have legs."

Hassie smiled. "You look very nice. Whatcha been up to?"

"She has a boyfriend," Kenny said. "He goes to Columbia."

Norma said, "Shut it, Kennedy. You're just jealous."

Kenny laughed. "Did you hear that? She called me *Kennedy.*"

"Well, honey, that's your name."

"I could call you Julian if you prefer," Norma said. The two of them made faces at each other.

Kenny motioned for Norma to sit and then said, "So, Mom, tell me again why this Charles guy is calling you now."

"I told you," Hassie said. "He's an old friend passing through town."

He shook his head and Norma asked, "Who is it, Hassie?"

"A friend who lives in England, and he's visiting New York."

"Maybe he wants to take you to dinner—or something," Norma said, and then released a low, guttural laugh.

Kenny glared at her. "Shut up. Her husband just died."

"So? Life goes on. And look at her," Norma said, nodding her head toward Hassie. "She still looks pretty good for an old lady."

Hassie stood and walked over to the desk. "Okay, you two. I'm not looking for anyone to do anything with right now. But... thanks for the compliment?"

Norma reached into her oversized patchwork satchel and pulled out a cigarette.

"You know you can't smoke in here," Kenny said.

"I'm not smoking it, you dork." Norma held the cigarette between her index and middle fingers, occasionally waving it around. Kenny rolled his eyes, trying not to laugh.

"Seriously, Hassie. Uncle Zach wanted you to get on with your life," Norma said. "He told us that more than once."

Kenny glared at her again. "Yeah, but I don't think he meant for her to do it the day after he died."

Norma shrugged. "It's been over a week."

"Oh, well, excuse me. A whole week." He looked at Hassie. "You probably already have a full calendar."

Hassie sorted through the mail and said, "You must have things to worry about other than my social life." She dropped the mail in the bin and then walked past the bronze urn, stopping to look at it again. Since the day she realized that Zach was going to die, she'd felt that he would never really leave them. So much of her life with Kenny involved Zach, and despite the fact that they'd lived separate lives, she knew he'd be there for anything she or the kids needed. It would be strange to make her own decisions. She'd already caught herself expecting to sit down with him when she got home—to ask what he thought about something she'd debated with Ruben or other members of their production team. His instincts were never far from the mark. She would miss his clever barbs and his ability to make her laugh. She would simply miss having him around.

She turned toward the kids and asked, "What are you guys doing now?"

"I blew off my classes this afternoon. What about you, Norm?"

"None of your business."

Kenny looked at Hassie and said, "That means she's meeting *him*."

"What's his name, Norma?" Hassie asked.

Norma stood and said, "Hiram. Hiram Ishkabibble."

"It's William." Kenny stood beside her. "William Somebody-who-needs-his-sanity-checked-for-dating-my-weird-sister."

Hassie walked over to join them. "I'd like to meet him, honey. Why don't we have dinner with Ruben this weekend? He's been asking about you guys. I think he'd like to see you."

"No can do for the weekend," Norma said. "How about tomorrow night?"

"Kenny?" Hassie asked.

"Whatever."

"Okay, I'll check with Ruben and let you know."

"Come on, Mizz Ishkabibble. I'll walk out with you," Kenny said and then looked at Hassie. "I meant what I said about leaving this apartment. You can do whatever you like."

She nodded. "But please don't make a hasty decision. Please believe me when I tell you that it's important for you to hold onto the memories that keep him close to you. As time goes on, those memories will change shape. But I promise, you'll never forget him, no matter where you live or what you do."

Kenny and Norma left, and Hassie walked back to the desk. She undid the clasp on the envelope she'd received from the British courts and removed the set of documents. While perusing them again, she heard Chaz's words—*I can't help realizing that you're no longer married to two men.* But the document was very clear. Chaz intended to annul the marriage that should never have happened in the first place. She opened the desk drawer, searching for a pen, and came across an article from the New York Times back in May. It was basically a report about a disease called GRID—Gay-related immune deficiency, also referred to as AID—Acquired Immunodeficiency Disease, "gay cancer" and "gay plague." Someone had sent it to her anonymously. She'd skimmed it briefly, and then, feeling completely overwhelmed, had hidden it in the desk drawer.

As she read the article, seeing the word "gay" over and over jarred her senses and sounded somewhat foreign to her and, at that moment, she couldn't bear to think what her life, and her son's life, might be like now if Zach hadn't gotten sick. Even after he insisted that he'd simply made a big mistake with Andrew—that he wasn't gay and that he truly loved Hassie and their *family*—she never believed that he ever really got over Andrew. She'd never know if Zach actually did know the cause of his illness and that if, in the end, he'd felt that there was poetic justice in his death like some sort of punishment for his sins. She took no pleasure in these thoughts and would never repeat them to another soul. But, after the conversation she'd just had with Kenny about leaving the apartment for good, she couldn't help but feel that all of the negative swirling around them now might have been avoided. And for that she was truly sad.

She walked to the bar and poured a shot of vodka. She stood silent for a moment, then touched her glass to the bronze urn with the knowledge that she would never really want to leave that apartment or live anywhere else. For, despite it all, this was where she'd remain close to Zach and could talk to him and feel his presence in every piece of exquisite furniture and every flickering bulb in an antique lamp and every creak in the floorboards and every cherished recording—all that he had selflessly shared with her and her son. She took a sip of the drink, left the glass on the bar and then went to change her clothes.

chapter thirty-seven

It was the first day the company had access to the Ethel Barrymore theater for auditions. The show was slated to begin previews in less than two months. Hassie arrived ahead of the production team and hung in the back of the theater to gather her thoughts and take it all in. *Sands of Time* was going to happen, and today's callback auditions for the lead role of Nia Jackson were possibly the most critical few hours the team would experience.

Hassie had done little more than sit through the first auditions for the girls on agent recommendations. According to Ruben, she'd been hypercritical. Zach had talked her through moments of wanting to quit, reminding her that if she relinquished her voice in the final casting and didn't like the production team's choice, she had no one to blame but herself. Still, it seemed impossible that she would ever be happy with anyone who was meant to represent all that a young Hassie Calhoun had been through during those years in Las Vegas at the Sands.

She'd grown to recognize that she had to trust the script and believe that a good actress, in the hands of their preeminent director, would deliver exactly what the role called for. After all, how many women—or people for that matter—are immortalized in a story that has every chance of living on long after they're gone? And, as Zach had reminded her, someone who hadn't experienced Hassie's life would have a much better chance of bringing that honest edge of naïveté that gave the story its grit.

So Hassie sat while the team arrived and organized. As the women set to audition showed up, she observed that they seemed exceptionally young, which validated Ruben's point that she was too old to play the role of Nia, and she felt foolish. What had made her think that, at forty years of age, she could portray an eighteen-year-old? She'd been so convinced that she was the only one who could bring the role alive, she'd totally blocked out the issue of her age. She laughed at the thought that she would never really want to return to her eighteen-year-old self, in any shape, form or fashion. So she decided to approach the callbacks with an open mind—to disregard the expectations of the woman she saw in her mind's eye when she conjured those key, critical scenes. And, anyway, considering the numerous debates she'd had with Ruben over the content of those scenes, what made her think that the process to find the right actress should be easy?

Ruben entered the theater, walking past her, and she called out, "Hey, partner."

He turned to her and said, "What the hell are you doing back here? Come on. We're late."

She joined him as they greeted the others, took the headshots and notes from previous auditions from the company manager and sat with Ruben five rows back on the left side of the house. The director took charge, and within half an hour they'd seen and heard three of the women they'd all seen before, at the end of which, Ruben leaned into Hassie and said, "So you're not enthused, but at least you're not fidgeting and sighing heavily like you usually do."

She laughed. "I was thinking about how many times I've been in the same position as these girls—giving it everything I possibly could and still knowing that I wasn't good enough."

"Is that what you think? None of these so far are good enough?"

She sat pensively and then said, "They *are* good enough. They're just not quite right."

He put his hand on her leg. "I agree a hundred percent."

The director returned after a short break, and the next girl was called. She walked out—medium height, slim and feminine, wearing black leggings and a loose-fitting white sweater. Her dark auburn hair was fashionably twisted into a loose bun with what looked like a chopstick holding it in place. She wasn't classically beautiful, but Hassie noticed that everyone intently watched her.

She stated her name and age—twenty-four—and Hassie suspected that she would come across as too old for the lion's share of the show. She tapped Ruben's arm, ready to dismiss what had looked promising when the young woman began reciting lines from the opening scene. She seemed to transform herself into a clueless ingénue with a degree of confidence that Hassie recognized but hadn't known she possessed at the time. How else could she have walked into the Sands hotel and practically demanded that she be given the job she'd been promised and then land in the grips of a man that turned out to be everything that was bad for her? It now seemed impossible that she could have been so stupid and reckless. But as she watched the woman's interpretation of who Nia Jackson was, she wanted to call out... *Don't lose who you really are. Don't let that man drag you down to a place where you can never be happy. Stay strong. And for God's sake, don't go back.*

Derek played the intro to one of Nia's solos in the finale. Hassie stood up and interrupted, "Hi..." She glanced down at the headshot and then continued, "Hi, Regina. I'd like to hear you sing one of Nia's ballads."

"Sure," Regina said. "Which one?"

"Whichever you feel most comfortable with," she said, sitting down.

Regina walked over to the piano. Derek flipped through his score and played the intro to "Do I Know You?" Hassie took shallow breaths as the girl sang the first few lines and remained still until the song was over. The theater was quiet until Derek stood up and asked, "Was that what you wanted, Hassie?"

At the mention of Hassie's name, Regina turned in her direction and slowly smiled. Hassie simply said, "Thank you." Regina left the stage.

They saw and heard several more candidates, but the benchmark had been established, and Hassie felt that further discussion was unwarranted. She excused herself, intent on taking the annulment papers to the Algonquin. She walked up the aisle to the theater entrance, half-dazed and relieved that they may have found their star. About two-thirds of the way up the aisle, she saw that someone—apparently a man—sat in the back row. As she got closer, she knew exactly who the man was. She stopped at the end of the row and said, "These are closed auditions."

He laughed. "You found your Nia."

"You think so?"

"I doubt you're capable of seeing her the way I do, but I'm pretty sure you recognized it." Jake stood up and walked to the end of the row. "Where are you going now?"

"I have plans."

He stepped out beside her, put his hand on her back and said, "Walk with me."

They exited the theater and walked along 47th Street toward Broadway. "I hope Ruben gave you my condolences after your husband died. I tried to speak to you, but there were too many bulldogs guarding the post."

She laughed. "I heard that you called. Thanks. We're slowly coming to grips with it all and honestly, I'm glad it's over. It's terrible to watch someone die like that."

"Was it worse than being told that your lover had been beheaded and left for dead in the desert?"

She stopped. "What do you want, Jake?"

He held her shoulders and said, "Don't you think it's time for you to accept that I'm alive and let me back into your life? Isn't it time for you to come back to me?"

She pulled away from him and turned south onto Broadway. "Why would you think that I'd ever go back to you? I've done nothing but push you away."

"You were being the faithful wife at the bedside of a dying man."

"Zach's death makes no difference to me where you're concerned. Our relationship is in the past. It's over, and I'm more sure of that now than I've ever been."

"So you're not going to even give me a chance to prove to you that I've changed? It means nothing to you that we have a son?"

"Kenny has nothing to do with this either. First of all, he's a young man now. He can have his own relationship with you whether I'm in the picture or not. And so can Norma."

"But you do admit that I've heeded your wishes to the letter with regard to those two. Doesn't that mean anything?"

"Yes, it does. It means that everything has happened the way I told you it would. Zach is gone. He can't be hurt by your showing up and bullying your way into Kenny's life after he practically raised him."

"Bullying? That's harsh, Hassie. Even if you think I deserve it, it's pretty harsh."

"Look. You say that you've changed. Well, I've changed too. I'm not the young, innocent girl that was swept into your crazy world. I'm asking you to accept that everything about our past is in the past. I'm not going back."

She stepped off the curb just as a taxi careened around the corner. Jake grabbed her elbow and pulled her back, holding her close to his chest as he said, "You'll never forgive me for hurting Julio, will you?"

She resisted his grip, fighting tears. "You didn't hurt him, Jake. You killed him. And you could've killed me." He let go of her. She looked him square in the face, touched her eyebrow and said, "I can always feel this scar. It's deep, and it's permanent. But more than anything, it's a constant reminder of who you really are, and your behavior does nothing to convince me that you've changed. So why the hell would I give you another chance?"

He sighed heavily. "You obviously need more time. But are you ever going to agree that I can meet my children? Because, in reality, I don't need your permission. I've honored your wishes but—"

"Are you free this evening?"

"I could be."

"I'm meeting the kids and Ruben for dinner. If you want to come to the restaurant, I'll introduce you to them, and then we'll play it by ear. If they don't freak out, I'll leave you to talk."

"You'll trust me to talk to them alone?"

"It would probably be best, but you need to think about what you're going to say. They both believe that you were killed, and that's all they ever need to know—no gory details. I have no idea how you'll tell them you're alive. It's bound to be a shock. You really need to think about that. And, by the way, I still don't know your whole story."

"If you'll ever give me the chance, I'll tell you everything you want to know. And I'll warn you, the story I tell the kids won't be the whole story. At least not right now."

"I've imagined a dozen times what this news might do to them."

"One day I'll tell them everything. For now, I want my children to know that they have a father. And I promise, I'll be good to them."

"Just be honest and don't screw them around and don't ever forget how..." She meant to say *don't forget how close Kenny is to me* but stopped as she realized that she could no longer honestly make that claim.

"Don't ever forget what?" Jake asked.

"Never mind."

They reached the corner of Broadway and 44th Street. Hassie stopped and said, "I need to leave you for now, but I'm meeting them all at seven o'clock at a restaurant downtown. If you want to join us, call me at home around six, and I'll give you the exact address."

He kissed her cheek. "Thanks. I'll call you later."

"Jake, I'm serious. You need to take your plans to win me back off the table. Don't make me sorry I let you into our lives."

"See you tonight."

Hassie turned left onto 44th Street and walked to the end of the block. She gazed into the next block and the vicinity of the Algonquin hotel. It was lunchtime. Would Chaz still be at the bank or would he have come back to the hotel for a midday break? If he was there and she saw him, what would she say to him? Would she ask him to sit with her for coffee? Would she quickly sign the papers and tell him she had another appointment? Would she beg him to give her another chance? Something like the way Jake had been begging her to give him another chance? The dichotomy of the moment leapt at her. Jake was determined they had a future. He'd pleaded with her to give their so-called *family* a chance. Her pulse raced as she at once realized what she'd done where Kenny and Norma were concerned. Did she really think it wise to spring the father that they'd believed to be dead on them at the dinner table? She could cancel the dinner and tell Jake they'd made other plans. But that would just delay the inevitable. And she still had passing, sanguine thoughts that Kenny's getting to know his father could have a positive effect on all of them. She suddenly felt tired and that the fatigue had punched her in the gut, inviting nausea. She looked for a taxi to take her home.

* * *

Just before seven o'clock, Hassie walked into Zach's favorite Armenian restaurant. Kenny and Norma were seated in a booth; Kenny waved her over. She sat across from him and said, "Ruben's running late and says we shouldn't wait for him to order."

Norma rolled her eyes. "That man's gonna be late for his own funeral."

"You want a drink?" Kenny asked.

Hassie's stomach was still bound in queasy knots, but her nerves could use the alcohol. But she might leave after Jake arrived, so she rested her elbows on the table and said, "I think I'll wait. You two order whatever you want."

Kenny motioned for the waiter.

Norma poked Kenny. "Get me a beer, Kennedy."

Kenny ignored her, looked at Hassie and asked, "How's the show going?"

"Good. We've just about finished the castings and will start rehearsals soon."

Norma propped against the table. "Are we ever gonna get to see this show?"

Kenny perused the menu as he said, "Sure. We'll go on opening night."

Hassie shook her head. "I'll be a bundle of nerves, but you guys will definitely be there." She checked her watch and glanced at the door.

The waitress set the drinks on the table. Hassie sipped her water and then touched Kenny's hand as she asked, "How's everything at school?"

He stiffened and pulled his hand away. "It's okay."

"I haven't heard you mention the job at the bookstore lately," she said. "How's that going?"

"You know, Kennedy won't tell you himself," Norma said, "but he's been playing his tacky little keyboard with a couple of the guys he works with."

"Stop calling me Kennedy."

"Sorry, old chap, but I like that name. It's regal. Prince Kennedy." She raised her hand, twisting it from the wrist in an odd sort of waving motion.

"What the hell are you doing?" Kenny asked.

"It's the royal wave—like Princess Diana does."

Kenny stared at her. "Are you on drugs?"

Where was Jake? Hassie hadn't expected him to keep them waiting. She was consciously trying not to appear anxious and caught Kenny looking at her as he said, "Let's get you a drink. And I think we should do as Uncle Ruben said and go ahead and order."

"Yeah, I'm starving," said Norma. "And I've got to finish studying for a test."

The waitress returned. Hassie ordered a glass of wine and then buried herself in the menu. While Kenny and Norma ordered, she thought back on the conversation she'd had with Jake when he called for the restaurant's address. He'd said he would see them at seven. He'd sounded fine—normal and calm and sincere. Ruben agreed to stay away so that Jake could talk to the kids alone. It was all simple enough—if Jake showed up.

"Hassie, what do you want to eat?"

She started, hearing her son call her by her name, but didn't look up. She had a last look at the menu and then closed it and said, "I'll wait. You guys need to get on with your night."

The kids continued their jostling repartee. Hassie struggled to stay in the conversation without glancing at the door. When the food was served, Hassie ordered a second glass of wine.

They chattered on about nothing in particular. Kenny appeared to pick at his food. His body language said that he was unhappy to be there. But he teased Norma unmercifully about her boyfriend, most of which she ignored.

"I've said it before, and I'll say it again," Norma said. "You're just jealous, Kennedy Calhoun."

Hassie chimed in, "He sounds very nice, Norma, but I'd like to meet this young man."

"He's not so young," Kenny said and elbowed Norma. "He's like almost thirty or something."

"Well, I hope he treats you well. Life's too short to spend it with someone who's not good for you."

"You'll meet him," Norma said. "He'll like you even if you did spawn this one." She motioned toward Kenny with her thumb and then punched his shoulder. "Move it. Gotta go."

Kenny scooted out of the booth, saying, "Yeah, me too. Tell Uncle Ruben we're sorry he couldn't get his lazy ass here on time."

Norma waved at her. "Sorry to eat and run. Thanks for the chow."

Hassie waved as they turned away and then quickly stood up and called out, "Kenny?"

He turned toward her, his hands in his jeans pockets and said, "Yeah?"

She walked up to him. "Is everything all right?"

He shrugged. "Sure. Why wouldn't it be?"

He walked away, and she sat down at the table and drained the last sip of wine. She was worried about Kenny's aloofness, but the bigger issue was that Jake hadn't shown. She'd never considered that a possibility. He'd been so persistent about meeting his children. What made him change his mind in that short space of time since she last spoke with him? She asked for the check and then left the restaurant and decided she'd walk for a while. She could feel the onset of winter, but the fresh air felt good. As she neared the corner, she spotted Ruben coming toward her, waving his arm in the air. She waited for him to cross the street and then asked, "What are you doing here?"

"Jake came to see me. He asked me to tell you that he's leaving the city for a while and that he wouldn't be here tonight."

She shook her head and started walking. "He's a real son-of-a-bitch."

Ruben held her elbow, walking alongside her in silence until she stopped, then looked at him mournfully and said, "He just has to do things his way. I'll never in a hundred years understand his evil mind." She took off walking at a fast pace. "And after all he put me through—guilting me into introducing him to Kenny and Norma. Pretending that it was the most important thing in the world to him. What a joke."

"Whoa. Slow down."

She stopped, stared at her feet and then asked, "Did he give you the rest of the money he promised?"

Ruben shook his head.

"Did you ask him about it?"

"No. He seemed irritated and preoccupied, and I didn't think it was a good time to turn into a beggar." They walked along in silence for a moment before Ruben asked, "Hassie, what did you say to him in your last conversation?"

"I told him he could meet and get to know his children, but that there could never be anything between me and him again. I've told him this a dozen times, but he refuses to believe me."

"Maybe he believes you now, and maybe that's why he's leaving town. Maybe he decided he's better off not knowing his kids right now."

"That makes no sense, Ruben. He's been after me to meet Kenny and Norma since practically the moment we met."

Ruben shrugged. "He's a complicated guy. I don't know what he's thinking, and he'd never let on to me that he has any sort of issues with you. But remember what I've always said about Hades."

Hassie walked ahead with purpose and said, "Oh, Ruben. That's enough of that mythological crap. Jake is Jake. Pure and simple. And it's his loss if he chooses to play some silly game with me at the expense of getting to know his own children. I'm done with him. Money or no money."

"Okay, say what you will, but I'm not wrong. Hades expects Persephone to return to him, and she always does—just like clockwork."

She shook her head. "You're wrong about me being that Persephone chick. And I don't want to hear another word about it. I'm not going back to Hades or Jake Contrata or anyone for that matter. I'm going to get on with my life, Ruben. One more little task and I'm a free woman."

At the next corner, Hassie stopped, looked at him and said, "You were really counting on that money, weren't you?"

He nodded. "Yeah. It'll be a blow if he reneges." He put his arm around her shoulder. "But don't worry, honey. I'll figure something out. I may have to dig a little deeper into my own pockets after all."

chapter **thirty-eight**

Charles left his bag with the doorman and went to have breakfast before leaving for the airport. He found a table by the window, removed his leather jacket and placed it on the opposite chair. The Algonquin had been a nice place to stay for the few days he was in New York, and part of him wasn't ready to leave. He'd hoped to accomplish that last bit of closure with Hassie. He'd actually hoped that he might see her—maybe when she came by with the papers. But she'd yet to leave them off, and, given the circumstances, he felt it wrong to call her again. Maybe he should've offered to collect them from her. Losing her husband couldn't have been easy. Looking back on that day at the café in Rockefeller Center, he realized that Zach must have been very ill—possibly dying. She should have told him, but then he'd probably have done the same thing.

"Shall I bring you the menu, Mr. Beauclerke?" the waiter asked.

Charles smiled. "A portion of toast and orange marmalade, please. And I suppose I'll have some of that tea you serve."

"Right away, sir. I'll have the newspaper sent over as well."

Charles nodded and peered out the window at a dreary, battleship gray day, which reminded him of what he'd most likely be returning to in London. The waiter returned with the newspaper. As he walked away, Charles called out to ask for milk with the tea and spotted Hassie standing at the entrance to the lobby lounge. She was wearing a long, red wool coat that brought focus to her face and dark hair, which was pulled back, clasped at the nape of her neck, a tan leather bag over her right shoulder. He stood and walked over to her; she appeared lost or confused. He moved closer until he stood in front of her. She looked up at him and said, "Hi."

"Hi. Are you looking for someone?"

"The concierge asked me to wait."

"You brought the papers?"

She nodded. "I took your suggestion to have my signature witnessed here."

He touched her arm. "Then join me for a cup of tea?"

She nodded, amused. "You and your *bloody* tea."

Charles led her to the table and helped her remove her coat. He pulled out the chair for her and picked up his jacket. She touched it and said, "I always loved this jacket."

He laid both coats on the chair beside him. "It has a little age on it now. But then, don't we all." He sat across from her as the waiter arrived with the pot of tea and asked, "Can we have another cup for my wife…" His face reddened. He barely caught her eye as he said, "Sorry about that."

"Well, technically, I'm still your wife." She smiled, and for a moment it felt like the first time they'd sat down together.

The waiter set the cup and saucer in front of her. Charles started to pour milk in her cup and then paused before asking, "Do you still take your tea with milk and sugar?"

"Honestly?" she replied. "I don't think I've had a cup of tea since I left London."

He poured a dollop of milk. "I don't blame you. This—what's it called, *Lipton* tea would put anyone off."

She helped herself to a spoonful of sugar and stirred it into the tea as he poured, just like old times. "I shouldn't be having all this sugar," she said. "I seem to have inherited my mother's tendency for broad hips."

He leaned down to assess for himself, raised his eyebrows and said, "You look pretty good to me. And I see that you're still wearing Barbara's scarf."

She sipped the tea. "Yes," she said and lightly fingered the well-worn piece of silk. "I didn't expect you to be here at this time of day. I meant to do this days ago but—well, it's been a little hectic."

"How are you holding up? You do look at bit tired."

"I won't say that everything's fine. It's been a rough few weeks, and I had no idea how difficult it would be to accept that Zach's gone. It's a strange feeling, Chaz. I'm not sure I can describe it."

"I have a better idea of what it's like to lose someone you care about than you probably know."

"So why are you here this morning?" she asked.

"I finished my work late yesterday. My flight's in a few hours. I'm killing time over breakfast."

"I guess the timing's good." Whether it was the awkwardness of the situation or the fact that she was recovering from her husband's death, she seemed subdued and soft in a way that Charles didn't remember. When he thought of her after she left London, he usually remembered the cheerful, slightly zany side of her personality—the thing that he'd become enamored with all those years ago. He furtively watched her, and she finally said, "After I sign these papers, the annulment basically means that we were never married. Is that correct?"

He pondered the question with melancholy that snuck up on him and then nodded. "The marriage is simply void."

"Then the upside to all this is that, even without Zach having died, I'm no longer a bigamist."

"Actually, you're no longer married to two men, but you'll always have been a bigamist."

She looked down, her cheeks flushing as she said, "Oh."

Although he was serious about what he'd said, his heart went out to her. She'd obviously had a bad time of late. He watched her, and then asked, "How's Kenny dealing with your loss? I imagine the two of them got quite close over those years."

She nodded. "They were like father and son—probably more like best friends at times. And, yes, Kenny's had a terrible time. But he's busy and has lots to keep him occupied. We all just need time."

"Of course." The waiter arrived with a plate of toast and a glass pot of marmalade. Charles looked at Hassie and said, "I didn't ask if you'd like something to eat."

"I'm fine, really, thanks."

Charles slowly spread the marmalade on a piece of toast, thinking carefully and choosing not to look at her as he asked, "Did you ever wish we'd had a child?"

He'd either shocked her or caught her off guard. She gazed off into the distance. "Did you?"

He shrugged. "I often fantasized when I was at sea about the children we'd have, picturing you fussing over them and teaching them your annoyingly charming American ways. I envied the relationship you had with Kenny from the first time I met you and he was still a little boy. You were such a wonderful mother."

"Really, Chaz? Have you forgotten that I left my son in someone else's care over three thousand miles away for the better part of four years? That hardly qualifies me for mother of the year."

"Hmmm. Well, it sounds like he survived, and I'm sure your relationship now is stronger for it."

"That's kind of you to say and, yes, well, it's all still pretty emotionally intense but…" She pressed her lips together while he took a bite of the toast and then said, "To answer your question, of course I wanted to have a child with you. But given all the circumstances of those first years of our marriage—"

"I'm sorry I mentioned this, Hassie. And, of course, I know that it would ultimately have been a bad thing—given all the circumstances."

She appeared to be preoccupied with something or someone at a table behind him. He was tempted to turn and have a look when she said, "There's something that's been bothering me since I saw you in October."

"What's that?"

"Why didn't you pursue this annulment right after I left London?"

He poured more tea. "I don't have a good answer to that question. You have no idea how many conversations I've had with myself about this and whether the argument was rational or not, the conclusion was always a resounding *Get on with your life, you pathetic git.*"

She wrinkled her brow, inquisitively, and asked, "So why didn't you?"

"Because I couldn't stand the finality of it. I believed that when you didn't hear from me or my solicitor, you'd do what you needed to do to rectify the problem for yourself. I'd deal with it in due course." He could see the confusion on her face. "I suppose I'm admitting that I wasn't sure what I wanted to do."

She waited until he swallowed a bite of toast and then said, "So you really didn't want the annulment?"

He shook his head. "I really didn't want you to have married me while you were married to another man. But I never stopped wanting you to be my wife."

She blinked several times and tried not to look at him. He wasn't sure why the hell he was saying these things to her and realized that he would soon leave for the airport. He finally reached over, put his hand on hers and asked, "Did you ever wish that you had just told me that you were married when you had the chance?"

"You mean when we first met?"

He nodded. "Then or certainly when I asked you to marry me. I've never understood why you just didn't tell me that you'd made a mistake marrying Zach and that you were willing to divorce him."

"Would you have accepted that? Would you have minded being someone's second husband and waited patiently while I tried to get out of that marriage?"

"I think I could've accepted the circumstances and maybe even helped you."

She breathed deeply. "Sadly—or stupidly—I never considered telling you the truth. In the beginning, I naively believed that I could go back to New York, tell Zach I wanted a divorce, and then come back to be your wife with you none the wiser. That sounds absolutely absurd now, but it's how I felt at the time."

"Well, the issue now is that we can't go back. You can't undo that bit of bad judgment, and I can't pretend that I'd have been the understanding second party."

She contemplated what else to say. Their eyes met, and they

stayed locked in each other's gaze until she finally said, "Your toast is getting cold."

He pushed the plate away and rested his elbows on the table. "I don't know why, but I feel the need to tell you my side of the story where Peggy is concerned. Do you mind?"

She shook her head, her mouth tense and unable to hide her discomfort.

"Mind you, Peggy would be very unhappy to know that I'm telling you any of this, but I feel like being honest with you today."

Hassie remained still. Charles shifted his weight in the chair that felt too small for a man his size and then said, "I suggested the last time we met that I'd been wounded in battle."

"I got the feeling that it's the reason you're retiring."

"It's one of the reasons, but, nonetheless, after I returned to the UK, my dear mother—I'm sure you remember Gwen—insisted that I spend my recuperative days with her in Brighton, which was sensible and, I suppose, tolerable in the grand scheme of things. But then Peggy started coming 'round to visit, and it didn't take long for Gwen's plan for Peggy and me to rekindle our relationship to happen. Peggy helped me move to the house in Rottingdean, and within days she was living there as well. She had the good sense, in the beginning, to stay in a guest room. But as I regained my strength and started behaving like a healthy thirty-eight-year-old—well, I don't think I need to spell all that out, and the next thing I knew I was part of Peggy's family, and my mother was deliriously pleased with everything I said and did."

Hassie tried not to laugh, and he smiled, knowing that the two of them could have a jolly good laugh about all this. He waited while she turned serious and said, "So you fell in love and decided to get married."

"That's hardly what I said at all. And I don't mean to be unfair to dear Peggy. She's a lovely woman, and if you can imagine it, she worships the ground I walk on."

Hassie giggled. "I can't imagine anyone thinking that way about you."

Do I Know You?

Charles tapped the top of her hand with his forefinger. "And who was it that swore to me that no one had ever been as important to her than I?"

She laughed again, raising her right hand. "That would be me."

He nodded, suddenly taken with this playful side of her. "Well, Peggy claims the same feelings. But there's one—albeit major—problem."

"What's that?"

"I don't feel the same way. I never have, and I never will."

"Then why did you agree to marry her?"

He shifted his weight again, discomfited by the reality of the situation but eventually said, "It's time for me to settle down. I'd like to have those couple of kids now, and I know that Peggy would be a good mother. Her parents would be marvelous grandparents. The pieces all fit together well enough. And besides, I've already had the love of my life."

Hassie blinked several times, swallowed and then gently asked, "Would you really marry someone you don't love?"

"I didn't say that I don't love her. She makes me happy in a lot of ways, and she'll be a good wife."

"But..."

He felt perturbed and reacted by saying, "What do you want, Hassie? Do you want me to admit that I'll never love her the way I loved you?"

"Well, will you?"

He looked away, but she kept her eyes on him. He preferred to let the thought die so that he could move on without admitting the obvious, but she sat patiently, holding onto the silence until he said, "I hate to admit this tired, old *woe is me* aspect of the story." He looked at her and said, "I love her, but I'm not *in* love with her."

"And that's okay with you?"

He shook his head. "Not really. It's just the way it is."

An awkward moment passed before she said, "You intimated when I last saw you that Peggy more or less insisted that you apply for the annulment. Is that so she—you could effectively say that you'd never been married... that you and I were never really married."

389

Having this conversation now would serve no useful purpose. He hesitated, trying to appear unaffected by the question and quietly asked, "Could we please change the subject?"

"Sorry. But I can't stop thinking about what our lives would have been like if—"

"Don't." He reached over and held her hand with an intensity that made her tearful.

She took a deep breath and nodded as she said, "I really want you to be happy. If you tell me you are, then…"

He gave her a moment and then said, "It seems that your *other* marriage was quite a successful one."

She tilted her head. "I, uh... I'd rather not talk about that right now."

"Did you love him?"

She nodded. "I did love him, but like you with Peggy, I wasn't *in* love with him."

"Never? Even in the beginning?"

"Think about it, Chaz. Zach and I had only been married a few months when you and I… got together. Do you really think I'd have been able to fall for you so fast and hard if I was madly in love with Zach?"

"I suppose not. But I'm sure you didn't count on meeting a dashing British sailor who'd sweep you off your feet, so much so that you'd lose hold of your senses for a while and make a dreadful mistake."

"And since you're partially responsible for that dreadful mistake—"

He laughed. "Oh, so now I'm responsible for your becoming a bigamist?"

"Well, you were the one who insisted that I stay on in London, and you worked very hard to make me fall in love with you."

He studied her fiercely; the delicate lines at her eyes and around her mouth brought attention to the years they'd been apart. Her beauty had mellowed, giving way to the seasoned, elegant woman that she was destined to be. He felt closer to her than he could ever remember and realized that he was nowhere near ready to leave her. He stood up, touched her shoulder and said, "I'll be back. Don't run away."

Do I Know You?

He went into the lobby, thinking that he was possibly going to cross a dangerous line. But he couldn't help himself. He'd never pretended that he didn't miss the life that he'd intended to have with Hassie. Seeing her now brought those feelings to the surface, and he didn't know what he wanted to do about it other than give himself more time. He spoke with the concierge and then accepted a room key from the desk clerk. When he returned to the table, their coats remained in the chair, but Hassie was gone. His first thought was that she'd left in such haste that she'd forgotten her coat, but then she walked up behind him and said, "Everything okay?"

He faced her. "It is now." Her bag slid off her shoulder. He pushed it into place, put his hands on her arms and asked, "Would you mind terribly if we continue this conversation in my room?"

She slightly winced. "I thought you were leaving for the airport soon."

"I've asked the concierge to move my booking to a later flight." He kissed the top of her head. "I'm not ready to leave you, but I don't feel like sitting in this lobby." He held her hand, and she tensed. She finally looked into his eyes, and he said, "If you'd rather not, I'll understand."

With a nervous smile, she asked, "Is it too early for a gin and tonic?"

"Never."

* * *

Charles had checked out earlier, but the room he'd previously occupied hadn't yet been serviced. A used towel and dressing gown were strewn across the bed, which he quickly collected and hurled into the bathroom. Hassie laughed and said, "At least there aren't any women's things lying around, or any trinkets left behind."

"If you're referring to that first night in my flat in St. John's Wood—"

"Of course I'm referring to that night. You were hilarious—hiding wine glasses and trying to keep me out of your bedroom until you were certain the coast was clear."

He led her over to an armchair by the window. "Do you seriously want a drink?"

"Only if you'll join me."

He took her in his arms and held her close but not too tight. When she didn't resist, he said, "I think I should keep a clear head here."

She pulled back from him, saying, "Chaz, what are we doing?"

"I'm not sure. And that's the God's honest truth."

She sat in the chair and gestured him over to the edge of the bed. As he sat, he knew damn well what he wanted. For even in those deepest, darkest days of willing himself to hate her and casting out the demons that she'd left behind, he'd never stopped wanting her.

"Are you thinking about Peggy?" she asked.

His face warmed as he realized that Peggy was nowhere in his thoughts. "You seem determined to keep her in the room."

"She's your fiancée."

"And you are my wife." He stood and pulled Hassie out of the chair and into his arms where, this time, he didn't let go. He kissed her neck and removed the clasp from her hair. She made a couple of sounds in protest, which he muffled with his mouth on hers, and as her passion erupted and their clothes fell to the floor, he entwined her naked body with his and everything that he thought he'd forgotten about being with her returned—with ease and comfort, though not without familiar pain.

* * *

They sat in two comfortable lounge chairs, a small square table between them. Chaz ordered a whiskey and a gin and tonic and then settled back in his seat, content and tortured all at once. Scraps of emotion dangled in the space around them. He still couldn't read Hassie's demeanor, and she seemed hell-bent on not giving anything away. He playfully cleared his throat before saying, "Penny for your thoughts."

She sat straight-faced, considering her words and then asked, "Was this a mistake?"

"Probably."

"I think it was all your idea, Chaz."

"Relax, darling. It was a mistake because I had no idea that, after all these years—after all that I've been through where you and we were concerned—I never expected my feelings for you could... Well, now I'm really in a sticky wicket."

"You've already admitted that you're not in love with Peggy—that your marriage to her would be one of convenience."

"Yes, I did say that, didn't I?" He looked away with a flash of memory back to those many years before when he'd told Peggy that he'd met Hassie and that he intended to marry her. It had taken years for Peggy to forgive him for that cavalier dismissal of her feelings relative to her place in his life. But she'd put all that aside when he returned from the Falklands and selflessly given herself to him all over again. He pushed those thoughts away and asked, "What else is on that beautiful mind of yours?"

She took a deep breath. "I miss England."

Her rueful tone sent him to another time, and he felt genuinely sad—for her and for himself. He'd relived that dreadful day in his apartment when he'd confronted her about her *other* life a thousand times, desperately wanting it to have all been a mistake. How could anyone do something so undeniably wrong to someone they claimed to love so much? But as much as it was all in the past, it was still there with them in this elegant room like the proverbial giant elephant.

She tilted her head to one side and then asked, "Do you miss the navy?"

He considered the question for a moment and then said, "I probably do miss it. But I don't miss the regimented lifestyle and the unspoken threat of battle."

The drinks arrived. Charles touched his glass to hers. "Cheers. And thank you for making this a day I'll never forget."

She nodded, stifling a pained expression, then sipped her drink before saying, "Tell me more about the war when you were wounded."

"The Falklands War was a brief one by any historic standard, but it was very intense. About halfway through the conflict, my ship was bombed, and twenty-two of my shipmates were killed. It was simply a harrowing experience that I try not to think about."

"It must've been awful for you."

He paused with thought of the funerals that he'd been unable to attend when he got back to England. "Those of us who weren't actually hit tried to help our comrades, which meant we were exposed to the noxious smoke that engulfed the ship as it burned. It was impossible not to inhale the smoke, and my lungs were badly damaged—hence the protracted recovery."

"But you had a complete recovery."

"To look at me there are no scars, but my lungs will never be the same. I'm told I should be careful of lung infections and the like. I suppose I'm lucky to be alive, really."

"And Peggy nursed you back to health."

"Yes, she did. I could be unkind and say that she did it because she had an ulterior motive, but the fact remains—"

"She loves you very much."

Shamefaced, he looked down before asking, "Where are the papers now?"

"In my bag. Don't worry, they're safe."

"Before we get into that, there's something else I should tell you."

She squirmed in the chair, tugging her skirt over her knees.

"Goldman's have offered me a job in New York. They'd like me to work here for a couple of years, which would mean a move within the next thirty days, shortly after the New Year."

Hassie quietly asked, "And are you considering the offer?"

"I'd be silly not to. But now…" He'd not seriously considered the move an option until now where, in a crazy mixed-up moment, he thought that basing himself in New York City would give him and Hassie another chance at their marriage. But this would mean ending things with Peggy, and that seemed unforgivably cruel. What could he say to her that would abate the devastation that leaving her behind again would do to her? He simply didn't know if he could do it. Hassie waited for him to continue his sentence. He moved to the edge of his seat and asked, "So what would *you* say if I were to take the job in New York?"

"Do you intend to bring Peggy over?"

Do I Know You?

A small cut-glass chandelier shimmered above her head. He focused on it as if it were a crystal ball and could reveal the answer to his conundrum if he simply asked it to. He could feel his pulse in his neck and finally looked at her, carefully picking his words. "If I take the position here, it'll be bloody hard work, and I'll travel between here and London. You're busy with your own project—or so it sounds." Her tightly knitted brow appeared to relax, and he continued, "We're both busy, but we can see each other when time allows and *carefully* work into a new relationship. We won't force it, and if it works out, we'll resume our marriage. If it doesn't, well, we know the options."

She started to speak and then hovered over her thoughts before asking, "Did you just say that you want to move to New York and... I guess, *date* again?"

He shrugged, sheepishly. "It's not a terrible idea, is it?"

"Do you really think that we can successfully get over this awful period of time and have a life together?"

He stood with a jolt and shoved his hands into his trouser pockets while walking away from her. She followed him; he stopped as she touched his arm and asked, "Could you really abandon your plans with Peggy just like that?"

He turned to face her and gently ran his forefinger across her lips, whispering her name. She held his hand, kissing his finger as she said, "I've wished a thousand times that you would give me another chance. And I swear on my son's life... I would never do anything to hurt you again."

He pulled his hand away and said, "Let's sit." They sipped the drinks as Chaz stared out into the room, wishing he could replay the previous hour and do it all differently. He finally looked at her and said, "Forgive me. I'm talking a load of bollocks here. Of course I'm not going to leave Peggy behind. I've put the woman through too much as it is. But the fact remains that I love you, and I'm sure I always will. Please forget what I just said, and forgive me for toying with your feelings today."

"Is that what this has been? You toying with me?"

"I've behaved like a hopelessly lovesick school boy, and for that I'm deeply sorry. Will you forgive me?"

She reached for her handbag and removed the envelope of papers. "You'll need these."

He took the envelope from her and opened it, removing the set of documents. He thumbed through to the last page, studied it briefly and then said, "Thank you."

She focused on her glass and quietly said, "I hope you'll go through with the annulment this time."

He had hurt her feelings or pride or both but thought it pointless to try to convince her that he hadn't planned their little rendezvous. He moved to the edge of his chair and said, "You understand that this will never be easy, but it's for the best. It means we can both get on with our lives."

She slowly stood. "Goodbye, Chaz."

He stood in front of her and slipped his hands in his pockets again as he said, "I didn't mean for this to be goodbye."

"There's really no other choice." And then she was gone.

chapter **thirty-nine**

So Hassie had been nothing more than a sounding board for Chaz to rid himself of a lot of crap that he'd kept pent up for so many months—a catharsis of sorts, which meant that he had used her and that he obviously felt it his right to do so. Maybe she deserved it. Maybe she didn't. But she'd consciously, soberly taken the bait—fallen into his trap and come out the loser. So be it.

She poured a shot of vodka and sat in the leather chair behind the antique desk where she felt the imprint of Zach's butt—the many years of his sitting there and where she still felt his presence. His death had stirred so many emotions, the least of which was her current state of happiness. Zach's words echoed in her head: "You're responsible for your own happiness, Hass. But you can't put yourself ahead of all others and expect unconditional contentment in return. It's a matter of choice—your choice." He'd convinced her to forgive herself for her mistakes where Kenny was concerned. But despite all her efforts to make amends, she wasn't sure that Kenny had forgiven her, and that was all that really mattered. "Give it time," Zach would say. She knew he was right, and some days were filled with positive gestures, and she felt a son's love and she felt hopeful. But some days were the opposite, and the distance between them seemed to broaden, and no matter what she said or did, he put a metaphorical hand in her face, and she backed away, hoping with all her being that he never found out about the mistake she'd made with Chaz—the crime she'd committed and the pain that she'd caused. Her excuses weren't valid. What she'd once dismissed as *complex* had simply been selfish rationale.

She sipped the vodka, thinking of the moment when she'd looked up and seen Chaz standing in front of her. He still had that boyish charm—his hair a little unruly and his complexion slightly ruddy. In truth, she wasn't sure what had hurt her more—the fact that Chaz had lured her into his bed, taking advantage of her vulnerable state, or that he hadn't remembered that today was her birthday. But then, realistically, she'd no reason to believe that he would remember the date. It's not something that men are apt to do, never mind that he now had another woman's birthday to remember.

She noisily sighed and thumbed through the pile of bills and circulars she'd collected from the lobby mailbox. She was expecting Kenny in a couple of hours. Would she have to remind *him* that she was another year over-the-hill?

Taking a closer look at the mail, she recognized the handwriting on the envelope of what appeared to be a greeting card. In all the years she'd known Clay, and even when she'd been a bad friend, he'd never forgotten her birthday. He used to call. But after his marriage to Carolee, he'd sent cards. She tore open the envelope and took in the front of the card—that benign bouquet of flowers and luxuriantly scripted, *For Someone Special*. She opened it to the standard greeting followed by Clay's "Thinking of you and wishing you a happy day." She laid the card on the desk and considered calling him to thank him for remembering her. But she knew he'd see through the gesture as an excuse to speak to him—or anyone. He'd know that she was spending the day alone, and she didn't want to feel his pity.

So Hassie Calhoun is forty-one years old and has no one. Except Kenny. And Ruben. And Norma. And, she guessed, Clay. She picked up the photo of the day she and Zach were married—Kenny looking miserable at having to wear the suit and tie. She took a closer look, and for the first time she saw misery behind Zach's smiling façade and misery in her eyes as she pretended to be the happy, blushing bride. It had all been a ruse and all with a means to an end and in a sick, funny sort of way, it had been a roaring success.

She kissed Zach's image in the photo and then thought of the many times she'd begged him to let her go and that if she'd been able to divorce him, she'd probably be living with Chaz and their children now, and there would be no Peggy and no sickening ache in her gut. But that's not how this story had gone, and there was no sensible reason to go backward now.

The phone rang, and she hoped it wasn't Kenny telling her he wouldn't be home after all. She answered, and a voice said, "Happy birthday."

"Oh, hi."

"*Oh, hi?* That's all you have to say?"

"Where are you, Jake?"

"Far, far away."

"First of all, I don't believe you. Secondly, why didn't you show up to meet your kids?"

"Because you weren't ready for me to meet them."

"It was my idea."

"I know it was, but I think you were trying to appease me or get me off your back, and that's not a good enough reason."

"Whatever. You have pretty well exhausted me over the last several months, and now I need to concentrate on getting my show open."

"Yes, you do. And I'm going to leave you alone. I'll figure out how to meet Kenny and Norma on my own. They're big kids, and I'm an old man. I can handle this."

She breathed deeply and said, "Okay. Just don't screw it up."

Jake laughed. Hassie was on the verge of saying goodbye when she remembered the issue with the money he'd promised Ruben. "I need to ask you something else."

Silence.

"Why did you leave town—if you actually left—without honoring your pledge to help fund the show?"

"How do you know that? Ruben?"

"Of course. Ruben told me, and I'm really disappointed. He works so hard—"

"Hold on a second," Jake said, and then exhaled forcefully. "You'll get your money. I don't have to be sitting in New York City to make that happen. So relax." Before she could comment, he said, "Now let me ask *you* something."

Silence.

"Do you remember that night you arrived at the Sands? What were you—seventeen?"

"Closer to eighteen, and of course I remember."

"If you'd known then what you know now, would you have made that big bus trip to Vegas and gotten involved with a wicked character named Jake Contrata?"

"Oh, hell no." She laughed lightly and then considered the question and said, "I'd have to be insane to admit that I would knowingly subject myself to you and that demented lifestyle. But if I hadn't, I'd never have known Julio and Henry and Dotty and Frank Sinatra, and I wouldn't have a story to put on stage and most importantly... I wouldn't have Kenny."

"That's nice—except for the Sinatra part. But I'd also like to think that I meant a little something to you as well."

"You were the first man I truly loved, even though I didn't really know how to love and to *be* loved..." Her throat tightened, and she inhaled deeply through her nose as she said, "You're my son's father. He's the only bond between us."

Jake hesitated and then said, "Well, thank you for taking care of my son—and my daughter. I know you've been good to them."

"Don't wait too long to get to know them, Jake. They'll soon have lives of their own."

"Happy birthday, Hassie."

She hung up the phone, thinking that Clay and Jake had remembered the day. Ruben would probably forget and then be reminded somehow and spend a week trying to make it up to her. Zach would have remembered, presenting her with a huge bouquet of the flowers he loved and treating her to a nice meal in one of his favorite restaurants. Chaz claimed he still loved her and that he always would. Chaz hadn't remembered. Chaz was gone.

She finished the vodka and left the glass on the desk. She went back to her bedroom, wondering exactly where Jake was when he called. If there was peace in the moment it was the recognition that she and Jake were finally where they belonged as parents and friends whose past was behind them and whose future was yet to be determined. There were still dozens of unanswered questions as to where Jake had been all those years she'd believed him dead. But she wasn't sure it still mattered. Rather, she wasn't sure she wanted to know.

She reached inside the closet, pushing aside a pile of clothes while locating an old shoebox tucked in the far corner. She pulled it out and sat on the bed, taking time to remove the cardboard top. As she carefully sifted through the collection of keepsakes, she was drawn back to a different time—one that she'd always believed had been easier and simpler. She could smell the pancakes and maple syrup that she used to eat at breakfast in the local diner with her father on Saturday mornings. She pulled out the small chiffon scarf that he'd given her when she was a girl. It was soft and light with bright, colorful flowers with leaves of chartreuse and deep forest green and a narrow, royal-blue border. She remembered how much she'd loved it and how she loved her father. Little did she know that the scarf would come to represent one of the most heart-breaking and difficult times in her life.

She carefully folded the scarf and placed it in the box, at once spotting a photo of Kenny as a newborn. It used to bother her that she had such difficulty remembering that time surrounding Kenny's birth. She'd been in a terrible state and wholly dependent on Clay. Now, she could look back and recognize that, despite it all, her survival of that dreadful time had been a victory of sorts. She'd emerged stronger and more resilient. And she'd promised herself—and Clay—that she would never let anyone or anything drag her to those depths of despair again. She was not, and never would be, Ruben's Persephone.

Today, as she approached middle-age as a single woman, she knew one basic truth—she needed a simpler life… one that would enable her to ride the forward motion that she'd worked so hard to put into play. She needed to focus on the positive things—the things that brought joy to her life. And even if she could count those things on one hand, they were there, and they were real. Outside of rehearsals and work to perfect the show, she'd probably spend a lot of time on her own. Maybe she would discover that she actually liked her own company.

Zach used to accuse her of enjoying being the victim. He'd shame her for being ungrateful for all she had—her talent, her good health, her good friends, her loving and forgiving son. She used to despise him for shaking sense into her and pushing her to grow up and be the woman he believed she was meant to be. But had he been right in his assessment? She hoped so. And had he ultimately forced her in the direction that she now faced? Of course he had. And she realized that despite how much she believed she once loved Jake, and despite the doleful feeling that she still loved Chaz, Zach was the only one with whom her heart had been entangled in that authentic, warts and all, this-is-what-it's-all-about way. Zach was the only man who truly knew her as she knew him, and she'd not really appreciated that until now.

On his deathbed, Zach had insisted that she get on with her life, and as she placed the shoebox back in its place in her closet, she recalled a song that Pat Benatar had written and recorded the year before: "Precious time, precious time, precious time. Oh, precious time. Life is too short, so why waste precious time?"

She closed the closet door and went into the living room to wait for her son.

END

about the author

Pamela Cory hails from Charlotte, North Carolina where she received a Bachelor of Music degree from Queens University. After fifteen years of working as a cabaret singer and vocal coach in the Southeastern USA, Pamela spent the next twenty-five years living in London, Paris and Dubai where the story of Hassie Calhoun was born out of her love for music and strong ties to an international arena. Pamela currently lives in Fort Lauderdale and New York City.

www.ingramcontent.com/pod-product-compliance
Lightning Source LLC
Chambersburg PA
CBHW030030030726
47500CB00001B/39